Florida Land Grab

Florida Land Grab

A Novel

DAVID FORSTER PARKER

iUniverse LLC
Bloomington

Florida Land Grab
A Novel

Florida Land Grab is a work of fiction in which the story, as well as the characters and their activities, have no relation to real persons. However, the state of Florida, its environment, history, urban settlements, politicians and historic land developers, as well as state laws and regulations, are real. Observations about this state and its development are entirely my own, as are any errors in relating historical and current facts.

iUniverse books may be ordered through booksellers or by contacting:

iUniverse LLC
1663 Liberty Drive
Bloomington, IN 47403
www.iuniverse.com
1-800-Authors (1-800-288-4677)

Because of the dynamic nature of the Internet, any web addresses or links contained in this book may have changed since publication and may no longer be valid. The views expressed in this work are solely those of the author and do not necessarily reflect the views of the publisher, and the publisher hereby disclaims any responsibility for them.

Any people depicted in stock imagery provided by Thinkstock are models, and such images are being used for illustrative purposes only.
Certain stock imagery © Thinkstock.

ISBN: 978-1-4759-8793-5 (sc)
ISBN: 978-1-4759-8795-9 (hc)
ISBN: 978-1-4759-8794-2 (ebk)

Library of Congress Control Number: 2013907789

Printed in the United States of America

iUniverse rev. date: 08/09/2013

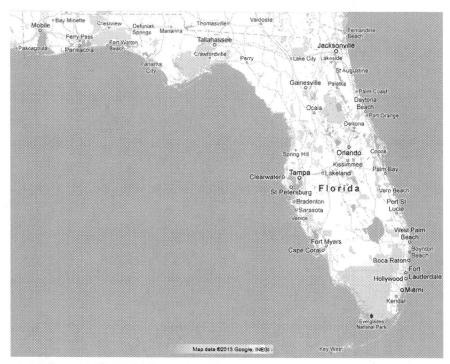

Exhibit 1:
Current map of Florida.

ACKNOWLEDGMENTS

Although this novel is a work of fiction, it contains a compendium of my knowledge, information and observations based upon thirty years of market research and strategic planning for Florida real estate developers. As with past publications, I have relied upon my sister, Margaret G. Vincent, for initial editing, as well as criticism of the storyline and other components. My son, David W. B. Parker, once again served as publishing advisor and final book designer through his company, PTC Communications. Of course, the research and observations are my responsibility as author.

I consulted many books about Florida which are listed in the accompanying Additional Readings, but I am responsible for transmission of dates and data appearing in this text. All of the historic figures, communities and land developers identified in the text are factual, but the novel's current characters and their possessions are all fictional.

In addition to growth-management laws enacted over the past fifty years, much of Florida's current environment owes a debt of gratitude to the members of the Civilian Conservation Corps (CCC) established by President Franklin Roosevelt in 1933 and active through 1942 for the purpose of enlisting unemployed American youth to restore and improve the nation's land. A total of almost three million young people served in forty-five hundred CCC camps across the country, planting some three-billion trees, building eight-hundred parks, restoring four-thousand historic sites, and spending six-million days fighting forest fires, under the motto "We can take it!"

A total of fifty-thousand "CCC Boys" served in Florida, re-planting ninety-thousand acres of public and private land and building eight flagship parks, in addition to hundreds of other civic projects.

PROLOGUE

October, 1775

It was a beautiful fall day in a green, sun-drenched meadow that was interspersed with spreading oak trees decorated with long strands of grey moss. In the distance, the meadow was bordered by a wood-land of tall pine trees, some appearing to extend over one-hundred feet into the cloudless blue sky. A small group of men was gathered on the edge of this tranquil setting in the northern part of the land called Florida. It had been so-named initially by the Spanish explorer Ponce de Leon in the early sixteenth century, and continued in the seventeenth and eighteenth centuries by Spanish settlers in the town of Augustine on the Atlantic coast some fifty miles to the east.

A tall, slim white man in his mid-thirties, with brown hair down to his shoulders under his wide-brimmed straw hat, was chatting with three male members of the Creek Indian tribe in their dialect. The Creek tribe originally had been located in the Carolinas to the north, but recently had begun to migrate south into northern Florida to settle in the hunting and gathering lands of the Timucua tribe, and the neighboring Apalachee tribe to the west, whose members had been mostly wiped out in the sixteenth and seventeenth centuries by diseases imported by Spanish Benedictine Monks seeking to convert them to Christianity.

The Indians were clothed only in leather loincloths and tribal headbands adorned with their tribal symbols, and they clearly appeared on friendly terms with the white man, whom they called "Bart"—the first syllable of his last name, easier for them to pronounce than his first name of William. He had arrived on horseback with his hunter companion, another white man of similar age who remained in the saddle of his horse, and a black slave boy in tattered clothing and bare feet, leading a pack mule.

"Bart" was William Bartram, a botanist and naturalist from Philadelphia who had been living in the wilds of the Carolinas, southern Georgia, and northern Florida for over three years studying plant and animal life before returning north to write a book on the subject of his explorations. Although he spent most of his time alone with his two companions, exploring the mature forests and open meadows and lakes of this beautiful land, he had taken time to make friends with Indians throughout the Southeast and to learn their manners of speech. He had found them to be very intelligent and eager to communicate with him, a distinct change from his first trip into this land ten years earlier, accompanying his father, the eminent John Bartram, appointed by King George III as "Botanist" for Britain's North American colonies.

The older Bartram, a migrant to Philadelphia from his native England, feared the Indians, whom he considered savages ready to destroy any white men at the slightest provocation. Needless to say, the Indians living in the forests of the southeast part of this vast continent reacted to John's animosity with their own fear, as well as anger toward him and others of his race. But, in more recent years, his son had created friendly relations with these Native Americans and became comfortable living among them.

In 1739, John Bartram and his wife became the parents of twins: William, whom they always referred to as "Billy"; and Elizabeth, who eventually married and moved to Lancaster, Pennsylvania, where she maintained little contact with her parents or twin brother. Billy was a talented artist who produced a large graphic collection of American plants and animals. He became known as the first native-born American to devote his entire life to the study of nature. William Bartram and his father are revered as the leading American horticulturalists of the eighteenth century, although William extended his own interests beyond plants and animals to author two pioneer books on Indians of the Creek Confederacy ("Muscogulges") in the Carolinas and the newer multi-tribal Seminoles in the Florida Territory (mostly descendants of the Creeks). The transfer of this Florida territory to the British as part of the Treaty of Paris in 1763 stopped any further Spanish colonization beyond the seaside towns of Augustine (now St. Augustine) on the Atlantic coast and Pensacola on the Gulf of Mexico.

Upon returning to his base in Charleston in 1775, for a brief respite before he extended his travels, the young William wrote an upbeat letter to his father (and sponsor):

"Honored and Benevolent Father, I am happy by the blessing of the Almighty God by whose care I have been protected and led safe through a Pilgrimage these three and twenty months till my return to Charleston two days since. I was threatened by hostile Indians, was struck down with a malarial fever for two months, met important people, and saw amazing things. The Alachua Savannah, for one, is vast and beautiful beyond description. The face and constitution of the country is Indian wild now and pleasing . . . I am resolved to . . . continue my travels another year. I am ever your faithful son."

During William Bartram's almost four-year exploration, the American colonies, along with the Florida Territory, fought and won their freedom from the British. However, the young naturalist was oblivious to politics and war. His mind was devoted to the land and its plants and animals. Although his relationships with and understanding of the Indians established a basis for mutual habitation and well-being between them, other white men did not share his compassion. The century following his journeys and publications featured a series of wars between these two races that resulted in subjugation and re-settlement of most of the Seminole tribes, in order to make way for uncontrolled land development for both agricultural and urbanization purposes, directed toward the objective of economic progress.

The result of this development over the following two-hundred years produced an environment far removed from William Bartram's vision of small farms and villages complementing the meadows and forests of what are now northern Florida. His commitment to the natural evolution of man and nature turned out to be diametrically opposed to the entrepreneurial spirit of the pioneers and politicians who followed him into the Florida wilderness. A few symbols of Bartram's vision remain in the form of dedicated hiking trails and preservation parkland, with occasional lakes and woodland that resemble the natural beauty he described so eloquently in his books and drawings.

John Bartram died in 1777, shortly after his son William returned to the family home from his travels in the wilderness. He was seventy-eight years old. William lived until the age of eighty-four in 1823. He never married. The two men were praised at that time and afterward as "botanical explorers". Both father and son lived long lives devoted to the study and analysis of nature. Hopefully, the subsequent Florida conundrum between the state's natural beauty and economic development to profit from this beauty can be resolved through a more creative balance of greed and nature than has been experienced to date.

Wednesday, March 24, 2010

"Look Mark, just above the Intracoastal Waterway Bridge. Could that be Nash Logan's helicopter?" Bobbi Wilkins, an attractive brunette in her early 50s, attired in a stylish pant suit to complement her slim figure, pointed her arm south from the Fernandina Beach riverfront helipad area to a rapidly approaching helicopter. Her husband, a handsome, tall and fit man of about seventy, with a grey 'Van Dyke' beard and moustache to match his full head of grey wavy hair, raised his hand to shade his eyes before responding in his low-pitched voice.

"No doubt about it, honey! I believe that our luncheon host has arrived. And he is right on time, too."

As Mark Wilkins finished speaking, the brightly-colored, five-passenger "Bell Ranger" swooped down from the cloudless sky to settle gently in the middle of the circular helipad, cordoned off by a rope barrier on the edge of the waterfront concrete parking area.

The rotor was still turning as the rear door opened and a fit-looking, white-haired man of about sixty, dressed in casual slacks and golf shirt, jumped to the pavement and strode toward them. He was undoubtedly the well-publicized Nash Logan, chairman and principal stockholder of Canada's largest homebuilding company, the very man who had phoned Mark the prior evening to invite the two of them to lunch aboard his yacht moored in the St. Johns River in downtown Jacksonville. He had asked them to meet him at the waterfront helipad a few blocks from their turn-of-the-century home in the historic section of this small city at the north end of popular Amelia Island, Florida. He said he would land at ten, and Bobbi glanced at her watch to confirm Mark's observation that Mr. Logan was right on time.

"Bobbi, Mark," exclaimed Nash Logan with a big smile on his face. "How good to meet you! With the telephone description I got from Harold Abrams, I would have recognized you anywhere. He told me just to look for the most elegant retired couple in Fernandina Beach. And here you are!" He offered his hand to Bobbi first before turning to Mark.

"Thank you for accepting my invitation on such short notice. I know you must be busy people and I am fortunate to find you home."

"Well, after all," Mark returned Logan's smile, "it isn't every day we get invited to lunch on a yacht, especially via a brightly-colored air taxi."

"Yeah," replied Logan in a softer voice, "our colors are rather bright. However, my Marketing VP claims that these bright colors attract attention wherever we go, and that's part of the mystique of selling new homes. But, enough small talk, let's get aboard. Mark, how be you sit up front with Jake Johnson, my pilot, so you can point out local attractions as we head back into the city? Bobbi and I can ride in the back."

Logan assisted Bobbi up the steps to the right rear seat and directed her how to attach the seat belt and don the ear phones and microphone so they could all talk to each other during the flight. Then, he and Mark hopped aboard and strapped in to their places. Mark shook hands with the pilot, Jake Johnson, who was a good-looking man of average height with a ready smile and an obvious Canadian accent, complete with hard-sounding vowels and the frequent addition of "eh" to the ends of sentences.

"All set, Jake, we are ready to fly whenever you are," Logan advised the pilot.

"Yes sir, Mr. Logan, here we go." The helicopter lifted off the concrete and quickly accelerated to about one-thousand feet altitude, moving slowly toward the north end of the island a few hundred yards from the waterfront dock.

"So Mark, tell me about this place," spoke Nash's voice in their earphones. "Why do you live here?"

"Wow," replied Mark. "That's a big question, Mr. Logan."

"Hey," said Logan, "please call me Nash. I came to Florida to learn everything I can about this state and I am anxious to get started. So, please help me learn."

"Okay," said Mark. "It turns out that you came to the right place to get started.' He proceeded to describe the unfolding scene below. Fernandina Beach is one of the oldest settlements in Florida. For many years, beginning in the 1850s, it was the southernmost stop on the east coast reachable by railroad. So many northerners came here for winter vacations. Florida's oldest operating hotel, Florida House Inn, was built here in 1857 by railroad pioneer David Yulee, one of the primary leaders in Florida's achievement of statehood in 1845, and the first United States Senator from Florida. Unfortunately, the current owners closed its doors because of financial problems earlier this year. The famous Henry Flagler, of Standard Oil, built a luxury hotel here for northern tourists in the 1880s, but it burned down in the early twentieth century and was not re-constructed. Prior to that, according to local historians, eight different flags flew over the city at different times as a variety of armies took possession of this strategic island colony.

"Up here on the north side of the island," continued Mark, "you can get a good look at Fort Clinch, named for a somewhat controversial army officer of the infamous Indian Wars in the mid-nineteenth century. It is still standing as an historic monument to guard the ocean entrance into the Fernandina Beach settlement. And across on the northern shore of the St. Marys River, you can see the historic fishing village of St. Marys, Georgia. So you are literally at the northeast corner of Florida. As to why Bobbi and I chose to live here in a one-hundred year-old house, we decided, after searching several options over a two-year period, that Fernandina Beach offers the most interesting and relaxing atmosphere for a newly-married older couple of any alternative location known to us."

"Dynamite," responded Nash. "What are those structures north of St. Marys?"

"We are not allowed to fly over there, Jake," replied Mark, as he felt the copter move north. "It is the King's Bay Navy Base for nuclear submarines and they do not welcome uninvited guests. I suggest we fly south along the Atlantic beachfront and I will show you two very popular resort communities beyond this area of Fernandina Beach." As Jake turned the aircraft to the south along the beach, Mark continued, "By the way, you can see the local executive airport to the west, fronting along the Intracoastal Waterway. East of the airport is the twenty-seven hole Fernandina Beach Public Golf Course, and coming into view along the beachfront is Summer Sands Resort Community with its eighteen-hole golf course. Very expensive mid-rise condominiums line the shore here, on either side of the Ritz-Carlton Hotel.

Mark explained that Summer Sands originally was the northern part of a large tract purchased by the Sea Pines Company of Hilton Head Island, South Carolina, in the early 1970s to plan and develop the southern half of Amelia Island Plantation. Sea Pines was founded by Charles Frazier, who many regard as the originator of recreation communities after he developed Sea Pines on his family's land on Hilton Head Island, beginning in the 1960s. Unfortunately, the recession of 1973-74 drove Sea Pines into bankruptcy just as it completed the first phase of Amelia Island Plantation and the property subsequently was split into two parts. The southern eight-hundred acres was acquired by an Ohio coal mine owner named Cooper who enlarged it to over thirteen-hundred acres and directed its development into a profitable resort community, with three golf courses and a championship tennis center, before he died in the 1990s.

Mark paused to point out another area of interest: "We are coming up on Amelia Island Plantation now where the large condominium buildings line the beachfront and lower-density attached and detached homes extend all the way across the island to the west. The northern part of the original property was acquired by a local group of investors who were equally successful in developing Summer Sands resort community. Both properties now are completely developed."

"That's a great description," interjected Nash. "What's on the next island south?"

Mark continued to describe the coastal terrain, pointing out that State Route AIA, which extends from the Georgia border down the coast three-hundred and fifty miles to Miami, traverses Amelia Island and crosses a recently re-constructed new bridge to Talbot Island—actually two islands, with the north portion named Little Talbot Island, but the divider creek is too small to be noticeable from the air. Except for a couple of small out-parcels, the entire double island is a state park with very nice picnic facilities and trails, as well as a magnificent sand beach.

State Route AIA then crosses on another bridge and swings west along the north bank of the St. Johns River to the Ferry Dock, where it crosses by ferry to the little fishing village of Mayport. The paved road continues on up the north shore of the river a few miles to the N. B. Broward Bridge, usually called the Dames Point Bridge by local residents, reflecting the narrowing of the river at that point.

"Holy Mackerel," exclaimed Nash. "Look at all those navy ships moored across the river. It must be a major Navy Base, eh?"

"That it is," replied Mark. "Mayport Navy Base is one of the largest military ports on the east coast and former home base for two aircraft carriers, both since retired. Currently, it is planned to re-fit the base as home-port for a nuclear carrier. You best stay on this north side of the river, Jake, to avoid any conflict with the base airport. You can follow the river for fifteen miles right into downtown if you like."

"Roger that, Mark," answered Jake, as he turned the helicopter to the west upriver. "This is an easy route to follow."

"The channel in the St, Johns River is about forty feet deep," continued Mark. "But it is about to be dredged another ten feet to accommodate the larger ships due to sail through the new Panama Canal when it is completed in 2014. Ahead, you can see the high-level bridge completed fifteen years ago and named for former Jacksonville native and Florida Governor Napoleon Bonaparte Broward. Many of his descendants still live on remaining portions of his property farther west along the river. I consider it rather ironic that Broward's major claim to notoriety, during his brief term as Florida's Governor in 1905 to 1909, was to initiate the disastrous drainage of the Everglades in south Florida, and then current state officials ended up naming a bridge after him. Just beyond the bridge, on the north side of the river, is the new Matsui Shipping Terminal on one-hundred acres already open to inter-ocean shipping. A neighboring terminal for Hanjin of Korea is planned for construction prior to 2014. We also anticipate a new cruise ship terminal, either at this location or in the village of Mayport—a location decision still being debated by local politicians and the Jacksonville Port Authority.

"Around the next bend in the river you can see the Matthews Bridge, often called the red bridge by locals because of its color. Beyond are the green or Hart Bridge, the blue Main Street Bridge, and the newer Acosta Bridge which is lighted with purple neon strips at night. The red, blue and green colors reportedly are symbolic of the colors representing Jacksonville's colleges of higher education. All of them serve downtown Jacksonville, which you can identify by the high-rise buildings around the next bend in the river. By the way, this city originally was named 'Cowford' because residents and animals had to ford the river on a sandbank at this point. But, wait, I believe I see your easily-identifiable colored yacht moored alongside the North Bank Riverwalk adjacent to downtown, so I guess my travel talk is completed."

"Right, take her down, Jake; and thank you, Mark, for an excellent description of the sights along our route," said Nash. "My contact was absolutely right about your knowledge of this state."

On the south bank of the St. Johns River, directly across from the Logan yacht moored on the north bank, three well-dressed men sat on the patio of the Crown Plaza Hotel bar. All three had drinks in front of them, but their attention was riveted on the helicopter landing on the deck of the yacht.

Exhibit 2:
Downtown Jacksonville from the
Southbank across the St. Johns River.

The oldest of the three was small of stature and almost completely bald, except for a fringe of white hair on his head. He had a pleasant-looking face that belied his seventy years of age. Despite his disarming appearance, Albert Siegal was the reputed controller of the largest money laundering operation in Florida for a Colombia drug cartel. He invested large sums in real estate developments that usually were completed in record time due to rapid local government approvals aided by rumored corrupt bribery of officials. The investor's share of the profits flowed to seemingly respectable business enterprises in other states controlled by Colombia's Esperanza family.

The two younger men on either side of Siegal appeared to be in their early fifties: one was a tall, handsome man with blond wavy hair who rarely smiled; the other was equally slim, but of average height and characterized by a full head of black hair combed straight back and shiny with hair dressing. The tall man was Siegal's attorney Kurt Richter, from Orlando, where all three men resided. He was well compensated for handling the illicit money flow from The Bahamas into Florida, and dividing it into deposits and short-term savings instruments in a variety of small banks and credit unions, until it could be transferred into longer-term land development investments. The shorter man was Jack Swift, an Orlando real estate broker who was responsible for identifying new investments for Siegal. His job had become increasingly difficult since the start of The Great Recession in late 2007, and the subsequent halt in new real estate development. Their Colombian masters were impatient with Swift's declining ability to invest their funds, a problem that was beginning to attract attention from federal bank examiners to their growing deposits.

Thus, Siegal had taken a personal role in micro-managing Swift's activities. He and Richter had accompanied their associate north to the Jacksonville waterfront for a personal look at Swift's latest prospect: the wealthy Canadian builder Nash Logan, who was rumored to be searching for a large land purchase upon which to build a new community. Evidently, the Canadian economy was not affected by the American recession and real estate development was continuing to expand. Swift had contacted Logan's office in Toronto, but only succeeded in leaving a message that he is the most knowledgeable land broker in Florida. He received no response from Logan! So, at Siegal's insistence, the three men decided to have a first-hand look at their new investment target, who had arrived in Jacksonville the previous night by air from Toronto.

Siegal was holding binoculars to his eyes, and he appeared to be focused on the passengers disembarking from the Logan Homes helicopter that had just landed on the stern deck of the yacht across the river.

"Do you recognize the helicopter passengers?" asked the older man.

"Yes sir, Mr. Siegal," replied the fast-talking Jack Swift. "The man in the passenger seat is Dr. Mark Wilkins, the well-known urban planner now retired from the international architectural, planning and engineering firm, Roberts, Jones and Vale (SJ&V), headquartered here in Jacksonville. That is his wife emerging from the rear seat. She is a successful free-lance writer for a number of national magazines.

They have been married only a couple of years and live in Fernandina Beach. My new contact on board the yacht told me that Logan would pick them up from there and bring them here for lunch. That is Logan disembarking from the other rear door. My informant tells me that Logan brought them here to recruit Wilkins to assist him in his Florida property search."

"Why the hell hire a planner," interjected Kurt Richter? "Why didn't he hire a real estate broker like you? Didn't you contact him at his Toronto office when you learned about his interest?"

"Yes I did," replied Swift, somewhat defensively, "but all I received was a polite brush-off from his secretary. And, yes, before you continue questioning, I tried to contact him several times without success, before I hired an informant on his yacht in preparation for a meeting here in Florida."

"Alright, gentlemen," said the older man, holding up both hands, "that is enough squabbling. We have seen our quarry and Mr. Swift is on his trail. That is all we can do here today. Let's return to Orlando and discuss our strategy for getting into his pocket."

The helicopter had landed on the stern deck of the luxury yacht, also brightly decorated in the primary colors and logo of Logan Homes. The name across the stern and on the bridge superstructure was boldly displayed as "Victoria".

As the motor died out after the helicopter was tied down and the passengers disembarked, Bobbi turned to Nash and said, "This is a magnificent craft, Nash, how long is it?"

"Yes, it is very comfortable, all two-hundred feet of it, although I believe that number is slightly rounded up a few feet by our public relations people. I will give you both a little tour before lunch. Come forward with me and we will begin with the bridge." He led the way toward the front of the superstructure and up a narrow outside stairway to the upper level control room, or bridge, facing the bow. Although Captain Ericksson and his Engineering Officer were ashore, Nash appeared to be very knowledgeable about the intricacies of the controls, and he explained them in some detail to Bobbi and Mark as the latest technology available for ocean-going yachts.

After a brief glance at the upper-level sun-deck behind the bridge, he then took them below to the main lounge which opened onto the stern deck where they had landed. It was a large room with comfortable furnishings in several conversation clusters with a well-stocked bar at one side of the double stairway where they stood. Nash explained that the room is adaptable to a variety of furnishings which are stored in a closet next to the bar, so it can function as a reception area, dining room or even a work room depending on need. Today, a single table was set for three near the bar area.

Then, they followed Nash down a half level to his well-appointed office before descending further to have a look at the lavishly appointed staterooms, which Nash preferred to call cabins, and they even visited the spotless engine room before returning to the main lounge.

"How about a drink before lunch?" offered Nash, as he stepped behind the fully-stocked bar at the forward end of the lounge.

"Just iced tea for me," responded Mark, "unsweet if you have it."

"You bet," said Nash. "How about you, Bobbi, will you join me in a glass of white wine? It is imported from the Okanagan Valley in the Canadian Rocky Mountains."

"Well," replied Bobbi with a bright smile, "I suppose it would be impolite to refuse, especially with the intriguing name of Burrowing Owl Winery on the bottle."

"Absolutely, it would be un-Canadian, eh," chuckled Nash, as he opened the bottle and poured two glasses of the light liquid. "This winery is owned and managed by a friend of mine. He and I went to boarding school together near Toronto and a few years ago he offered a few of his friends the opportunity to invest in this winery, so I joined his small consortium and very quickly developed a liking for his products. I have a standing order to keep our yacht and my personal homes supplied with an ample supply at all times. Cheers to both of you. I am glad you are here."

"And cheers to you as well," responded Mark. "I am eager to learn the reason for this impromptu invitation."

"And so you shall," said Nash with a smile, "but first let's sit at the table and enjoy the delightful light lunch my chefs have prepared, featuring Canadian wild salmon flown in from Haida Gwaii, formerly known as the Queen Charlotte Islands, on the west coast of Canada. We Canadians are slowly moving ahead with overdue recognition of our native people. This new name is the latest land area to return to a name in the Indian language."

The three of them sat down and were immediately served by two white-coated stewards whom Nash introduced as Jose and Alfredo. The smaller Jose appeared to have a permanent smile on his face, whereas Alfredo was somewhat taller with a darker complexion and serious efficiency. Jose was clearly in charge.

The two guests chatted with their host about current events in Florida, a subject introduced by Nash. Both Bobbi and Mark also extolled the wonderful taste of the cold salmon salad—perfect food for their normally health-sensitive dietary choices. The crème caramel dessert was not so diet-sensitive, but neither one of them hesitated to consume every delicious bite of it. They both agreed to try table-brewed Canadian Red Rose Tea for a post-lunch drink, and then looked expectantly to Nash for his explanation of why they had been invited to this wonderful luncheon on the banks of the St. Johns River in downtown Jacksonville.

"Mark," began Nash, "I know that you are retired from your lengthy successful career in planning communities and lesser developments all over the world, and I know that you and Bobbi are enjoying the quiet and relaxing atmosphere of Fernandina Beach. But, when I questioned my old friend Dean Abrams at the School of Urban and Regional Planning of the University of North Carolina about the single best person to advise me on planning a dream community in Florida, you were his first and only recommendation. He claimed that you were not only the best student he ever taught in his long academic career, but that you continued to keep him apprised about your career issues and opportunities long after receiving both Master's and Doctorate degrees from his school. He assumed that you would turn me down because of your retirement and new bride; but he urged me to try my best because, in his opinion, nobody knows this state and its development any better than you.

"Now, before you protest this lavish praise, let me expand a bit on what I have in mind. I understand that you do not know me, except by possibly-exaggerated press releases. Therefore, there is some risk in you agreeing to work with me. This pamphlet written by our public relations firm summarizes my life to date; you can review it this evening if you like. Second, you do not have any idea about the entitlement potential or marketing feasibility of what I have in mind, another possible element of risk for you professionally. Third, you appear content with your retirement decision as well as to spend all of your time with your new wife, Bobbi,

"Let me just respond to these three issues. First, although I make no pretense about wanting you to help me realize my dream town, my current proposal is to retain you for only two weeks, as a tour guide of Florida, to help me select the best location for my new community. You would have no commitment beyond this two-week period. We would schedule a flying tour in the helicopter with Jake driving and you and me looking, along with my male Executive Assistant to take notes—just four of us. The yacht would follow us as a moving hotel, providing excellent accommodations and dining. We would discuss issues of feasibility, both during the tour and in the evening, to ensure that I end up the preliminary tour with a do-able project location. If two weeks' absence from your wife is too great a burden, she is welcome to join us on the yacht for all or part of the tour and join us for meals each day. I realize that she is a professional free-lance writer, so I must ask both of you to sign a pledge of confidentiality until the project is officially announced. Finally, I am prepared to pay you five thousand dollars per day for your counsel, a retainer of thirty-five-thousand dollars upon your agreement and a like sum at the end of your two weeks, without anything except oral input from you. I would like to start tomorrow. What do you say, eh?"

"Wow! I have never heard such an offer. I am truly humbled, both by Harold Abrams' kind words as well as by your extraordinary confidence in my capabilities. It sounds more like a two-week vacation than a work assignment. However, I do believe Bobbi may have an opinion that I would like to hear before giving you a response. Would you mind if we could speak in another room?"

"Not at all," replied Nash with a sincere smile. "Why don't the two of you retire to my office-sitting room down a half-level of stairs at the front of the lounge? Jose, our waiter, will show you the way and bring you another pot of tea. I will be on the rear deck whenever you want to resume. And, by the way, Jake is at the ready to return you to Fernandina Beach whenever you like. Does that sound okay?"

"Absolutely," responded Mark. "We'll see you within the hour."

Nash arose and beckoned to Jose, who immediately appeared at the table and ushered the Wilkins couple down to the reading room. After making sure they were comfortable, he hurried off to prepare tea. Bobbie and Mark sat in opposing chairs and stared at each other before speaking.

"Bobbi, I am absolutely flabbergasted by this whole thing. Nobody ever offered me this size of daily fee, especially for just doing what appears to be a pretty pleasant vacation trip. What do you think about it?"

"I agree, Mark, the whole thing is positively overwhelming, especially since he offered me a rather appealing opportunity as well. But, it seems to me that we should at least make a couple of calls on our cell phones to see if we can acquire some independent opinions on Mr. Logan, other than this publicity piece he just handed to us."

Just then, the smiling Jose knocked on the door and entered with a tray holding another pot of tea with cups and saucers, along with a plate of what appeared to be homemade cookies. He set the tray down on the coffee table between them and nodded politely before retreating and closing the door behind him.

While Jose delivered the tea tray, Mark proceeded to scroll through his cell phone memory in search of colleagues whom he might consult. It being a Wednesday afternoon, he assumed that there was a good possibility of reaching them. Without further consultation with Bobbi, he dialed the private cell number for Dean Harold Abrams in Chapel Hill.

"Hello, Harold, this is Mark Wilkins calling. Can you take a minute to speak to me about Nash Logan?" He pressed the speaker button so Bobbi could listen in.

"Mark, I am delighted to hear from you. It turns out that Nash Logan is a longtime acquaintance of mine. He hosted me years ago when I was a guest speaker at the annual convention of the Canadian Homebuilders Association in Toronto, and since then he has sponsored graduate student critiques of some of his community plans for our students, even including site trips for them. I joined a couple of the site trips to Ontario communities and had the good fortune to stay in his home and meet his wife Victoria and his two sons and daughter. The children are all grown now and two of them work for Logan Homes. Unfortunately, Victoria died of an unexpected heart attack three years ago, and Nash increased his already busy work schedule to overcome his sorrow. It was during this period that he began to get interested in the dream of his longtime associate, Nathan Rosenberg, to revolutionize housing production through application of non-oil-based-synthetics to construction materials. They invited my critique on their plans and on the actual prototype dwellings manufactured in a secret operation they set up in an old factory in the town of Ajax just outside Toronto. I must admit being intrigued by the combination of strength and efficiency as well as the attractive designs they have produced in the initial three prototype buildings.

In respect to why you are involved, Nash has expressed interest for several years in expanding his business to Florida, and this current recession has convinced him that this is the best time to purchase land. Also, he began to explore the potential of launching their new housing concept in a free-standing new community. But, as has always been his custom in his extraordinary career, he wants advice from knowledgeable professionals in this market. He asked me for advice, and, without hesitation, I told him to start with you. Since he and his executive assistant were already planning to fly to Jacksonville, to look at land, I assume he called you immediately. It has never been his style to waste time."

"Golly, Harold, this is a lot of fascinating stuff for a retired guy. It sounds pretty irresistible. Clearly, his relatively-modest offer of only a two-week commitment touring Florida is just the tip of the iceberg."

"Yes, I am certain that is true. Remember, Mark, Nash Logan rose to the top of his profession in Canada by being very adept at motivating people. I must assume that the very fact you called me for advice indicates that you are already under his influence. And, as an admirer of Nash, I must warn you that his personality is contagious in attracting people to his point of view. On the other hand, in recommending you, I knew that this whole concept is right up your alley. I suspect, unless Bobbi objects of course, that you will find it increasingly irresistible."

"Well, Harold, as usual in our discussions, you have created as many problems as you have solved. But, I thank you, dear friend, both for recommending me and for this exciting story of a potential new adventure. Please convey my best wishes to Alma. Both Bobbi and I look forward to having dinner with the two of you at the upcoming APA Conference."

"Goodbye, Mark, and good luck dealing with my friend Nash."

After disconnecting the phone, Mark looked at Bobbi and said: "I am beginning to feel the same way I did prior to our marriage; being pulled into a relationship I didn't pursue, but find impossible to resist."

"You're right Mark," smiled Bobbi. "But do you feel that you should look for another opinion, despite Harold Abrams' solid reference?"

"Frankly, Bobbi, my trust in Harold's opinion has always been justified. And, after all, this is just a two-week commitment. Unless you feel concerned, I believe we both should come aboard."

"I agree. Let's go up and tell Nash the good news. But I would like to suggest that you do not reveal everything that Harold related to you. I think you should let Nash spring it on you in his own charming fashion."

"In fact," Bobbie continued, "I think that I should hang around to provide moral protection for you. But, I would like some protection of my own, so what do you think of me inviting my younger sister to join us for the cruise? She has been miserable since the divorce, and a couple of weeks in the sun would be good for both of us."

"I think that would be a great idea," replied Mark, smiling broadly at his wife's clever idea of capitalizing on this opportunity. "If she can't fly down here immediately, she can join you en route. Do you want to call her from here or wait until we get home?"

"I will wait. Let's go up and tell Nash that we accept his offer so we can go home and pack."

DAY 0

Thursday, March 25, 2010

A few minutes after one o'clock on a typically beautiful sunny day in Jacksonville, the brightly-colored Logan Homes helicopter touched down on the after-deck of the equally flashy Logan Homes yacht. Mark and Bobbi Wilkins stepped down from their helicopter seats and greeted Nash Logan who was waiting for them by the entrance to the yacht's main lounge. The three of them had parted company on this same deck at three o'clock the prior afternoon, after shaking hands on Nash's offer of a two-week assignment, accepting the retainer fee of a check for thirty-five-thousand dollars, and agreeing to meet for a late lunch the next day, which would give them time in the morning to prepare for the trip.

Jake Johnson unloaded two small suitcases and a large plastic storage box from the luggage compartment of the helicopter and handed them off to a sturdy deckhand to deliver the suitcases below-deck.

"Please put all their luggage in Guest Cabin A, Carlos," advised Nash. "Mark and Bobbie, this is Carlos who is at your service throughout your stay." The deckhand, clearly of Latin origin because of his bronze complexion and black hair, smiled briefly at both of them but remained silent. They would learn later that, although he understood commands in English, he was unsure of his own speech. He usually relied upon Jose and Alfredo to speak for him.

"Excuse me, Nash," interjected Mark, "but we will need the contents of that storage box for our discussion this afternoon, so it would be better left wherever we plan to meet."

"Okay, great, then. Carlos, please set it inside the lounge next to the large round table we have set up in the rear corner. We can move there after we have lunch. Speaking of lunch, I am starved, so let's move to the dining table set for us inside." With that said, Nash held the door for his two guests and they all moved to the lunch table.

Once again, Mark and Bobbi were impressed by the flavorful lunch served up by Jose and his assistant steward, Alfredo. A fresh spinach salad with light dressing was followed by broiled grouper fillets garnished with salsa and accompanied by steamed broccoli. Dessert was a sherbet topped with fresh strawberries. Without asking, Jose brought the Wilkins a pot of Red Rose tea to complete the meal, just as they had ordered the previous day.

"Okay, Mark, let's plan the afternoon, eh?" began Nash. "I would like to begin touring first thing tomorrow morning and I am relying upon you to be the guide. However, before we begin, my lawyer in Toronto emailed me this one-page confidentiality agreement for each of you to sign. Please read it over now, so we can dispense with the formalities. I have not prepared any contract for you, Mark, because I am comfortable with our oral agreement of five-thousand dollars per day for fourteen days in return for your advice. Is that okay with you?"

"Ordinarily, I prefer a written contract, but, after a lengthy phone conversation with our mutual friend, Harold Abrams, I too am comfortable with an oral agreement. However, there are a couple of caveats I would like to propose. First, of course, you agreed yesterday before we left to accommodate Bobbi's sister as a traveling companion for Bobbi. Her name is Linda Cummings and she will fly down tomorrow afternoon from her home in Atlanta, where she is the Director of Emergency Room Nursing at Emory Hospital. Bobbi plans to take a taxi out to the airport to meet her and bring her back to the yacht. At this point, Linda has arranged to spend at least ten days of her vacation time with us."

"No problem," smiled Nash. "We will be pleased to have two female passengers. I have arranged to have her occupy Guest Cabin B right across the hall from your room. Of course, I must ask her to sign the same confidentiality agreement you have in front of you."

"Great, I am sure that confidentiality for Linda will not be a problem, and that the two of them will have a good time.

"My second request is a new thought that Bobbi and I discussed last night after our telephone chat with Harold. We understand from him that you plan to introduce a revolutionary new kind of dwelling design and construction in your planned community, therefore making it a unique development in Florida and perhaps the world. As you know, Bobbi is a free-lance writer for several of this country's major magazines. She would like to write the premier article on your plans and our hunt for an appropriate site. Of course, she would provide a draft for your approval, and await your release from the confidentiality agreement, prior to submitting it for publication; but she would like your permission to sit in on, and tape-record, our on-board discussions. Naturally, she receives remuneration for such articles, but she believes the publicity would be a good trade-off for you. What do you think?"

"I am glad you brought it up," replied Nash with a smile. "If you had not, I would have introduced it myself. Having someone of Bobbi's talents aboard is too great an opportunity to waste. In fact, after we complete this trip, I would like to invite you both to fly up to Toronto, as my guests, to view our prototype factory and learn more of our plans. I hadn't intended to bring up this idea until the end of our tour, but, since Abrams spilled the beans prematurely, let's first of all agree to include Bobbi in our discussions to do her thing. Agreed!"

Bobbi smiled her acknowledgement and remained quiet as Mark continued.

"The last item is better left to our route plan, but I will include it now for Bobbi's interest. I spent part of last evening and this morning planning the most efficient route for our tour, and I will propose a route beginning with the far west Panhandle, about four-hundred miles from here, and work our way through the state to complete the tour at the southern end of the peninsula, exclusive of the Florida Keys which offer no opportunities for large-scale development. If you agree, and we travel west tomorrow, it would be much more efficient to spend tomorrow night in the Panhandle than return here and then go back almost as far the next morning. I suggest we park the helicopter at Destin Airport and stay in Destin overnight at one of my former client's facilities. It is the height of the spring season over there, but I believe we can arrange accommodation. If you agree to this one night away from the yacht, then Bobbi should know who is in charge."

"Right, that all makes sense to me," replied Nash. "You both will meet Captain Franz Ericksson at dinner tonight. He is in full charge of this vessel and I promise that he will do everything in his power to make your stay comfortable and safe. Now, I suggest that Jose show you to your cabin to freshen up, and we meet back here at the large round table in the rear corner in about fifteen minutes. Does that sound okay?"

Both Bobbi and Mark nodded their agreement and then followed Jose down to their room. Nash followed them to his own master cabin in the stern.

When Bobbi and Mark re-convened in the main lounge, their corner table was laid out with a large map of Florida in addition to a stack of yellow writing pads and several pens and pencils. Five chairs were grouped around the table and a pleasant-looking black-haired young man with a bronze complexion stood beside Nash and Jake Johnson.

"Hi Bobbi and Mark," said Nash. "I would like to introduce you to my Executive Assistant, James Quickfoot, better known as Jimmy. He will accompany us in the helicopter as well as attend all of our meetings to keep a record of the entire tour. He already knows about you two. I also asked Jake to join us so he can be involved in the route plan."

Bobbi and Mark both shook hands with Jimmy Quickfoot and greeted Jake before everyone took seats. Bobbi pulled out her small portable tape recorder and set it in front of her on the table. She was not surprised when Jimmy set up a laptop computer in front of his place at the table.

"Okay, Mark, we are in your hands," said Nash.

Mark opened his storage box and pulled out several sheets of paper that he set aside for reference, and then addressed the map of Florida on the table.

He began by describing the basic statistical data of Florida—a state of almost sixty-six-thousand square miles including about four-thousand-seven-hundred square miles of inland water and another thirteen-hundred square miles of coastal waterways within embayments, as illustrated on this large map of Florida on the table. Although many visitors envision Florida as being flat and swampy, it actually has extensive hill country in the north-central and west portions of the state, rising to a maximum elevation of three-hundred-and-forty-five feet above sea level on the Panhandle, with a mean statewide elevation of one-hundred feet above sea level. Over eighteen-million people currently live in this state, despite a small decline in population in 2008, the first decline in over thirty years, as Florida consistently has been among the highest-growth states in the nation. Projections by the University of Florida Bureau of Economic and Business Research—the official state forecasting agency—add another six million new residents between 2010 and 2030 to total over twenty-five million residents, an average new growth of almost three-hundred-thousand persons per year, compared to an average of over four-hundred-thousand new residents per year during the first half of the past decade. Since projections for 2010 and 2011 are low-growth, consistent with slow recovery from The Great Recession of 2007-09, annual growth is expected to exceed three-hundred-thousand new residents during the years following the recession.

"So, Florida should remain a strong market for new homes after we throw off this vexing recession, but I would be less than straightforward if I failed to warn you that our historic state leaders have not managed state growth in optimum fashion. Many problems have been created in terms of conservation of natural resources, land, water and air pollution, transportation, and efficient land use that have caused, and continue to cause, serious problems of growth management. These problems, in turn, have generated legislation that makes land development an increasingly-complex issue for even the best developers."

"Darn it all, Mark," interrupted Nash, "this sounds just like home, eh!"

"Perhaps so, Nash, but, with all due respect, Canada contains a great deal more land for experimentation than Florida. In fact, this state already contains well over half of Canada's population in a fraction of Canada's land area. Although you will see ample open space on this statewide tour, this state is using up arable land for urban development at a frantic pace; or, at least it was at a frantic pace until the recession virtually halted new housing development and migration in the fall of 2007."

"I do understand your point, Mark, and excuse me for being flippant. But, I came to Florida with my eyes wide open and with the experience of over thirty years wrestling with increasingly difficult growth management in five of Canada's ten provinces. I am prepared to spend the necessary time, money and personal energy to realize my dream town. So, please keep on teaching me about my new second home."

"Right," smiled Mark. "I'll give it my best shot."

He went on to explain that, in terms of history, Florida is a rather young state, despite boasting the oldest settlement of Europeans in the nation at St. Augustine, where Ponce de Leon was reputed to have landed in 1513 to claim the land he named La Florida for Spain (historians still debate Ponce de Leon's actual landings, but St. Augustine's tour guides remain dedicated in their devotion to his appearance on the site of their "historic city"). The Spanish priest, Don Pedro Menendez de Aviles, actually generated the first settlement at St. Augustine in 1565, some four-hundred and forty-five years ago. The prolific Florida author and historian, Gary Mormino, claims that Florida's first great land boom occurred from 1782 to 1784 when British Loyalists escaped the new United States by moving south to settle in St. Augustine, and farther south along the St. Johns River, resulting in the British colony's population to jump from about six thousand to seventeen thousand residents.

State estimates indicate that over one-hundred-thousand Native Americans lived in Florida prior to the Spanish occupation during the seventeenth and eighteenth centuries, and the introduction of European diseases that virtually wiped the Indians out. Most of the additional Indian migrants arriving after the departure of the Spanish were subsequently killed or forcibly re-settled out of the state in three successive Indian Wars during the first half of the nineteenth century. A few remained by hiding out in south Florida swamplands. The Indian Wars were fought by American Militia that had been solicited by European settlers who established large cotton and sugar plantations, in addition to logging operations in the northern areas of the state, with slave labor imported from Africa. The port of Fernandina (later enlarged to become Fernandina Beach) became notorious as a major slave-trading center in that era.

"Excuse me," interjected Jimmy Quickfoot. "As a full-blooded Indian, I am naturally interested in what appears to be a massacre of the Florida Indians. Do I hear you correctly?"

"I'm afraid so, Jimmy. Although the demise of Indians during the seventeenth and eighteenth centuries could be attributed to bad management by well-meaning Franciscan monks, the Indian Wars of the nineteenth century were wanton bloodshed by over-eager soldiers of the new United States of America. The plantation owners believed the Indians to be disruptive to their profitable operations through stealing and hiding runaway slaves, so they simply asked the militia to take care of the problem. The militia was trained to kill people as a primary means of conflict resolution. It also managed to send a great many to the new government Indian reservation in what became the state of Oklahoma—a trek west that became known as the 'trail of tears'. Ironically, the slave owners' complaints were dissolved a few years later after Reconstruction through the Civil War in the 1860s, when they were forced to give up their slave labor, and eventually terminated their plantations because of increased labor costs. Despite the end of slavery, segregation and race relations remained a continuing issue in this state. The Florida lynching rate between 1890 and 1930 was the highest of any southern state. By 1950, not a single Florida school was racially integrated and only one school (in Dade County) was integrated over the next decade. Even beaches were segregated with only a few reserved for African-Americans. These are the sad historic facts of a beautiful state."

"Of course, your summary is correct, Mark," interjected Bobbi, "but it should be noted that these atrocities toward Indians and

African-Americans were commonplace throughout the south. Florida's shame was shared by many early Americans."

"That's true, Bobbie. Thank you for adding that clarification. But let me continue with my historical summary."

The railroad era spread to Florida in the 1850s, primarily to serve logging operations. David Yulee constructed the first major rail line from Fernandina Beach to Cedar Point on the coast of the Gulf of Mexico in 1857 to provide a shortcut for goods to travel from the Atlantic Ocean to the Gulf. Other rail lines soon followed, both for hauling Florida agriculture and timber products north to more populated states, and for bringing affluent tourists south to enjoy the climate and natural features of this virgin land.

"When Florida achieved statehood in 1845, the site for the new state capitol was chosen as Tallahassee, half-way between the two primary Spanish settlements of St. Augustine and Pensacola on the two coasts. Although the largest city in Florida at that time was Key West, it was accessed only by ship and not considered a factor by the new state government. The federal government financed a road across the northern part of the state linking St. Augustine and Pensacola through Tallahassee, but it took a week's travel to reach the state capitol from either city. Railroads provided much more efficient means of travel and two wealthy men became responsible for opening up the new state to development through their railroad construction. Henry Plant linked his rail network with logging lines down coastal Georgia from Savannah and extended his lines through the state to Tampa, thereby providing transport of citrus crops as well as lumber from this vast central area of the state, previously accessible only by riverboats and wagons pulled by oxen or horses. Henry Flagler, longtime partner of John D. Rockefeller in Standard Oil and one of the richest men in the country, developed more ambitious plans for rail lines and tourist hotels south from the Georgia border along Florida's entire east coast, and eventually to Key West.

Flagler first visited Florida in 1876, on orders of his wife's doctor to have her vacation in a warmer climate than winter in New York (Mary suffered from chronic bronchitis). He was distressed with the condition of both St. Augustine and Jacksonville. He believed that accommodations and transportation were dismal, relative to accommodations in other resort settings for affluent consumers that he had experienced, and he vowed not to return. But, in 1882, he did return to St. Augustine after his wife's death and he expressed pleasure at the positive changes in the city. It was here that he determined to make profitable changes in both transportation and lodgings, in order to open up the natural beauty of this new state to affluent tourists. He began by hiring two New York architects to design a luxury hotel to complement the sixteenth-century Spanish style of buildings in that city. They took liberties in their extravagant design to ensure the building's appeal to New York's wealthy clientele. This resulted in one of the earliest and largest cast-concrete buildings in the United States, when completed in 1887 and opened in January 1888. He added to his patrons' enjoyment by the purchase of a small local railroad from Jacksonville to St. Augustine (and south to Daytona Beach), so that visitors could travel in relative comfort from boat to train, into the historic city where he built the first of many hotels to come—the magnificent Ponce de Leon Hotel remains today as Flagler College in the heart of St. Augustine.

The response from Flagler's New York friends and neighbors was outstanding and encouraged him to devote the rest of his life (1830-1913) to developing the eastern coast of Florida. As Flagler's railroad continued south (to Miami by 1896, and then on to Key West in 1912, finishing in January, just eighteen months before his death in May of 1913), he built magnificent resort hotels as he went, and simultaneously gave birth to the cities of Ormond Beach, Palm Beach, West Palm Beach and Miami. Only one of his hotels, The Breakers in Palm Beach, is still operational today (although the Casa Monica which he purchased across the street from the Ponce de Leon re-opened ten years ago and continues to operate as one of St. Augustine's premier hotels). For the last twenty-five years of his life, Henry Flagler committed his energies to development of Florida's east coast and can rightfully be considered as the "father of Florida tourism".

Exhibit 3:
The Breakers Hotel in Palm Beach, constructed by Henry Flagler.
Photo by Nick Juhasz of the Breakers Hotel

"Now, we can move on to the results of Plant's and Flagler's initiative in terms of Florida growth over the past one-hundred years, including the extraordinary American population shift after 1950 when migrants poured into Florida from every part of the United States, as well as the Caribbean, Latin America and even Asia.

During the last half of the twentieth century, fellow Sunbelt states, Texas and California, tripled in population while Florida increased by a factor of six, from under three-million to sixteen-million residents, an astounding growth rate of about seven-hundred persons per day. Nine of the nation's "fastest growing cities" were in Florida during this period. Florida dominated the list of fastest-growing Metropolitan Statistical Areas (MSAs)—areas defined by county boundaries to account for suburban growth around central cities.

Mark then explained that the city of Jacksonville remains the largest city in the state, primarily because other large cities retained their original boundaries whereas, in 1969, Jacksonville amalgamated with surrounding Duval County to become the largest geographical city in area within the continental United States.

Mark distributed letter-size copies of the outline of the state of Florida showing the boundaries and names of the state's eleven planning districts superimposed on the state's sixty-seven counties.

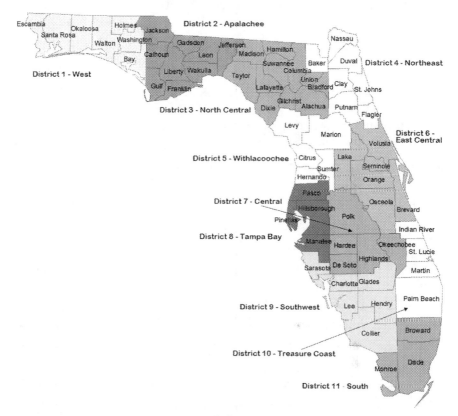

Exhibit 4:
Florida Planning Districts.

"There are sixty-seven counties in Florida, each with local land-planning responsibilities and controls, usually separated from similar powers vested with cities, all of which are monitored by a state planning agency known as the Department of Community Affairs. Florida's growth management laws are now amongst the most restrictive in United States, since new laws were put into effect beginning in the 1970s. Before that time, land development control was fragmented and relatively ineffective, resulting in a great deal of inefficient land use, as well as both visual and physical pollution accompanied by environmental destruction. We will witness many areas from the air that exhibit extensive wasteland resulting from lack of government control or badly regulated growth management.

"I have wrestled with the best way to introduce this state to you within two weeks and I have come up with a program utilizing the helicopter for daily trips to all portions of the state north of the Florida Keys. During these trips, I can describe each portion and simultaneously provide summaries of historical and contemporary events. I have passed out copies to each of you of the eleven state planning districts superimposed on county boundaries, to illustrate what I believe to be the most efficient route to tour the state by helicopter, covering one planning district per day in numeric order of their identification. You can compare these districts to the large-scale map of Florida to orient them to cities and transportation routes.

"The eleven planning districts illustrated on your handout encompass all sixty-seven counties in the state and, in my opinion, are numbered in logical order for an air tour of the state. I propose that we examine one of these districts each day for the next ten days and that the Logan yacht 'Victoria' proceed down the Atlantic coast to selected moorings as a nightly base of operations. This program will ensure that the yacht is always in reasonable proximity to each day's helicopter tour.

"The first two planning districts are exceptions to the nightly return schedule. Since Planning Districts 1 and 2 cover the Florida Panhandle, three-to-four-hundred miles distant from here, I suggest that this general plan be interrupted tomorrow night by parking the helicopter at Destin airport, about fifty miles west of Panama City, for an overnight stay in a local hotel. All other nights can easily be accommodated on the yacht according to the schedule I have discussed with Franz Ericksson.

"Jake, I have typed this proposed schedule for you and Captain Ericksson to review this afternoon with the objective of finalizing it before dinner, so you both can begin making any necessary arrangements before we begin our first tour tomorrow morning—the four-hundred-mile trip west before we begin touring District 1. I realize this is short notice, but can you meet with the captain this afternoon, so we can finalize the plan before dinner?"

"I'll give it my best try, Mark. What about routings for each district tour?"

"Ah, now I'm afraid we cannot plan those so far ahead, Jake. I believe the best we can do is brief you in the evening of each day prior to departure. However, I did bring along a detailed atlas of Florida showing the land at larger scale. Here it is for you to review the first District before tomorrow. I assume you must file a flight plan tonight if we are to lift off at daybreak."

"Roger that, Mark," replied Jake with his usual smile. "I had better leave now and get to work, eh." And Jake smiled his departure to everyone as he rose to leave.

"So, any other questions or suggestions on the route plan?" continued Mark. "If not, I would like to turn to a second agenda item."

"Yes, Mark," responded Nash. "You certainly have put some careful thought into this schedule and I cannot see any problem with it at the moment. But let's defer it until we hear back from Jake and Franz later this afternoon. In the interim, I suggest we take a twenty-minute break before we move ahead with the next item on your agenda."

Mark and Bobbi went back to their cabin to freshen up. Once inside, Mark asked Bobbi her opinion on the introductory session.

"Mark, you were magnificent, just as I expected you would be—a concise historical overview followed by an efficient tour plan. I believe you thoroughly enjoy being back in the saddle again."

"Well, darling, I must admit that this is fun, but I am not angling for a long-term commitment. I just demand excellence at my chosen profession, and this assignment simply draws upon knowledge already stored in my idle brain from forty years of practice. Do you feel that I am throwing too much at them too fast?"

"No, not at all," replied Bobbi. "They were all fascinated with your presentation, even Jake, who has no direct commitment to the subject area."

"Yes, I found his attention surprising as well. In fact, Nash has assembled a great little team here. My feedback thus far indicates that I will enjoy working with them. And Nash himself appears to be a very intelligent person as well as charming."

"Well, after all, he didn't make all that money by accident. I suspect that he purposely masks a very calculating mind behind his casual demeanor."

"No question about it," smiled Mark. "So let's go back up and throw some more serious information at him."

When Mark and Bobbi returned to the main lounge, they found everyone seated and ready to hear the next phase of Mark's presentation.

"Welcome back, everyone. The next item on my agenda is Nash's development concept. In order to help you find an optimum location for a new community, we need to have a common concept of what this community is to be: what kind of land uses, what kind of residents, what kind of employees, what kind of on-site amenities, what kind of off-site amenities, what kind of access, et cetera. You need to tell me about your dream and allow me to clarify the parameters of the site that will suit the dream."

"Excellent," replied Nash. "I am not sure I can answer all of these questions, but let's get started and see what we can do. Remember, everyone, you are all pledged to confidentiality on what I am about to reveal.

"First of all, I need to give a little background. I started Logan Homes with a loan from my uncle in 1973. I was twenty-three years old and I had been working for a homebuilder for two years in my hometown of Kitchener, Ontario. Kitchener was then a small city about sixty miles west of Toronto. It was founded by German immigrants to Canada and originally named Berlin, but in 1916, during World War I, the city leaders diplomatically changed the name to that of the famous English General Kitchener. It actually adjoins the city of Waterloo, the home of what is now Waterloo University, and the twin cities were normally referred to as Kitchener-Waterloo. Today, it is the hub of a metropolitan area including Waterloo and the neighboring city of Cambridge with over four-hundred-and-fifty thousand residents, the fifth largest metropolitan area in the province of Ontario. I had received a landscape design degree from nearby Guelph Agriculture College and I handled all of the landscape design and planting for the builder. But, after my Dad died suddenly in a senseless traffic accident, my uncle received a half-million dollar payoff from a partnership insurance policy with my Dad, and he decided to set me up in business with one-hundred-thousand dollars of his payment. So, despite what you may read in press releases, that is how I got my start. My Uncle Ted is long gone now, but I am pleased to report that I paid him back with healthy interest before his death.

"Because of my inexperience, I initially partnered with the superintendent of construction of the builder who employed me, and we began building houses on the heels of the recession that swept the United States and Canada in 1974. I brought in a second partner who was a design architect and we quickly gained a reputation in central Ontario for innovative housing. Over the years, as we grew to establish operations in other cities, I bought out my initial partners and established a marketing firm to ensure our personal growth at minimal cost. It worked and we out-hustled some very tough competition to become one of Canada's biggest homebuilders in 2005, with operations in eight major cities stretching from Montreal to Vancouver.

"In 2001, I was introduced to a brilliant young architect named Nathan Rosenberg who had just won the Canadian Housing Design Council Award for the best small house design in Canada. He was just thirty years old. I immediately hired him as Vice President of Design and Development and, within two years, Nathan had completely re-designed all of our offerings to be more appealing designs at less cost and subsequent lower prices than our competition. Now, we were not only recognized as innovative and good quality, but the best buy as well. Nathan was the cause of our rapid rise to number one, and I made him Executive Vice President with free rein to become even more innovative. So, in addition, to managing the business operations of a cross-Canada builder, Nathan set to work on a plan to revolutionize the house-building industry.

"It turned out that Nathan's older brother, David Rosenberg, was a senior chemist in one of Canada's biggest chemical companies, that was experimenting with a wide range of products based upon non-petroleum derivatives, primarily extracted from plant sources. In casual conversation, they discovered that several of the chemical company's emergent products contained amazing strength capabilities in addition to being susceptible to production in many forms. That is, they were like a chameleon in terms of being adaptable to designs resembling virtually any traditional building material. But, better, they could be bonded to other materials through chemical applications rather than nails, screws, superglue or duct tape. The result is 'packaged housing' that is stronger, cheaper, and as good-looking as anything on the market. In short, we have the capability of re-producing any kind of house or mid-rise condominium in stronger format at less cost than traditional methods. By the way, plumbing, mechanical and electrical conduits can be built right into the structure with no-leak capacity. And, on top of all this, we can produce the housing units in a factory in one-third the time it requires for stick-built dwellings and even faster than any manufactured housing on the market today.

"How do I know all of this is true? The answer is that we purchased an old industrial building in the east-Toronto suburb of Ajax two years ago and equipped it as a prototype factory for producing prototype houses. To date we have three detached dwellings complete, ready for on-site foundations, and a new 'Lego Block' apartment for stacked construction. Each of these prototypes comes in reduction and/or expansion plans for varying size products—over thirty house types and eight apartment types to date. Finally, they all are designed to be partitioned for highway or railway travel prior to being chemically rejoined on-site. We are ready to launch this entire product line subject to marketing materials and the right location.

Of course, everything I have been telling you has been accomplished under strict security. You are the only people outside a small group of Logan Homes' staff that are privy to this information.

"This leads me to why we are all here. The Canadian housing market is a little over one-tenth the size of the American market in normal times. Florida is about to become once again one of the top three or four markets in this country. Currently land prices are at the lowest point we have seen in a couple of decades. And, in case you haven't noticed, it is a lot warmer down here than in my homeland. Voila, this is the place to launch our new product. Questions? Mark?"

"Nash, this is an extraordinary story. Thank goodness that Bobbi has it all on tape because I must listen to it several times to digest everything you said, especially the chemical advances about which I would like to learn more."

"And you will," interrupted Nash with a smile, "but I am not the right person to brief you on these details. You can learn more when you meet Nathan in a couple of weeks."

"I look forward to it," replied Mark. "But the important aspect for this tour is to dissect the land uses and transportation needs of this concept so we can narrow down site options. For example, you stated that you must have a factory operation for production of these houses. How much land will it require and how many people will it employ at what level of wages?"

"Excellent questions, but we do not yet have a complete answer for them, to date. It depends on how far we can ship these units economically before constructing another factory. But Nathan's initial estimate is that we should allow about one-hundred acres for the factory and essential suppliers, including expansion potential for up to twenty-five completed units per month. We haven't discussed employment projections, but early indications are that we might average four-hundred square feet per employee in a five-hundred-thousand square foot building, or twelve-hundred-and-fifty employees in our factory plus another five-hundred in supplier facilities and another five-hundred in community services occupations—say twenty-two-hundred-and-fifty employees on-site. I believe expansion over a ten-year community build-out would boost total on-site employment to three-thousand, of which eighty percent, or twenty-four-hundred, would elect to live on-site in about two-thousand dwellings."

"How much would you pay them, or, put another way, would it be your objective to provide housing suitable for all of them on-site?"

"Absolutely, that is our plan. However, I am not so naïve as to believe we could capture them all, even with special incentives for employees living on-site. I believe our lowest-paying employees would earn fifteen dollars per hour, or about thirty-thousand dollars per year in today's dollar values. Average household income for that primary wage earner, assuming a second basic wage earner, would equal about forty-five-thousand dollars per year.

"I believe that the concept of financing infrastructure and amenities through Community Development Districts in Florida has failed, given the huge number of such districts currently in default. But, regardless, we plan to set up a Community Land Trust for the entire residential portion of the community and thereby spread out land purchase and infrastructure costs over fifty years; thus following the formula made successful many years ago by mobile home parks.

"In addition to the lower cost of our 'packaged housing' dwellings, this would enable us to sell detached homes to families with children having a household income of less than forty-five-thousand per year in current money value. If we provide these prices as an incentive to persons employed within the community, our capture rate should be over 80 percent on employees."

"How about catering to retirees, Florida's biggest import?"

"Absolutely, we would be derelict to ignore this market, and also we want to sell this community as 'Logan Lifetime Living' for employees to eventually retire here with a continuation of their employment incentive, as well as attracting non-local retirees. We do not want to be labeled as just a company town. I conceptualize about half the community in retiree housing and half in employed housing, say about four-thousand total dwellings on a site of about twelve-hundred acres. The important point for government officials is that we plan to develop a self-contained community where most people live in proximity to their work, thus responding in positive fashion to those who are concerned about contributing to daily traffic congestion."

"That is an outstanding objective, but your land estimates are a little low for Florida," said Mark. "We must allow for wetland in almost every area of the state. Nevertheless, from what you have given me, I can estimate Florida land use for your concept. "I have listed my estimates on the sheet of paper which I am duplicating in clearer writing for Jimmy to copy."

	Acreage	Dwellings
Industrial Park	100 acres	
Mixed Use Commercial Center	50 acres	400 dwellings
Peripheral Highway & Institutional Uses	20 acres	
Residential Uses (at 3.5 per acre)	800 acres	3,200 dwellings
Amenities (incl. public golf course)	200 acres	
Major Roads	50 acres	
Water Retention (at 12% + 3% golf)	170 acres	
Conservation & Open Space	100 acres	
Total Site	1,490 acres	3,600 dwellings
Conservation Contingency	50-500 acres	
Gross Site Acquisition	1,500 – 2,000 acres	

Exhibit 5:
LoganTown Concept Plan Land Uses and Dwellings.

Mark continued speaking, after writing down the above list for Jimmy to type and make copies for everyone. "So I suggest that you may be searching for a Florida site of around fifteen-hundred to two-thousand acres to accomplish your dream. It depends a great deal on the amount of wetland on any given site, a major factor in estimating land use in Florida. In addition, on average, each new development must provide about fifteen percent of its gross area for storm water retention.

"I also believe that transportation access is a major factor for shipping your products to other cities, as well as receiving materials to construct your 'packaged housing.' I imagine that such access should include rail, as well as interstate highway, access."

"You are absolutely right, Mark," interjected Nash. "High volume transportation is essential for both incoming and outgoing products."

"With respect to migrating retirees," Mark continued, "we must keep in mind that a high proportion of them prefer to live within an easy drive—say an hour—of a major metropolitan center so they can avail themselves of shopping, cultural, sports and entertainment facilities only available in such centers. For example, the late Harold Schwartz and his son Gary Morse have developed the biggest and best-selling retiree community in Florida in the center of Lake County between Leesburg and Ocala, at less than an hour's drive from Orlando and Tampa. We will visit 'The Villages' on our tour of District 6.

"Your point on the virtual collapse of Community Development Districts, Florida's widely acclaimed solution to deferring costs of acquisition and development costs for resident payments over time, is right on target. Current reports indicate that there are over one-hundred and twenty-five CDDs in default across the state and another ninety on the watch list. Clearly, this method of financing new development must be re-considered in future. Your plan to establish a long-term community land trust will be welcomed by public officials, assuming of course, that you have patient money to invest in the proposed land trust. Please keep in mind that the establishment of such a trust may require additional permanent conservation land be included in your site, thereby increasing the overall size by ten percent or more. On the positive side, as you noted earlier, the land trust concept can be presented as a very strong marketing tool.

"These are the major concept criteria I wanted to clear up before we get started, Nash. We now have a good set of parameters for site selection. So, I suggest we move on to my fourth and final agenda item for this preliminary session—the process of large-scale development approval."

"Good," replied Nash as he checked his watch. "Let's take a break now and resume after dinner, with the objective of saving time for a decent cocktail session prior to dinner with Captain Ericksson here at seven pm. Does that sound okay?"

"Works for me," said Mark, as he gathered up his notes, took Bobbi by the hand, and headed for their cabin.

Dinner aboard the "Victoria" was another taste treat for Mark and Bobbi Wilkins as well as their fellow diners, beginning with shrimp cocktail, followed by Caesar salad, New York strip steaks grilled to perfection and béarnaise sauce on the side, with fresh asparagus garnished with a light cheese sauce and a dessert of very light chocolate mousse. Of course, Jose offered both red and white wine choices from the delightful Burrowing Owl collection, but Mark and Bobbi both limited themselves to one glass, having each enjoyed two mixed drinks before dinner. Jose and Alfredo hovered behind the seven diners, eager to fulfill everyone's slightest culinary wish.

In addition to the Wilkins and their new colleagues, Nash Logan, Jimmy Quickfoot, and Jake Johnson, the yacht's Captain Franz Ericksson and his Chief Engineer, Tim Wilson, joined them for cocktails and dinner. All seven of them sat around a single round table with the conversation centered on the proposed yacht schedule down the Atlantic Coast as far as Fort Lauderdale and the good and not-so-good aspects of each proposed port. Ericksson was a large man with blonde hair, at least five inches over six feet tall, with a slight accent from his Swedish upbringing that gave added charm to his appealing personality, especially magnified by his handsome white uniform with captain's insignia in gold on the epaulets and sleeves. He exuded the confidence that gave both of the Wilkins comfort about the management of their new floating home. Wilson was a smaller and younger man of less than six feet and athletic-looking in his white uniform. He did not have the outgoing personality of his captain, but responded politely when questioned. At the end of the meal, Nash introduced his pair of smiling chefs, Pierre and Marie Bouvet (pronounced in the French manner ending in "ay"), who were natives of Trois Rivieres, Quebec, and spoke English with a pronounced French accent. Both were short and rather plump, a fitting image for chefs.

Bobbi sat next to Jimmy Quickfoot during dinner and learned that he was a full-blooded Mohawk Indian, also from the Province of Quebec, raised on a farm near the Vermont border in the part of the province called the Eastern Townships. Although pleased to be invited on this tour, he expressed a confidential disappointment at missing the early spring skiing at Jay Peak on the Quebec/Vermont border. Bobbi mentioned that she recently read an article claiming that this border was a little-publicized location of smuggling operations. Jimmy smiled and responded that the border actually runs right through the middle of his hometown, so one misstep could put you across the border. It was no surprise to him that smuggling was a regular enterprise that occupied the attention of many local citizens. The issue for border residents is not whether you smuggle, but rather whether you get caught, he had stated with a smile.

At the completion of dessert, Nash offered after-dinner drinks and expressed some disappointment that only Jake and Franz joined him in a Remy Martin brandy. The others, including the Wilkins, appeared sensitive to the scheduled evening session yet to come.

As Nash Logan was enjoying dinner with his companions on the "Victoria", Albert Siegal was joining Jack Swift and Kurt Richter in the latter's law office conference room in central Orlando. After exchanging terse greetings, the two younger men turned their attention to Siegal.

"Gentlemen, I just finished a call on my cell phone from our Caribbean benefactor, who reminded me in rather strong language of our Florida objective. We have too much cash in our accounts waiting for long-term investment. Kurt cannot continue to open new accounts without attracting the attention of federal agents, and our patrons cannot, and will not, risk identification."

"Did he actually threaten you?" asked Kurt.

"No, I am certain that he felt threats to be unnecessary. He is well aware of his family's reputation in taking care of non-performing associates, and he knows that we are equally aware. Failure will not be tolerated. In short, our very lives are at stake. We cannot delay additional investment projects any longer. Mr. Swift, what about it?"

"Albert, you know very well that the entire development industry is at a standstill. My very best prodding and pushing is not generating any new activity."

"Except for the Canadian," interjected Richter.

"Yes, he is our only candidate at the moment," responded Swift, "but I have not been able to break through his people for a personal interview."

"Up until now!" spoke Siegal in a quiet voice. "You must report progress tomorrow, no excuses." The older man looked directly at Swift and asked "Do you understand, Mr. Swift, no excuses?"

The usually vibrant Jack Swift turned visibly pale before answering in a subdued voice: "Yes sir, I understand." Then he pushed back his chair and left the room without another word.

Back in the "Victoria" main lounge, everyone had finished dessert and after-dinner drinks. Nash Logan stood up from his chair and received immediate attention from his companions.

"Alright, everybody, let's adjourn to the corner table to learn some more from Mark about land planning and development in Florida," announced Nash in a louder voice than usual, as he rose from his chair and led the group to the corner table. The large Florida map, that had been on the table during the afternoon, now was mounted on an easel facing the table; leaving the table surface clear for other material. Jimmy immediately set up his computer and Bobbi readied her tape recorder to preserve Mark's new presentation.

"First of all," said Mark after taking a seat, "I should ask Franz and Jake if they have any problems with my preliminary yacht schedule?"

Jake looked toward Franz, and the captain replied with a gracious smile before stating "We have reviewed it thoroughly, Mark, and I believe it to be an excellent plan. I already have been in touch with Camachee Cove in St. Augustine, as you suggested, and fortunately they can accommodate us for three nights on the end of their dock. I have never been there, but the website indicates a very pleasant mooring on the river, just a short taxi ride into the old city. I will proceed with the rest of the arrangements tomorrow morning."

Mark then turned to Jake: "I too have been busy booking a parking spot at Destin Airport, and Mark kindly arranged with a former client to accommodate us at one of the newest condo hotels at the mouth of the inlet in the center of town. So we are set to depart at seven tomorrow morning for the four-hundred-mile ride over to Pensacola, during which I will look forward to more explicit instructions from Mark."

"Excellent," interjected Nash. "I am eager to see this young state."

"Young is correct," replied Mark, "at least in terms of European settlement. Florida was a relatively wild frontier prior to the railroads extending beyond Jacksonville in the latter half of the nineteenth century. Except for the sailing port at Fort Pierce, and small docks at Fort Lauderdale, and an anchorage at what is now Miami, as well as the cattle export dock at Punta Rassa west of today's Fort Myers, and docks for shallow draft boats at Tampa and at Pensacola, transportation in this state was by horse and wagon. Key West, the site of a United States Navy Base, was our largest city, but essentially in another country on an island Now, of course, it's heralded in song as 'Margaritaville' and proclaimed as the 'Conch Republic' by local residents." Mark continued to summarize the state's land use history.

Up until the beginning of the twentieth century, most of the Florida interior south of what is now Orlando was open range much like the old west from cowboy movies. The laissez-faire attitude of Florida settlers right up until the 1960s generated a great deal of uncontrolled development and permanent damage to the environment, perhaps the most dramatic being the invasion of the Everglades by agricultural interests from the north and urban developers from the east.

Florida's growth management laws were first introduced in the 1970s and revised several times since to make Florida one of the most difficult and expensive states in this nation in which to develop land and construct housing.

"I believe this introduction is a necessary prerequisite to exploring potential new community sites, beginning tomorrow. I hope that you all agree," concluded Mark.

"By golly, folks," interrupted Nash loudly, "we sure snared the right man to lead this tour. Lead on Mark."

Blushing slightly, Mark continued: "Thank you, Nash, but I suggest you save your applause until we finish the job. There's no telling what mistakes I have yet to make. Then, he continued to explain Florida growth management.

Government land use control throughout Florida prior to 1970 was sporadic and subject to the goals of dozens of competing interests. Some of the disastrous results of this laissez-faire attitude will be visible from the planned helicopter tour. Economic growth was paramount in Florida and government corruption was common.

These negative results eventually motivated both politicians and professional planners to work together toward a comprehensive approach to growth management, that resulted in two 1972 pieces of legislation entitled the "Florida Environmental Land and Water Management Act" (ELMS Act, revised over subsequent years) and the "State Comprehensive Planning Act". The first was designed to control growth and the second to "provide long-range guidance of the orderly social, economic and physical growth of the state". The Legislature also passed the "Land Conservation Act" (and approved in public referendum in November of 1972) which allowed the state to purchase environmentally threatened lands. A decade later, in 1985, the Florida Legislature passed the "Growth Management Act" which mandated the most detailed plans ever prepared for Florida counties and municipalities. It included a "concurrency" provision requiring local governments to pay for infrastructure (adequate roads, water, sewer, hospitals, libraries and schools) concurrently with new growth—a "pay-as-you-build" policy.

Despite the carefully drafted provisions of these strong legislative actions, the state of Florida continued to experience difficulty regulating new growth. Pro-growth advocates extolling economic benefits consistently overpowered the objections of planners and environmentalists. Government officials frequently were indicted for accepting bribes for votes. Comprehensive plan amendments at the local level became common activities as developers argued successfully that increasing property taxes would pay the costs of local services. Development of unincorporated areas across the state proliferated with septic tanks instead of sewers and congested local roads becoming the norm.

The very active Sierra Club defined "sprawl" as separation of residential areas from daily homeowner destinations (employment, shopping, schools, recreation) causing increasing traffic congestion; and this nationwide conservation advocacy group conducted a 1999 study that cited Florida as the nation's leader in "edgeless sprawl" (i.e., beyond municipal jurisdictions). The Orlando metropolitan area was proclaimed the leading generator of such sprawl in the country, a good deal of which was attributable to the Disney magic that, along with its collegial theme parks, became the world's largest consumer attraction.

Proponents of "new urbanism", that was initiated in Florida with the model vacation community of Seaside, identified the generic definition of sprawl as lying at the root of the country's nineteenth-century gridiron patterns. But developers and builders reacted to majority consumer attraction to contemporary lower density suburban patterns, with continuation of horizontal growth throughout this state and across the nation. With the stimulus of exotic mortgage instruments from unregulated financial institutions, home ownership nationwide grew to almost seventy percent of households, as the American dream of home ownership appeared to come within reach of people from all walks of life.

Accelerating demand for larger houses and lots in the new century drove up prices concurrently with municipal costs. Builders reacted with increasingly expensive new home products and municipalities countered with local impact fees that drove up new home prices even higher. The latter revenue source became even more popular as state and federal aid programs declined, so Florida local governments increased impact fees. Spiraling prices soon attracted investors who perceived higher returns in new housing than in alternative investments, especially with the cooperation of low-price mortgage lenders.

The housing feeding frenzy, that drove nationwide production to over two-million new dwellings per year, coupled with the globalization of the secondary mortgage market providing international buyers of American house mortgages, resulted in The Great Recession of 2007 to 2009, with the lasting negative impact extending into 2010 and beyond. Buyers disappeared, foreclosures skyrocketed and property prices of all kinds fell rapidly. The term "short sale" came into vogue, that described a sale transaction in which the value of the property is lower than its mortgage amount. These conditions are expected to continue beyond 2010, as accompanying high unemployment and the international credit lockdown contribute to the vastly diminished consumer demand for new homes.

"Of course," Mark stated, "the nation and Florida will recover from this worst manmade disaster since World War II, but it will be a recovery tempered by widespread price sensitivity and interest in value versus status symbols—in fact, value may become the new status symbol of a much more frugal American population.

"Florida is overstocked with entitled and even improved land inventory which will influence low property prices for several years. New development will be restrained by this over-supply, as well as by more cautious consumers. Governments at all levels already are being pressured by consumer groups to exert stronger controls over developers and to exercise greater watchfulness over lobby groups attempting to direct their legislation. Although many believe that growth mistakes of the past may be too overwhelming to re-direct toward sustainable development, the fact is that responsible professionals representing both public and private interests must forge new dimensions of cooperation in order to make a new start in Florida. The entry of Logan Homes may provide a special opportunity to initiate this new start."

"Amen to that Mark," interjected Nash. "That is precisely why we are here—not to tell Florida officials how it should be done, but rather to offer a cooperative approach to producing a better living environment for all income groups. I believe we can do that, and I am elated that we have a man of Dr. Wilkins' experience and knowledge to guide us. Carry on, Mark."

Florida has literally dozens of agencies at four levels of government that become intimately involved in the approval or rejection of every large-scale development. Title VIII, Chapter 186, of the Florida Statutes defines planning and growth management within this state. As is true throughout the United States, all local governments are creatures of the state and subject to state law for governing their jurisdictions. Therefore, although cities and counties throughout Florida are responsible for governing local land uses, they must do so within the confines of a comprehensive plan approved by the state. The regulating agency here is called the Florida Department of Community Affairs (DCA). Any change in land use must be submitted to the local government for a change in that jurisdiction's comprehensive plan, and subsequently submitted for approval to the DCA.

Those land use changes, including marinas, that may impact areas beyond the local jurisdiction, also must be approved by the relevant Regional Planning Council, of which there are eleven, corresponding to the eleven Planning Districts. The members of each Regional Planning Council are appointed by the Florida Governor, and include at least one representative from every political jurisdiction in that district.

The definition of regional impact is determined by the scale of the proposed land use change. Impact thresholds for each jurisdiction are defined for each land use and published annually by the state. Regional Planning Agencies have discretion not limited by these impact thresholds, but they generally abide by them. These thresholds of regional impact always have been an issue of debate in the law, insofar as they are calculated according to each jurisdiction's population, rather than to specific impact criteria; that is, the larger the jurisdiction's population, the larger the threshold. Those that exceed the threshold are termed a Development of Regional Impact (DRI) and are subject to a much more rigorous approval process.

The land management debate centers on the fact that knowledgeable developers carefully acquire land that accommodates housing, or other land uses below the threshold, to avoid the rigors of the DRI approval process; or, conversely, developers planning a large scale community with state-of-the-art planning and amenities are considered penalized by more arduous approval regulations compared to rules applied to smaller subdivision developers with few or no amenities. Consequently, the issue of regional impact is under constant re-examination and occasional experimentation in terms of its being the primary solution to responsible growth management. However, anyone contemplating large-scale development in Florida must assume a difficult multi-agency approval process generally requiring at least two years and over two-million dollars in costs for consultant studies, advice and reports—a high risk decision, insofar as there is no guarantee that all of this time and money will result in a satisfactory outcome.

"Excuse me a moment," interjected Nash, "but you are rolling along at a pretty good clip with a pile of important information. Jimmy, are you keeping up with Mark, or should we re-visit some of these subjects?"

"No problem, Mr. Logan. I believe I have kept up with Dr. Wilkins so far—not verbatim, you understand, but I have all of the significant highlights."

"Okay, great. Let's move ahead Mark. Excuse me for interrupting."

"I would be remiss in explaining this process if I did not mention two other pieces of legislation from last year, and a proposed constitutional change going to the electorate next November. House Bill 697 includes new land use regulations on five different components: (1) energy-efficient land use patterns; (2) greenhouse gas reduction strategies in transportation buildings; (3) energy conservation; (4) energy efficiency in design and construction; and (5) use of renewable energy sources. Each of these components is designed to make new land development more responsive to energy concerns. They increase long-term efficiency at the expense of higher initial development cost, thereby tending to drive up the cost of housing, in support of statewide energy conservation and support of 'green' programs—a noble objective which may reduce opportunities for affordable housing for modest income households that provide essential employees for both public and private enterprises—another paradox in the continuing Florida development conundrum of trying to accommodate new employers and migrants at the expense of environmental hazards.

"Senate Bill 360, on the other hand, reduces initial development costs for projects in 'Designated Transportation Concurrency Exception Areas' (TCEAs), a new term defining areas in cities or counties that are already urban centers, according to a rather modest criterion of one-thousand people per square mile of land area. These areas become exempt from state-mandated transportation concurrency requirements and the DRI review process for new or expanding development. Concurrency, you will recall from my earlier discussion, is a legal term which means that existing infrastructure is sufficient to accommodate planned new development. So this law provides an incentive for development in existing urban centers, in comparison with less developed areas of the state, presumably reducing sprawl by encouraging developers to target existing urban centers.

"However, SB 360 goes further in bolstering existing urban centers by mandating that local governments must adopt 'Transportation Strategies' into their Comprehensive Plans. These strategies include alternative modes of transportation, and local governments are encouraged to adopt complementary strategies that reflect the Planning District's 'Vision' for its future. Such multi-mode transportation reflects federal funding to support alternative forms of transportation in lieu of existing primary reliance upon subsidized highways. Clearly, Nash, this law provides incentives to large-scale developers for incorporating more efficient forms of transportation."

"Excuse me," said Jimmy, looking up from his computer note-taking, "does this mean that we must respond positively to these issues in order to gain development approval?"

"Absolutely, Jimmy. And, furthermore, I strongly suggest that you launch your initial promotion with direct attention to innovation on these exact concerns. Pre-empt expected criticism by joining hands with the environmentalists and conservationists in planning to produce a better and more economic place to live, work and play.

"The biggest event in growth management this year is the scheduled vote on the so-called 'Home Town Democracy Amendment' to the State Constitution. You need to understand that Florida laws are based upon the State Constitution that requires a two-thirds majority vote to change (the primary reason that this state is not likely to ever have an income tax). The supporters of the 'Home Town Democracy Amendment' have been gathering petition signatures for several years to put this amendment on the ballot. Their name for the amendment certainly has proven appealing to a great many Floridians, especially those who have not taken the time to study the cost implications of this proposed amendment. In essence, it mandates that every proposed land use change to the comprehensive plan would require a public referendum vote in the affected political jurisdiction to achieve approval. The result would be enormous new costs on local governments as well as a severe constraint on new development. Supporters of the proposed amendment claim that it would put such decisions in the hands of the people rather than leave them up to public officials who are unduly influenced (they actually use stronger language) by wealthy developers.

"Opponents cite both excessive cost and inefficiency in applying this legislation through the process of local government, as well as tremendous job losses in the restrained construction industry. You can expect to see major publicity campaigns from both sides over coming months. But, as a prospective new developer, you would be well-advised to plan a government land use change submission prior to the end of this year to safeguard a 'grandfather' provision under existing law. Your current emphasis on speed appears to be wise."

"Wow," exclaimed Nash. "I know that approval is difficult in Florida, but your description puts some definitive parameters on it. Can you give us some idea of what is involved in the DRI process?"

"Yes," answered Mark. "I dug out an Application for Development Approval (ADA) from my files which, as you can see, is about six inches thick, and that doesn't include additional submissions for responses to agency questions on the ADA, often requiring two or three rounds of submissions. The application process includes answers to thirty questions relating to the proposed development plan and its economics and revenues in addition to its impact on: Vegetation and Wildlife, Wetlands, Water, Floodplains, Water Supply, Wastewater Management, Stormwater Management, Transportation, Air Quality, Hurricane Preparedness, Housing, Police and Fire Protection, Recreation and Open Space, Education, Historical and Archaeological Issues.

"As you can see, each submission usually contains several appendices of details supporting the question answers. Copies must be delivered to a host of government agencies. These agencies vary in number depending on the property location and local agencies in each jurisdiction, but suffice it to say that the submission requires a great many copies. In order to prepare the submission and responses, the applicant's study team also must include a large number of specialists, such as: Legal Services (usually the application coordinator), Project Planner, Market Research, Economics, Civil & Transportation Engineer, Environmental Consultant, and Land Surveyor.

"This very thick example is from a land-locked site plan. A site located on a waterway would have additional participants. You are welcome to examine the sample application in more detail at anytime throughout our tour, and I will be pleased to try and answer any of your questions about the process. It includes a host of meetings between team members and government agency officials as well as formal presentations to public agencies. Now, Nash, I suggest we adjourn, so that I can have time to plan tomorrow's agenda for Planning District 1."

"Absolutely, Mark, and thank you for such a comprehensive introduction to our tour! I believe you will have plenty of time to brief us about District 1 on the helicopter tomorrow morning. Jake says wheels up after daylight at seven-thirty am. Good-night everyone. I am grateful that each of you can be here."

DAY 1

Friday, March 26, 2010

Daylight Saving Time had been moved forward to March 14 this year, so the sun was just peeping over the eastern horizon to greet Mark Wilkins as he stepped out of the yacht's main lounge a few minutes after seven o'clock, upon completing a light breakfast of coffee and toast. Bobbi was still asleep in the cabin below-decks, planning to arise in plenty of time to meet her sister's flight from Atlanta in mid-morning. Jimmy Quickfoot and Jake Johnson were waiting for him by the Logan helicopter that appeared to be idling in preparation for takeoff. Nash Logan joined them a few minutes later and suggested that Jimmy ride in the front seat with Jake, leaving the spacious rear seat for Mark and himself. Jake stored their overnight bags in the luggage area, and the four of them climbed aboard, quickly donning their earphones and mikes for cabin conversation. Jimmy carried his laptop computer, and Mark had a briefcase full of information about the Florida Panhandle.

"Everyone buckled in?" questioned Jake, as he glanced at his three passengers prior to bringing the engine up to take-off speed. After clearing his airspace with Air Traffic Control, Jake piloted the red, yellow and green Bell 206L-4 up into the morning sky over downtown Jacksonville, and pointed it due west on the four-hundred-mile journey to Pensacola.

Once the helicopter settled into its flight altitude of five-thousand feet, Mark retrieved some reports from his briefcase in preparation for briefing his companions about their destination: Florida Planning District 1: West.

"Now that we are underway," began Mark, "let me tell you about District 1 well in advance of our arrival. This flight should follow Interstate 10 which is a straight road west, with increasingly higher elevations until we are well past Tallahassee. There are no special features except the city of Tallahassee on the left at the one-hundred-and-fifty mile mark and the huge Eglin Air Force Base on the left at about the three-hundred mile mark. But, if you have any questions along the way, please interrupt me at any time. In the meantime, I will proceed with the briefing."

"Mark, this is Nash. We are crossing what appears to be a major railroad yard east of a four-lane, north-south highway to the west of Jacksonville. Can you explain?"

"Yes, certainly.! We are just leaving Duval County. The railroad yard is the CSX railroad facility at the village of Macclenny, that is in Baker County to the west of the four-lane highway. The highway is U.S. 301, a major route into Florida prior to construction of north-south Interstate Highways 95 through downtown Jacksonville and 75 from Atlanta which we will cross over in a few minutes just north of Lake City. Highway 301 is still used by truck traffic as a shorter route to Ocala and points southwest from Jacksonville than going farther west to I-75. There are potential sites for you on this highway which we will tour in District 4 on Sunday."

"Good," replied Nash. "This area looks promising."

"Now, on with District 1! It is named West Florida Planning District, although most Floridians refer to it as the Panhandle because of its shape relative to the rest of the state. It is composed of seven counties, five of which adjoin the Gulf of Mexico with beautiful white sand beaches kissed by the Gulf Stream and referred to as the 'Emerald Coast'—a major summer playground for adjacent states as far west as Texas. It is bordered by the state of Alabama on the north and west with the west border being Escambia County linking Pensacola, Florida with Mobile, Alabama. The city of Pensacola extends to the state border along the Gulf Coast. The entire district contains over nine-hundred-thousand residents, most of whom live close to the Gulf Coast, and over a quarter of these in Pensacola.

"Pensacola residents claim the city to have been founded by Spanish settlers in the early sixteenth century, prior to the permanent founding of St. Augustine on the Atlantic coast, but national records cite St. Augustine as this country's oldest city. Pensacola's location on the Gulf Coast and its excellent climate motivated the founding of Pensacola Naval Air Station which served as a major training facility in both World Wars. Additional smaller Navy facilities and air fields also are located in and around Pensacola."

Mark referred Nash and Jimmy to the state map of Planning Districts and counties that he had handed out the previous day. He was prepared with extra copies, but both men quickly produced their own copies to use for reference.

After ensuring that both of his new colleagues had reference maps, Mark continued his description of Planning District 1. The other major government facility in this planning district is the massive Eglin Air Force Base—the largest air base in the free world—which extends across Okaloosa, Walton, and Santa Rosa Counties, encompassing nearly a half-million acres of land north of Fort Walton Beach. The primary Eglin airfield on the north edge of this small city also serves as a commercial airport for the central Panhandle. A low security federal prison is located

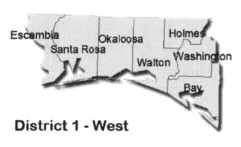

District 1 - West

Exhibit 6
Planning District 1—West.

adjacent to this airfield. As a result of the last military base reduction program (BRAC), Eglin received increased facilities devoted to high technology research projects. These projects generated a great many well-paid migrants to this area, leading to new housing developments north of the beachfront all the way up to and beyond I-10, particularly expanding the small city of Crestview. The entire area north of I-10 to the borders of Alabama and Georgia is farmland surviving from former slave-plantations which produced cotton and sugar cane up until Reconstruction banished slave labor, and effectively put them out of business.

The entire Gulf coast of the Panhandle is heavily developed with resort hotels and vacation homes in both low- and high-rise structures, serving consumers primarily within a five-hundred-mile radius of here, but also including Canadian winter visitors who take advantage of winter rental rates in this part of Florida being much lower than in south Florida."

"Are you suggesting that 'Canucks' are cheap, Mark?" said Nash with a touch of cynicism in his voice.

"Certainly not," replied Mark slyly. "As a planner, I just deal in facts, and the facts about Canadian spending habits in Florida are well documented; so there is no suggestion implied." His voice was followed by laughter from both Jake and Jimmy through the earphones. With that encouragement, Mark added: "I assume you gentlemen know the Florida definition of the difference between a Canuck and a canoe? Hearing no response, the answer is that a canoe tips." This time he was rewarded with laughter from Nash as well the others.

In a lighter tone, after his apparently successful attempt at humor with his new Canadian colleagues, Mark continued, "I am delighted to hear you are awake, Jake, because I would like to suggest that you request permission to set down at Pensacola Airport on the edge of the bay for a coffee break—no more than a half-hour, unless Nash wants to look at downtown Pensacola. Then, I propose that you skirt the Naval Air Base to the west and take a relatively low level run along the entire coastline from there to Panama City—about one-hundred miles—where we can set down the helicopter for lunch at a fine restaurant nearby. After that, Panama City being the eastern end of this District, I propose that we swing north past DeFuniak Springs and I-10 to show you the undeveloped land north of I-10 and extending west to Crestview and on to the Alabama border. I can point out some other interest areas along the way."

"Sounds like a good plan to me," responded Nash. "I am about ready for the airport men's room."

Jake was busy talking to Pensacola Tower, and got approval to land within the next fifteen minutes. The helicopter began its descent.

The rest room and coffee break at the Pensacola Regional Airport were a welcome respite from the two-hour flight in the helicopter. It took about thirty minutes for Jake to file a flight plan for the rest of the day. During that time, Nash was on the phone to his office in Toronto. When he finished his call, they all climbed back aboard to continue the first day's tour. As Jake expertly controlled the lift-off and headed southwest according to Mark's instructions, Nash spoke to Mark over the intercom: "Mark, my office tells me that they have received several phone calls from Florida realtors eager to speak to me about available parcels, but I left word that we are not considering potential acquisitions until after we complete this statewide tour. Does that make sense to you?"

"Absolutely," replied Mark, nodding his head. "I suggest that you do not even consider speaking with any real estate agents until we show you the entire state north of the Florida Keys."

In the interim, the helicopter moved toward the Alabama state line intersection with the Gulf Coast at Perdido Key State Park. On the flight over central Pensacola, Mark pointed out the large waterfront site of the Pensacola Naval Air Station, as well as wooded residential suburbs west of the city. As they flew out over the beautiful white sand beach of Perdido Key, they could see central Mobile, Alabama to the northwest, and miles of Gulf Coast shoreline to the east.

"Thank you, Jake," came Mark's voice through the helicopter earphones. "We are sitting on the southwest corner of Planning District 1 at the Alabama state line. That is the major seaport of Mobile on the shore of Mobile Bay to the northwest. Our interest is to the northeast. But, as an introduction to this District, I have asked Jake to take a low-level flight along the 'Emerald Coast' from here to Panama City, so you can get a feeling for this summer playground. You can see the derivation of the name 'Emerald Coast' from the beautiful green color of the water in contrast to the sugar-white sand of the beach. So, have at it, Jake, and we can pause anywhere anyone wants a closer look."

Mark had planned for this trip in advance by sitting on the right side of the helicopter to ensure that Nash had a full view of the coast on the left. The Canadian was clearly in awe of the brilliant color contrast between the turquoise and blue water next to the white sand and green trees and plants adjacent to the beach. Mark occasionally commented on specific projects he knew about from prior client assignments, but mostly he sat quietly and let Nash enjoy the scenery.

"We are coming up to the eastern end of Santa Rosa Island. You can see the small city of Fort Walton Beach beyond the narrow Santa Rosa

Sound, and immediately north of the city is the large Eglin Air Force Base which also contains the Okaloosa County Air terminal—one of the few instances where a military base doubles as a public airfield. The entire Eglin Air Force Base contains several airfields, with its area extending over three counties north of the coastal settlements. As I mentioned previously, the base now includes a number of transferred research projects which employ a large civilian workforce that stimulated a brief housing boom centered on the small city of Crestview north of I-10. We will have a closer look at it this afternoon.

"Right below us now is the small-boat cut from the Gulf of Mexico into Choctawhatchee Bay—an obvious Indian name left over from the nineteenth century, prior to early European settlers driving most of the native Indians (not killed on the spot) out of Southeast United States and sending them to reservation land in the sparsely-settled future Oklahoma—a sad chapter in American history. Choctawhatchee Bay is very shallow with a sand bottom, and the channel is dredged through the center to accommodate large pleasure boats using the Intracoastal Waterway which extends from Maine to Miami and across the Gulf Coast to New Orleans (often misspelled and mispronounced as 'inter-coastal waterway'). Its channel extends along this coast west from Fort Walton Beach on the inside of Santa Rosa Island and Perdido Key to Alabama. Choctawhatchee Bay is over twenty-seven miles long and up to five miles wide—a great amenity for pleasure boats of all kinds during the six-month summer season on the Emerald Coast, when the local population expands by over one-hundred-thousand seasonal visitors, mostly from southern states.

"On the east side of the small-boat cut is the booming resort village of Destin with its adjoining executive airport where we are scheduled to park our helicopter tonight. So you will be able to get a closer look at the famous 'Emerald Coast' white beach sand later this afternoon. A few miles east of Destin you can see the beachfront condominium towers and Hilton Hotel of the Sandestin Resort. Sandestin contains three golf courses and a huge water park under the ownership of Canada's Intrawest Company, known primarily as a winter resort developer. A few miles east of Sandestin you can see the high-price communities of Water Color and Water Sound developed by the St.

Joe Company, formerly Florida's biggest land owner (that dubious honor having since passed to a timberland investment company named Plum Creek), on some of its beachfront property. It is adjacent to the trend-setting Seaside community that launched the New Urbanist planning movement over twenty years ago. Note the low-rise, high-density development that set the precedent for this movement."

"Mark, I would like to walk through Seaside and Water Color. Can we land somewhere?" asked Nash.

"Before Jake gets concerned about finding a landing place, let me suggest that we defer your request until this afternoon when we return to Destin. He can inquire about a local landing place when we are in Panama City for lunch, or we can rent a vehicle in Destin and drive over here in twenty minutes. I have been here several times and can serve as your guide."

"Sounds good to me," responded Nash.

"Prior to this coastal area being completely overrun with vacation facilities, the state managed to preserve the green woodland you see on your left: Point Washington State Forest. It is bisected by US 98 Highway cutting back to the coast from the east end of Choctawhatchee Bay. Beyond that is Florida's second largest freshwater lake, known as Powell Lake. Adjoining its north side is the Wild Heron Resort Community, developed around a Greg Norman golf course and financed by the Hillman Company of Pittsburgh. This community was awarded the 2009 Golden Aurora Award for the best residential development over five-hundred acres by the Florida Association of Home Builders. Along the coast, you can see the spinoff communities from Seaside, the most well-known being Rosemary Beach, which followed Seaside's higher density model, and, over ten years ago, set some new Florida price records for its tiny lots.

"Now, as you can see by the tall condominium towers along the beach in front of us, we are approaching Panama City Beach at the eastern end of the 'Emerald Coast.' This beach used to be known as the 'Redneck Riviera' because of its attraction for southerners from rural Georgia and Alabama. It also welcomed annual 'Spring Break' students who added to its low-price reputation. The Chamber of Commerce has spent a great deal of money over the past decade on publicity to change this image, and, to the extent that the high-rise condominiums are sold out, it appears they are succeeding.

So that's a quick look at 'Emerald Coast' which, up until the recent Great Recession, was one of Florida's most popular resort areas. Jake, if you would just hover offshore for a few minutes at a slightly higher altitude, there is one more information piece I would like to provide."

"You bet, Mark, just let me know when you are ready to go down for lunch."

"I mentioned the St. Joe Company briefly a few minutes ago. This company was founded in 1936 as the St. Joe Paper Company with its former major paper mill just a few miles east of here in Port St. Joe. It was funded by the Alfred I. duPont Testamentary Trust established by the wealthy Alfred I. duPont who moved from Wilmington, Delaware to Jacksonville in 1926 with his wife, Jessie Ball duPont, who originated from Jacksonville. Earlier, in 1933, duPont had purchased the Apalachicola Northern Railroad and two-hundred-and-forty thousand acres of land in and around Port St. Joe. Alfred duPont died young in 1935, and the Trust and related business interests were turned over to the sole management of his brother-in-law, Edward Ball, who subsequently became one of the most powerful men in Florida.

"Ball directed the use of Trust funds to buy additional large tracts of wasted farm and forest land across North Florida in the 1930s. The company re-planted the land with fast-growing slash pine to feed the pulp and paper factory started in St. Joe. The St. Joe Paper Company eventually owned over a million acres of North Florida land, a portion of which you can see north and east of Panama City. It also acquired the Florida East Coast Railway Company in 1960 and Talisman Sugar Company in South Florida in 1972, properties that later pitted Ball against unions and conservationists in major disputes. Edward Ball was reputed to be an arch-conservative personality known for his openly racist and anti-communist tirades, as well as for his violent union-busting techniques. Ball died in 1981; but, during his thirty-year reign over the duPont Trust and the St. Joe Paper Company, he had control over twenty-three box plants and thirty-one banks in Florida, as well as the Florida East Coast Railway and the vast land holdings centered in this part of Florida. Ed Ball was a true Florida icon.

"Since Jessie Ball duPont (Ed Ball's sister) was a Florida native, she and her husband were regular winter visitors to Jacksonville before moving their primary residence there in 1926. Jessie's husband, Alfred DuPont, became well-known locally for his financing of the San Jose Estates in 1925—a planned development of several hundred acres along the east bank of the St. Johns River. Remaining buildings from San Jose Estates include the hotel (now the Bolles Private School), the adjacent golf course and clubhouse (now San Jose County Club), his mansion (listed on the Historic Register, and now the elegant clubhouse for Epping Forest—a fifty-two acre residential community and yacht club on the St. Johns River), and twenty-one (of the thirty-one originally built) other residences in the Mediterranean Revival style. The development was terminated in the Florida real estate bust of 1926 and the remaining land was slowly subdivided for residential use over subsequent decades.

"After Alfred's death, Jessie duPont became well-known for entertaining many world leaders, including President Franklin Roosevelt and Prime Minister Winston Churchill, at her twenty-five-room, fifteen-thousand-square-foot mansion named Epping Forest (after her family's ancestral home in England), prior to her death in the 1970s. During the 1980s, the Epping Forest estate was transformed into one of Jacksonville's most prestigious residential communities, under the sponsorship of self-made multi-millionaire Herbert Peyton, father of the current Mayor of Jacksonville.

"After Edward Ball's death, and the decline of the pulp and paper industry over the next decade, the St. Joe Paper Company sold the paper mill in 1996 and dropped the word 'Paper' from its corporate name. The paper mill closed in 1998. In 1997, the St. Joe Company hired a new CEO with a distinguished real estate background (including the Arvida and Disney Companies), named Peter Rummell, to re-direct the company into disposing of its million-acre property in real estate ventures.

In 1999, the company report stated that it wanted to sell up to eight-hundred-thousand acres of its million-acre holdings. That same year, the State of Florida paid more than one-hundred and thirty-three million dollrs for St. Joe's Talisman Sugar Company land for Everglades restoration and, in 2000, the company sold its shares in Florida East Coast Railway.

Rummell arranged for the purchase of community development and commercial real estate companies to expand St. Joe's development capacity. But the vast majority of its assets were, and are, in the area of Florida where we are now, mostly second-growth pine forest with few natural amenities other than a couple of rivers, a few small lakes, and a relatively modest area of Gulf Coast beachfront.

"Rummell set about developing the best locations first: master-planned-communities outside Jacksonville and Tallahassee; and, of course, the coastal land west of Seaside that we just flew over, in addition to some riverfront land. But his long-range plan was to upgrade Panama City and its environs into much more appealing locations for industry and other business interests. The key, in his view, was to build a new and better airport outside this city which would attract more visitors and industrial developers.

Exhibit 7:
Epping Forest, former riverfront home of Alfred
and Jessie duPont, Jacksonville.

"Both Panama City and coastal Chambers of Commerce jumped on the St. Joe bandwagon to boost Northwest Florida. And St. Joe took the big step of financing a new airport north of the city to replace the existing airport confined by the water of West Bay and existing urban development. The result is still in the future. After Peter Rummell left St. Joe for another position, the company re-directed its operations to diminish primary development activities and concentrate on property value enhancement and disposition. Earlier this month, the company announced it is moving its headquarters from Jacksonville to a location within its land holdings in Bay County.

"In the interim, the new airport is reported to be on schedule for an opening within the next couple of months. St. Joe announced the Venture Crossings Enterprise Centre on a one-thousand-acre site at West Bay near the new airport. It will contain a mixed development of retail, office, hotel and industrial uses, including the new headquarters for the St. Joe Company. This development is the first step in the seventy-five-thousand-acre West Bay Sector Plan near the new airport. This is a potential site location for Logan Homes. Now, Jake has gained permission to land at the old airport site which is close to Panama City dining establishments. So, Jake, with Nash's approval, I suggest you take us down to have lunch."

"Sounds like a great idea to me," responded Nash, as the helicopter headed north across the city and descended toward the old airport.

"What a great lunch," uttered Nash, sitting back in his chair with a contented look on his face. "Thank you, Mark, for recommending this restaurant."

"I am just thankful it still is operating under the same owners after all these years," replied Mark, who, by the pleasant look on his face, appeared to have enjoyed the seafood gumbo they had both selected, just as much as Nash.

"On a serious note, Mark, this has been a great morning. I have learned more about Florida in the last two days than I learned in the past six decades . . . and I have seen only a tiny amount so far. Thank goodness I can rely upon you for good notes, Jimmy, because I don't believe my mind can keep up with all the information Mark is presenting. So, before we get up, Mark, what is on the schedule for the rest of the day?"

"This afternoon I would like to show you the northern part of this planning district, an area almost barren of trees because of its original use in large cotton plantations operated on slave labor, prior to Reconstruction. Tree growth was so efficiently cut down that new seeds did not re-seed, and farming reverted to grazing and some grain crops. In general, it is among the least expensive land we will visit over the next ten days, so you need to remember it as a baseline for other potential sites. In terms of transportation, I-10 runs east and west, but you must travel back east to I-75 or west to Alabama for an interstate highway heading north; the Bayline railroad runs due north from Panama City and alternative railways run north from Mobile, as well as east-west tracks to Jacksonville and New Orleans.

"So, if you are all ready, I suggest we return to the helicopter and get to work."

Within ten minutes after Jimmy paid the luncheon bill, they returned their rental car to the airport and boarded the helicopter ready to take off. Jake started the engine and checked his instruments before confirming with Air Traffic Control that they were cleared to tour up to DeFuniak Springs and then north of I-10 with a final destination at Destin as long as they stayed well away from Eglin Air Force Base air space. Jake piloted the craft up to an altitude of 1,000 feet and proceeded northwest toward DeFuniak Springs, the county seat for Walton County. This small city of just over five-thousand residents is at the intersection of US 90 (east-west) and US 331 (north-south) near its intersection with I-10 and about twenty-three miles north of its intersection with US 98, a few miles east of Sandestin.

Mark had received reports of a new subdivision south of DeFuniak Springs and north of I-10, so he was alert to signs of progress at that point; and indeed, a few rooftops did appear at that location, but not enough to make a significant change in the population. In fact, he was disappointed because he had hoped this area of inexpensive land might provide a solution to the severe shortage of workforce housing for employees in resort employment along the coast—but it was not happening at DeFuniak Springs. Mark continued his description of the area.

"Below is DeFuniak Springs, the county seat for Walton County which extends down to the coast, but there is no significant new development here. Some consider it among the most charming of Florida's small cities. It was settled in the 1880s around an oval spring-fed lake. It became the winter home to the Chautauqua Movement, which had its birth on Lake Chautauqua east of Jamestown, New York in the 1870s, and flourished as a center for world-renowned speakers, many of whom appeared here during the winter months.

"Please keep flying north for a few miles, Jake. I believe there are lakes north of here that . . . yes, the large lake directly ahead is Juniper Lake with organized housing development on the west and north; and, to the west across US 331, is Holly Lake with additional development. Please keep north at a higher altitude, Jake, to ensure that I am right in my assumption that the only new development is along US 90 and I-10 that parallel each other through to Alabama. The farmland you see below us continues all the way up through Alabama, and much of it was in huge slave plantations until the Reconstruction ban on slave ownership in the 1860s."

As the helicopter increased altitude while moving north, it became clear to everyone that there was no additional development north to the Alabama state line and beyond; so Mark directed Jake to return to an altitude of one-thousand feet and veer south to the junction of US 90 and I-10. Just west of the junction of the two roads, he spotted an incomplete large-lot development on the north side of the two highways that he remembered from past years.

"Gentlemen, the gridiron pattern of roads just below us is one of the scourges of Florida—a subdivision of large lots with dirt roads and no water or sewer infrastructure. It has been sitting here for fifty or more years with very few houses scattered across it. You will see more of these graveyard subdivisions all around the state, many much larger than this one—too many scattered owners to rescue and re-plat it for efficient land use. There is a second one just to the west of us, and a third on both sides of US 90, just after it separates from the I-10 right-of-way. Swing north here for a couple of miles, Jake, and we will see some even worse examples of sprawl, with lots of up to five acres legally subdivided on dirt roads so that a few of them can be sold with the majority left for long-term wasted land. Okay, now follow down to the city of Crestview to the southwest and circle around the perimeter. Thank you. That's great."

"Crestview is a city that has grown by 50 percent in the past ten years, primarily because of the shortage of modest price housing in the coastal areas to accommodate resort employees; and, as I mentioned this morning, new employees at Eglin Air Force Base. Crestview's population has increased from under fifteen-thousand residents in 2000 to over twenty-one-thousand residents today—not high in terms of large urban areas, but huge in this county. Fully-serviced subdivisions have been added, primarily in the northwest sector, but not completed because of The Great Recession. There is more development south of the city at the intersection of I-10 and SR-85 leading into Fort Walton Beach. This is all of the primary home development in Planning District 1, except for the eastern Mobile suburbs extending into Escambia County south from the city of Milton and north from Pensacola around Blackwater Bay and Escambia Bay. But this urban development pattern has been growing very slowly over a long period. Escambia County grew by only 7 percent during the past decade, and Pensacola actually lost population during this time period.

Exhibit 8:
Example of Florida large lot platting from 1950s.

"So, as we head back down to where we started in Pensacola this morning, and then along the coast to Destin, I believe we can sum up Planning District 1 as containing lots of open land that can be developed with strong support from local governments, but suffering from low population growth and less than optimum transportation potential to outside markets."

"Thank you, Mark, a perfect summary" said Nash. "Now, Jake, what about landing at Seaside? Can we do it?"

"Actually, Mr. Logan, there is a helipad at Seaside, but it is reserved for residents arriving between four and six pm. As a backup, I have arranged for a driver with a minivan to pick us up at Destin Airport upon my call-in, drive us to Seaside and Water Color, and then return us to our condo hotel in Destin before dark—the entire trip for seventy-five dollars. I think that's your best deal for seeing Seaside."

"Okay, Jake, finalize that by phone. Then, let's head to Destin Airport."

Within twenty minutes, Jake was setting the helicopter down at Destin Airport, where a light-colored minivan was waiting beside the helipad. Jake preferred to stay behind and attend to his machine for tomorrow's flight. He said he would grab a taxi and meet them at the condo hotel. So the other three transferred their luggage and hopped into the van for the twenty-minute drive to Seaside.

At this same time, back in St. Augustine, Bobbi and her sister Linda, who had arrived from Atlanta earlier that day, were strolling out of the old town pedestrian area, about to hail a taxi to return them to the Victoria now docked just north of that city. They had enjoyed a wonderful lunch at the renowned Columbia restaurant and were looking forward to returning to the yacht. Suddenly, a dark-haired man of slim stature stepped in front of them with a bright smile and addressed her by name: "Mrs. Wilkins", he stated, "my name is Jack Swift of the Swift Property Company."

"I'm sorry, Mr. Swift, but I do not believe we have ever met," replied Bobbi, somewhat indignant that this man had the audacity to accost her on the street without a prior introduction.

"Yes, that's true," Swift continued, "but I am anxious to speak with your husband and Mr. Logan on a most urgent matter. I would be grateful if you would take my business card and give it to him upon his return from the Panhandle." He held out the card to her.

"How do you know he is in the Panhandle?" asked Bobbi, her natural curiosity aroused by this stranger's apparent knowledge of their travel plans.

"Well, Ma'am," Swift replied quickly, "I am in the information business and I pride myself in keeping up with new events in this state. Your husband's new liaison with Nash Logan is a hot piece of news. I have been trying to contact Logan for weeks, but he does not return my phone calls. I have intelligence on land availability in Florida that he needs to know about."

"Really? Well I am afraid that is Mr. Logan's business. I am not involved in his business, and I certainly am not a messenger for either him or my husband. But, I will agree to pass on your card, Mr. Swift, when I see them again, which will not be today."

"I know, I know," said Swift in his rapid-fire manner of speech. "But, when they return tomorrow, please tell him that I am staying at the Crown Plaza Hotel in Jacksonville. I can meet him there or on the yacht at any time. Thank you, Mrs. Wilkins. I am sorry to trouble you, but I can assure you that it will be well worth their while to speak with me." He then slipped way into the crowd, leaving the two sisters staring at each other in amazement.

Destin Pointe is a relatively new condo hotel on the peninsula in Choctawhatchee Bay. The developer's local agent, Tom Parsons, a former colleague of Mark's at Sandestin many years before, ensured that each member of their group had a beautifully appointed room looking down upon the clear, shallow waters of the bay. Tom Parsons met the four of them for dinner at Pat O'Brien's Restaurant in the impressive Emerald Grande entertainment center, which is planned to be the anchor of the Destin Harbor re-development plan. Unfortunately, the developer of Emerald Grande was out-of-town and could not join them. But Tom Parsons had lived and worked in Destin all of his professional life and was able to offer credible information on all of their questions about the evolution and future growth of the Emerald Coast.

When Jake expressed enthusiasm about his hotel room with a view of the clear water of Choctawhatchee Bay, Tom replied, "You should come back in the summertime when the bay is full of small boats. On the Fort Walton waterfront you can usually see over one-hundred boats anchored in the shallow water, where a giant party is taking place, with scantily clad people standing on the sand bottom throwing footballs and Frisbees, drinking beer and munching burgers from the floating snack bars. There is even a little skiff cruising around selling ice cream. It truly is a sight to behold."

Nash was enthused about his late-afternoon tours of Seaside and Water Color, and he questioned both Tom and Mark extensively about the origin of Seaside and the later development of Water Color and adjacent Water Sound. Nash was already familiar with the founding of Seaside by Robert Davis on his family land in 1979. He hired the husband-wife architectural team of Andres Duany and

Elizabeth Plater-Zyberk from Miami to design the town plan as a beachfront resort with private vacation homes for residents. Walton County then had no zoning ordinance, and the planners were able to design the plan to their own standards of lot density and street rights-of-way. They created circulation way dimensions and building regulations based upon future use and compatible aesthetics rather than on historic tradition.

The resultant Seaside plan and subsequent development were heralded as the prototype for what became the 'New Urbanism' movement of mixed-use, pedestrian-oriented plans that were reminiscent of nineteenth century small towns. This movement spread across the country (and beyond) over the following thirty years, strongly promoted by the designs and speaking talents of Duany, and supported by conservationists, environmentalists and the 'Green' movement.

The popularity of New Urbanism among urban planners and architects today is much stronger than its popularity among consumers, according to reputable consumer surveys. These surveys, conducted frequently over the past thirty years, indicate that up to one-third of Americans are interested in living in higher density urban environments, compared to those preferring more contemporary suburban large lot communities. Thus, New Urbanism has become a controversial topic among land developers and builders committed to creating popular living environments to generate profit for their investors.

As Nash pursued this topic, he revealed that the cost of land in Canadian cities where his company builds new homes drove developers to develop smaller lots and higher density attached and multi-family housing to attract modest income consumers. However, a substantial proportion of their housing consumers continued to accept longer commute times to purchase lower density housing in formerly rural areas farther from the central city.

"The City of Toronto is now spread up to one-hundred miles from the city center and we continue to struggle with local and regional governments over density. There is no question that higher densities are more efficient, but they only prove successful if consumers accept them. This is one reason why I plan to build in Florida where we have many examples of local and state governments supporting free-standing new communities, especially those with an employment base to reduce commuting trip-lengths."

"One of the major criticisms of Seaside," responded Mark "is that both the street system and the architectural standards are too rigid. The former adopts the strict grid system prevalent in American towns and cities of the nineteenth century, whereas the latter dictates conformity of exterior style and materials that, according to some critics, limit freedom of expression unnecessarily. The British system of controlling architecture in new developments has resulted in some truly dull suburban and new-town living environments that must rely upon landscaping to mask the uniform building facades—an issue not dissimilar to rows of look-alike detached homes in some of our American suburbs—but the latter are caused by insensitive builders, whereas the British problem is due to government design officials. In both cases, however, we are leaving a legacy of less-than-optimum communities for future generations. So there is a concern that, despite the infrastructure and travel efficiencies attributed to New Urbanism, we may be 'throwing out the baby with the bathwater', insofar as diversity is at the heart of this country's strength."

"Although I agree with Mark's point on diversity, both social diversity as well as physical diversity," responded Nash. "Nevertheless, the mixed-use principles and higher density tenets of New Urbanism undoubtedly have created interesting neighborhood environments, as well as contributed to operating efficiency in many cities across this country and Canada. I would like to create a new town that can incorporate the best of all these principles coupled with better forms of transportation. The much greater problem, in my view, is the cost of higher density solutions. Clearly, dwelling prices are higher in the New Urbanism designs (for example, in Celebration and Baldwin in Orlando) than in larger lot subdivisions in that same market. And, as we are all finding out after this Great Recession, price continues to be an important factor in consumer choice of new housing."

"Well said," replied Mark. "Your initial objectives to reduce costs of both buildings and infrastructure in your new community should attract the interest of government officials, as well as consumers. Virtually every city in Florida suffered from lack of workforce housing prior to the recession and the same problem will emerge again once normal price inflation reappears in coming years."

"Amen to that," chimed in Tom Parsons. "You are sitting in the center of a market that has ignored costs in its frenzy to charm vacation-home buyers with bigger and better developments. The end result is too many empty condominium dwellings owned by financial lenders and we still haven't solved our workforce housing shortage. County and regional politicians are finally waking up to the problems of unrestricted resort development, and it is a costly lesson for everyone. However, gentlemen, as much as I have enjoyed your company, I must retire to my overtaxed residence. It has been a real pleasure meeting all of you. And, Nash, if we can help you in any way to achieve your dream in Florida, please give me a call."

Everyone rose to bid Tom good-night and then they headed back to their rooms at Destin Pointe to rest up for Day 2.

DAY 2

Saturday, March 27, 2010

"That is surely one of the finest breakfasts I have ever experienced," uttered Jake as he leaned back with a contented smile on his face. "Somebody please thank Tom for recommending 'Another Broken Egg' for breakfast here on Destin's main street. It is the best!"

"I agree," said Nash, "but Mark has another big day planned for us, so let's hop in the minivan and get over to the airport." Everyone headed out to the minivan taxi while Jimmy paid for their breakfast with a Logan Homes credit card. When they reached the Destin Airport a few minutes later, Mark accompanied Jake to the flight room to help him describe their tour route, while the others sat in the waiting room. Ten minutes later, they were belting themselves into their seats as Jake warmed up the engine prior to takeoff.

Mark's voice came through everyone's earphones: "Today we are going to tour Planning District 2 known as the Apalachee District, in memory of the displaced Indian tribe that once lived here. I have asked Jake to take us back to Panama City where we will begin our tour at the southwest corner of the District. I see he is ready to go, so I will continue en route."

A few minutes later, as the helicopter re-traced the prior day's route east along the coast, Mark continued his briefing: "With Nash's approval, I have asked Jake to take a counter-clockwise route around the periphery of District 2 from our starting point at Panama City, followed by a final west-east route through the center, crossing over the city of Tallahassee. This city is, of course, the original and continuing capital of Florida, as well as home to the large Florida State University. Later this afternoon, we will make the return flight to the 'Victoria', now moored in the historic city of St. Augustine.

Mark once again referred Nash and Jimmy to the handout illustrating planning districts, as he began his description of Planning

District 2. They both found their copies and located the southwest corner of this district in Gulf County, just east of Panama City.

"Planning District 2 contains nine counties with a population approaching five-hundred-thousand residents, of which over half live in Tallahassee—smaller in population than Planning District 1 because most of the rolling terrain of this district is covered with pine forests, and wetland near the coast, a large portion of which are protected in the Apalachicola National Forest.

"On the left side of our flight path, you can see Panama City where we were yesterday, and just ahead on the long peninsula is Tyndall Air Force Base—yes, another military base, which I believe was located along the Gulf Coast because of the vast expanse of neighboring water for training flights. Tyndall is much smaller in size than the huge Eglin Base we passed yesterday and it is still located in District 1. We do not officially begin District 2 until we come to the very long spit of land in front of us, named St. Joseph's Peninsula, that encompasses St. Joseph Bay and Port St. Joe. I mentioned yesterday that the town of Port St. Joe was expanded for employees of the St. Joe Company's large wood processing plant which has now been abandoned on the edge of the bay. Just to the north of the town, you can see the Gulf Coast Canal that links the bay and the Intracoastal Waterway paralleling the coast a few miles inland. You might also notice the logging railroad heading into the interior from Port St. Joe. It also has been abandoned along with the company logging operations. Everything on the horizon to the north is the huge Apalachicola National Forest, a tract of five-hundred-and-fifty-five-thousand acres encompassing the historic Indian hunting grounds, and later logging operations, of white settlers.

"The St. Joe Company has prepared a plan for enlarging St. Joe into a new community of several thousand acres at this location, but any development has been deferred because of The Great Recession and the re-direction of the company. I have no current information on the progress of this plan.

Now we are approaching the much larger St. Vincent Island which is entirely a National Wildlife Refuge. South of it is the long barrier island of St. George Island (and Little St. George Island) which many say boasts the best beach on this continent, if not in the world. It is accessible by the causeway across Apalachicola Bay and St. George Sound that serves the small beachfront village on this island and the St. George Island State Park on the south end of the island. I have been told that one must reserve a year in advance for a summer campsite in this park.

District 2 - Apalachee

**Exhibit 9:
Planning District 2—Apalachee.**

"On the mainland, at the mouth of the Apalachicola River, is the historic city of Apalachicola which only contains about twenty-five-hundred residents and their wonderfully restored old Victorian houses. I felt certain you would like to see this town, Nash, so I have asked Jake to set down at the Municipal Airport where we can rent the town's only taxi to give us a brief tour."

"A super idea, Mark," responded Nash, as Jake expertly set the helicopter down beside the tiny terminal building. "How does this remote community continue to survive?"

"You will see in a moment as we leave the airport—tourists, oysters and fishing. Apalachicola Bay oysters are touted as the finest in the south. A small fleet of charter fishing boats takes tourists into the Gulf of Mexico for sport fishing. I understand that many fishermen arrive at this airport by private plane. But why don't you go ahead and visit the men's room, and when you return, and before we get started on the tour, I would like to tell you the rather odd circumstances leading to the success of this town in the nineteenth century."

The four men returned a few minutes later, and resumed their seats. Nash and his two employees appeared eager to hear Mark's story.

"As I described earlier, the rush of settlers to establish profitable slave-plantations for growing cotton was huge in the early nineteenth century. Their choice of shipping points was limited to Fernandina or

St. Michaels on the Atlantic Coast or the much closer Apalachicola on the Gulf of Mexico. But, the story of how Apalachicola became the Florida Territory's earliest boomtown dates back to the Spanish ownership of this land, prior to trading it to the Americans for Havana in the 1783 Treaty of Paris. All of the land in this part of the territory was platted as a Spanish grant, which Spain sold to a British firm called Forbes and Company. Early settlers coming to this area either bought land from Forbes or simply squatted illegally. An American firm called the Apalachia Land Company contested the Forbes ownership and the case went to the young United States Supreme Court in 1835. The court sided with Apalachia and voided the Forbes grant, leaving settlers without title. The Apalachia Land Company demanded the then-exorbitant price of thirteen-thousand dollars cash to repurchase titles; so the deposed residents decided to create a new town west of Apalachicola on St. Joseph's Bay which they named St. Joseph. The new town grew quickly to four-thousand residents by 1839, and threatened the dominance of Apalachicola for shipping cotton and other goods.

"But, in 1841, the population of St. Joseph was decimated by an outbreak of yellow fever, and then hit with a hurricane and tidal surge. The few remaining residents left the new town to thieves and scoundrels, with many of the remaining residents re-locating to Apalachicola. Thus, Apalachicola became the sole port on the Gulf Coast for shipping cotton and it grew to become the third highest-volume port on the northern Gulf, behind New Orleans and Mobile. Almost a century later, in the 1930s, the St. Joseph Bay site was revived by DuPont and Ball for their pulp and paper company, and the adjacent town named St. Joe, the same name they gave their company."

After thanking Mark for this interesting piece of history, all four of them climbed into the taxi for the tour of Apalachicola—a charming little town of Victorian houses set amidst tall southern oak trees with Spanish moss trailing from their branches. The commercial area was equally charming, with appealing tourist shops and tiny restaurants featuring local seafood specialties. Jimmy was snapping pictures at a rapid rate on the small digital camera he carried with him.

It was too early for lunch, and, as they had a sumptuous breakfast in Destin, they resisted the allure of the local offerings and continued back to the airport.

As they climbed back into the helicopter, Nash said "Mark, this place is a gem. Thank you for bringing us here to a place which we would never have seen without your guidance. How did you discover it?"

"As a matter of fact, I found it by accident rather than referral. When I worked in Sandestin thirty years ago, I decided to travel back home via US 98 just for fun. Adjacent St. George Island is better known as a summer vacation destination, and many tourists go there by car without ever visiting this town—a major oversight on their part."

Jake took them back onto the assigned route, and Mark pointed out the little waterfront village of Carrabelle a few miles east. The waterfront along this part of the coast inside the barrier islands was void of beaches as the forest came right to the water's edge. To the north they could see the huge expanse of the Tates Hell Swamp which covers hundreds of square miles north of Carrabelle, effectively ruling out any development in this part of the state. The northern coast of Apalachee Bay is marshland, much of it in the St. Marks National Wildlife Refuge, with wetland extending inland from the coast for several miles southeast of Tallahassee, where its larger buildings are visible in the distance. Jake changed his direction northward along the Aucilla River marking the eastern boundary of Jefferson County and Planning District 2. The land elevation increased as they crossed I-10 and passed the little town of Monticello, then west across a large shallow lake.

"That is Lake Miccosukee in the northeast corner of District 2," continued Mark, "with the Georgia border just to the north and suburban Tallahassee coming into view to the southwest. The land is high and dry, with frequent farming as well as woodland in this area. Later we will see the small beginnings of a six-thousand-five-hundred acre new community southeast of Tallahassee named Southwood that was planned and launched by the St. Joe Company several years ago, but it never sold beyond the first phase. The size of the Tallahassee residential market is less than two-thousand new homes per year in normal times. The land is pretty in this part of Florida, but employment growth is too modest to support major new development.

"The string of lakes we are crossing now has attracted many unfulfilled development plans, in addition to the sporadic large lot homes around their shorelines. The southernmost Lake Jackson is a popular suburb for affluent residents employed in Tallahassee.

"We will return for a closer look at Tallahassee this afternoon. In the interim, we are coming up on the agricultural center of Quincy, a city of over seven-thousand-five-hundred residents employed mainly in farm service industries. It's well after high noon now, and there is a nice little 'mom and pop' restaurant at the small airport here that serves excellent southern barbeque, if you gentlemen would like to try a southern lunch?"

"By all means, Jake, y'all take her down fer some barbeque an' hush puppies," replied Nash with his best southern accent (which did not mask his Canadian hard vowels).

"Well now," exclaimed Jake, stretching his body over the back of the lunch booth, "I don't know diddley about land development, but Mark, you sure are a first class restaurant guide. Thank you for leading us to another great meal."

"My pleasure, Jake! I enjoyed it too. And, furthermore, it is probably the best price bargain we will have on the entire trip."

"In that case," interjected Nash, "Logan Homes thanks you too, Mark" as he motioned to Jimmy to pay the bill. "And the best part of all is that the helicopter is right outside the door."

"Even better," added Jake, "I had the gas tank topped up while we ate, so we can leave immediately." All four men clambered out of the booth and thanked the smiling owners as they left to climb in the helicopter and waited for Jake to warm up the engine.

Once they were airborne, Mark directed Jake to the northwest before speaking into his microphone. "As I mentioned before lunch, this is farming country which extends up into Georgia and west to Alabama. Directly in front of us is Lake Seminole, a manmade lake of several miles in length on the Georgia-Florida border that feeds the Apalachicola River, restrained by an earthen dam—the same river they had visited briefly at its mouth this morning. This is one of several rivers that flow from Georgia into Florida, and they are the subject of controversy for both flooding and scarcity at different times. However, the dam controlling the flow out of Lake Seminole is in Florida, so residents of this state have fewer concerns. The Florida-Georgia border swings north here to meet the Alabama border in the midst of farmlands in all three states. Jake took a quick swing around Jackson County to view this farming country before heading south for the pass through the middle of District 2 over the state capital.

"As we travel south into Calhoun County you can see more areas of uncontrolled land subdivision with gridiron patterns of streets which have only a few scattered houses dating back to the Florida land rush days of the 1920s, and again in the 1950s and 60s. I will return to this sordid period of rampant land subdivision as we move farther south in our tour of the state, but suffice it to say here that no part of Florida was immune to this scourge.

"As Jake turns eastward at approximately the center line of District 2, we cross the flood plains of the Chipola River and then the Apalachicola River before entering the Apalachicola National Forest. This vast preserve of conservation land adjoins the Bradwell Bay Wilderness on the south next to the floodplain of the Ochlockonee River that flows from the Lake Talquin Reservoir west of Tallahassee.

"I am asking Jake to make two circles around Tallahassee so you can first see the suburbs and then the university-government complex adjoining the city center. The entire city is circled by a beltway called Capital Circle Drive. On this first swing outside the beltway you are witnessing the largest gridiron subdivision we have yet witnessed, approved for development in the 1950s with only limited settlement. Moving north, we are crossing the Southwood Plantation new community, planned by a subsidiary of the St. Joe Company in the 1980s for development over a twenty-five-year period. However, as you can see, only a small segment has been developed on the north end after twenty years. This land use, however, differs from the gridiron, south of it, insofar as the undeveloped portion is under single ownership and can be re-planned for alternative uses. I might add that this, and other entitled parcels, may constitute efficient options for your concept, Nash, since the basic planning approvals are in place."

"I was thinking the same thing, Mark, although this parcel seems to lack multi-mode transportation access."

"True enough, but keep that thought in mind."

"I will, but feel free to remind me again as we continue to see other opportunities."

"The north side of the city is most heavily developed," continued Mark, probably because I-10 was routed across vacant land here in the 1960s. Development to the west has been more sporadic. Now let's have a look downtown, Jake.

"Tallahassee was planned as the capitol for Florida when the state was first declared a political jurisdiction in 1845. The location was selected as half-way between the two principal Spanish colonial cities of St. Augustine and Pensacola, and a city plan was prepared with the state capitol building as its centerpiece. Of course, that plan was exceeded many decades ago with the development patterns you have just witnessed added to its outer boundaries. But the capitol on the hill remains. A small state college for women adjacent to the government buildings was expanded to become the full-fledged Florida State University, now with over forty-thousand co-ed students. Both of these state institutions have long since outgrown their initial sites and spread to larger facilities. Employment in both institutions has grown faster than the state population increase, but other types of industries have not grown at the same rate despite promotion efforts by the St. Joe Company and others, thus limiting Tallahassee as a housing market.

"Gentlemen, unless you have questions or additional inspection preferences, this wraps up the tour of Planning District 2. Jake knows the way to the yacht's new mooring in St. Augustine and I will be happy to respond to any questions you may have along the way."

"Yes, Mark," replied Nash, "we have an hour's trip ahead of us to St. Augustine. I would like to use some or all of this time to discuss your biases in this business, and at the same time reveal mine to you, so we can better understand each other in the days ahead. Is that acceptable to you?"

"Yes indeed, Nash, I think that is a good idea, one which I probably should have addressed in my introductory remarks in Jacksonville. But this is as good a time as any."

"So Mark, what can you tell me about your background, education and work experiences that affect your outlook on land development?"

"Okay, first of all I am an only child who was raised by church-going Protestants in a suburb of Milwaukee, Wisconsin; and I attended local schools without incident. I preferred individual sports rather than team sports and I was good enough at tennis and track and field events to make the varsity teams in each sport. As an adult, I preferred long distance hiking and outdoor camping and I still go trekking in the mountains a couple of times per year. Luckily, Bobbi also enjoys the outdoors, so this common interest serves us well.

"I was attracted toward plants and animals from an early age; and, after high school graduation, I enrolled in the Landscape Architecture Program at the University of Wisconsin. I enjoyed the learning experience, but a career of garden design did not feel sufficiently exciting, so I asked my parents for financial assistance to enroll in the Graduate School of Urban and Regional Planning at the University of North Carolina. I chose this school with some care, after discovering that the faculty at that school had authored a number of the leading textbooks in this field. Teachers like Stuart Chapman and Shirley Weiss were acknowledged leaders in this field, and I wanted to learn this subject from the best people available. This turned out to be a wise decision because they stimulated me enough to apply for a scholarship that paid my way through both the Master's and Doctoral programs.

"After I had completed my doctoral degree, Dean Abrams approached me about joining the faculty as an Assistant Professor, but, after careful consideration, I decided that I would prefer to learn from practitioners rather than continue in academia. So, I expressed my gratitude to the Dean, but explained my preferences to him and went on to apply for several positions in both government and private consultant practice. I ended up accepting a job with the Mississippi State Planning Office in the state capital city of Jackson where I moved with my new bride in 1962 when I was twenty-five-years-old. The position did not pay as much as other options, but the office had only a small staff dealing with a large state plagued by environmental and social issues. That environment presented an opportunity to learn a great deal in a short time period. And I did! This was a time of racial tensions in the schools, corruption in the government and profit-hungry land developers, so attempting to initiate a state planning operation was a formidable challenge and kept up my interest despite the considerable frustrations of attempting to change a hundred years of procedures.

"After two years in Jackson, one of our state consultants, RG&V, the large international architecture, planning and engineering consultant firm in Jacksonville, solicited my interest in becoming a principal planner with their firm. After my wife and I visited Jacksonville as guests of the company and met with the key partners, there was no doubt that we wanted to make the change. So, in the fall of 1964, we moved to Jacksonville and I began a career with RG&V that lasted forty-two years with assignments all over Florida as well as in twenty-four other states and sixteen other countries. It was a great adventure that I enjoyed thoroughly and ended it with regret. But luckily, after two unsuccessful marriages, I discovered my life companion and I have enjoyed my two years of living with Bobbi both in Fernandina Beach and in traveling to other destinations.

"That's very helpful, Mark, but I want to delve further into your values and decision parameters. What are your politics and what charities do you support?"

"Right! Let's see if I can be more helpful about my personal outlook. First of all, although my parents were devout Presbyterians, I drifted away from church activities after leaving home for college and I have never been moved to return. The organized church appears to me to have the same decision problems as government and business bureaucracies, problems which I encountered both in Mississippi and at RG&V, as well as with government consultant assignments. Regardless, I still consider myself as Christian in outlook, and I have empathy with persons of all races and creeds throughout the world. I have associated with persons of a wide variety of backgrounds and skin colors without any difficulty in communication or friendship. At the same time, I am not an ardent supporter of social or political causes of any type. As an urban planner, I have adopted the view of interested independence from such issues. Politically, I have always been a registered Independent who tends to vote in favor of social justice and fiscal responsibility.

"The history of Florida is a sordid example of bigotry toward other human beings of different racial backgrounds and social class as well as reckless disregard for our natural resources. The land you are seeing from the air this week is marred by countless examples of the latter problem which were further exasperated by unbelievable atrocities committed by Europeans against Native Americans and African-Americans. We can go into details later in our trip, but, hopefully, these few insights into my character give you a better idea of my decision-making framework."

"They do, indeed, Mark, and I am pleased to report that they coincide remarkably close to my own outlook. I have always believed that I can be a profitable developer of real estate and concurrently a person who upholds principles of conservation of natural resources and social justice. I am convinced that my adherence to these principles has contributed in no small measure to the success of our company. But, I am still woefully ignorant of Florida history and I look forward to your teaching me about it on this trip. So far, you have been exceptionally informative.

"But, talk about great timing, I feel Jake beginning his descent into what I hope is St. Augustine. Is that right, Jake?"

"Right you are, Mr. Logan, I have a visual on the 'Victoria,' moored at what I assume to be Camachee Cove, and I have notified Franz of our arrival. We should be on the deck in a few minutes."

Jake guided the helicopter in a wide turn across the Tolomato River, also known as the Intracoastal Waterway, and came in low across the water to make a perfect landing on the rear deck of the "Victoria". Before his passengers disembarked, he notified Nash that he planned to take off immediately for a quick trip north a couple of miles to the St. Augustine Airport to fuel up for tomorrow's flight. He would have one of the yacht crew take their overnight luggage to their cabins when he returned within the hour. Nash confirmed that arrangement and followed the others out of the helicopter into the main lounge where Bobbi and her sister Linda waited to greet them, along with Jose standing by with a tray ready for drink orders.

Mark approached his wife for a hug and brief kiss, before turning to greet his truly beautiful younger sister-in-law with a second hug. Whereas Bobbi was of medium height with dark brown hair, her younger sister was two or three inches taller on a statuesque body, and with natural blonde hair tied back in a fashionable ponytail. It was hard to imagine a woman of this beauty being divorced. With his arm still about his sister-in-law's slim waist, Mark then turned to introduce Linda Cummings to Nash and Jimmy.

"Welcome aboard, Linda," said Nash, with a big smile. "We are delighted to have you join us. By now, after your cruise down from Jacksonville, I assume you are acquainted with our entire crew: Captain Franz Ericksson, Chief Engineer Tim Wilson, Chefs Pierre and Marie Bouvet, Stewards Jose and Alfredo, and Deckhand Carlos. They are all at your service, along with me, of course."

"Thank you so much, Mr. Logan," smiled Linda back at her genial host. "All of them already have made my time here enjoyable. I am truly grateful to you for allowing me to accompany you on this trip."

"Believe me," countered Nash. "It is we who are fortunate to have two such beautiful women aboard our vessel. But, please call me Nash, so I can feel free to address you as Linda. Everyone here should be on a first-name basis. Now," he continued turning to Jose, "please give your drink order to Jose, so we can properly begin the cocktail hour."

⁓

When Bobbi and Mark sat down together on an appropriate love-seat, she recounted the story of Jack Swift encountering the two sisters on the street in St. Augustine. Mark looked alarmed, but Bobbi assured him that, although Swift was not her favorite kind of person, he certainly did not appear dangerous. Linda nodded in agreement from her chair close by. Just then, Nash approached to report that he had overheard their conversation. It turns out that Swift was one of the Realtors who had been phoning his Toronto office, attempting to schedule a meeting with him. "I must admit that the guy gets an 'A' for aggressiveness, although it is quite annoying that he is privy to our travel plans. I had better have a word with my staff this evening to track down the information leak. Now, Linda, please do me the honor of sitting beside me at dinner so I can get to know you."

It was well after seven when they all finished dinner: fillet of grouper, broiled to perfection, with a light garlic sauce and baby potatoes and fresh green beans, finished off with a delightful pineapple sorbet. As they sipped their coffee—tea for the Wilkins—the yacht's two officers excused themselves for the evening. Nash turned to Mark with a request that, despite the fact that Planning District 3 was on the agenda for tomorrow, he would be grateful if Mark first could address the highlights of St. Augustine for the ladies' activities, prior to his planned briefing on District 3.

"Of course, I can do that," replied Mark, "but, since Bobbi is a veteran shopper and luncheon planner in the historic city, I feel that I can keep my remarks brief . . . especially since tomorrow's planned tour is on the largest District in terms of counties that we encounter: no fewer than eleven counties in District 3, otherwise known as North Central Florida. However, I first invite you all to join me at the corner table where you can examine the mounted state map on which I have now highlighted the borders of each planning district.

The round conference table now was surrounded by the five project participants, with Jake and Linda diplomatically choosing chairs behind the rest of the others. They all could see the outline of Planning District 3 on the map, as well as the red circle around central St. Augustine. This circle encompasses the protected harbor inside the barrier island channel to the sea which separates Vilano Beach village on the north and Conch Island on the south. The latter comprises a major portion of Anastasia State Park, as marked on the map.

Mark began: "Now that my audience has grown to seven, I may suffer some stage fright."

"Not a chance," interjected Bobbi, generating laughter from everyone, including Mark.

"The city of St. Augustine is about a mile south of where we sit. It is located on both sides of the Matanzas River which flows from the south to join the Tolomato River from the north in this protected bay crossed by the historic Lions Gate Bridge. The bridge currently is under construction for restoration, but traffic continues to cross on a temporary bridge. The high bridge visible from our deck is the Vilano Narrows Bridge, built ten years ago to replace a former draw-bridge. Traffic turns north here to reach Jacksonville Beach, about thirty-five miles north. A second high-level bridge crosses the Matanzas River, just south of the old city, to carry traffic to Anastasia Island and south along the coast. Most of you know that Ponce de Leon is reputed to have landed at this location in 1513 to declare the land for Spain. Some accounts claim that he first landed north of here on what is now Ponte Vedra Beach and then sailed south until he came across the natural inlet. But old records are not specific about his landfalls in terms of current geography. They do agree that he christened the land as La Florida and claimed it for Spain.

"The settlement here claims to be the oldest continuously-occupied city in North America (from 1565), a fact often disputed by the Pensacola Chamber of Commerce which also likes to claim this honor. Regardless, these two Spanish settlements became the initial two cities on the Florida mainland; and, in 1845 when Florida was granted statehood from the new government of the United States, the capital was located half-way between these two settlements at Tallahassee which we overflew earlier today.

Exhibit 10:
Central St. Augustine at the confluence of the
Tolomato and Matanzas Rivers.

"The Spanish fort overlooking the harbor, named Castillo de San Marco, is the most-visited federal monument in Florida with over 500,000 visitors annually. Uniformed guards (actually college students) patrol the fort and fire the cannon at noon daily. Across the street from the fort is what remains of the historic city, clustered around a single main street, called St. George Street in honor of King George III of England. That King's troops battled the Spanish garrison and captured the city, thus converting it to an English colony (although today it is always identified in terms of its Spanish roots). St. George Street (pedestrians only) runs through to King Street which is the main east-west street, and boasts the original Ponce de Leon Hotel, first built by Henry Flagler in 1886-88, and now occupied by Flagler College. This street is bordered by several historic buildings, including two other hotels once owned by Flagler—Alcazar (now a city museum) and Santa Monica (formerly named Cordova when owned by Flagler). The original offices of his Florida East Coast Railway are farther west on King Street. I urge you all to take advantage of the trolley tour of St. Augustine which explains all of the details surrounding these and many other historic structures."

"But Mark," spoke up Linda, "you haven't addressed the critical question of where Bobbi and I should have lunch tomorrow while you are off touring. This history is all very interesting, but it shouldn't take precedence over really important issues like lunch and shopping."

"My most humble apologies, dearest sister-in-law, but I assumed that Bobbi has already taken you to one of her favorite lunch places, the Columbia, located in the heart of St. George Street, where I suspect the two of you shared a pitcher of refreshing Sangria prior to this establishment's famous salad mixed at tableside—all of this while we are studiously examining fields and forests. Furthermore, I feel certain that she already has a second charming restaurant selected for tomorrow, so my suggestions would be of little importance to you."

After the laughter from this exchange had subsided, Nash held up his hand to restore order to the group. "Thank you, Mark, for that introduction. I am sure we all feel better informed about this mooring, and I am relieved that Linda's primary concern has been addressed. Now, Jose is at the ready to freshen your coffee or tea and bring you an after-dinner drink. I will have a Remy Martin in a snifter please, Jose. So, Mark, please tell us about what we helicopter people will see tomorrow."

Mark approached the Florida map to point out the huge North Central Florida Planning District stretching from the Georgia border on the north to the Gulf of Mexico on the southwest and over to the St. Johns River on the east.

"Tomorrow morning, we will begin our tour of Planning District 3 in the southeast corner of the District, just south of the historic river town of Palatka on the northeastern boundary of the huge Ocala National Forest, where it adjoins the shores of Lake George in the channel of the St. Johns River. This is one of the largest forest preserves in Florida, extending all the way south to the central Florida Lake District which we will explore in Districts 5 and 6 next week. I propose to undertake this tour in a clockwise route, traveling around the periphery and then looping back around the City of Gainesville, home of the University of Florida, before heading back to our base. I propose a late lunch in Gainesville to give you the feel of Florida's major college town (and allow Jimmy to rate the co-eds for his personal record). I asked Jake to line up a mini-van taxi to meet us at the Gainesville Airport for this excursion.

"District 3 is larger in both area and population than District 2 which we toured yesterday—approximately five-hundred-thousand residents (excluding most university students, who maintain their hometown addresses). Both districts contain large areas of wetland and preserved forests, and both were heavily populated by Native Americans, prior to their shameful treatment by early settlers and the militia of our new country in the first half of the nineteenth century. I will tell you more about the Seminole Wars and this shoddy chapter of early American history after our tour of District 3. In the interim, I wish you all a pleasant evening. Jake plans lift-off again at half-past seven tomorrow morning."

DAY 3

Sunday, March 28, 2010

Jake and his three passengers were all on time for the helicopter lift-off the next morning. He immediately pointed the helicopter southwest, away from the piercing rays of the early morning sun, and headed toward Palatka on the west bank of the St. Johns River.

"Mark," said Nash over the intercommunication system, "I have been thinking about your final remarks last night concerning the plight of Native Americans in Florida at the hands of European settlers and the United States Militia. We tend to associate Florida Indians as Seminoles living in the Everglades. Did they live up in these northern areas as well?"

"Yes, indeed," replied Mark. "Historians estimate that over one-hundred-thousand Indians lived in all parts of what we now call Florida. They were of many tribes and customs, but most of them were wiped out in the eighteenth century, primarily through disease and violent contacts with the Spanish invaders and the Franciscan priests who accompanied them. Later, they were replaced by migrating Creek Indians from what is now Georgia and the Carolinas. They too dispersed into smaller tribes, but the Spanish referred to them all by a derogatory term which became translated as Seminole. So, all of the Indians in Florida by the early nineteenth century were known as Seminoles. Their subjugation at the hands of the white man is my topic for later today, after you have completed this tour over the central part of their homeland."

Mark once again ensured that both Nash and Jimmy had their copies of his prior handout illustrating the Florida Planning Districts, and he referred them to the area defined as Planning District 3. which, along with the pine, were prized for building ships, forts and houses for early European migrants. Lesser species of pine became prized for making turpentine, a high-demand commodity in that era. Some of that environment has been preserved in our National Forests and Swamps, but most of it was ravaged beyond redemption along with the natives that lived in its shade. Both the trees and the men are

District 3 - North Central

Exhibit 11:
Planning District 3—North Central.

sad symbols of a bygone era when greed and ignorance overwhelmed common sense. We will continue this historical sketch later. For now, you can see below you the mighty St. Johns River that drains a large part of Florida north through Jacksonville to the ocean."

At this point, Mark passed around a picture of the preserved environment along the Santa Fe River (located in the western part of Planning District 3) to illustrate the beauty of the historic Florida environment.

Exhibit 12:
Preservation of Historic Florida Environment along the Santa Fe River.
Photo by David Byrd

"The lakes and wetlands we are crossing now are what William Bartram, the eighteenth century naturalist from Philadelphia, termed one of the most beautiful parts of Florida—the Alachua Savanna, now called 'Payne's Prairie', which is a vast lowland (actually a huge sinkhole)—over fifty miles in circumference, collecting the drainage of a substantial area of north central Florida. Bartram described it as extensive green meadows without trees of any kind, bordered by fertile hills which he projected would be home to thousands of residents and domestic animals in future years. Drainage here goes underground into the limestone foundation of Florida, which I will explain further next week. For now, you can see that Bartram's projection came true, with fertile farms covering the high ground all the way up to and beyond the city of Gainesville to the north and the twenty-one-thousand-acre preserve of Payne's Prairie Preserve State Park, established in 1971 as Florida's first state preserve, and later designated as a 'National Natural Landmark'. It continues to exhibit the natural meadow of years gone by. By the way, the name Payne's Prairie, comes from the eldest surviving son of Chief Ahaya the Cowkeeper, often referred to as the first chief of the Alachua band of the Seminole tribe, which dominated this area in the early nineteenth century."

As Nash was scanning the photograph, he happened to glance out the window and asked Mark: "I assume that the city to the right is Palatka?"

"Correct. You'll have a better view when we return on the west side. Ahead you can see the vast expanse of Lake George, about twelve miles long and seven miles wide, through which the river passes through from south to north. All the forest land you can see to the west of the lake is part of the Ocala National Forest. Now, as Jake brings us back north up the west bank of the river, you can see the small city of Palatka, with its over eleven-thousand residents, commanding a strategic bend in the river for early steamboat traffic that served a large portion of the lake district to the south and west, prior to the emergence of railroads and highways. I have asked Jake to head west across the state. You will notice a large canal on the left with U.S. 19 crossing it on a high-level bridge. This canal and the adjoining Rodman Reservoir are all that's left of the attempt to construct a coast-to-coast barge canal across the state as a short-cut for water transport to the Gulf of Mexico. It was successfully halted by conservationists in the 1980s after construction had been underway for several years. The conservationists' primary concern was the potential disruption of the natural waterways and wildlife in this pristine area of the state.

"So, when Bartram visited here in the eighteenth century, this land was all populated by Indians," asked Nash?

"Absolutely, and unlike his fellow countrymen in the next century, Bartram made friends with the Indians who reciprocated by guiding him through the wilds of their homeland. As we move west across vast areas of farmland, you can see other large wetlands extending from north to south prior to reaching the large Suwannee River flowing all the way from Georgia to empty into the Gulf of Mexico to the southwest. The neighboring Santa Fe River to the east actually disappears in a whirlpool south of today's O'Leno State Park, just west of I-75, and reappears farther south.

This area of the state approaching the Gulf of Mexico is low-lying land and sparsely populated, until we move north past the seven-thousand residents in the farming community of Perry and up to the even smaller community of Madison in the midst of the former slave plantations of the mid-nineteenth century. These huge areas of northern Florida were scraped clean of their magnificent long leaf pine trees to meet the demand for timber used in building ships, forts and buildings of all types in eastern seaboard cities. The forests were replaced with cotton plantations (and sugar cane closer to the ocean). In addition to the huge pine trees, that could be transported only by ox carts with wheels of twelve feet in diameter to traverse the often-wet terrain, Bartram had earlier reported giant bald cypress trees measuring over ten feet in diameter and with straight trunks extending fifty feet high before branching off into their magnificent green domes of foliage."

"You mean virtually all of this land we are crossing over was timbered and turned into agriculture plantations?" questioned Nash. "It appears to be mostly forest today."

"Yes, but if you look closely, you can see that these pine trees are second and third growth slash pine cultivated for pulp and paper operations, and even those are no longer economically viable. The major forests of Florida are long gone, with primary forest resources exhausted by the early twentieth century after railway expansion had improved the ability to move cut trees to markets.

"We are now passing over the small community of Dowling Park on the banks of the Suwannee River. It claims to be Florida's first retirement community and it remains a thriving church-operated retirement community today. But, it originally was founded in the late nineteenth century as a sawmill powered by the flowing water of the river and supplying finished lumber for the Sears-Roebuck company in Chicago. Sears-Roebuck was selling packaged houses advertised in its catalogue for under one-thousand dollars, and the material originated from Dowling Park, prior to shipment to Chicago by train.

"A somewhat similar story precedes O'Leno State Park that I mentioned a few minutes ago. Its site was formerly a small logging community on the banks of the swiftly-flowing Santa Fe River. The residents named it Keno to advertise the gambling game available in its small commercial center. Later, after logging declined, church-going settlers stopped the gambling and changed the name to Leno. In the twentieth century, the village eventually became a ghost town. But, in the 1930s, this beautiful site on a bend in the Santa Fe River was selected by the federal Civilian Conservation Corps (CCC) as a location for a new state park which they called 'Old Leno' and that name changed to O'Leno when the completed park was handed over to the State of Florida.

"In 1860," continued Mark, "at the height of the slave plantations, the new state of Florida recorded seventy-seven plantations of more than one-thousand acres, two-hundred and eighty with five hundred to one-thousand acres, eleven hundred and twenty-three farms over one-hundred acres, and forty-six-hundred-and-seventy-six smaller farms. Most of them were in this north Florida area and worked by slaves imported directly from Africa to raise cotton (much of it the high-demand Sea Island cotton that grew better here than in the Carolinas), as well as corn and other food crops.

This slave society was similar to that in other parts of southern United States, with the richness of the historic north Florida soil providing the plantation owners with greater profits. These former northern European migrants guarded their lifestyle with care, particularly against the native Indians who, they were certain, threatened their livelihood through stealing and providing refuge for escaped slaves. Despite the presumed freedom for slaves after the Civil War in the 1860s, and the subsequent demise of Florida plantations because of both labor costs and soil decline, Florida grew rapidly with its population increasing from above one-hundred-and-forty-thousand residents in 1860 to over two-hundred-thousand by 1880—an impressive start toward the major population surges yet to come.

"Before I brief you on the Indian Wars, I see that Jake has followed my prescribed route back south to the city of Gainesville, a university town of one-hundred-and-twenty-five-thousand residents, exclusive of most of the more than forty-thousand students at the University of Florida and over ten-thousand non-local students at Santa Fe Community College. I have asked him to fly over the middle of the city so you can see the university complex from the air before we land at the airport east of the city. Nice work, Jake, in making a double pass so everyone gets a good view of the campus."

Although the luncheon food at the student restaurant across from the campus was better suited to young appetites than to the more mature tastes of Mark and Nash, it suited the much younger Jimmy Quickfoot admirably. Jake Johnson, of course, appeared to relish any kind of food. But, after the minivan taxi tour of the campus, they all enjoyed the energy of students who all seemed to talk at once as they devoured their lunches and hurried back to class. Central Gainesville was a beehive of activity, in sharp contrast to the quiet tree-covered residential areas they drove through on the way in from the airport.

After lunch was completed, Mark suggested that they convene at a table in the waiting room of the airport while Jake checked on the helicopter and his flight plan.

The airport waiting room was deserted in the early afternoon, providing a satisfactory meeting spot for Mark's synopsis of Indians in Florida. "The two decades from the 1820s to the 1840s marked the tumultuous culmination of fifty years of struggle between the native Indians and the incoming white men for possession of Florida. The Indians lost, but not without a series of heroic struggles referred to as 'The Seminole Wars.'

"Archeologists report that Indians inhabited the Florida peninsula over six-thousand years ago, and they began making pottery in 2,000 BC, eight centuries before other native groups in North America. Around 1,000 BC, people in southeastern North America began cultivating vegetables and developed ceramic vessels for cooking and storage. Most of these people lived along the coastlines of both the Atlantic Ocean and Gulf of Mexico and depended on shellfish as their dietary staple. Archaeological examination of village remains in the Tampa Bay area indicates that social organization, including potential religious ceremonies, existed by 500 AD.

"At the time of Ponce de Leon's arrival in 1513, the Indian population throughout what is now Florida is estimated to have been one-hundred-thousand persons in a variety of tribes, including half in the Timucua Confederation, twenty-thousand Calusa, twenty-five-thousand Apalachee, and five-thousand in several smaller tribes. The Calusa in the southeast were reported to be the most highly-organized society with small towns, cultivated fields and construction of canals for access to the towns.

"It appears that an Indian village existed adjacent to the St. Augustine inlet in the 1560s when Jean Ribault and his French Huguenot colonists took refuge there after being chased from their Fort Caroline site on the St. Johns River by a Spanish fleet led by Pedro Menendez. The Spanish routed the French from St. Augustine, and subsequently chased them back to France from the St. Johns River. Menendez is credited with establishing the Spanish colony that became St. Augustine. After a devastating raid by an English ship in 1668, the Spanish settlers began constructing the fort called Castillo de San Marcos, which survives to this day.

"In the interim, the Spanish Franciscan priests, who accompanied the invaders, began to establish missions in Florida to convert Indians to Christianity, particularly in northern Florida. Over a period of less than two decades, the brutal imposition of European cultural and religious practices reduced the Indian population from an estimated one-hundred-thousand at the turn of the century to fewer than eleven-thousand by 1674, mostly located in Apalachee. By the turn of the century, all of the Indian tribes in Florida were approaching extinction.

"Excuse me," interrupted Jimmy Quickfoot, who had remained a relatively quiet note-taker up until now. "Are you telling me that these presumably well-meaning Franciscan priests were responsible for killing most of the Indians in Florida?"

"Well, Jimmy, that is putting it rather bluntly," replied Mark. "But the short answer is yes. The Franciscans of that era believed that their God approved of harsh measures to spread Christianity to the uneducated natives, and at the same time their own lack of knowledge about basic hygiene caused disease to spread among the Indians. The Spanish Franciscans failed to accomplish their objectives, and they subsequently closed all of their missions in Florida."

"But, apparently well after the damage was done," said Jimmy. "As an indigenous native myself, I find this to be an appalling story."

"It is appalling, Jimmy," chimed in Nash. "But, if I understood Mark's opening remarks, the worst atrocities against Indians are yet to come. Is that right, Mark?"

"I'm afraid that's true, Nash, the rest of the story is even worse."

"After establishing a settlement in 1699 at what is now Pensacola, the Spanish began to lose interest in a land that had no gold to mine. In 1783, the Spanish signed the Treaty of Paris which ended the Seven Years War and reconfigured ownership of North American colonies. Spain traded La Florida to the English for Havana, and the Spanish took the last of the indigenous Indians back to Spain (two-hundred-and-sixty survivors from the Tekesta and Apalachee tribes, their fate in Spain unknown). So Indians disappeared from Florida, which then appeared to revert to a few European colonists in St. Augustine and Pensacola.

"Slowly, over subsequent years, the Creek Indians from Georgia and the Carolinas began migrating into the giant forests and rich soil of northern Florida. They eventually proliferated in a line between Apalachicola to the St. Johns River. They were disliked by the Spanish, who began calling them 'cimarron' (meaning 'wild or abandoned sailors'), a term pronounced by the Indians as 'Seminole.' Northern European settlers migrating into northern Florida to establish logging operations and slave plantations on the rich forest soil were equally annoyed by these Seminole Indians whom they accused of stealing their crops and harboring runaway slaves (imported directly from Africa).

"In 1814, the battle-seasoned Andrew Jackson was appointed Governor of Florida and he acted upon the complaints of his wealthy land-owner constituents by sending troops in to attack Indian villages across northern Florida (although the city of Jacksonville was later named in his honor, Jackson actually never set foot in the river city). William Duval succeeded Jackson as Governor in 1821 and attempted to settle the dispute between settlers and Indians by negotiation. At that time, there were a reported five-thousand Seminoles living in forty villages in Florida's north-central highlands. In 1823, thirty-two chiefs of the various Seminole tribes gathered south of St. Augustine to sign the Treaty of Moultrie Creek, in which they relinquished all claims to Florida land except for a four-million-acre reservation in the interior of South Florida, and a smaller area in the Apalachicola Basin. These chiefs ceded twenty-eight-million acres to the United States and also agreed to turn in runaway slaves and fugitives, as well as cease separate trade with Cuba. They were given twenty years to move to their new lands.

"But the plantation settlers continued to expand across North Florida with their cotton and sugar plantations. Tallahassee was named the territory capital in 1824, and an east-west road was constructed across the northern part of the state—a second north-south road was built from New Smyrna to Cowford (later to become Jacksonville). Initial railroads were constructed in the 1830s to haul logs and cotton to northern markets.

"In 1825, a severe drought caused famine and a return to hunting by the Indians. The slave plantation owners once again demanded action. A new treaty was presented in 1832 to pay the Indians eighty-thousand dollars for their four-million-acre reservation (two cents per acre), but Chief Micanopy denied signing this treaty. Thus began the Second Seminole War, in which the great chief Osceola became leader of the intransigent tribes. He led attacks on the plantations, destroying the crops. The United States Militia was called upon to retaliate, first under the command of Duncan Clinch, who was replaced in 1836 by Winfield Scott (most of whose officers resigned rather than fight in the heat and insects of Florida). The officers rose to skeptical fame as the creators of the 'flag of truce' to lure Indians into capture. Chiefs Coacoochee and Osceola were captured and the latter died of malaria in jail in 1838, later becoming a folk hero with his name featured in dozens of political jurisdictions, a park and a national forest.

The army seemed incapable of defeating the Indians and the conflict continued unabated until a new commander, William Worth, with five-thousand troops, brought the war to a close in 1842 with an estimated three-or four-hundred Indians still at large throughout the state. Worth informed them that they could remain south of a line from Charlotte Harbor to Lake Okeechobee—thus the modern association of Seminoles with the Everglades. By then, almost four-thousand Indians had been shipped to the reservation in the Arkansas Territory (later to be part of Oklahoma).

"This truce lasted until 1849 when a group of five white men were found murdered and settlers again cried for the elimination of all Indians from 'the promised land.' This cry occurred concurrently with drainage and agricultural encroachment on the Everglades where the Indians were domiciled. In 1855, the United States Secretary of War, Jefferson Davis, issued orders 'to clean out the Indians.' The Third Seminole War had begun. This time, even private bounty hunters were employed to capture Indians. But the hunt for Indians gave way to the bigger conflict of the Civil War among the states. An estimated one-hundred Indians were left in the swampland of the Everglades, but it was not until 1934-37 that the Seminoles finally signed treaty agreements with the United States, formally marking the end of the wars of removal and fixing the boundaries of their South Florida Reservations. Tensions still persist between the few remaining Indians and the 'white men' who continue to develop their hunting grounds and restrict their indigenous rights—a sad chapter of American history which lingers on."

"It is a sad story, indeed, Mark," said Nash, "but one which I appreciate hearing about. We European descendants have inflicted undue hardship in many parts of the world and we need to remember them with remorse. As Jimmy well knows, the history of European settlement in Canada bears its share of mistreatment of indigenous Indians that is not a proud part of our brief history." Jimmy just nodded in solemn agreement with his employer.

When the helicopter returned to the "Victoria" later that afternoon, Linda and Bobbi were on the deck to greet them and recount the shopping and lunch adventures they had enjoyed in St. Augustine. Nash asked them all to meet in the main lounge for an important announcement. Except for Jake, who immediately took off again to fuel up at the St. Augustine Airport, the others moved inside to hear Nash's announcement.

"Ladies and gentlemen, we have just completed our successful third day of touring and learning about this great state and I believe it appropriate to celebrate with a special dinner this evening. I have learned from Mark that St. Augustine is home to one of Florida's finest restaurants; so, with Jimmy's help, I have booked a table for all of us. Please gather here for drinks at six o'clock. Transport has been arranged for a seven o'clock dinner.

"Mark, you will just have to defer your preamble on Planning District 4 until tomorrow morning."

"Sounds good to me," said Mark, with a broad smile. And everyone adjourned to their cabins to dress for dinner.

✑

As Captain Franz Ericksson and Chief Engineer Tim Wilson had prior commitments, there were only six of them seated at a round table in the second-floor dining room of the Raintree Restaurant on St. Augustine's main vehicular street north of the "old city". Nash arranged the seating with Bobbi, Jake and Mark across from Jimmy, Linda and himself. As earlier suggested by Mark, everyone was attired in casual clothing suitable to St. Augustine informality. The moderate spring temperature proved comfortable without jackets or sweaters.

This restaurant was a consistent winner of the "Golden Spoon Award" given to Florida's best restaurants annually by the popular *Florida Trend* magazine. All of their menu selections were spectacular dishes, and all of the guests from the "Victoria" praised the superior cuisine.

Bobbi was pleased to note that her sister, who had been sorrowful over their lunch about her recent divorce, appeared exceptionally animated in conversation with their host. Nash, of course, always seemed sincerely interested in everyone he spoke with, but Linda's response was the most cheerful that Bobbi had witnessed all day. Maybe, she thought to herself, this cruise could be a better idea than she had imagined.

Bobbi's smile quickly disappeared with the sudden appearance of the smiling Jack Swift at her side: "Good evening, Mrs. Wilkins and Ms. Cummings. What a pleasant surprise to find you all together. Mr. Logan and Dr. Wilkins, my name is Jack Swift of the Swift Property Company. As I believe you know, I asked Mrs. Wilkins to present my card and request a meeting where I can present some vital information to you."

Although Mark was not surprised by Swift's appearance, his arrival at their table seemed too timely to be a coincidence. He looked at Nash for reaction, but the personable Canadian gave no hint of annoyance.

While Swift was speaking, Jake and Jimmy both rose from their chairs to take whatever action Nash Logan might feel appropriate, but Nash smiled warmly at Swift and responded, "This is not the time or the place to discuss business, Mr. Swift, but we can spend a few minutes with you at seven-thirty tomorrow morning if you could come by my yacht at Camachee Cove."

"I would be honored to be present at that time, Mr. Logan."

DAY 4

Monday, March 29, 2010

Rather than an early helicopter start, last night's celebratory dinner and the impromptu early morning meeting scheduled with Mr. Swift prompted Mark to suggest an after-breakfast meeting on the yacht following their proposed meeting with Mr. Swift at seven-thirty. He would introduce the day's proposed agenda at that time. Since they were docked within Planning District 4, the tour would be of somewhat shorter duration, and they could afford a later start. So, at 7 am, Mark was joined by Nash, Jimmy, Jake and Bobbi at the breakfast table in the "Victoria" main lounge. Promptly at seven-thirty, Carlos, the deckhand, ushered Swift to the rear entrance of the main lounge where he could be seen by Nash Logan. The Canadian immediately excused himself and strode to the rear sliding glass door which Carlos slid open for him as he approached.

"Mr. Swift, right on time, I see," as Nash offered his hand in welcome.

"Good morning, Mr. Logan," replied Swift. "This is a beautiful vessel. I am privileged to be invited aboard."

"Please come in and have a seat here in the corner. The others are just finishing their breakfast, so you and I can chat privately here. Jose, please bring us some coffee and water over here if you would." The smiling waiter nodded his head vigorously in response and proceeded to serve them without speaking.

"So then, Mr. Swift, what is on your mind?"

The slick-looking guest set down his coffee cup and dabbed his lips with a napkin before speaking: "Mr. Logan, friends of mine in the state government have made me aware of your inquiries about land development in Florida, and I am prepared to offer you some special assistance to achieve your objectives."

Logan immediately raised his hand for Swift to stop talking and then motioned to Mark. "Mark, would you mind joining us over here for a few minutes. Mr. Swift apparently wants to talk about land development in Florida, so I believe you should sit in."

"You bet," replied Mark as he rose from the breakfast table and nodded his apologies to his table companions before approaching the seating group at the corner table.

"Please pull up a chair, Mark. You already met Mr. Swift last night."

"I did indeed, good morning, Mr. Swift."

"It is a good morning," replied Swift, "and I intend to make it better for your land hunt. I represent a syndicate of investors who would like to assist you in your mission. We not only control agency listings on most parcels over one-thousand acres in size throughout the state, but we have unusually fine connections with both appointed and elected officials at the local and state levels of government who can help achieve your entitlement objectives in rapid fashion."

"Well, I am really sorry to hear that, Mr. Swift," countered Mark. "I have no interest in being involved in any attempt to influence government officials in an unseemly and possibly illegal manner . . ."

"Please, Dr. Wilkins, I am sorry to interrupt, but, I did not for a moment mean to imply any impropriety. Heaven forbid that I should be accused of such a thing. Our group acts completely within the law. Having said that, your lengthy experience in state planning should include many examples of land-use entitlements that are achieved much faster than others, without any accusation of wrongdoing."

"Well, yes, I suppose that's true. But, just what is it that you are proposing?"

"Very simple, Dr. Wilkins, our group would like to procure a modest equity investment position in Mr. Logan's land acquisition. In return, as a junior partner, we are prepared to expedite the acquisition and development process for you—and for us too, of course. As you are well aware, large scale land acquisition and development entitlement have become increasingly difficult over the past few years as both conservation and citizen rights groups have banded together in opposition to any developer, no matter how well-meaning he might be. Our group operates completely behind the scenes to ensure your success. The need for our participation has never been greater than this year, when the development industry is facing its greatest threat from the supporters of Constitution Amendment 4, popularly called the 'Hometown Democracy' amendment. And the best news is that we actually supply investment funds at no fee, rather than bill for our services. You only have seven months to beat the election date."

"Frankly, Mr. Swift," responded Nash, with a grim look on his face, "if I were certain that everything you have just said is not true, I would have you thrown overboard for suggesting potentially criminal collusion to circumvent the Florida development process. As it is, I am going to defer judgment until my legal staff investigates you more fully. Therefore, I invite you to return next week when we are docked in Fort Lauderdale . . . at your own risk, of course, depending on what I find out about you in the interim."

"I can assure you, Mr. Logan, that I have an unblemished reputation in the Florida real estate business. Furthermore, I will be delighted to return in one week to discuss details of our new working relationship." With that, Swift rose from the table and reached his hand out to Nash Logan with a comfortable smile on his face. After a few seconds' hesitation, Logan shook the outstretched hand and bid Mr. Swift farewell. Mark never moved from his seat or spoke a word as Swift quickly left the yacht.

"Nash," said Mark, after a moment of silence, "that man makes me feel uneasy. There is an aura about him of dishonesty, regardless of what your attorneys may discover."

"I do not disagree with you, Mark, but I am reticent to close out any option solely on the basis of intuition. Let's see what happens when my lawyers in Toronto investigate. Perhaps you have sources here in Florida who might assist?"

"Yes, I do," answered Mark without hesitation. Please defer our introduction to Planning District 4 for ten minutes while I go to my room and phone a good friend in Orlando, who also happens to be one of the best land-use legal minds in the state. Excuse me."

When Mark reappeared in the main lounge about fifteen minutes after his departure, Nash, Jimmy, Jake, and Bobbi were all seated at the round conference table.

"Sorry to keep you all waiting," he began, "but my phone call was urgent."

"Not a problem," smiled Nash, "but we are more than ready to learn about our tour of the day. So, please begin when you are ready."

Mark immediately moved to the mounted map and pointed to the boundaries of Planning District 4. "As you all are aware, today we are scheduled to tour Planning District 4, also known as the Northeast Florida Regional Planning District. It contains seven counties, including Duval County that is virtually coterminous with the city of Jacksonville—a union dating to 1969 that created the largest city in area in the United States, over eight-hundred-and-forty square miles of land and water area and almost forty miles from side-to-side. Four of the seven counties in this district are designated by the United States Census as the Jacksonville Metropolitan Area: Duval, St. Johns (encompassing St. Augustine), Clay (including Orange Park), and Nassau (containing Amelia Island and Fernandina Beach, where Bobbi and I hang out when we are not on luxury yachts). Of the other three counties, two are predominantly rural—Baker to the

**Exhibit 13:
Planning District 4—
Northeast.**

northwest and Putnam to the southwest (containing the city of Palatka)—and the third contains a large planned community named Palm Coast, that for many years made Flagler County the fastest-growing county in the state. Now, if you will refer to your copy of the planning district map once again, you can follow along with my description of our route for today."

After Nash and Jimmy produced their maps, Mark continued with his description. "The Northeast Florida Regional Planning District contains over one-and-a-half million people of whom nine-hundred-thousand are in Duval County. For our tour today, I propose we go south to Palm Coast and Flagler Beach and then follow the coastline all the way up to Fernandina Beach before circling west across the north side of Nassau County, with a quick look at the farms and forests of Baker County before heading south through the west side of Duval, Clay and Putnam Counties. Then, I suggest we follow the St. Johns River north over the city of Orange Park and over central Jacksonville east to the Intracoastal Waterway, and follow it back south to St. Augustine. The President of the Jacksonville Chamber of Commerce has invited us to join him for lunch at the University Club, on top one of the city's higher buildings where Jake can park the helicopter on the roof of the adjacent parking garage.

"I believe most of you know by now that Jacksonville was one of Florida's early settlements. It was originally known as 'Cowford' because of the need to ford the river at this point when going south, prior to construction of any bridges. It was re-named Jacksonville in honor of Andrew Jackson who served as Governor of Florida during the First Seminole War that I summarized yesterday. This city's strategic location on the river, and as an oceangoing port, stimulated its growth to become Florida's largest city. And, by virtue of its amalgamation with the county, it remains so.

"You mean its population is greater than Miami's?" asked Jimmy.

"That's an excellent question, Jimmy. The major urban areas of this state, like those in many other states, are centered on cities that encompass only a small part of the urban growth area. Thus, for example, the city of Miami has a population of only about four-hundred-thousand, within an urban area of almost two-and-one-half million in population. So, it is recognized appropriately as a much larger city than Jacksonville, whereas the Miami jurisdiction has a much smaller population than that of the much larger land area of Jacksonville. Similar comparisons can be made for Fort Lauderdale, West Palm Beach, Tampa and Orlando—all smaller in population than Jacksonville, but all in the center of urban areas with populations larger than the population of metropolitan Jacksonville.

"In addition to being a seaport, a function that is destined to grow substantially with the opening of the new Panama Canal in 2014, Jacksonville's growth is due to its regional location as a center for health and financial services to northeast Florida and southeast Georgia. It also serves a large Navy population in two air and sea bases. And, Jacksonville's former Naval Air Station, Cecil Field, was a third large Navy base since World War II and prior to the closing of bases (including Cecil Field) in 1988 by the Base Realignment and Closure Commission (BRAC). This city also was home to several manufacturing industries which have declined over recent years, particularly three large pulp and paper mills that formerly generated serious air pollution.

"Growth occurred on the three non-ocean sides of Jacksonville, but primarily to the south where major employment generators were, and are, located. Clay County and its city of Orange Park, west of the St. Johns River, achieved rapid growth because of its excellent school system. Its population remains higher than that of St. Johns County east of the river, despite the disadvantages of its location west of the river for center city commuters.

"The city has few buildings dating from the nineteenth century because of a devastating fire that swept through the central part of Jacksonville in 1901. However, reconstruction after that date provided particularly fine residential architecture in the Riverside and Springhill neighborhoods that adjoin the central city. The Epping Forest mansion, mentioned earlier as the longtime residence of Jessie Ball duPont, is listed on the National Historic Register as one of the city's best examples of pre-World War II architecture.

"We already have discussed the historic city of St. Augustine which is one of Florida's major tourist destinations, despite the fact that it is primarily an attraction for day visitors rather than overnight tourists. Its beaches and other attractions do not compete favorably for longer-term tourists. Farther south, in Flagler County (named after the wealthy turn-of-the-century pioneer developer of Florida's entire east coast, as I described earlier), a retirement community was planned in the 1960s by ITT on forty-two-thousand acres of slash pine forest used to feed its Rayonier pulp and paper mills. The company built four signature golf courses and an oceanfront hotel to attract retirees to modest-price housing at this location, a promotion that made it the fastest-growth county in Florida for many years. However, the company reported a consistent financial loss on this venture and eventually sold out the remainder to other development interests who have continued its growth. A few years ago, the city of Palm Coast became chartered and continues with self-government for over forty-thousand residents.

"Like most parts of Florida, this region was hard-hit by The Great Recession of 2008-9 and currently still contains an inventory of entitled, but undeveloped, lots numbering over twenty-five-thousand, the major share being in St. Johns County. In addition, it contains abandoned master-planned communities that were partially or fully processed through entitlement. Similar situations exist in Orlando and Tampa as well as South Florida. One possible alternative for your quest, Nash, may be to acquire one of these planned communities and adapt it to your objectives.

"A recent news article in the *St. Augustine Record* newspaper quoted St. Johns County planners as estimating sixty- to eighty-thousand entitled homesites in this one county, the majority in fourteen developments of regional impact, which I described previously as defined by size standards in state legislation. Several of these DRIs are lying vacant without any homes; some without any construction at all. The Regional Planning Director, Brian Teeple, was quoted as saying that all of these planned communities will be absorbed over time, and he referred to the twenty-five- to thirty-year build-out periods programmed for most of these DRI communities, as well as to historical community build-outs substantially below original entitlement projections. Nevertheless, growth plans for metropolitan Jacksonville are well beyond current growth rates, and this suggests that there may be future public reticence to continue approving large community developments.

"With that introduction, I suggest we go have a look at the Northeast Florida Regional Planning District."

"Once again, Mark, you have excelled at providing useful information," responded Nash. "Jake, I propose wheels up in fifteen minutes."

"Right you are, Mr. Logan."

❧

It was another beautiful day for flying, and the flight proceeded down to Flagler Beach over the new city of Palm Coast, and then north past miles of clean sand beach. Just before they came to the southern tip of Anastasia Island at Matanzas Inlet, Mark asked Jake to drop down and circle over one of the most distinctive incorporated cities in Florida with a current population of six residents on a small beachfront area bisected by the SR AIA highway.

"This is what is left of what used to be one of Florida's most popular tourist attractions, called Marineland. It was initiated in 1938 as a partnership between two wealthy men: Cornelius Vanderbilt Whitney (the commander's grandson) and Ilya Tolstoy (the count's grandson) as a film studio for marine life, and, by the 1950s, its acclaimed oceanarium attracted over half-a-million visitors annually. Although originally conceived as a motion picture facility for marine life, it became famous for the antics of bottlenose dolphins that performed daily for admiring crowds. Its location, just west of US 1 leading to Miami, was a convenient stopping point for tourists driving farther south. But, after the emergence of Sea World next to Disney World in the 1970s, Marineland lost its popularity and remains today as a quiet marine research center."

They continued north past St. Augustine Beach, Anastasia State Park, Vilano Beach, Ponte Vedra Beach, Jacksonville Beach, Neptune Beach, Atlantic Beach, Talbot Island State Park, and Amelia Island Beaches, to the mouth of the St. Marys River. It was a pleasant vista interrupted with no conversation, except the answers to a few location questions. Once again, Mark had arranged the trip so that Nash had the prime view through a left window of the helicopter.

One question from Nash concerned the number of golf courses clustered into Ponte Vedra Beach. Mark had to pause for a moment and count seven courses containing a total of 135 holes of golf in this large cluster of recreation communities, centered on the Professional

Golfers' Association of America Tournament Players Club course and headquarters' offices southeast of central Jacksonville.

Once Jake had changed course to the west along the St. Marys River, Mark felt it necessary to add more information. "Much of the land in this northern sector of Nassau County is still owned by Rayland, the subsidiary of Rayonier and ITT. The land, once the source of slash pine trees for processing paper products, became redundant after the parent company closed its pulp and paper plant at Fernandina Beach.

"So, Rayland has been actively selling land here and in St. Johns County for the past thirty years and still owns a great deal of unimproved land in both counties. Most of the vacant land right up to the St. Marys River is Rayland property.

You can see all the way down I-95 at this point to the Jacksonville International Airport and beyond to the tall buildings in downtown Jacksonville. The large estate along the river bank west of I-95 is White Oak, the former home of the now-deceased owner of a large pulp and paper plant in St. Marys, which closed and was demolished after his death. The plant property, within the city of St. Marys, was purchased by LandMar of Jacksonville, a subsidiary of Crescent Resources of Charlotte, North Carolina. That company, which in turn is a subsidiary of the Duke Power Company, declared Chapter 11 bankruptcy over a year ago but still has not disposed of its assets—some dozen master-planned communities in Florida and Georgia in various stages of completion. You might make a note to explore one or more of them for your project."

"Thank you, Mark. Please make a note of that Jimmy."

"Yes sir, Mr. Logan. I've got it."

"There are several large land ownerships in this western area of Nassau County and south into Duval County, in addition to Rayland holdings. Two railroads run through here. If this area looks promising for you, land acquisition would be straightforward. The St. Marys River takes a big curve southward here and extends Georgia into Florida. Straight ahead is Macclenny; and the rail yard, which you inquired about on our first day, is adjacent to U.S 301 on the east, with the north-south four-lane highway to the west of the railroad tracks. To the west is Osceola National Forest where it is reported that one or more Florida cougars are still living. Below us is a tract of three-thousand acres in Baker County planned for a new community served by I-10, but listed for sale last year. I believe it is still listed. As you can see by the tree growth, only the land around Macclenny is suitable for agriculture or development in Baker County.

"Returning now to Duval County, you can see the former Cecil Field Naval Air Station. It encompasses almost twenty-thousand acres to the east, and effectively blocks suburban development on the west side of Jacksonville. As I noted earlier this morning, Cecil Field, first opened in 1941, was declared surplus in 1988 (National Priorities List, 1989) and officially closed in 1999 during its transfer from the Navy to the city of Jacksonville. The city adopted the NAS Cecil Field Base Reuse Plan in 1996 and followed with a multi-use Planned Unit Development (PUD) ordinance in 1997.

"After more than ten years of planning, negotiation, coordination and expectation, city officials distributed, in January 2009, a Request for Proposal to developers across the United States, inviting them to submit credentials and a concept plan to become a contract master developer. Only five proposals were received, of which one was accepted in April: Jacksonville/Cecil Commerce Center LLC, headquartered in Dallas, Texas (owned by the Hillwood Company of Dallas). The city is now completing a final draft of an agreement with this developer to develop and sell parcels of land for thirty-one million square feet of commercial and industrial buildings, as well as six-hundred hotel rooms on thirty-five-hundred acres of the Cecil Field property over a thirty-five year period—an enormous undertaking that is to be controlled by interim sales targets required within the first ten years and every five years thereafter. This focus on new jobs and related economic growth still leaves the bulk of Cecil Field land uncommitted—a potential opportunity for your plan, especially since this public property is exempt from DRI approval and already has completed a four-lane connector highway to I-10 north of the site. However, I should temper this possibility with the fact that the site is reputed to contain a high proportion of wetlands.

"The Cecil Field opportunity certainly is interesting, Mark, but it suffers from throwing me into the public spotlight where the attention is not always welcome."

"Very true," replied Mark, "although your marketing staff may disagree with you on publicity. But I have many more possibilities to come. Ahead to the east, along the 301 corridor past the Jennings State Forest, there is a large tract of close to two-thousand acres just inside the northern boundary of Clay County that was withdrawn from DRI processing in 2008—it is owned by an investment syndicate familiar to me. As you can see, the suburban fringe extends southwest from the city of Orange Park into Clay County. Transportation has been a problem in this county; however, a new beltway road is in the planning stage for private toll road participation that will link to I-95 in St. Johns County and cross the river turning north to link up with I-10.

"Jake, you need to swing east here to miss the Camp Blanding Army base dead ahead. The army is not friendly to unannounced visitors from the air. If you stay to the east of the north-south two-lane highway, you will be fine."

"Will do," replied Jake, as the helicopter moved left.

"South of Camp Blanding we enter Putnam County, which is predominantly farms and forests, with a still-operating former Georgia-Pacific paper plant on the river to the east, marked by the high smoke-stack just north of the city of Palatka. Stay south of the city, if you will, Jake, and head right into Flagler County. The large lake coming up ahead is Crescent Lake, Nash. We participated in planning over eight-thousand acres on the east side of that lake, but it never attracted enough investment interest to proceed to entitlement. Straight ahead is the sprawling community of Palm Coast, but you can turn north here, Jake, over the large-grid road network representing another example of wasted land divided into one-quarter acre lots for sale to northerners, but never completed as a community.

"That's really ugly," remarked Nash. "It is such a needless waste of land, eh!"

"Okay, Jake," interrupted Mark. "You can see the St. Johns River. Please fly right up the center until we get to downtown Jacksonville. Our landing spot is on the top of a parking garage right across the river from where the yacht was docked when we began this journey."

"The river separates the two counties here with St. Johns on the right and Clay on the left. Suburban development will emerge after we pass the old ship-building community of Green Cove Springs on the left. The bridge across the river here is due to be replaced by a four-lane controlled-access highway as part of the planned west side 'outer beltway'. You can see extensive development to the river here in Clay County, but development in St. Johns has been delayed by the launch of a forty-three-hundred-acre new community called 'River Town' by the St. Joe Company, which has promised to preserve the river edge. Now, we are re-entering Duval County, with the Naval Air Station on the left and downtown straight ahead.

"Mark, the St. Johns is a beautiful river, but what about pollution problems?" asked Nash.

"Excellent question, Nash. The three-hundred-and-ten-mile-long St. Johns River drains much of eastern Florida and has suffered from pollution since the earliest settlements along the river one-hundred-and-fifty years ago. State legislation passed in the 1970s and 1980s established regulations to stop raw sewage and other untreated pollutants from entering the river and its tributaries, but pollution problems persist. Many parts of the river system experience large algae blooms that reflect excessive levels of nitrogen and phosphorus which harm both fish and plants. A number of springs that feed the river are producing less water than in the past and they are showing signs of pollution. In addition, residues from pesticides and industrial waste have seeped into small creeks and streams that drain into the St. Johns. All of these issues are a source of concern by both local and state environmentalists and politicians in coordination with the non-profit St. Johns River Alliance, which monitors river conditions, along with the St. Johns River Water Management District, a state agency with responsibilities extending across the river's entire watershed. Clearly, it is one of the state's major natural resources and deserves the care it is receiving from these agencies and legislators.

"Jake, you can short-cut across to our parking garage here if you like. I see you have a visual on the helipad, so I will stop talking."

Lunch on the twenty-second floor at the University Club was a real treat. Not only was the food good, but the views out three sides of the building were spectacular. The beaches were visible fifteen miles to the east, and the river view to the south was equally impressive. Everyone enjoyed the luncheon as well as meeting the president and two senior executives from the Chamber of Commerce. They were full of information that Nash and Jimmy were devouring faster than their food. Mark had explained to them the purpose of Nash's visit and they were eager to be of assistance.

Mark took this occasion to summarize the history of Jacksonville after the great fire of 1901 burned most of the city. The re-building of the neighborhoods closest to the city center produced many fine examples of residential architecture, featuring both Victorian and the 'prairie' designs popularized by the famous architect Frank Lloyd Wright. However, by the 1950s, the prosperous city center was surrounded by ugly slums and illegal activities. Poverty was rampant. But the Florida population explosion of the 1950s and 1960s generated headquarters for insurance companies, banks and health-care facilities that pumped new vitality and employment into the city. New military facilities added another strong dimension to the local economy. Suburban sprawl strained the city's infrastructure and center city merchants' abilities to compete with new suburban shopping malls. Although the completion of I-95 through the center of the city improved access to the suburbs, it left racially-segregated slums behind, in the shadow of downtown office buildings.

"August 27, 1960 was arguably the most infamous day in Jacksonville's history, called 'Ax Handle Saturday.' It was on this day that black youths, frustrated by the segregation conditions in the city, staged a lunch counter sit-in at Woolworth's store in downtown

Jacksonville. As they emerged from the store, after the manager refused to serve them, they were attacked by a gang of angry white men, marching in Confederate uniforms and carrying ax handles and baseball bats. The battle was then joined by a large group of black youths calling themselves the Boomerangs, and downtown Jacksonville streets soon became covered with the blood of wounded contestants and bystanders. Major news services carried the story nationwide: 'Angry bands of club-swinging whites clashed with Negroes in the streets of Jacksonville today. At least fifty persons were injured . . .' as reported by United Press International.

"Jacksonville at this time was, by some accounts, the worst city in Florida for African-Americans. The after-effects of the segregation era continued in the form of wide disparities in economic opportunities, education and health. These disparities were highlighted in a 1946 study called 'Jacksonville Looks at Its Negro Community'. High rates of prison admissions, infant mortality and unemployment among blacks were key results of segregation in every facet of community life. In post-War Jacksonville, there was not a single public swimming pool, beach or park open to blacks, the only city in the state without such access at that time. There were no African-American police officers in this city where 27 percent of the population was black. Segregationist policies in schools, stores and businesses remained in force at the time of the 1960 uprising.

"In August, 1960, the Jacksonville NAACP Youth Council organized peaceful sit-ins at downtown lunch counters. They were joined at an August twenty-fifth sit-in by a white Florida State University student named Richard Charles Parker, who, two days later, was found on the street with a broken jaw and was imprisoned for two months. Subsequently, he was refused re-admission to Florida State University.

"On August twenty-seventh, the demonstrators first went to W. T. Grants' lunch counter, whereupon the management turned out the lights and closed the store. Others went to Woolworth's where they were refused service and attacked by white segregationists as they left the store. Mayor Hayden Burns called an emergency meeting with law enforcement officials to restore order; and, by mid-afternoon, police began arresting people (primarily blacks) downtown. By evening, violence spread throughout the city, perpetuated by both blacks and whites.

"The following day, the NAACP Youth Council voted to discontinue the sit-ins and proceed with a boycott of downtown merchants. They also called upon the United States Justice Department to investigate local law enforcement for failing to protect peaceful demonstrators. Although the uprising was widely reported across the nation, the local Jacksonville papers ignored it. In September, Mayor Burns met with NAACP members, but refused to appoint a bi-racial committee to ease the racial tension. However, downtown merchants did initiate discussions with the NAACP. In November, lunch-counter sit-ins resumed; and, in December, a black mother sued, on behalf of her children, to end Duval County's segregated school system. By the following year, meetings with business leaders resumed and downtown lunch counters became fully integrated by Spring 1961. In 1962, a U.S. District Judge ordered the School Board to submit a plan for integration; and, in 1963, the first thirteen African-American children were enrolled in Duval County Public Schools. Thus, the long road toward ending segregation in Jacksonville was initiated and continues to the present time.

"In June of 1964, the nation's attention turned to St. Augustine, where Martin Luther King, Jr. and seventeen others were arrested after trying to integrate the Monson Motor Lodge Restaurant. An attempt to swim in the Lodge's pool was met with acid dumped in the pool while demonstrators were in it. Hundreds of protestors, including blacks, whites and sixteen Rabbis were arrested. Later, after the lodge temporarily integrated, it was bombed. Thus, Northeast Florida was a central focus of the movement to bring equitable integration to the United States. Jacksonville's Mayor Burns would soon recover from his resistance to social justice to lead his city into a new political era."

"During the 1960s, a progressive Mayor Hayden Burns re-organized city government and proposed amalgamation with Duval County to achieve more efficient government. Residents supported the mayor's proposal by a two-to-one vote in 1969, and Jacksonville became the largest territorial city in continental United States, on a land area of 840 square miles. Over the next three decades, a succession of committed city leaders transformed Jacksonville into a modern city with a variety of private and public amenities, including a convention center (former railway station), a performing arts center, a new city hall, a riverfront commercial and entertainment center with boardwalks and water taxis, a riverfront park adjacent to a new sports complex containing football and baseball stadiums, as well as an indoor arena.

Downtown developers followed with high-rise housing that completed several buildings prior to The Great Recession, which halted even more ambitious plans. Through the generosity and foresight of the Davis family, the founders of Winn-Dixie Supermarkets, land was donated for the prestigious Mayo Clinic's first satellite center, to add to the city's already-strong health-care system. Concurrent with these improvements, city officials concentrated on neighborhood improvements in the northern (primarily African-American) urban areas to instill pride by the over seven-hundred-thousand residents of Florida's largest city."

It was after three o'clock by the time they said goodbye to their new Jacksonville friends and took the elevator down to the crosswalk to the parking garage where another elevator took them to the roof. Within a few minutes, Jake had them airborne again and heading south over the Southside of Jacksonville.

"The large area of undeveloped land ahead is a fifty-thousand-acre preserve owned by the Davis family. It contains a number of species of exotic animals, but is not open to the public. The southern part of the initial sixty-five-thousand-acre tract was committed a few years ago to a fifteen-thousand-acre new community called 'Nocatee' (yet another remembrance of our former Indians). You can see, as it comes into view, that the major roads have been completed and housing is being developed in four villages. This community is being developed and financed by the Davis family as a profit-making venture over a twenty-five-year completion schedule. Given the recession period, they appear off to a good start with about 400 new homes occupied."

"Is the family actually managing the development?" asked Nash.

"No, they have a long relationship with a local development company called The Parc Group."

"On the east side of the Intracoastal Waterway up ahead is the Guana River State Park, a preserve with natural marsh and dune preservation. Across from it on the west side of the Waterway is a new community called Palencia, with its championship golf course in the foreground. Nash and Jimmy, please note the extent of retention lakes required in a Florida development of this scale. Next, we are approaching the St. Augustine Airport with which Jake is already familiar. He knows the route from here, unless there is anything else you want to see, Nash?"

"No, this has been another good day, Mark, but that sumptuous lunch has made me sleepy. I think I will need a power nap before dinner. Please take me home, Jake."

After another delicious dinner in the main lounge of the "Victoria", the yacht officers and Jake excused themselves to attend to preparations for trips by both the yacht and the helicopter the next day—the yacht was destined for a new mooring at Port Canaveral while the helicopter was scheduled to tour Planning District 5 on the west side of the peninsula. Linda once again joined Bobbi as observers to the evening discussion at the corner table with Mark, Nash and Jimmy.

"Although we summarized Henry Flagler's impact on the development of Florida at the beginning of our tour, I thought, since we are sitting here in the first city that he promoted, it would be helpful to re-visit his exploits," began Mark.

"That makes sense to us," said Nash, "particularly with respect to all of the major cities he initiated on this coast."

"Okay! First, there is little question that Flagler became an elitist through his extraordinary success with John D. Rockefeller and the Standard Oil Company. They went from modest beginnings to become two of the richest men in the world through the success of this company. Flagler initially set foot in Florida with his first wife, Mary, at the age of forty-six, and then returned in 1882 (after her death) at the age of fifty-two and spent the next thirty years developing the east coast of Florida, until his death in 1913. He firmly believed that providing rail transportation and exclusive hotels for affluent tourists in this undeveloped land was a great contribution to mankind, in addition to being a profitable business enterprise. He was hailed as one of the richest men in the world upon his death."

"Mark, can you be more specific about his actual accomplishments?" asked Nash.

"Certainly! During his second trip to St. Augustine in 1882, he decided to build vacation accommodations for the affluent residents of New York and other parts of northern United States; and he wasted no time in retaining two New York architects to design an elaborate hotel for the site which he had purchased on King Street in St. Augustine. He instructed them to make the design compatible with the sixteenth century Spanish architecture of the old city, but they went well beyond the Spanish Mission style to a much more elaborate design that became the image of Flagler's Florida. It has survived the test of time as one of the most-admired buildings in Northeast Florida (now it is the home of Flagler College).

"The Ponce de Leon Hotel proved an immediate success when it opened in 1886; success that moved Flagler to build a less expensive hotel called the Alcazar across the street for vacationers of more modest means. He then added an indoor swimming pool, bowling alleys and other amenities to the Alcazar Hotel. In later years, the Alcazar was converted into the St. Augustine City Hall, and, more recently, to its present use as a museum. The site immediately east of the Alcazar had been purchased by another developer, who built the elaborate Casa Monica Hotel in direct competition with the Ponce de Leon. But it was unsuccessful, so Flagler bought it and changed the name to the Cordova Hotel. He had a covered connection built on the second floor to connect the Cordova to the Alcazar, so that the Cordova guests could enjoy the amenities he had installed in the Alcazar. In recent years, the old Cordova was purchased by new developers who re-named it the Casa Monica Hotel.

Exhibit 14:
Flagler College, formerly Flagler's
Ponce de Leon Hotel in St. Augustine.

Flagler was concerned about transporting his guests to St. Augustine and purchased the Jacksonville, St. Augustine and Halifax railway to ensure their comfort while traveling from Jacksonville, where they arrived from the northern states by rail or steamboat. His St. Augustine success stimulated him to further expansion and he built another hotel in Ormond Beach which also was served by his railway. His old partner, John D. Rockefeller, enjoyed the Ormond Beach location so much that he built a mansion in this town where he spent all his winters until his death in 1917. It has been preserved as a museum.

"In the interim, Flagler extended his railway farther south to New Smyrna in 1892, to Rockledge (between Titusville and Melbourne) in 1893, to West Palm Beach in 1894, and to Miami in 1896. He was enamored with the island of Palm Beach and built two hotels there: The Royal Poinciana, followed by The Breakers, both large and elegant vacation destinations for wealthy northerners. The Breakers is the only one of his hotels still operating today. He went on to

**Exhibit 15:
Henry Morrison Flagler.**

construct the Royal Palm in Miami and two hotels in The Bahamas—The Colonial and The Royal Victoria—which were served by his own steamship line (it also served Havana, but he chose not to build a hotel in that city). In 1900, he constructed The Continental Hotel in Fernandina (later expanded to become Fernandina Beach) which would be a shorter journey from the north, but it did not prove successful, and it was never re-built after fire destroyed it in 1919. Along with his fishing camp on Key Largo, all of Flagler's hotels could accommodate up to forty-thousand people at one time.

"Flagler's masterpiece was completion of his railway across the Florida Keys to link the city of Key West to the mainland. He was convinced that this city had a great economic future which would be enhanced by his rail connection. After a long planning period to determine the best route, his work team began construction from the town of Homestead south of Miami in 1905. In 1906, a devastating hurricane killed 200 of his workers, but he replaced them and pushed his men relentlessly toward his goal of completion by 1912, despite additional hurricanes in 1908 and 1909.

"Henry Flagler died in 1913, at age 83, after completing five-hundred-and-twenty-two miles of his railroad down the east coast of Florida and on to Key West. His empire was completed before his death, although the link to Key West proved unprofitable. On Labor Day in 1935, long after Flagler's death, a massive hurricane demolished the major bridges of his masterpiece, thus ending the rail link to Key West. The State of Florida purchased the railroad right-of-way from the bankrupt Florida East Coast Railway and the state completed a highway to replace it in 1938. Henry Flagler and his Florida East Coast Railway (later to be purchased by the duPont estate and transferred to the St. Joe Company prior to its separation as a public stock company in the 1990s) provided the stimulus for the development of Florida's east coast.

Jimmy Quickfoot leaped to his feet upon the completion of Mark's monologue on Flagler. "There is no question that this man achieved success in opening up the east coast of Florida, but isn't it true that he caused enormous disruption of the natural environment?"

"Absolutely true, Jimmy, and I'm glad you raised this issue. But, he was not alone in initiating this problem. Later in the week, I will tell you about the dredging activities of Flagler's contemporary, Henry Disston, and the railway and hotel exploits of his competitor Henry Plant. These men contributed to what can be rightfully considered a mass attack on the Florida environment, all the while believing that they were serving the progress of mankind.

"Florida's population doubled from one-hundred-and-eighty-eight-thousand residents in 1870 to three-hundred-and-ninety-one-thousand in 1890, and up to seven-hundred-and-fifty-thousand by 1910. As the state's largest city, Jacksonville grew to twenty-eight-thousand, followed by Tampa at sixteen-thousand, and Miami at eleven-thousand. This growth continued to triple by the start of the War years in 1940. As you know, we now have over eighteen-million residents in Florida and we have projections for adding another six\-million over the next twenty years. In the meantime, we have converted over 75 percent of the state's wetlands to agriculture and urban development. Mankind has altered more than one-third of Florida's land.

"So, this is a prime example of sprawl," responded Jimmy. "Are we then about to contribute to extending this environmental destruction by developing here in Florida? It seems to me, with due apologies to Mr. Logan, that this is a serious question facing our development decision to come to Florida."

"No apologies required, Jimmy," responded Nash. "We are all in this together and I request and respect your opinion. It is the land developer's conundrum: provide for population growth by destroying the natural environment. I believe we can have both, but in different proportion as our population expands. Early developers like Flagler were not concerned about the natural habitat; they believed they were serving the people by converting the wilderness to a habitable landscape. With the wisdom of hindsight, we now know they were wrong in this belief, but they were convinced they were doing good work for mankind. The real question for those of us who choose to continue creating habitable communities is how to do so in the most efficient manner. The creation of optimum living environments with minimum disruption to the environment should be our goal."

"Yes," said Mark, "You have stated the conundrum and a feasible solution in principle. The real issue, I believe, is to get beyond principles to positive action. The suburbs of Jacksonville that you flew over today clearly illustrate the inefficient use of land by developers convinced that the majority of Americans still yearn for a detached house with private yard. The proof of their conviction is in the continuing sale of these houses."

"Of course, you are right," said Nash. "The solution lies in producing a better product, and that, Jimmy, is why we are here. I believe we have invented a better building. Now, we must combine it with equally innovative land-use patterns. This is a major reason I asked Mark to direct this tour. Frankly, I am hoping to extract his best ideas on this topic. Before we end this discussion, Mark, I would be grateful if you would share your thinking on this topic of sprawl and how to beat it."

"Alright," said Mark slowly, clearly organizing his thoughts on this most difficult topic, "let me try to summarize some of my views."

"Over the past few years, many writers have confused urban development sprawl with density—the lower the density, the greater the sprawl. Others have simply used sprawl to describe any type of urban development they personally find distasteful. The word has become a cliché for a wide variety of urban conditions without specific definition.

"Webster's Dictionary describes sprawl as 'to spread or develop irregularly'—a definition that applies to a great many urban areas at any density. The linear blight caused by major city streets suffering from unregulated peripheral development, both old and new, is likely to be accepted by most observers as fitting the negative image of sprawl. On the other hand, a pleasantly wooded subdivision of well-maintained homes and lawns does not deserve the same designation just because of its low density. Yet, the latter often is classified by this negative term simply because it is part of a low-density suburb that generates traffic to employment, schools and shopping centers.

"Few urban planners would argue with the public efficiency of servicing urban areas of high-density in comparison with suburban areas of low-density. And fewer still would argue with the private efficiency of living in a neighborhood sufficiently dense to support shops and other facilities within walking distance. And a significant segment of our society (recent estimates suggest about one-third) appear to prefer to live in these more efficient higher-density neighborhoods. But an even larger segment appear to prefer lower-density housing locations, despite the annoyance of higher utility costs and the inconvenience of longer travel distances to support facilities. And, of course, an unfortunate minority has very little choice in living environment because of limited resources (and we have both high-density city slums as well as low-density rural slums).

"These are choices open to a majority of Americans. Public planners and other officials are free to influence persons to select more efficient lifestyle locations. And they can also attempt to influence developers to build more dense neighborhoods and housing. But they are not charged with regulating such decisions except as specifically defined in public legislation (and minimum density is seldom included in legislation, only maximum density).

"Therefore, whereas the term sprawl is a negative term for 'irregular' development, planners and politicians should refrain from using it generically to describe urban growth that is equated to lower density. Higher rather than lower density does not equate to good and bad. It does equate to more efficient services and walking distances, but the value of these elements is judgmental for most persons. Americans will select the types of living environments they prefer, regardless of definitional inconsistencies from advocates of higher density environments.

"Before leaving this topic, however, I would like to add one caveat. Land developers and home builders, like politicians, often claim to know what Americans want, and they proceed to try and guide public opinion by their interpretation. We will see many unfinished developments in Florida developed on that premise, which leave behind committed land that is not used for anything, but reserved for a use that will never occur. At present, we have excellent and economic means of finding out what people really want. We do not need to rely upon one man's or one company's intuition. In sum, I hope Logan Homes will conduct consumer research as an integral part of the planning process."

"That is very well stated, Mark," said Nash, "and you can rely on us to follow your logic. This has been a highly useful discussion. Jimmy, I thank you for your input. Now, I suggest we call it a day and look forward to another great day tomorrow. Mark and Jimmy, I expect to see you both for another breakfast get-together at seven o'clock. Oh, Bobbi and Linda, just a minute before you go. Franz will be cruising down to Port Canaveral in the morning. Tim Wilson has been there before and told me of a wonderful restaurant on the main street in the nearby town of Cocoa. So, I wonder if the two of you and Mark might like to join me there for dinner tomorrow evening?"

"Sounds great," Bobbi replied with a warm smile. "I'll check with Mark but I am 90 percent certain he will want to join us. How about you, Linda?"

"Count me in," replied Linda brightly. "I don't have to check with anyone."

Tuesday, March 30, 2010

By seven o'clock the next morning, the four helicopter travelers were seated at the "Victoria's" breakfast table being served by Jose. Although they all were looking forward to the day's tour over Planning District 5, Mark had suggested a pre-trip introductory meeting again similar to the previous day. So, with second cups of coffee in hand, the four men left the breakfast table for their customary seats at the round meeting table at the rear of the yacht's main lounge. Bobbi joined them a few minutes later.

"Bobbi and gentlemen, thank you all for being on time," began Mark. "Today, as you know, we are touring Planning District 5, the Withlacoochee Regional Planning District—another name memorializing our lost Indians. Actually, it is now the name of a very pretty river draining a large watershed in Central Florida, which contains some of the lakes which you may recall from our southern route over Planning District 3. The source of this river is in the Withlacoochee State Forest in Hernando County about fifty miles north of the city of Tampa and it flows north and then northwest, emptying into the Gulf of Mexico just west of the town of Dunnellon.

Exhibit 16:
Planning District 5—
Withlacoochee.

"Dunnellon was known in Florida history for the first large-scale phosphate mining which ravaged hundreds of acres north of the Withlacoochee River. The phosphate was extracted from the surface sand leaving barren wilderness behind. Phosphate mining subsequently was carried out in many parts of the state with a few areas, such as Ponte Vedra Beach outside Jacksonville, re-surfaced into golf courses and resort homes, but most areas were left in their barren form. More recently, the world's biggest phosphate company, Mozaic, has conformed to government regulations and successfully reclaimed the bulk of its phosphate lands in Polk County for agricultural use and potential urban development.

"Now, I would like each of you to pull out your Florida Planning District Map that I handed out in our first meeting together. Here are extras for anyone who has not got one at hand. Please follow along with me in Planning District 5 marked on the map.

"The Withlacoochee Regional Planning District contains over seven-hundred-and-fifty-thousand residents, of whom over fifty-thousand live in the city of Ocala. There are other smaller incorporated cities in the five counties of this District—Brooksville, Inverness, Bushnell, Wildwood, Belleview, Crystal River, Williston—but the vast majority of the population lives in unincorporated areas, including several retirement communities dating back to the 1960s. This district and portions of the neighboring Planning District 6, which we will tour tomorrow, cover the primary water aquifer in Florida, which will be my primary topic at the end of the day.

"In the interim, I propose that we tour this district in a counter-clockwise direction, first beginning at the source of the Withlacoochee River in Hernando County and witnessing the extraordinary growth of retiree development in this county, which was initiated by the first of two massive lot developments by the Deltona Corporation—Spring Hill—and then proceeding north past Crystal River to a second Deltona development called Citrus Springs. These two pioneer land developments are encompassed by many others in Hernando and Citrus Counties, and beyond into Marion County. The large expanse of Levy County to the north is primarily farmland and of little interest to you for development because it lacks suitable infrastructure.

"I have arranged with Jake to set down at one of Florida's oldest attractions—Silver Springs—which is the headwaters of a major tributary to the Ocklawaha River and the most magnificent example of one of the dozens of major springs in central Florida. Some of you may remember it from movies shot here over the years for the television series called 'Sea Hunt', starring Lloyd Bridges. We can have lunch here and take a brief tour prefatory to my later discussion of Florida's water supply. After lunch we will complete the tour down the east side of this district over recently-expanding Sumter County. So, Jake, I am ready whenever you are."

"One moment, please," interjected Nash. "Jake, I need to have a few words of confidential discussion with Mark before we depart, so I suggest you plan to lift off in about fifteen minutes."

"No problem, Mr. Logan. I will be ready to leave when you are."

Nash motioned Mark to join him at the seating alcove in the opposite corner of the lounge, where the two of them could chat without interruption.

"Mark, I remain concerned about our visitor of yesterday, Mr. Swift. I have asked my lawyers in Toronto to investigate him, but I am anxious to know whether you learned anything from your attorney friend in Orlando?"

"As a matter of fact," replied Mark, "I did manage to speak to my old friend and respected land-use attorney, Tony DiMartino, yesterday; and I have been waiting for an opportunity to report back to you."

"Does he know Swift?"

"Not personally, but by reputation. It seems that Swift has been a moderately successful real estate broker in Orlando for the past twenty years, dealing almost exclusively in land transactions of various types. Although, to the best of Tony's knowledge, Swift has never been accused of any illegal activity, he does have the reputation of being a 'wheeler-dealer' in terms of involvement in a number of grand schemes for large-scale development around the state—schemes that appear to have faded away over time. My friend promised me that he would make some phone calls to colleagues and get back to me today. So, I suggest we wait until we return this afternoon before calling him."

"Very well, I don't want to jump to conclusions, but my initial impressions of him are negative. I am sure you feel the same way."

"I do, Nash, but let's go on our tour and come back to this subject later in the day."

"Alright, but I need to seek your advice on a related issue. I have been quite careful about my plans for this venture and for my trip down here. I will grant you that our company displays garish colors on our means of transport to announce our presence, but that does not account for Swift being knowledgeable about our activities to date, and even knowing where and when to contact Bobbi and Linda on the streets of St. Augustine. How does this apparent inside information strike you?"

"I must admit that it is too detailed to be coincidence. It appears to me that Swift may have the confidence of one of your staff on the yacht."

"That is exactly my conclusion. But who? Or, of greater importance, how can we identify our corporate traitor?"

"Well, Nash," replied Mark with a smile, "I am a mere urban planner, but I do read a great many mystery books for recreation. If we were with the CIA, we might use disinformation to separate members of your staff and see which lead Swift pursues."

"Excellent! Let's devise a plan over dinner tonight with the ladies. I have often found women to be particularly adept at subterfuge, and your wife and her sister strike me as quite clever people."

"Okay, let's do it." And the two men arose and headed for the helicopter.

Jake pointed the helicopter south by southwest, heading back down the St. Johns River past Palatka and across the northern end of Lake George where they had started their tour of Planning District 3 two days previous.

"As I mentioned to you a couple of days ago," began Mark over the intercom, "this river was home to a large number of steamships in the 1850s and again after the Civil War in the 1870s, prior to the extension of railroads and motor vehicles. Both Jacksonville and Palatka were major ports with ship-building facilities, particularly in what was called the 'golden age of Florida steam-boating' from 1875 to 1887. Over one-hundred steamboats were estimated to be on the river during that time. Railroad facilities took over most of the traffic thereafter.

"The St. Johns River was the major thoroughfare to and from the interior of Florida. Passengers could travel all the way south of Kissimmee or over to the coastal waterways past present-day Melbourne. They also could take somewhat smaller boats into the Central Florida Lake District via several rivers and lakes, the most popular being along the Ocklawaha River which was later dammed in the unsuccessful scheme to build a cross-Florida barge canal to Yankeetown at the mouth of the Santa Fe River on the coast of the Gulf of Mexico. The initial stage of this project is the canal crossing under the high level bridge over US 19 below. The large lake beyond, named the Rodman Reservoir, was caused by the dam and locks on the Ocklawaha River in the first stage of the canal construction.

"The concept of a ship canal across Florida was first documented by the Spanish in the sixteenth century when they were losing many valuable cargoes in the treacherous waters rounding the Florida Keys. The idea kept surfacing at intervals throughout the history of modern Florida. Funding of studies became available in the 1920s, however, the report was unfavorable. But, undeterred, promoters rose again in the 1930s and revived efforts after the Second World War defined it as a barge canal rather than a ship canal, no doubt to lower the public profile. Finally, in February 1964, President Lyndon Johnson officiated at the start of the barge canal that literally destroyed over forty miles of the Ocklawaha River and surrounding wetlands in the Ocala National Forest, a result of the diligent construction by the United States Corps of Engineers. But the newly-formed 'Florida Defenders of the Environment' produced a report in 1969 recommending that the project be halted, to stop further damage to the ecosystem. In 1971, President Richard Nixon directed the Corps of Engineers to abandon the project, but a 1974 ruling by a federal judge reversed his decision. Finally, in 1976, under the leadership of Florida Governor Reubin Askew, the project was voted down in Florida; but since it was a federal project, it remained on the active public works list until 1985, when it was dropped on condition that existing structures should remain in place and be maintained. So we now have passed this monument in the woods to the Florida conundrum of growth versus environment, which continues to plague state politics. I will return to this topic when we reach south Florida where the bulk of the environmental damage in this state occurred.

"In the interim, we have passed over the three-hundred-and-sixty-six-thousand-acre Ocala National Forest, entirely within Marion County, and we are heading into Sumter County. The development expansion into this formerly-rural county is the westward growth of 'The Villages', this country's most successful retirement community which we will examine tomorrow. The town to the east is Leesburg in the heart of the Lake District which we also will cover tomorrow. Sumter County is known for only three things: Henry Plant's railway switching-yard at Wildwood (developed for whites only, blacks had to live in Coleman, a few miles south), the western terminus of the Florida Turnpike from Wildwood to Miami, and the state prison for women outside the county seat of Bushnell. At the southern end of this county we enter the Withlacoochee State Forest which extends over three counties: Sumter, Hernando and Pasco. At its southern end it becomes the huge Green Swamp which covers land in adjoining Polk County and provides a major water-retention area and game preserve.

"Jake is now traveling due west along the southern boundary of Hernando County and Planning District 5, marked appropriately by County Line Road. Jake, let's make a slight deviation from our route plan and head north along the Suncoast Expressway toll road that you are coming to now. It was completed a few years ago connecting the Tampa Airport up to the northern boundary of Hernando County, where its further progress up to Crystal Springs was halted by slow-growth citizen groups from that area. I understand that this opposition has been mitigated and the road will be extended north.

'The small city of Brooksville, which you see ahead, is the county seat and dates back into the nineteenth century. Just to the west of town is the restored family home of the Lykes family, one of Florida's most notable dynasties. Frederick and Margaret Lykes migrated to

Hernando in the 1860s and acquired a five-hundred-acre farm on which they grew cotton, citrus and cut timber. Their son, Howell Tyson Lykes, joined the Confederate Army, after which he studied medicine and returned to practice in Brooksville. However, he became more interested in business as his family of seven sons grew to adulthood. He and his sons sold beef cattle for the Cuban War of Independence by cattle drives from Hernando County down south through open range all the way to Punta Rassa at the mouth of the Caloosahatchee River (west of present-day Fort Myers), where the cattle were purchased for export to Havana, Cuba. Most of the cattle were wild (originally imported to Florida by the Spanish), so it cost nothing except labor to catch them, and Lykes had plenty of family labor. The increasing revenues from cattle sales allowed the family to expand its land holdings in both Florida and Cuba.

The next generation of Lykes expanded their wealth many times; and, after incorporating in 1910, the Lykes Empire grew to include meat packing, steel mills, banking (First Florida Bank) and the largest merchant fleet of ships in the United States, as well as increasing amounts of farmland.

By the 1970s, the Lykes Corporation was a billion-dollar company, ranked among the top one-hundred-and-fifty in the *Fortune* 500. After selling the fleet and the packing plant in recent years, the family has reduced its operations to about three-hundred-thousand acres of land encompassing three-quarters of Glades County and spilling over into neighboring counties north of the Everglades. Recently, they announced the development of a new community along US 27 south of Sebring, which appears to be deferred until the economy recovers.

"Jake, please swing to the east and head south down US 41. Just to the east is the highest point of land in Hernando County rising over two-hundred-and-ten-feet above sea level. You can see a clubhouse on top of the hill which anchors a Pete Dye golf course and the new community of Southern Hills Plantation, partially developed by the LandMar Group of Jacksonville.

LandMar is a subsidiary of Crescent Resources of North Carolina that is in Chapter 11 bankruptcy, leaving ten planned communities unfinished throughout Florida. I can provide you information on all of them, but I doubt whether they will fit your needs because of their advanced stage of development.

Exhibit 17:
The Southern Hills Plantation Community,
rising 210 feet above sea level.

"As we return to the southern boundary of Hernando County and Planning District 5, you can see solid development to the northwest which is centered on Spring Hill, the unincorporated result of another huge Deltona Development, initiated by the Mackle Brothers in the 1960s to sell unimproved lots (except for dirt roads and electric lines) to northerners (more about their exploits later).

"Although Florida is covered with many examples of incomplete large-lot developments, this one, less than an hour's drive north of Tampa, attracted many builders and smaller land developers who, in turn, attracted a steady flow of northern retirees over the past fifty years and rapidly expanded the population of Hernando County from eleven-thousand residents in 1960 to over one-hundred-and-sixty-five thousand today.

"As we turn north over U.S. 19, you can see solid development of single family homes on one-quarter acre lots (the minimum size lot for a well and septic tank allowed by the Florida Department of Health). On the east side of the highway is a very successful retirement community called Timber Pines, developed by US Home and completed several years ago. That company was later merged with Lennar Homes. Below, on the west side of the highway is one of Florida's oldest attractions, still operating as the Mermaids of Weeki Wachee, who perform in a giant aquarium over a natural spring.

"Citrus County, to the immediate north of Hernando, has a similar growth pattern, despite being dominated by the northern segment of the Withlacoochee State Forest. Deltona developed a second fifteen-thousand-acre tract into one-quarter acre lots here, concurrently with an adjacent smaller-lot retirement community of several hundred acres named Beverly Hills. However, the latter community was developed by a Long Island, New York builder named Sam Kellnor, who divided it into smaller lots and serviced it with water and sewerage from his own utility company. Sam built small two-bedroom concrete block dwellings specifically for retirees. He was respected by his buyers for being attentive to their needs and interests, particularly with an amenity center which was one of the best of its time (replaced in this century by more modern facilities provided by new owner Morrison Homes, which later sold out its remaining land). Both of these large retirement communities were started in the 1970s without the benefit of interstate highways or railway service. Other developers joined them in the 1980s to generate Citrus County growth from just over nine-thousand-residents in 1960 to over one-hundred-and-forty-thousand today. Just to the northeast, in Marion County, Deltona started a third large-scale development called Marion Oaks which is still incomplete.

"As we fly over Citrus Springs we come again to the Withlacoochee River which serves as the boundary between Citrus and Marion Counties. This river boasts an abundance of wildlife thriving under giant oak and cypress trees covered with Spanish moss, similar to pictures of a jungle river in Africa far from civilization. But, as you can see from the air, it is surrounded by a sea of single-family homes on one-quarter acre lots. As we cross the river at Dunnellon, you can still witness the scraped-off land of the early phosphate mining north of the river where a small executive airport is the only sign of civilization.

But, just to the west of that tract is one of the beauty spots of Florida called Rainbow Springs State Park. Originally a privately-owned amenity, it became the signature of the surrounding Rainbow Springs retirement community on rolling hills covered with second-growth pine trees. The forest hides many of the homes in this development which have been planned on variable lot sizes in a much more cohesive and pleasant setting than the Deltona large-lot communities.

A good example of this contrast is a development directly north of Rainbow Springs called Rainbow Lakes Estates, several thousand acres of gridiron lots and roads with a few houses dotting an open landscape that has not changed in fifty years. The farmland to the north is Levy County which is an agricultural area of very low density, particularly because the entire western sector is low-lying wetland adjacent to the Gulf of Mexico, marking the beginning of the Florida Panhandle where we started this adventure.

"As we head east over northwestern Marion County, you will notice very well-maintained ranches. This is the well-known 'horse country' of Ocala which is second only to Kentucky's Lexington area as a breeding ground for race horses. The hilly terrain actually is reminiscent of central Kentucky. Now Jake, if you will just head south to the east side of the pleasant city of Ocala, you can locate the helipad at Silver Springs."

The four men had an enjoyable time at Silver Springs as the guests of the management. After a sandwich lunch, their attractive young female guide named Cindy took them on a brief tour of the spring lagoon in a glass-bottom boat. She took obvious delight at their expressions of amazement at the clarity of the water and their surprise at learning they were looking down at over forty feet in depth. Jimmy was obviously disappointed when Mark reminded them it was time to leave. He vowed to return to test out the giant water slide and perhaps take another tour with Cindy in future.

After lifting off from Silver Springs, Mark directed Jake to swing south briefly, to fly over another retirement community southeast of Ocala named Silver Lakes which was developed by another Mackle Brothers enterprise named the General Development Corporation. "As I will explain later, the GDC actually pre-dated the Deltona Company. Although Silver Lakes was started later than Deltona's Citrus County developments, and with a more diverse street pattern, it too had public streets and large lots.

"Tomorrow we will tour the remainder of Central Florida's lake district which is home to a great many more retirement communities initiated in the 1970s and 1980s, including The Villages which has expanded into three counties. But for now I have asked Jake to head back north to Palatka up the course of the Ocklawaha River, which originates in the Marshall Swamp just east of Silver Lakes. Although this river suffered from the initial construction of the Cross-Florida Barge Canal, it was a major transportation artery into Central Florida prior to railroads and vehicular roads. This route still provides an overview of the historic natural beauty of internal Florida, a view that northern tourists seldom visit.

"This location in the middle of Florida overlies one of this country's largest water aquifers. It is contained in what is known as the Florida Plateau, a large rock formation stretching from South Georgia into a large part of the Florida peninsula. It is reputed to be one of the most geologically-stable regions of North America. Although this state's wetlands are only a fraction of what they were in the nineteenth century, the federal and state governments have managed to preserve some of the prime areas as seen below.

"The Florida Plateau is bordered on both sides by the coastal plains that wrap around most of the state—thirteen-hundred-and-fifty miles of coastline is second only to Alaska among American states. The Atlantic Coastal Ridge runs down the east coast providing a line of barrier islands rising twenty to forty feet above sea level and accommodating the major cities of the east coast. We will have more to say about those as our tour extends south. Similar islands extend along the west coast some two-hundred miles north from Marco Island, just south of Naples. The Central Highlands in South Florida rise one-hundred feet from the coast, peaking at Iron Mountain just north of the city of Lake Wales. But, the majority of lakes and springs rising from the aquifer are here in Central Florida. North, as we have seen earlier, the Tallahassee Hills run west for one-hundred miles along the Georgia border, extending up to three-hundred feet above sea level. This area receives the benefits of rivers flowing from Georgia, which nourished the rich soil and forests plundered by early settlers. West of Tallahassee are the Mariana Lowlands and beyond them are the Western Highlands, rising to a peak of three-hundred-and-forty-four feet above sea level—the highest point in Florida.

"The vast limestone aquifer underlying most of Florida is estimated to contain about 20 percent of the volume of water in all of the Great Lakes bordering Canada. The springs and sinkholes throughout Central Florida have created a network of lakes throughout this area, of which you will see more tomorrow. Of seventy-eight first-magnitude springs (discharging more than one-hundred-cubic-feet-per-second) in the United States, twenty-seven are in Florida. You just witnessed one at Silver Springs. In fact, this state has more springs than any other region of the world—three-hundred-and-twenty of them, discharging eight billion gallons of water per day. It also contains the largest spring in the world, located as a submarine spring in the Panhandle that discharges an amazing two-thousand cubic feet per second, or over a billion gallons per day. Most of the lakes are round due to their origin as sinkholes. These often-sudden depressions in the earth's surface are caused by the collapse of underground limestone formations because of fluctuations in water levels. They are always circular in shape and occasionally occur in developed areas, causing losses in vehicles and buildings that are swallowed by rapidly expanding sinkholes.

"Urbanization has decreased the water table by fifty-five feet since 1920, a process bound to continue as Florida attracts many more residents in future years. We have nearly eight-thousand lakes and seventeen-hundred rivers and streams in Florida. The St. Johns, now coming into view ahead, is the third-ranked in volume, draining some nine-thousand-one-hundred-and-sixty square miles along the east side of the state.

"So, gentlemen; despite the huge aquifer underneath, water supply is becoming an increasing problem throughout all parts of Florida. Although northern parts of the state receive winter storms, most of the peninsula receives the majority of its rain in the summertime—about a fifty-four inch annual average—from afternoon thunderstorms emanating from the Gulf of Mexico and moving east across the state. Occasional hurricanes, mostly from the southeast, also bring rainfall, although they are not welcomed by most of our residents.

"Now that we have reached the St. Johns River, Jake is turning southeast to Port Canaveral where the 'Victoria' should have arrived earlier in the day. Are you in touch with Captain Ericksson, Jake?"

"Yessir, I am. He sends greetings and reports that the 'Victoria' is well moored and ready for our arrival. We are just going to follow I-95 down to the small city of Cocoa and slip over Merritt Island to where the yacht is berthed. We will be skirting Cape Canaveral to the left for any of you who want to catch a glimpse of our Astronaut launch pad."

"Damn, Jake," uttered Mark with a rare expletive, "that's pretty good guide talk. You sound sufficiently knowledgeable to take over my job."

"Not a chance, Mark, just a little info I picked up from my charts, eh!"

"I'm glad to hear that," rejoined Mark. "You had me worried for a minute. By the way, everybody, the terrain below is all part of Planning District 6, known as East Central Florida Regional Planning District. We will have a busy day tomorrow learning about it. And just let me add my thanks that nobody fell asleep during my explanation of water supply."

"On the contrary," replied Nash. "I felt you summarized it admirably, and it is a vital topic for our planning program. I trust that you have recorded all the salient points, Jimmy?"

"I gave it my best shot, sir," said Jimmy, "but I will probably ask Mark to re-check my numbers after I print a draft."

"No problem, Jimmy, I will be pleased to respond, either on this trip or afterward. Just transmit whatever you have and I will give it priority attention."

"Okay, gents," interrupted Jake, "I have a visual on our yacht. Please make sure you are belted in and I will have you on the deck in a few minutes."

Bobbi and Linda were enjoying a drink in the main lounge of the "Victoria" when the helicopter landed, and they decided to stay inside, out of the wind. The three passengers soon came inside to greet them, and all three announced that they would join the ladies after repairing to their rooms to freshen up and check their phone messages. So, in anticipation, both ladies asked Jose for a refill and awaited their return. They noticed that Jake took off again, no doubt for a local airport to refill his fuel for the next day.

Although Port Canaveral is a cruise ship terminal, no ships were at dock this day, so, except for four other large yachts, the harbor was relatively deserted. Port Canaveral is a manmade extension of the barrier island into the Banana River that separates the Cape Canaveral barrier island from Merritt Island, which in turn is separated from the Florida mainland by the Indian River. The small cities of Cocoa and Merritt Island are on either side of the Indian River and beachfront communities line the outer barrier island all the way south past Patrick Air Force Base to the larger city of Melbourne about twenty-five miles south.

Jimmy was the first of the three travelers to return to the lounge and he came directly to the table and took a seat next to Bobbi, then ordered a light beer from Jose.

"Welcome back," smiled Linda. "Did you have an interesting day?"

"We really did," responded Jimmy. "The highlight was our lunch stop at Silver Springs where a gorgeous girl named Cindy was our tour guide after lunch. Aside from marveling at the crystal clear water of the springs, the best part was acquiring Cindy's home phone number for arranging a future tour."

Both women were laughing at Jimmy's excitement when Nash and Mark arrived simultaneously, pausing only long enough to order drinks from Jose, before taking seats at the table beside the other three.

"Jimmy, I'm glad to see you are entertaining the ladies," began Mark. "Is it a story of your younger days in the Quebec countryside?"

"Heavens, no," said Bobbi. "Jimmy just related his successful conquest of your young tour guide at Silver Springs."

"I guess I must have missed part of that tour," responded Nash with a smirk, "because I did not witness any conquest."

Jimmy flushed noticeably as he said: "Gee, I guess I must have given the wrong impression, Mr. Logan. All I meant to say is that Cindy offered me her phone number for possible future consultation. I didn't mean to imply . . ."

"Of course not, Jimmy. I can't imagine you committing any impropriety."

"Or at least not in front of onlookers," chimed in Mark with a serious tone.

"Alright, you two," rebuked Bobbi. "Quit picking on this man, or I'll have to tell some stories of my own. The important point here is that Jimmy is spreading Canadian goodwill among the locals and that is worthwhile. Now, what Linda and I want to know is what time is our dinner date at this nifty Cocoa restaurant that Nash promised?"

"Excellent question," said Nash, before turning to beckon to Jose. "Jose, Mrs. Wilkins wants to know what time is our reservation for dinner?"

"Yes sir, Mr. Logan. That would be at seven o'clock," replied Jose with a smile, "and the taxi will be here at quarter of seven."

"Well, that just leaves me an hour to get ready," responded Bobbi, "so I better get started."

"Me, too," added Linda, rising from her chair.

"Hold on, ladies," said Mark. "This is just an informal little Florida restaurant."

"I certainly hope so," replied Bobbi as she rose to join her sister, "or I would need to have started an hour ago. See you later." And the two sisters departed for their rooms.

"Well, Jimmy," added Nash after their departure, "you are making friends everywhere today. Those two are certainly in your corner."

"Yes sir, Mr. Logan," retorted Jimmy with a wide smile. "I guess it's just my natural aboriginal charm, eh?"

"Undoubtedly," added Nash. "Under the circumstances, I believe I will require another drink to toast your success. Will you join me Mark, and you too, Jimmy?"

Both men nodded in unison and Jose responded immediately. The three of them then launched into a more serious review of the day's events until it was time to get ready for dinner.

The historic-revival section of Cocoa is a delightful architectural experience and the recommended "Black Tulip Restaurant" on the corner contained a turn-of-the century décor that complemented the distinctive offerings on the menu. Nash ordered a couple of bottles of Cabernet Sauvignon, remembering the prior wine selections of his three guests, which the experienced waiter opened in advance while they studied the menu. After everyone had selected their dinner choices and wine had been poured all around, Nash raised his glass to his guests.

"Ladies and gentleman, I cannot begin to describe how delighted I am to have each of you aboard my vessel. I raise my glass in sincere thanks to Harold Abrams for bringing all of us together."

After everyone had taken an initial sip of wine, Nash continued: "I neglected to inform you upon issuing invitations to this small dinner that there is a fee for attending."

As he paused for effect, Linda turned to Bobbi with a mock frown, and said, "You should have warned me about these foreign men. I didn't even bring any mad money."

"Ah, no problem, Linda," Nash replied with his best engaging smile. "The fee is not monetary, but rather advisory. I have a problem with which I need sage advice and I suspect that you ladies may be able to provide wise counsel."

"Do we get dessert, too," questioned Bobbi innocently, "or must we provide additional advice for each course?"

"Ah, you have me there," laughed Nash. "I didn't think that far ahead. How be I just describe the issue and see how far we get by dessert time?" The two women nodded their assent.

Nash paused for a moment while salads were served, before continuing: "The issue on which I need your advice is the apparent collusion of one of our yacht companions with the mysterious Jack Swift, and what to do about it. His knowledge of our helicopter travels is too complete to be coincidental . . ."

"In addition to his recognition of Linda and me in St. Augustine," interjected Bobbi.

"Precisely," added Nash. "So, for a number of reasons, including company loyalty, I want to identify this person, or persons, and terminate him, her or them from my employ."

"And just how to you plan to identify this person or persons?" asked Linda.

"What I have in mind is to seek advice from two beautiful women at a pleasant dinner here in Cocoa," replied Nash, with his charming smile focused on Linda.

"Implying that we have devious female minds?" questioned Bobbi somewhat impishly.

"Well, frankly, yes," smiled Nash. "What do you think?"

"Enough of this sparring around," interjected Mark with a good-natured smile. He had been silent throughout the conversation thus far. "Nash broached this subject with me earlier, and I believe we must simply spread some disinformation to different staff members and see which message stimulates action by Swift. This will reveal our culprit in short order."

"That sounds like a good approach to me," responded Linda, "but what kind of disinformation will you use?"

"Precisely where you ladies come in," smiled Nash. "We need several trap messages that are all sufficiently plausible to cause action by Swift. What do you suggest?"

At this point, the waiter arrived with the main course, and all conversation ceased while the four diners all began eating their dinners and each one exclaimed over the taste treat. Nash accepted compliments over the choice of restaurants, which he duly passed on to Mark who had recommended it to him. As their separate meals neared completion, the conversation turned once again to the topic of the evening.

"So," queried Linda, "how many separate disinformation stories do you need?"

"Good point," answered Nash. "First, I think we can assume that Franz Ericksson is not involved, and besides, we will need his cooperation for route changes. That leaves Tim Wilson, in addition to Jose, Alfredo, Carlos and our chefs, Pierre and Marie. Also, I'm afraid we must include Jake and Jimmy, much as I dislike the idea of it being either one of them. That's a total of seven separate messages."

"Perhaps not," smiled Linda. "If you like, the suspects could be divided into two or more packages over a period of two or three days. Then, you could reduce your options to two or three messages. In fact, if you drew a blank the first time, you might use the same options for a second round."

"Brilliant! Why didn't I think of that?" exclaimed Nash.

"Perhaps because you don't have a devious female mind," replied Linda without hesitation.

"Point well taken! Using your formula, we could leave Jimmy out for the present, and devise three messages for half of the others. Mark, which ones do you feel are the highest priority suspects?"

"Wow, Nash, that's a tough call. I don't know them nearly as well as you do. On the other hand, I am inclined to believe that a bribe would be most effective with a lower-paid staff member who may have money needs that are unknown to us. What do the rest of you think?"

"That reasoning makes sense to me," said Linda, and her older sister nodded in agreement, just as the waiter returned after removing their dinner plates to pass out dessert menus.

"While you are considering dessert," said Nash, "I would like to follow up on Mark's idea before we lose track. By salary criterion, he would place the initial messages with Jose, Alfredo and Carlos. Does that sound right?" The other three all nodded in agreement. "Okay, then the dessert fee is three diverse messages and how to deliver them?"

"In that case, since our attentive waiter is standing by," smiled Linda, "I will have the crème brulee with black coffee." The others quickly added their orders. "By the way, I believe the delivery can easily be accomplished by Bobbi and me during the morning while you are gone. It shouldn't be difficult to isolate each of them for a casual reference to your plans."

"Curses," exclaimed Nash, "that will probably cost me another onshore dinner."

"Absolutely," exclaimed the two sisters in loud unison.

Mark once again broke his silence: "I believe the three messages should be quite distinct from each other and be designed to stimulate rapid response from Swift. For example, a business emergency necessitating Nash's immediate return to Toronto with a departure time within twenty-four hours and an indefinite return time. Another might be a mechanical problem with the yacht requiring immediate departure to an unrevealed ship repair port. A third could be deferring tomorrow's program so Nash can tour a hot property opportunity. What do you think?"

"Darn, Mark, now you have successfully usurped our fee, and I didn't bring any money to pay for my dessert," grumbled Linda with a grin.

"She's right, darling," added Bobbi. "Those are perfect messages to cause Swift to show his hand today. If he doesn't, I suspect we could use the same three messages with the others tomorrow. Linda and I just have to massage them a bit for effective delivery. What do you think, Nash?"

Their host smiled at all three before answering: "I think we have a plan. Our evening is a complete success. Thank you all." And with that, he handed his credit card to the waiter and noted that the taxi was waiting outside, exactly as requested two hours after their arrival. Upon returning to the "Victoria", the two sisters accepted Nash's offer of a nightcap, so that they could discuss tactics for their morning subterfuge. Mark begged off, in order to prepare for the next day's tour.

Wednesday, March 31, 2010

"The East Central Florida Regional Planning District is composed of six counties encompassing the City of Orlando," began Mark, after his usual group had completed breakfast and were seated around the corner conference table. All eyes were focused on the portion of the map of Florida he was describing for today's helicopter tour. "This district is one of our most interesting tours since it extends from open prairie on the south up to the high growth city of Orlando in the center and on up to the lake district and its extensive retirement communities in the north. Expansion of Orlando has been occurring on all sides of the city, only constrained by wetland which is literally everywhere in Florida. Clearly, despite The Great Recession, land tends to be more expensive around Orlando than in other parts of the state we have visited to date. If everyone will please refer to Planning District 6 on the handout of Florida Planning Districts you received earlier, I will begin my trip summary."

"There are over three-million residents in Planning District 6, with over one-million in Orange County, including Orlando. From 2000 to 2007, prior to The Great Recession, the district population grew 22.6 percent, but Osceola County grew 54.3 percent (all in the northern end, adjacent to Orlando) and Lake County grew 36.1 percent. Orlando grew at about the same rate as the district and currently the city contains about two-hundred-and-thirty-thousand residents.

"Once again, I propose we begin at the southeast corner of the district and tour counterclockwise, heading northwest up the angular boundary to Disney World; and then do a loop around the edge of Orlando prior to continuing north into Lake County up to its intersection with Marion and Sumter Counties where The Villages continues to be the fastest-growth active retirement community in the nation. I have arranged with the developer, Gary Morse, for a trolley-bus tour of this community and lunch afterward, so that you can experience the appeal of what Morse likes to call his 'Disney World for Retirees.' Afterward, we can head east across Seminole and Volusia Counties to view their growth on the north side of Orlando before heading south down the sparsely-settled land east of I-95 back to Port Canaveral. You witnessed the waterfront on the way here yesterday, and we will begin with the southern waterfront this morning. My statewide topic for today is agriculture since the southern part of the state had its agriculture start along the coastal waterways of this district. Unless you have any immediate questions, I propose we climb aboard and let Jake perform his skill."

**Exhibit 18:
Planning District 6—
East Central.**

After the touring party lifted off, Linda joined Bobbi at the breakfast table to begin their assigned duties of the day. Their first target was Jose who remained on duty in the main lounge, awaiting their usual eight o'clock arrival. They carefully timed their conversation to include the information on Nash being called back to Toronto when Jose was within hearing distance. At the end of breakfast, Bobbi actually asked him if he had heard anything about staying in Port Canaveral for additional days until Mr. Logan returns from Toronto. Jose quietly assured them that no such news had reached his ears, but he would let them know if he heard anything.

Their next target was Carlos, who always washed the decks at this time of morning. So, the two ladies unwrapped their outer garments to reveal swimsuits and deliberately occupied two deck chairs that they knew would be obstructing Carlos's usual deck-washing pattern. As he approached within listening distance, they began their dialogue on the alleged boat problem and its probable move to an announced repair location. Finally, when he was almost upon them, they jumped up and moved their chairs despite his protests. Then, before leaving, Linda asked Carlos if he had any news of when and where they would move. Of course, he was absolutely blank on this subject, but he promised to make an inquiry and report back to them (Bobbi had already received word from Nash earlier that morning, informing her that Captain Ericksson was briefed and would provide innocuous corroboration if questioned on this topic).

Their third target was Alfredo, who customarily cleaned their rooms around nine each morning, after being certain that they had left them. So they crept below silently and, sure enough, Alfredo was busily engaged in his morning clean-up of the visitor cabins. As soon as they arrived in the passageway outside the open door to Linda's cabin, they began their dialogue about Nash's great opportunity to purchase a perfect property for his needs. Then, as if by accident, they discovered Alfredo, and Linda asked him if he had any news on this topic. Of course, Alfredo was taken aback by the question and assured them that he knew nothing. But, after Linda's gentle coaxing, he agreed to report any news that he might pick up for them. They expressed their heartfelt thanks and returned to the deck with reading books in hand. Their mission was accomplished.

The flight path south from Port Canaveral was not unlike the trip from St. Augustine to Fernandina Beach two days previous, except this time Mark insisted that Nash take the right-hand seat so that he would have an unobstructed view of coastal development. As they approached Patrick Air Force Base, Jake was directed by ground control to circle out to sea prior to returning to the coast at Satellite Beach and continuing south by Indian Harbor Beach, Eau Gallie Beach (where Jimmy felt obliged to point out the French influence on place names, even down here in Florida), Paradise Beach, Melbourne Beach, Floridana Beach, and eventually Sebastian Inlet, which marks the southern border of Brevard County and Planning District 6.

"As you can see, gentlemen," Mark said into the intercom, "all of these beaches have a certain sameness. We will see some changes farther south in a couple of days. The waterway behind the barrier island is the Indian River Aquatic Reserve; and south of the state park at the inlet is the Pelican Island National Wildlife Refuge, a major conservation area managed by the federal government. I have asked Jake to jog northwest here to give you a glimpse of an early General Development Company community called Port Malabar. Almost all of GDC's communities were named port 'something.' The name for this one has all but disappeared since a portion of it was incorporated many years ago under the name Palm Bay. You can see the original gridiron street system of quarter-acre lots intermingled at intervals with more recent parcels of variable streets and smaller lots. The thousands of lots and multi-family sites in this community sold better than other GDC sites because of the location eventually bisected by I-95 after the community was underway. When GDC went into Chapter 11 bankruptcy in 1990 (a story for another day) the scattered unsold lots in this community were sold in bulk at a very low price, and resales to consumers are still continuing at a steady pace.

"Now Jake is heading west by southwest across Florida's huge prairie land that was open range up until one-hundred-years ago when the state government required land owners to fence their properties. During the nineteenth century, this prairie was like stories of the old west with round-ups of wild cattle for massive cattle drives over several weeks to Punta Rassa on the Gulf of Mexico, where the cattle were sold for shipment to Havana. Florida historic novelist Patrick Smith relates this era in his memorable novel, *A Land Remembered*. Some suggest that his novel was based upon the Parker Brothers' Ranch farther west outside Arcadia, where Reading Parker was a patriarch controlling thousands of acres of land and using a steamer trunk as his only bank. Today, the holdings are separated by fences (since 1949) to hold the largest cattle herd of any state east of the Mississippi River—almost two-million animals.

"We are now heading northwest along the central portion of this huge prairie, following along the course of the Kissimmee River, which once was a steamboat waterway carrying freight and passengers all the way to Miami. It is the western border of Planning District 6.

"A wealthy investor recently attempted to achieve approval on an eastern tract of several-thousand acres in this prairie to develop what he claimed would be a model new town named 'Destiny'. State officials were not impressed, and I believe his dreams have been laid to rest.

"We are now over the large expanse of Lake Kissimmee with virtually no development around it except fishing camps. The next large lake is Lake Tohopekaliga, of which the northern end marks the southern boundary of Orlando suburban development. To the northwest is the county seat of St. Cloud, first established by the Florida Sugar Manufacturing Company in 1890 with an investment in land and development of one-million dollars. I'll have more to say about the rape of the southern prairie and Everglades in a couple of days.

"As we continue northwest, you can see the ambitious development of 'Reunion', partially completed south of Interstate 4, and farther to the northeast is the internationally-famous Disney World that succeeded in overturning several Florida water management laws in another triumph of economic promise over environmental conservation. In this case, Disney lived up to its economic promise, emerging as the top tourist destination in the world. Unfortunately, its creator, Walt Disney, did not live to see his dream come true.

"Prior to the opening of Disney World in 1971, Orlando had enjoyed significant growth from the Florida population explosion starting in the 1950s. Orange County, which encompasses the city, had tripled its population during those twenty years up to almost three-hundred-and-fifty-thousand residents. But tourism was not a major draw, although 'Gatorland' was a big attraction. The emergence of Disney World stimulated growth to over one-million residents today, and the four-county Orlando metropolitan area to over two-million residents. Tourism became Florida's biggest industry.

"Disney World is a story of worldwide scale. Since its opening in 1971, it quickly became, and remained, the single biggest tourist destination in the world. The over-seventy-million annual tourists visiting the many attractions in southwest Orange County cause an enormous strain on the infrastructure and facilities of this metropolis, as well as generating over fifty-thousand jobs. The more than one-hundred-thousand hotel rooms constitute the biggest concentration of accommodations in the United States.

"Walt Disney selected suburban Orlando for his east-coast theme park because of its combination of almost daily sunshine, sandy soil, and plentiful clear spring water. A reputable story relates that Disney first phoned Ed Ball about the availability of St. Joe property on the Panhandle, but Ball, with typical arrogance, refused to discuss property transactions with what he termed 'a carnival person'. So Disney settled on what turned out to be twenty-seven-thousand acres of land (compared to less than one-hundred acres in California's Disneyland) in Orange and Osceola Counties—an area twice the size of Manhattan—that he purchased quietly through many agents to keep the price down to an average of less than two-hundred-dollars per acre. When local and state politicians learned of his purchases, issues of water management, traffic impact and land use were resolved readily in Disney's favor to ensure that this potential multiplier of the economy would stay (including control of an entire water management district, the Reedy Creek Improvement District). Interestingly enough, Walt Disney originally came from Florida as a child and ended his life back in the same state in 1966, well before his vision was fully realized.

"In 1982, a decade after opening the Magic Kingdom, the Disney organization opened 'EPCOT' (Environmental Planned City of Tomorrow). It bore no resemblance to Walt's vision of a future city with twenty-thousand residents living in sight of tourists. But, this permanent 'world's fair' became almost as popular as the Magic Kingdom. It was followed by two additional Disney theme parks—MGM Studios (now Hollywood Studios) was introduced in 1989, and Animal Kingdom in 1998—as well as a variety of resorts, campgrounds and related attractions. In addition, theme parks by other interests emerged, most notably Sea World and Universal Studios. Today, five of America's top seven mega-theme parks are located in Orlando, making central Florida almost completely dependent upon tourism for its economy. These attractions not only dwarf all other attractions in Florida, but literally put most of them out of business, including Dick Pope's once-dominant Cypress Gardens (now being reborn as 'Legoland').

"From here, I want to deviate from prior trip patterns to make a circle around Orlando before heading northwest into Lake County, the state's major retirement destination. Any questions?"

"Yes, Mark," said Nash. "There is no question that the enormous Disney complex and its sister attractions have made a huge impact upon the Orlando economy in terms of employment and tourism expenditures. But, what about their impact on housing?"

"Good point! The great majority of the huge Disney work force, and the related employees in the tourist business, receive modest compensation, suitable primarily to support only rental accommodations. So you may observe a large number of rental apartment complexes and entry-level condominium developments in southwest Orlando. However, the real surprise for many builders has been the strong demand for single family homes by individual foreign investors, particularly from Europe, Canada and Brazil. The single family communities you see below and to the east contain a high proportion of this seasonal housing.

"As we move north of Disney, we come to one of the most expensive residential areas of metropolitan Orlando, centered on the Butler Lakes and the village of Windermere. Famous stars and athletes, like Shaq O'Neal and Tiger Woods, live in some of the mansions in this area. The very large lake to the north is Lake Apopka, which was virtually destroyed by lack of waste management, particularly by the runoff from vast vegetable farms on its northern shore, which I will describe more fully later in today's trip.

"Turning northeast, we cross over Wekiva Springs State Park which was acquired from private ownership to protect the headwaters of the Wekiva River that flows into the St. Johns River just north of the city of Sanford—the center of major early farming activities in Florida. Henry Sanford was a retired general in the Union Army who purchased twenty-two square miles of land on the shore of Lake Monroe in 1874, and established orange groves. But, terrible frosts of 1894-5 ruined his groves and he switched to vegetables, particularly celery, which became his best-known crop. Other agriculturists followed his lead, expanding cropland south of Lake Jessup just south of the present city of Sanford.

"After the turn of the century, a Czechoslovakian immigrant named Andrew Duda settled in the rich farmland south of Lake Jessup with a forty-acre vegetable farm at Oneida. A. Duda and Sons subsequently expanded to own one-hundred-thousand acres at several locations in central and southern Florida (and even in the western United States and Australia) to become one of the biggest agro-industries in the world. We will observe the Duda family's huge new town, called 'Viera', at the end of the day.

"Duda's expansion into Brevard County included acquisition of lands from other large ranches, most notably the one-hundred-thousand-acre ranch of the Platt family. At the same time, the largest ranch in Florida was being established in the same area by the Church of Jesus Christ of Latter-day Saints. The Deseret Ranch extends forty miles in length through Orange, Osceola and Brevard Counties, encompassing some three-hundred-thousand acres of land, used primarily for raising beef cattle.

"In the interim, before we turn south, the large community north of Lake Monroe is named Deltona, as the namesake of the Mackle Brothers company's extensive real estate holdings (which I will describe more fully in Day 9). It did not grow like Spring Hill (which you saw yesterday) until after the population boom generated by Disney in the 1970s.

"Returning to the agricultural expansion of the late nineteenth century, central Florida's growth relied heavily on the railway expansions of Henry Plant, who was responsible for opening up much of central and southwest Florida. In 1880, he extended his railway from Sanford's Lake Monroe docks to the hamlet of Winter Park in Orlando, where he anchored a resort with the Seminole Hotel, containing twenty-three-hundred beds, the largest such facility south of St. Augustine. In 1885, a wealthy Chicago native, Alonzo Rollins, endowed a college right down the street from Plant's hotel that still bears his name. Thus, Plant's railway carried tourists south into Winter Park from the St. Johns River steamboats and then carried citrus and vegetable produce north.

"During this same period, citrus production expanded over to milder coastal areas on Merritt Island and beyond, where new blends gave birth to Indian River Oranges, claimed to be the finest oranges in the world. From 1878 to 1893, the Florida citrus crop grew by a factor of five. It remained strong through 1949 when the invention of concentrate provided a great boost to the industry and gave rise to such international product names as 'Tropicana' and 'Minute Maid'.

"This nineteenth century growth period also was the era of Hamilton Disston, who may have been the biggest force of all in Florida's dubious triumph of economics over nature. But I will leave his story for a future trip, as we head south down the east side of Orlando, following the route of the State Route 417 toll road, which provides a traffic bypass all the way to Disney World at I-4. We are passing over the University of Central Florida campus which has grown to thirty-thousand students in thirty years. You will notice solid suburban development on this side of the city, undisturbed by theme parks or industry. You can see the tall buildings of the city center to the west as we move on down to cross State Route 528 toll road leading directly to Cape Canaveral; and just beyond it to the south is the constantly-expanding Orlando International Airport. The federal government has just approved the first stage of funding for a high-speed train from Tampa to this airport, in what should be the beginning of an integrated transportation system. The second stage will link this train to Miami.

"As Jake continues along SR 517, to the west, below the airport, we once again encounter solid suburban development which caused the population of Osceola County to increase 54 percent over the past decade, despite the fact that 80 percent of the county is wetland and ranch land. Just below to the south, is the headquarters of one of Florida's most successful sales persons, a woman named Brownie Wise. She moved to Plantation, Florida as a single parent in 1949 and proceeded to sell two-hundred-thousand dollars worth of a new plastic kitchen-ware marketed as 'Tupperware'. She pioneered and perfected the Tupperware 'home party' and made it so successful that the manufacturer stopped selling in retail outlets and specialized in home sales. The company made her Sales Director, and she built an empire of ten-thousand sales persons with annual sales of one-hundred-million dollars. Her product and her parties became a household word. The world headquarters moved to Kissimmee in 1952, and the company has continued to flourish long after Bonnie Wise died in 1992.

"We now are approaching the junction of Polk, Lake, Osceola and Orange Counties where we began the circle of Orlando. We will now head due north into retiree country, where a high proportion of the almost three-hundred-thousand residents of Lake County live in gated and high-amenity retirement communities.

On the way north, I would like to footnote my earlier comments on Florida's growth of agriculture with two later developments that took place in this part of the state north of Lake Apopka, the large lake to the east. Elwood Zell, a prominent Philadelphia publisher, settled a few miles north of this lake in the early part of the twentieth century, to farm the muck lands extending north from the lake. But the poor drainage hindered agricultural growth around his community of Zellwood, until the Florida Legislature enacted the Zellwood Drainage and Water Control District in the 1940s. This Act authorized the diking and drainage of two-hundred-thousand acres on the northern shore of Lake Apopka.

However, the subsequent agriculture bonanza on this recovered rich land caused severe pollution and silting in Lake Apopka, and, in the 1990s, the federal government took action by purchasing the farms and ending farming. The short-lived 'agriculture miracle' was over.

"Below, to the west, is the city of Clermont, with its twenty-three-thousand residents nestled between two lakes. It is now a suburban center west of Orlando. The Clermont Tower, on the highest hill overlooking Clermont, was a popular tourist vantage point for viewing the vast orange groves in every direction, until a series of freezing winters drove this crop farther south.

"We now pick up Florida's Turnpike, heading northwest from Miami to Wildwood at I-75; and to the north we see Little Lake Harris, part of a chain of lakes connected by canals that provide a cruising and fishing delight for the residents of Lake County. To the left as we approach the entry into Lake Harris, is the popular Mission

Inn resort, with one of the oldest golf courses in Florida (established in 1926), as well as a more recent residential golf course, with both vacation and permanent homes encompassing its fairways. This resort was founded as the guest quarters for the original investors from Chicago and other cities, who sponsored the vast orange groves of Howey-In-The-Hills, which was developed in the 1920s. The resort property was sold to the Beucher Family from Chicago in the 1950s, who expanded it to its current size. Over to the east, beyond pretty Lake Dora, lies the nineteenth century city of Mount Dora with its twelve-thousand mostly-retired residents, who enjoy its tree-covered streets and restored Victorian buildings. Its annual art show and antique boat show attract visitors from throughout the state and beyond.

"The city of Leesburg with its twenty-thousand residents is located at the west end of Lake Harris and south of Lake Griffin. It is bisected north-south by U.S. 27 that formerly was one of the major thoroughfares for Florida visitors from the Georgia border to Miami. This traffic prompted the entrepreneurial spirit of a northerner named Harold Schwartz in 1982, when he purchased a mobile-home community for retirees along this highway. It lies outside the village of Lady Lake, north of Leesburg, originally called Orange Blossom Gardens (probably named after the train from the north to Orlando, called the 'Orange Blossom Special'). This community had a manufacturing plant for mobile homes on-site to meet the increasing demand from Schwartz's advertising of 'free golf for life' in homes starting at under-twenty-thousand dollars, including lot.

"Harold Schwartz used to tour Orange Blossom Gardens in his golf cart daily to greet his residents, right up to his death at age 94; but he turned over management of the expanding community to his son Gary Morse (and eventually Gary's daughter Jennifer) in the 1980s. Gary dismantled the manufactured housing factory and began 'stick-built homes,' concurrently changing the name to 'The Villages of Lady Lake' and then just 'The Villages.' But, Morse kept the 'free golf for life' (at least on one of the sixteen golf courses) as his annual sales continued to mount (peaking at over five-thousand sales in 2006 prior to slowing during The Great Recession).

Exhibit 19:
Aerial view of part of The Villages retirement community.

"Gary Morse continued to improve upon the variety of activities that his father Harold had pioneered in what is now 'The Villages'. It has expanded into contiguous parcels in Marion and Sumter Counties and it is still growing toward one-hundred-thousand residents. Now, Jake, if you can set us down on the helipad next to the two-story Welcome Center, we can take a tour of The Villages and have lunch in the adjacent village center."

The four visitors from the sky were greeted by a Welcome Center hostess and ushered aboard a trolley bus provided with a resident guide, who admittedly was thrilled to live in The Villages. Her driver followed a route designed to view the many amenities and varying housing types offered to prospective residents, as the cheerful guide described life in The Villages. The developers had adopted the 1984 federal retirement housing legislation which restricted new residents to age fifty-five and above (with some exceptions), but grandchildren were welcome to visit under specific guidelines. The community is designed as a fun-filled living environment for active adults and its appeal is obvious from the high number of visitors and sales even during The Great Recession of 2008-09. It is touted by many experts as the most successful retiree community in America.

After the trolley ride, their guide led them into the Welcome Center to explain the overall plan of The Villages from a large wall display, and then answered their remaining questions, after which she recommended a luncheon place in the adjoining retail center. Her advice proved to be excellent as they enjoyed a pleasant luncheon, surrounded by cheerful grey-haired seniors.

As Jake maneuvered them back up in the air after lunch, Nash turned to Mark and commented: "Despite some criticisms I might have over specific details, including some inefficient land uses, there is no question that Harold Schwartz and the Morse family have created a very appealing environment for active adults at The Villages, Mark. I assume they are being widely copied by other developers?"

"No question about it, Nash. Community developers and their planners from all over the country visit The Villages on a regular basis to learn the secrets of its success. Unfortunately, most of them carefully copy the housing and facilities without realizing that the real success ingredient has always been the soft programs defining the myriad of activities offered to residents at and near this community. So, they come, they look, but they do not probe into the heart of The Villages' success. Years ago, the management of The Villages established a policy for sales persons: no visitors were to be shown model homes until they had spent at least a full day experiencing the program activities—in short, the management of this community understood, many years ago, that their residents purchased homes here primarily because of these activities. The home purchase was, and is, a secondary consideration."

"That is such an obvious revelation," responded Nash, "but I agree that few of us builders stop to recognize it. We all have heard that neighborhoods sell before houses, but we continue to pour our marketing dollars into new home graphics and features. I am as guilty as most of my colleagues, and I even told you that the reason for our rapid growth was keyed to the redesign of all our new home offerings, whereas, with the wisdom of hindsight, I realize that the locations which we selected just as carefully as the new designs, may well have played a bigger role in the actual purchase decisions. Thank you, Mark. You just may have paid for the entire trip. Jimmy, please boldface these notes in your diary and remember to remind me of their importance—although I doubt that I will forget such an important lesson, eh?"

"Yes sir, Mr. Logan, consider it done," replied Jimmy.

"Dawgone it, Jimmy, I think it's about time you begin addressing me as Nash. This constant 'Mr. Logan' stuff is making me feel old. How about it?"

"Yes sir, Mr. ah, ah, Nash," replied Jimmy, with a nervous laugh.

"And, Jake, that goes for you too. No more smart-ass formality, do you hear?"

"I hear you loud and clear, Mr. ah, ah, Nash," replied Jake with a hearty laugh.

"Good! I feel better already. What else are we looking at, Mark?"

"As I requested, Jake has been flying an easterly course across the north end of Planning District 6. That is the city of DeLand to the south, the Volusia County Seat and home of Stetson University. It is a small, but highly-rated, school, slightly off the beaten path, in a very pleasant town of twenty-seven-thousand residents. It is not a bad place for your development except that the terrain is quite wet between here and the coastal ridge. Daytona Beach is ahead of us, about twice the population of DeLand, but usually swollen with tourists, both for the famous historic race car beach and the current huge Daytona Speedway. A small school named Embry-Riddle is located here that has a far-flung reputation for producing aeronautical vocation specialists, as well as excellent schooling in other subjects.

"We are now heading south toward New Smyrna Beach, an early settlement which, for some reason unknown to me, has become a favorite winter vacation spot for Canadians."

"Probably because it's cheap," chimed in Jake, with obvious reference to Mark's joke a few days previous that Canadians may suffer from (or enjoy) that reputation.

"As a matter of fact, Jake, I believe it does have that reputation, but for a different reason. It is the closest ocean beach to Orlando and is a popular second-home location for many modest-income residents from that city. New Smyrna contains over twenty-three-thousand permanent residents, who mostly live in modest-price housing.

"This day's tour also includes one of the most famous places in the country: Cape Canaveral and the Kennedy Space Center. Although we are not allowed to fly over this center, I have asked Jake to go south past Titusville, a former steamboat stop on the Indian River. There is now a bridge over to Merritt Island which you will recall contains Cape Canaveral on its eastern point. It initiated operations on January 24, 1950 with the firing of a fifty-six-foot long, fourteen-ton rocket that reached a speed of two-thousand-seven-hundred miles-per-hour. The resultant space program accelerated the economy and the population growth of what became known as 'The Space Coast'; even though politicians failed to capture the manned space center, which was located in Houston, Texas.

"The end of today's tour now takes us past the seventeen-thousand residents of Cocoa to the city of Rockledge, an historic farming community, now a rapidly-growing retirement area. South of Rockledge is a former major farmland of the Duda Ranch which is now bisected by I-95—a thirty-eight-thousand-acre tract that the Duda family decided, twenty-five years ago, to develop into a model new town which they named Viera (a Czech word). The size was eventually cut in half through mitigation negotiations with the state, but it remains a very large planned new community still under development. You can see that the portion east of I-95 is virtually completed, with predominantly single-family homes, in addition to schools, parks, a golf club in the center and office buildings at the south end adjacent to Wickham Road, a major east-west thoroughfare.

"The west side of I-95 contains a regional shopping center in addition to a high school, county government buildings, and a baseball stadium which now serves as the winter training ground for the Florida Marlins (the only professional baseball team that travels north for winter training). I have asked Jake to take us west to a retirement neighborhood within Viera that was planned by the US

Home Corporation (prior to its takeover by Lennar Homes, a national builder headquartered in Miami). You can see that it is developed next to a public golf course provided by the developer—part of the purchase deal, so that the retirement community would have golf access without carrying the development and operations costs in its budget. Viera is planned to have an I-95 intersection in its center, but the construction funding has been deferred until a later stage of development.

"By the way, Joseph Duda, the current patriarch of the family businesses, has his home on that delightful little lake at the north end of the community. Because of its highly visible location on I-95, Viera has prospered with an influx of retirees from northern states, who make up a large portion of its residents in the diverse-age areas, as well as in the age-restricted retirement neighborhood."

Exhibit 20:
Aerial view of portions of Viera New Town bisected by I-95.

The first priority for Nash Logan upon his return to the "Victoria" was to huddle with Bobbi and Linda to see whether Jack Swift had responded to any of the three messages they had initiated. He found both women on the upper deck above the main lounge, enjoying the late afternoon sun. But before he even had time to ask, the two sisters nodded their heads from side-to-side in unison, indicating no response.

"Damn," muttered Nash. "There was no word from him at all, eh? I thought sure that the informant would be one of our lower-paid employees."

'Sorry to disappoint you," replied Linda. "But we can try again with the others in the morning. Each of the three got the message loud and clear this morning, and I am sure my collaborator and I can make it happen again tomorrow."

"Okay, great! I really appreciate the two of you cooperating on this. I am anxious to rid my staff of the disloyal culprit." With that, Nash hurried away to his cabin to check on messages.

Dinner that evening in the main lounge was dominated by Nash and Jimmy relating stories of their day's adventures, with The Villages dominating their conversation. They both agreed that The Villages appeared to be a huge success, and it did differ dramatically with the earlier Deltona communities, in terms of housing variety, amenities and landscaping.

But, at least from the air, The Villages did not appear to vary significantly in layout from Viera, over which they had flown later in the day. Each neighborhood contained its same size lots and houses, which varied from adjoining neighborhoods with other lot sizes and houses. Jimmy commented that both of them resembled super-markets with produce arranged in displays of uniform types, next to displays of other uniform types. The overall effect was attractive, but boring. Except for the golf courses, the concrete pathways were primarily sidewalks on the streets and collector roads. In fairness, Nash added, the main roads did have dedicated paths for NEVs (neighborhood electric vehicles), of which most were standard golf carts.

Mark did sum up their experience by reminding them of his earlier remark that the secret to The Villages' success was the program activities rather than the physical facilities. "Remember the words of developer Gary Morse that 'The Villages is a Disney World for retirees.' That is the message you should take away, rather than the community plan or model homes. Now, let's move over to the map corner where I can illustrate tomorrow's tour of Planning District 7."

Noticing that Tim Wilson was heading toward the exit, Linda glanced at Bobbi for approval, and then hurried after him. "Tim, excuse me, but I didn't want to bring this up in front of the group. I hope you don't mind if I ask you a question?"

"Certainly not, Linda, fire away."

"Well, Bobbi and I planned to meet a family friend in Fort Pierce tomorrow, but we wondered whether the Captain may have changed the sailing time?"

"No, why on earth would he do that," questioned Tim with a blank face.

"Well, because of Mr. Logan's urgent message to return to Toronto. I assumed that the Captain might prefer to wait for him to return here. I also assumed you would know about it."

"No, I have heard nothing about it. Are you certain of this information?"

"Oh yes, Nash and Mark were discussing it today and how they will need to defer the tour after tomorrow. I'm sorry if I upset you. I just assumed you would be in the loop, being the first officer and all," said Linda with a bright smile for the engineer.

"I will get together with the captain immediately and find out what's going on. Then I will make sure everyone is notified." He then walked toward the steps leading down below, rather than toward the bridge where Captain Ericksson had headed after dinner.

Linda slowly wandered back to a seat at the conference table where Mark was busy with his explanation of the next day's tour.

DAY 7

Thursday April 1, 2010

Three of the four tour group members were all at the breakfast table just before seven o'clock, when Jake suddenly burst into the lounge with his hands up in the air. "I'm sorry Nash, but I'm afraid we are grounded for today. I can't even tell you what the problem is. We will have to bring in a mechanic from the Melbourne airport. Oh, hi Jose! For breakfast this morning, I would like two large pancakes with two fried eggs over easy and crisp bacon. A man can't fly on an empty stomach, eh."

The other three men stared at Jake in amazement with their mouths open, as though to say, "What could he be talking about?" just as Bobbi walked into the room. She surveyed the whole scene for a few seconds and then burst out laughing.

"Bobbi," said Mark sternly, "what on earth are you laughing at?"

"Well, a pleasant good morning to you," reprimanded Bobbi. "I'm just amazed that three college-educated men can't recognize an 'April Fool's Joke' right in front of them. Congratulations Jake, you took them all in admirably."

"Yes I did," laughed Jake, as the others slowly began to understand what had happened and what day it was. "And it was a good thing too, Bobbi, because they were all sitting here too solemnly for such a beautiful day that is about to dawn in the east. So, don't worry, gentlemen, we will fly today just as soon as I fill my personal tank with fuel." And Jake set about demolishing the plate of food that the smiling Jose set down in front of him.

Mark, still somewhat red-faced from his failure to recognize the April fool joke, excused himself from the table and strolled over to the wall-mounted map of Florida to review their route for the day. The previous night after dinner, he had described Planning District 7, the Central Florida Regional Planning District. He summarized it as a sparsely-populated part of the state that had a rich history of ranching and farming prior to the twentieth century. The Indians herded wild cattle on this huge prairie in the center of the state, before they were chased south by white settlers who had no better claim to the land. Most of these white settlers were brash and tough and they had no compunction about claiming the land and wild cattle for themselves and relegating the Indians to a life of thievery and hiding from these terrifying white men.

He explained that Planning District 7 is composed of five counties, with a combined population of almost eight-hundred-thousand residents, the bulk of whom—about six-hundred-thousand—live in Polk County along the route of I-4 between Tampa and Orlando. Almost one-hundred-thousand of these Polk County residents live in the city of Lakeland, and another thirty-five-thousand live in the city of Winter Haven, both located in the I-4 corridor. Less than seventeen-thousand live in the county seat of Bartow, although that number is destined to multiply with the realization of annexation and development of Clear Springs, the seventeen-thousand acres of recovered phosphate mining land adjacent to the city. The farming counties south of Polk include Hardee and Desoto on the west and Highlands and Okeechobee on the east. The northeast sector of Polk County includes expanding suburban growth from Orlando. The northwest corner of Polk County is the extension of the Green Swamp from Sumter County to the north.

The tour route he described for the next day would take them from Orlando directly down the I-4 corridor to Lakeland and then south over the phosphate mining area to Walkula and then to Arcadia, the county seats of Hardee and De Soto Counties respectively. They would then travel east across the vast farmlands of Central Florida to the city of Okeechobee on the north shore of Florida's largest lake of the same name. Then they would go north up the sparsely-settled eastern sides of Okeechobee and Polk Counties back up to suburban Orlando. From there, he proposed flying down the US 27 corridor past Haines City, Lake Wales, Avon Park, Sebring, and Lake Placid—all populated by retirees. For lunch, he announced that he had arranged to stop at the planned community of Solivida in northern Polk County, which boasts a two-story town center built in advance of housing sales.

Once again, he asked his two flying companions to refer to the planning districts map handout he had supplied earlier for reference to the tour of Planning District 7.

After becoming airborne that morning, Mark decided to relate some of the history of this part of Florida: "The most notorious name in Central Florida's history was Hamilton Disston, who, many claim, ranks with Flagler and Plant as key figures in exploiting Florida's natural environment for white settlement.

"Flagler and Plant were beneficiaries of large tracts of land for building railways, but Disston preempted them both in 1881, when he agreed to drain twelve-million acres of wetland in South Florida in exchange for receiving ownership to half of that land. He already had bought four-million acres extending from Marco Island in the southwest to Tampa Bay to Titusville and back to Marco Island—a huge triangle of property. With the proposed twelve-million added to his four-million acres, Disston virtually controlled half of the state's area, much of it in swampland.

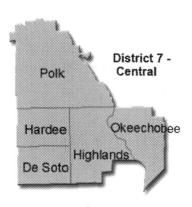

Exhibit 21:
Planning District 7—Central.

"Disston's role dates back to 1850 when the United States passed the Swamp and Overflowed Lands Act, which deeded vast lands to Florida, provided that they were reclaimed for agriculture production. In 1855, Florida legislators established the State Internal Improvement Fund to trade land for rail and drainage improvements by private entities

"Disston's plan was to build a cross-Florida canal using the lengthy Caloosahatchee River as the major drainage way, but it was not completed around Lake Okeechobee (or at least not during his lifetime). This waterway across Florida would have provided a major transport route, as well as a drainage way, for agricultural products to be grown in the rich silt underlying the northern portions of the Everglades. Disston vigorously promoted Florida land sales of forty-acre parcels for farming homesteads, both in Europe as well as in the northern United States. After having initiated a resort community at Tarpon Springs (north of Tampa) in 1876, he began other settlements at St. Cloud, south of Orlando, and he established a model village at Lake Conway.

"The Disston land deals focused attention on the palmetto prairie in the Kissimmee and St. Johns River basins, as well as the huge unfenced pastureland west of Lake Okeechobee. His land sales marked the end of the open range, and he was no friend of cattle ranchers in these areas. However, he succeeded only in digging a few miles of drainage canal, and therefore did not consummate his deal with the state. A nationwide recession in 1893 caused his financial ruin, and he died virtually penniless. However, Disston had started the real estate boom in Florida that led to several decades of entrepreneurial growth.

"Many decades later, the state government made another error when it created the Central and Southern Florida Flood Control District, the pioneer of later water-management districts throughout the state. But this first such district was responsible for what turned out to be some of the most ruinous water-control projects in Florida's history. In striving to rationalize the plethora of canals and levees around Lake Okeechobee and the upper Everglades, the new state agency constructed bigger and longer canals that ensured rapid drainage of water from the rivers, lakes and marshes, thus causing a major change in the ecological balance which is still being addressed with new retention measures.

"Now we are entering the northeast corner of Polk County, which, as you can see, has many housing developments, including the partially-completed new community of Reunion that I pointed out to you yesterday. Like many new communities in Florida, Reunion development was halted due to The Great Recession.

I-4, the major cross-state highway, is now six lanes wide between Orlando and Tampa. Most development has occurred on the southern side of this highway where the lakes make it more attractive for retirement communities. You can see the sprawling development around the lakes to the south, including Haines City, Winter Haven, Lake Alfred and Auburndale. Mobile home parks also are plentiful in this county and attract many modest income employees from both Orlando and Tampa to live here and commute to work in the larger cities.

Exhibit 22:
Florida Southern College featuring Frank Lloyd Wright architecture.

"The biggest city in Polk County is Lakeland, which is home to a great many distribution companies, including the headquarters of Publix Supermarkets, the largest food store chain in Florida. One of the more interesting components of Lakeland is Florida Southern College, designed by Frank Lloyd Wright, the biggest single-site collection of his buildings anywhere. Wright was coerced into designing this campus in 1938 by a Methodist minister named Ludd Myrl Spivey, who was president of Florida Southern College. The college was in need of expansion and he appealed to Wright's ego to create a "great educational temple in Florida." It still stands on the shore of Lake Hollingsworth as Wright's only venture into educational architecture."

"That is a sizeable baseball park down there for such a modest community," Jimmy pointed out.

"Yes, Jimmy, that is the Detroit Tigers' spring-training facility on the shore of Lake Parker, Lakeland's largest lake. The Tigers' complex is one of many pre-season baseball training facilities throughout south Florida (remember that you saw another one for the Florida

Marlins in the new town of Viera). The baseball teams have just about wrapped up their spring training for this year and are ready to fly north to start the baseball season. As we fly past the city, you can also see the relatively-new Polk Parkway looping around the pleasant city of Lakeland to the south and returning to the I-4 highway.

"South along SR 60, you can see the enormous piles of tailings from the Mozaic phosphate processing, formerly referred to as 'Bone Valley' because of the prolific fossil deposits buried in the sand. This area is now mined out, and you will see them working farther south in Hardee County. The city of Bartow is on your left. It is due to become much larger by annexation of over seventeen-thousand acres of recovered phosphate mining land, currently called Clear Springs. Phosphate mining has caused the underlying aquifer to be lowered by over fifty feet, causing termination of several springs in this area. The Peace River flows south from here as the main drainage way to the Gulf of Mexico at Port Charlotte. Continuing south along US 17, you can see farmland in every direction, At least three plans for master-planned communities have been announced in De Soto County, but none developed to date. Of course, land is cheaper in these rural areas of the state, but development has the disadvantage of being farther away from major amenities.

"You can see Port Charlotte to the southwest as we turn east to follow the southern boundary of Planning District 7 across the extensive farmlands of the prairie. The elevation rises in the middle of this prairie where the end of the limestone underlay extends to the north—thus the name Highlands County for the plateau in the middle, which contains spring-fed lakes just like those which we saw farther north in Lake County. We are moving northeast now to Okeechobee County, and you can see Florida's largest lake of the same name off to the east as we approach the city of Okeechobee on the lake's north shore. We also have crossed over a large boat canal leading into Lake Okeechobee from the north. This is the re-routed channelization of the Kissimmee River, which was a very expensive drainage-way joining Lake Kissimmee and Lake Okeechobee to make the land habitable and the river navigable a century ago.

"North of Okeechobee, you can see more farmland in every direction, a part of Florida not portrayed in publicity about this state; but agriculture is still one of the major employers in Florida. We are moving back into Polk County where the Gulf American development company (of which we will talk more about in a future tour) purchased forty-seven-thousand acres of forest and wetland in the 1970s, and named it 'Poinciana', to be developed in concert with Orlando's growth. The growth here, and in other areas, did not meet the company's expectations; and it was eventually re-organized under the name Avatar, which proceeded to carve out a retirement community in the middle of Poinciana named Solivita. Since the site is so far from urban development, the planners of Solivita decided on the bold step of building a two-story town center and an adjacent eighteen-hole golf course at the outset, to convince prospective purchasers that their daily needs can be met on site—a six-figure front-end amenity cost that will require many more years of housing sales to be recovered. However, it is a distinctive idea that I thought you should experience, so take us on down to the helipad, Jake and we will visit Solivita."

The helipad at Solivita is located sufficiently close to the town center to enable visitors to stroll into the center. The town center contains an elaborate visitor information facility along with a café and some retail establishments, but many of the buildings are occupied by community association and developer offices. Most of the second floor and some of the ground floor space appear to be vacant. The setting is very attractively blended into water features and urban landscaping.

Mark reported that during its peak year in 2007, it recorded annual sales of close to two-hundred-and-fifty new homes. So it seems that they were doing something right. After walking around the center and posing for Jimmy to record their presence with his camera, the four men entered the golf clubhouse at the end of the street for an enjoyable lunch.

"This is an enormous front-end cost to burden the financial plan," remarked Nash as they awaited their orders.

"It is indeed," replied Mark, "but it also is a calculated risk to lure residents this far away from suburban conveniences. I am not privy to the financials of this development and I could not secure any senior management to join us on short notice. But, if this is an important issue for you to discuss with them, I will arrange to get you a face-to-face meeting at a future date."

"Yes, I would like that, Mark. We can talk about scheduling later."

After lunch and a quick look at the Solivita golf course, they returned to the helicopter to continue the tour of Planning District 7. Jake flew northwest to the intersection of I-4 with the four-lane US 27 from the north, and then turned south down the route of US 27 toward Miami.

Exhibit 23:
Solivita Town Center.
Photo by Canin Associates

"This highway was the major north-south route through the center of Florida prior to construction of the Florida Turnpike and the interstate highways," began Mark. "Today it carries mostly local traffic as tourists tend to stick to the interstate highways. U.S. 27 parallels railway routes in this part of Florida. In fact, CSX Railway has announced plans for a major inter-modal center just a few miles west of here, in the center of Polk County, with a new multi-lane highway link to I-4. This could be an attractive amenity for your proposed community.

"Although citrus groves are quickly being overrun with development in the suburban fringe of Orlando, Haines City, coming up ahead, is still a major citrus distribution center. The profusion of lakes in this area has made Winter Haven and its environs a popular destination for seasonal retirees from the north (the folks we call 'snowbirds' in Florida).

"Just south of Winter Haven is the site purchased by Richard Pope Sr. in 1936, that he developed into Cypress Gardens, one of Florida's most popular attractions. for several decades, with his water ski shows and pretty girls attired in nineteenth century dresses as southern belles. But the profusion of attractions centered on Disney World caused the demise of Cypress Gardens, and the property was recently sold to the Lego Block Company. It has announced the opening of a new theme park called 'Legoland' on this site within the next year.

"Coming up on the left is Iron Mountain, the highest elevation in south Florida at 298 feet above sea level. This site was purchased by Edward W. Bok in the 1920s, an immigrant from Holland, who became the wealthy retired editor of the *Ladies Home Journal.* He retained the famous landscape architect Frederick Law Olmsted Jr. to design the site into a garden sanctuary and retained architect Milton B. Medary to design a 71-bell carillon tower of marble rising 205 feet on top of the mountain, as the centerpiece of his mountain sanctuary. President Calvin Coolidge presided at the opening in 1929. Bok Tower Gardens is considered one of the most beautiful park attractions in Florida.

"On the right side of US 27, you can see Lake Ashton, one of the most successful planned retirement communities in this part of the state. It is priced below Solivita and it has generated sales absorption in similar numbers. It is developed around a lake with a very impressive community center located on the lakefront adjacent to the main entrance.

"On the left is the charming city of Lake Wales, with a substantial proportion of the thirteen-thousand residents living around a lake in the center, and a couple of mature golf course communities on the eastern edge of the city.

Exhibit 24:
Bok Tower and Gardens
outside Lake Wales.
Photo by Averette of
Bok Tower—Averette
at en.wikipedia

"As Jake flys further south, you will see a proliferation of spring-fed lakes which are fed by the limestone aquifer. They present some very pleasant settings for the communities of Avon Park on both sides of the road, and Sebring around Lake Jackson. Sebring became a well-known car-racing center and it still draws large groups of fans for its annual race program. The farthest-south retiree community in the highlands is Lake Placid, snuggled between two large lakes and several small ones. The elevation then descends into the prairie farmland draining toward the Everglades."

As Jake turned the helicopter east back toward Okeechobee, Nash turned toward Mark to ask: "That strip of communities down US 27 looks very appealing, yet the locations are all relatively modest in size. Why didn't this area grow as rapidly as the lakes district farther north?"

"Good question, Nash. What you didn't see is the large number of abandoned subdivisions and planned communities in Highlands County, implying that other people besides you asked that question, prior to plunking their money down for parcels of land. But I believe that the buyers did not materialize for two reasons. First, we are so far south on the peninsula that fewer tourists venture into the interior, especially since we are a considerable drive from big city amenities. Second, nobody marketed this area of Florida, in contrast to the strong campaigns launched over the past several decades by the large communities in Lake, Marion and Citrus Counties as well as the oceanfront counties. The big developers of the 1960s, '70s and '80s never ventured into this part of the state, with the notable exception of the General Development Corporation's 'Port LaBelle', south of here in Hendry County adjoining the Caloosahatchee Canal linking Lake Okeechobee with the Gulf of Mexico. Port LaBelle turned out to be a failure, and it is still marked by a derelict hotel and acres of unused lots and roadways. Despite that, Highlands County was experiencing accelerated sales of new homes prior to the start of the 2007 recession, so it was being discovered by northerners as perhaps the best value in Florida."

"So, is land cheaper down here?" asked Nash.

"Well," replied Mark with a laugh, "property in Florida is relatively cheap everywhere during this recession. But, yes, Highlands County is still one of the lowest-price areas for raw land. But, if price is a high-priority consideration for you, then there are several areas of Florida we have already toured that can match or come close to Highlands County; and, frankly, given the extent of recent negotiations in high-demand areas, I might suggest that price is elastic and might be considered as a low-priority item, subject to adjustment."

"An excellent point, Mark! I will re-organize my thoughts on the purchase issue."

As the helicopter approached the helipad on the stern deck of the "Victoria", Jake suddenly broke his customary silence: "Nash, I'm afraid you have unexpected company waiting for you down below. I believe that is Mr. Swift waiting for you, accompanied by two tough-looking companions. Would you like me to change my flight plan to a safe haven?"

"Not a chance," responded Nash. "I think I just caught a talking skunk in my trap—not the skunk I expected, but a skunk, nonetheless. Please take us down, Jake."

"Yes sir, boss, but I'll be carrying my trusty spanner just in case."

"Rather than use your spanner, I would like you to ask a couple of port security people to drop by in about fifteen minutes. We may be having a little disagreement on board."

Two minutes later they were on the helipad disembarking; and Nash moved directly toward Jack Swift and his companions.

"Ah, Mr. Swift, I thought you were not due to return until next week?"

"Good afternoon Mr. Logan, I apologize for my early arrival, but I would appreciate a few minutes of your time to discuss an urgent matter?"

"Well, I believe we can arrange that. Are the gentlemen behind you part of this discussion?"

"My apologies, once again, Mr. Logan! Please let me introduce my associates, Mr. Jones and Mr. Johnson." Both men nodded stonily to Nash, without speaking.

"Well, fine, nice to meet you. Why don't we all go inside where we can talk more comfortably?" suggested Nash, as he nodded to Mark and Jimmy to join them.

Nash motioned the three visitors to chairs around the conference table, while he, Mark and Jimmy sat across from them. He then looked at Jack Swift expectantly.

"I realize that I was not to return until the first of the week, Mr. Logan," began Swift, "but a matter of some urgency arose that I need to address with you."

"Okay," replied Nash. "What is this matter of urgency?"

"At our initial meeting, Mr. Logan, I endeavored to make clear that our group is prepared to represent you in Florida land acquisition and entitlement approval. Nobody is better-equipped than our group to ensure your success. I urged you to make all necessary inquiries into my character and flawless background. But, just yesterday, I learned that you were contacting another realtor about acquiring land without consulting me. This action on your part is contrary to the oral contract I proposed to you and, therefore, I rushed over here today to inquire about your intentions with this other realtor, as we would like to detail our case for more cost-effective service to you."

Nash smiled back at Swift before responding: "Mr. Swift, let me first of all inquire as to where you heard that I was in contact with another realtor?"

Swift allowed a grimace to creep across his face before he replied: "Mr. Logan, I regret that I am unable to reveal my sources of information. Our intelligence network relies upon complete confidentiality to maintain its reliability . . ."

"I'll bet it does," interrupted Nash. "The fact is, Mr. Swift, this particular piece of information was known only to three people: me, the trusted person used to relay it, and the suspect on my staff who undoubtedly passed it on to you. Your arrival today on the premise set out in this piece of disinformation proves beyond a doubt that you have bribed a member of my staff to convey my activities to you. This is a criminal offense in Canada and I assume that it is illegal in Florida as well. So, gentlemen, be advised that you can expect to be charged accordingly. Now, if you'll excuse me, I see no reason to continue this meeting."

"But, but," stammered Swift, "you cannot turn your back on me. I must warn you that it would be dangerous to your personal health to ignore my group."

"Is that so?" stated Nash, now standing and glowering at the smaller man. "Then let me advise you, Mr. Swift, that it might be dangerous to your health to stay on this vessel another minute." As he finished this retort, two port security officers appeared at the sliding door and knocked politely. Jimmy jumped up to usher them inside. "Now, I am going to say this only once: get off my boat and do not return."

Even though his own two associates had risen to their feet ready for action, Swift was smart enough to realize that this battle was not his to win. As he quickly moved toward the open door, he turned to Nash and exclaimed: "You have not heard the end of this matter, Mr. Logan. We know how to take care of stubborn foreigners in this state." And he left, with his two burly associates close on his heels.

"The larger of the two security officers smiled at Nash and asked, "Is there anything else we can help you with today, Mr. Logan?"

"No, not a thing," smiled Nash, "and thank you very much for appearing so promptly. Your timing was perfect. Oh, wait, there is something else. Would you mind giving my associate, Mr. Quickfoot, the name and address of your pension fund? We would like to make a donation in your names. I see Jimmy already has copied them from your badges."

"Gee, Mr. Logan, there is no need for that. We are just doing our job."

"I know that, but you did it well, and I want to support your organization." Then he shook hands with both men and wished them well. He then turned to Captain Ericksson, who had entered the lounge during the end of this conversation with Swift. Franz, I would like to visit with you and Tim in my study right away." The captain turned immediately and left the room.

"Thank you, everybody, for being here and at least appearing ready to do battle for your employer," he said, chuckling at his little joke. "The excitement is all over now and I look forward to seeing you at dinner. Mark, I would be grateful if you would touch base with your friend Tony and ask if we can conference with him in half an hour. I will meet you in my study at that time."

Exactly twenty-five minutes after Nash's request, Mark climbed the steps from his room up to the study level. At the top of the steps, he was almost bowled over by Tim Wilson, who disappeared down below without uttering a word of apology. Of course, Mark was not surprised, insofar as he was quite certain that Mr. Wilson had just been terminated from his employment in very direct terms. Mark arrived at the study door just as Captain Ericksson was emerging. Franz excused himself, smiled and invited Mark to step in as he was just leaving. And he closed the door gently on his way out.

"Hi Mark, right on time as usual," exclaimed Nash from his chair by the desk. "Franz was aghast to learn of Tim's nefarious activities and he was in complete agreement with me that he cannot stay aboard another minute. So he has gone, and Franz is confident that he can handle the vessel without him, barring any mishap, until he finds a suitable replacement. Now, were you able to get hold of Tony?"

"Yes, he is waiting for our call," replied Mark, as he handed over a slip of paper with the Orlando phone number on it, for Nash to dial on his desk phone.

Tony DiMartino answered his private line on the first ring.

"Hi Tony, this is Nash Logan, and Mark Wilkins on the speaker phone in my private study aboard the 'Victoria' yacht in Port Canaveral. I hope this is a convenient time for you to talk about Mr. Jack Swift and his unnamed colleagues."

"Absolutely, good to speak with you both! Mark tells me that you endured a bit of a confrontation with Mr. Swift this afternoon."

"Yes," replied Nash, "a few minutes of unpleasantness which he brought to our unscheduled meeting, but that is water under the stern at this point. Our primary concern now is to keep this confrontation from escalating."

"You bet! My information is that Mr. Swift is the front man for some potentially nasty characters, so you need to take some security precautions."

"That bad, eh?" said Nash, slipping into his Canadian slang.

"I believe so; but let me take a few minutes to summarize, and then you can ask any questions that you feel pertinent. First of all, let me emphasize that this group is known to the FBI to engage in illegal activities of various kinds in Florida. They have informants in state government agencies that tip them off about inquiries, so they probably have had you under surveillance since you entered the country last week, or perhaps even earlier, if you or your staff engaged in correspondence with state agencies."

"Guilty," interjected Nash.

"Despite Swift's reputation for being a slick personality," continued Tony, "these people play rough, and they do not take 'no' for an answer. Just to be on the safe side, gentlemen, I recommend that you add some security to your yacht."

"Okay, that makes sense," said Nash. "Can you recommend someone?"

"Absolutely, the best in the business: Dan Houlihan right here in Orlando. And I happen to know that he is available personally, and also his fearless sidekick, Ling Ho."

"Ling Ho?"

"Absolutely the best fighter in the martial arts I have ever seen! This woman has black belts in everything. The only problem is that she rarely says anything."

"Fabulous, I like them already," replied Nash. "Can you make the arrangements?"

"You bet, I will phone him right away and ask him to confirm."

"Great, now let's get back to Mr. Swift and friends. What more can you tell us about them that we haven't learned already?"

"Alright, this group apparently came into existence a few years ago when land-use approval processing was really bogged down in most of Florida's major markets because of excess builder demand. They hid behind a law firm here in Orlando that is a small general practice by the name of Richter, Hansen and Morgan. Richter's uncle is Albert Siegal, a successful developer of shopping centers throughout Florida who was reputed to have off-shore financing—a plain name for drug money that is laundered through legitimate business enterprises, in this case, development of shopping centers. Evidently, according to a pretty good source I have in a federal agency, Siegal was being pressed by his drug kings to quadruple his investments, meaning that their illegal business was flourishing. Since he couldn't find locations for more shopping centers, he pressed his nephew to find him some larger development ventures. So, Kurt Richter began peddling financing among fellow lawyers and soon found several developers who needed more equity to enlarge their operations. Mr. Siegal became involved in the illegal end of the business by hiring Jack Swift to bribe public officials in locations where his new ventures were bogged down in the entitlement process.

"Thus, through the middle part of this decade, when demand for new housing exploded, the supply side became much more efficient through Siegal's easy money and corrupt public officials. And he didn't concentrate on just a couple of markets. Swift lived up to his name by hustling public officials, both elected and appointed, all over the state with the simple formula of equity investment plus entitlement processing consulting, supplemented now and then with some quiet strong-arm tactics when they felt it was absolutely necessary.

"This story may sound a little fanciful for those of us who live law-abiding lives. But, even though police agencies at all government levels are aware of these activities, Mr. Siegal stays well behind the scenes and lets Swift and Richter stay in the forefront—a couple of very savvy fellows who, so far, have evaded the law successfully. In addition, many of their joint-venture partners have taken their profits and run, after selling out to national builders who are financed from out-of-state."

"Now, I know what you are thinking: why pick on a foreigner who isn't even in the business in Florida? The answer is very simple. The Great Recession has literally halted new real estate development in Florida, and elsewhere. Their inability to fund new ventures has crippled their business and they are desperate to find new investment partners to meet the continuing money supply demanded by their business. So, they are unlikely to give up on you just because you called their bluff."

"Wow, Mark, this is incredible," exclaimed Nash. "What Tony is telling us all seems logical. Yet, here in the sunshine paradise, it just seems incredible. Is this all news to you, too?"

"Well, over past years, I have certainly come across corrupt public officials," replied Mark, "but this widespread involvement with drug smugglers is new to me. Perhaps if I was still in the business rather than retired, I might have learned about it. Tony, what do you advise? Should we just tell Nash to get on his horse and ride out of town to a more peaceful paradise? Or what?"

"I do have a suggestion for you, Mr. Logan, if you would like to continue with your plan to do business in our state. I am privy to all this information because of my beloved brother-in-law, Jonas Jensen. Jonas is the Florida Director of the DEA, the federal Drug Enforcement Agency. He is stationed in Tampa and is responsible for statewide operations. He knows that I am talking to you, and his price for allowing me to share this information with you is that I request you to meet with him at your earliest convenience. Will you help me keep peace in my family?"

"You bet I will," answered Nash without pause. "This is the kind of criminal operation that erodes law and order in this country and in Canada. I despise it, and I will be happy to assist your brother-in-law. Please tell him that we are scheduled to tour the Tampa area tomorrow, and we will be happy to have lunch with him, if he is free. We are travelling by helicopter, so a spot near a helipad would be preferred."

"Thank you, Mr. Logan. He will be pleased to hear about your interest. I will add a call to him right away, in addition to my call to Dan Houlihan."

"And Tony, I am truly grateful for your role in all of this. Please call me Nash from now on. I will ask my Toronto attorneys to phone you to set up a formal relationship; but, for now, please consider Logan Homes your client in Florida."

At half-past-six that evening, Nash had arranged to meet Mark, Bobbi and Linda prior to dinner, at the large table in the corner of the main lounge for drinks, and a quick recap of the afternoon events. Nash, first of all, thanked both women for their effective disinformation role in setting up both Tim Williams and Jack Swift, and he thanked Mark for suggesting the idea of disinformation. It achieved its objective perfectly. Nash went on to summarize the confrontation with Swift and the timely arrival of the two Port Security officers, thanks to Jake. He then described Tim's almost tearful confession to him and Captain Ericksson. His reason for being an informant was that he was in debt and needed the money—a reason that did not delay his immediate dismissal. Then, after explaining to Mark that he had decided to take the two sisters into his confidence, Nash asked Mark to report on the return phone calls he had received from Tony DiMartino and from Dan Houlihan, as well as from Tony's brother-in-law, Jonas Jensen.

"Well, I know Tony," said Bobbi, "but who are Dan Houlihan and Jonas Jensen?"

"First of all, for Linda's benefit," smiled Mark, "Tony DiMartino is a highly respected land-use attorney in Orlando who has been a good friend of mine for some twenty years. Nash and I asked him to provide information on Jack Swift, since Nash's Toronto lawyers were unable to uncover anything beyond general information. Tony revealed a rather sordid story of Swift being on the tail-end of a money-laundering scheme for drug revenues that provides financing for Florida land developers, and then bribing public officials to expedite the entitlement process for the financed developments. He recommended that Nash retain a top-notch security adviser from Orlando named Dan Houlihan to join our group while we are on this tour. Dan accepted the job, and he and his associate, Ling Ho, will meet the yacht after it docks in Fort Pierce tomorrow afternoon. By the way, Ling Ho is a woman with extraordinary skills in martial arts. So, you both should feel safe with them on board, in place of Tim Williams."

"Darling, I feel safe just with you on board," smiled Bobbi.

"Very comforting, my love, but these two will be on board twenty-four hours each day."

"Ah, good point, I guess they will be useful when you are away."

"Precisely! Now to continue my report, Jonas Jensen is the Florida Director of the federal Drug Enforcement Agency (DEA) who coincidently happens to be Tony's brother-in-law. He provided Tony with background on Swift in turn for an introduction to Nash. Nash agreed, and Jonas looks forward to meeting us for lunch around noon tomorrow at the Tampa Airport Marriott where Jake can land the helicopter, but he would prefer only Nash and me to be present. So that brings everyone up to date."

"Wow," exclaimed Linda, "now this is what I call a real vacation—never a dull minute! Thank you all for letting me share this adventure."

"Linda," replied Nash as he rose to his feet and extended his hand, "I told you earlier in the week, but I will tell you again. It is our pleasure to have you aboard. You light up the whole room. Now, please let me escort you to the dinner table, where I would like to learn more about the nursing profession."

Dinner on the "Victoria" that evening turned out to be another celebratory event. It so happened that the rather reserved Tim Wilson was not a favorite with the other staff members, and his dismissal generated some irreverent toasts from Jake and Jimmy, until Nash implored them to change the topic. Conversation turned to focus on their next mooring at the historic waterfront port of Fort Pierce, just a short trip south along the coast. Although this small city is the county seat, its growth was overshadowed by the rapid expansion of Port St. Lucie immediately south. Now, the retail core of Fort Pierce is growing as a boutique-shop area for tourists, and Bobbi and Linda were looking forward to a better environment for shopping and lunching than the rather sterile Port Canaveral.

After dinner, they all gathered to hear Mark's summary of the next day's tour of Planning District 8, the Tampa Bay Regional Planning District. When everyone was seated, Mark took up his laser pointer and outlined District 8 on the map, encompassing the four counties of Hillsborough, Pinellas, Pasco and Manatee, and containing the two major cities of Tampa and St. Petersburg, separated by the northern arm of Tampa Bay.

"You may be interested to know that development of Tampa and the entire southwest coast of Florida trailed the growth of the east coast by many years. The adjoining coastal plain was open range up until 1884, when Henry Plant extended his railway to this tiny Tampa settlement of eight-hundred residents. Plant projected great things for this little settlement on the bay, and he immediately set about building a large resort hotel to rival Flagler's Ponce de Leon in St. Augustine. The new destination attracted twenty-five-thousand tourists each winter after the hotel opened, and the settlement population grew at the rate of close to fifteen-thousand new residents annually.

"The Tampa of today consists of one-quarter-million residents within the Tampa Bay Planning District of almost three million residents. St. Petersburg contains about the same number of residents as Tampa within the surrounding Pinellas County of nine-hundred-thousand residents.

"Our tour tomorrow will be interrupted by a ninety-minute luncheon that Nash and I have arranged at the Airport Marriott Hotel. Prior to that, I propose another counter-clockwise circle tour, beginning in the farmlands of Manatee County to the south, and continuing over the city of Bradenton, across the edge of Tampa Bay and north across St. Petersburg and Clearwater up to the historic city of Tarpon Springs, settled by Greek sponge fishermen; and then north to the Hernando County border, before following I-75 south and then I-275 into the airport for lunch.

After lunch, we will head south past the city center to the waterfront, and then down the coast of Tampa Bay to have an aerial look at two waterfront communities before heading east to Sun City Center, one of the oldest and largest retirement communities in Florida, where I have arranged for a brief tour. After that, we can take a peek at Plant City, the strawberry capital of Florida, on our return to the east coast and our new berth at Fort Pierce. Any questions? Hearing none, I look forward to seeing my three traveling companions at breakfast."

DAY 8

Friday, April 2, 2010

"I can't believe this weather," exclaimed Jake at breakfast, "ten beautiful days in a row. Why, the helicopter almost flies itself. But, I'm not complaining. This is great. I'm ready to go."

"Yes," responded Mark, "this is the dry season when we customarily have our best weather, and coincidentally our biggest crowds of tourists. We'll fly over Disney World today and see their parking lots almost full at eight or nine o'clock in the morning. But before we begin, I would like to pause at the map to repeat your orientation for today—across the state to Manatee County, then north into Pinellas County and farther north into Pasco County and east to Zephyrhills, before heading southwest to the airport for lunch. After lunch, we go south to Tampa Bay and then east for a look at Sun City Center and Plant City, before we head back east to our new mooring at Fort Pierce on the east coast. If everyone has the trip route clearly in his mind, let's head out."

Once again, Mark reminded his companions to consult the handout on Florida Planning Districts, as a reference to this day's air tour of Planning District 8. Once up in the air again, Jake headed west to Orlando and then southwest to the southeast corner of Planning District 8 to begin their tour. Mark continued with another summary lecture on Florida history.

"On our way over to the west coast, I would like to brief you on Florida's great land boom of the 1920s. In general, it's fair to say that Florida's growth of immigrants has been pretty consistent since Menendez initiated settlement at St. Augustine in 1685. But the growth spurts after both world wars, in the 1920s and again in the 1950s, were spectacular and generated surreal visions of Florida for millions of people who had never set foot in the Sunshine State.

"The real estate boom of the 1920s had its beginnings much earlier, around the turn of the century, when speculators, lured on by the completion of railways and resort hotels on both coasts and in Winter Park, promoted cheap land in 'paradise'. The title of Florida's first real-estate huckster belonged to Richard Bolles, who purchased five-hundred-thousand acres for one-million dollars in the name of Florida First Land Company, and attracted northern buyers to come south. He launched the new town of 'Progresso' at Fort Lauderdale. But, in 1911, the *Washington Times* newspaper published a well-supported expose that accused Bolles and his cohorts of deception, collusion and fraud, thus ending the Bolles venture. In 1913, another visionary, Thomas E. Will, purchased land on the south shore of Lake Okeechobee and devoted the next ten years developing 'New Okeelanta'—a utopian community based on cooperative labor and joint ownership of town and utilities. But it failed. Other new community efforts followed, including Pahokee, Moore Haven, Chosen, Belle Glade, Canal Pointe and South Bay, with equal lack of success (only Belle Glade remains today). Transportation projects accelerated, in an attempt to keep pace with land sales (subsequently driving the Florida East Coast Railway into bankruptcy).

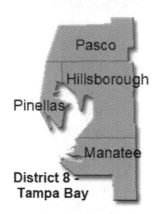

Exhibit 25: Planning District 8—Tampa Bay.

"Finally, in the 1920s, the land boom hit full stride with world-wide promotion of a healing climate with year-round recreation and abundant fertile ground. The state government added to the frenzy by abolishing inheritance and income taxes, through constitutional amendment, to attract elderly and wealthy new residents. Transportation projects accelerated, in an attempt to keep pace with land sales (subsequently driving the Florida East Coast Railway into bankruptcy).

"By 1925, northern banks were warning customers about the danger of investing in Florida land. Dark jokes persist to the present time about swindlers selling swampland to unsuspecting northerners.

"Amidst all of the hoopla and hucksterism, a genuinely honest developer, George Merrick, planned a new town on ten-thousand acres around his family home, west of Coconut Grove and Miami. Coral Gables was initiated in 1921 for one-hundred-thousand residents with canals, fountains, golf courses and hotels; Merrick even donated land for the University of Miami. His famous Venetian Pool above an artesian well was reputed to be the largest swimming pool in the United States. There was no question that Merrick started one of the most attractive communities in the United States. But the real estate collapse of 1926, followed by the stock market crash of 1929, caused his financial downfall. However, his creation lived on after him, and today Coral Gables is home to about forty-five-thousand middle class residents.

"During this same period, a developer named George Young launched a new town called Hollywood between Miami and Fort Lauderdale, and it remains viable today. Young also developed Port Everglades into a major harbor for international trade, adjacent to what is now the Fort Lauderdale International Airport. Carl Fisher, who had made millions from inventing automobile headlamps, spent most of his fortune improving Miami Beach into what became a world-class resort. And, on the west coast, advertising magnate Baron Collier acquired a million acres of land around present-day Naples; in 1923, he paid to finish the Tamiami Trail (US 41) through his domain, eventually completed in 1928. Regrettably, he did not live to see the rapid development of Collier County after World War II.

"Although the 1920s real-estate boom ended with a crash in 1926, sporadic development continued afterward. One notable development was achieved in 1930 when Charles Stewart Mott of General Motors and Clarence Bitting purchased bankrupt sugar companies around Clewiston, on the shore of Lake Okeechobee, and launched the United States Sugar Company. It expanded to produce 90 percent of Florida sugar cane, and became one of the biggest exploiters of migrant labor, as well as invading the natural grasslands of the upper Everglades. Recently, the State of Florida agreed to pay five-hundred-and-thirty-six-million dollars for seventy-three-thousand acres of U.S. Sugar corporation land in an effort to restore a large part of the Everglades. More recently, the state secured a federal grant of eighty-nine-million dollars to purchase use rights for almost twenty-six-thousand acres of ranch land to protect the wetlands in the Fisheating Creek watershed in Highlands County for conservation and restoration of the northern Everglades.

"That is a quick overview of the 1920s real estate boom which succeeded in establishing Florida's reputation, both good and bad, around the world.

"By coincidental good fortune, Jake indicates that we have just reached the border of Manatee County at the eastern edge of Planning District 8, where SR 70 heads northwest from the farming center of Arcadia up to Bradenton on the Manatee River. This highway bisects one of the largest new communities in Florida, which began housing sales in 1995 and now contains over seventy-five-hundred households and some four-million square feet of commercial office and retail space. Currently, it contains five signature golf courses (and a sixth on the eastern edge), an extensive open space and park network, both public and private schools for all ages, two small colleges, a hospital, a YMCA, and shopping centers, with dining establishments and entertainment facilities for its residents and visitors. It is named Lakewood Ranch, and it is part of the thirty-one-thousand-acre Schroeder-Manatee Ranch (SMR), which has operations in mixed agriculture, as well as in mining, providing limestone for highway construction.

"SMR is planned for continuing development through 2035, with current explorations into a possible city charter for Lakewood Ranch. Planning for the new community was initiated in the 1980s; and construction was launched in 1994 under the direction of SMR President, C. John Clarke, and New Communities Vice President, Roger Postlethwaite. After Clarke's retirement about ten years ago, Rex Jensen, who had directed the initial real-estate entitlements on the ranch, became SMR President.

"These men organized a development team and a set of home builders that sold over two-hundred dwellings in the first year of sales in 1995. In 2004, Lakewood Ranch sales peaked at over one-thousand new homes, but annual production dropped rapidly in concert with The Great Recession of 2008-09 to just over one-hundred new homes last year. As Jake completes a circle over the developed portion of the ranch, you can see the business park to the south, next to the Sarasota Polo Club in the Sarasota County portion of the ranch where residential development is planned to begin in 2014 around the lakes in former rock quarries at the south end of the property. The SMR property is owned by the Uihlein family, which was heir to the Schlitz Brewing Company of Milwaukee.

Exhibit 26:
Lakewood Ranch Country Club.

"As we progress over Bradenton, you can see the barrier islands along the Gulf Coast similar to those on the Atlantic Coast, although much lower in elevation. With very few exceptions, they are fully developed from north of Clearwater all the way to Marco Island south of Naples—an island about which I will speak in more detail tomorrow. Now, we are coming into view of the vast Tampa Bay, which extends almost thirty miles from the islands west of the Skyway Bridge, into Hillsborough Bay to the east and Old Tampa Bay on the west, separating the city of Tampa from the city of St. Petersburg and other municipalities, including Clearwater, on the western peninsula of Pinellas County which is now fully developed.

"We'll return to the Tampa waterfront this afternoon. For now, we continue north across Tarpon Springs, the home of Greek sponge fishermen who migrated there after it was launched as a resort by the infamous Hamilton Disston. As we cross into Pasco County, you can see that the coastal areas continue to be fully developed almost to Hernando County, where mangrove islands line the coast from there northward up to Apalachee Bay (which we saw in Planning Districts 2 and 3).

"I am asking Jake to fly east, across the northern suburbs of Tampa parallel to SR 54 which is the current major growth corridor. There are a reported forty-thousand entitled lots in Metropolitan Tampa, and the majority of them are in Pasco County north of SR 54. Currently, most have been purchased at very low prices by large investment companies, waiting for prices to rise in order to make a profit from them. If you decide to locate in metropolitan Tampa, you may note that north of here there is access to both the CSX railway and Interstate 75 highway.

"As we reach I-75, with the small city of Zephyrhills in sight to the east, I have asked Jake to follow this highway and then I-275 west to the Tampa International Airport. You can see the campus of South Florida University below, and then the Busch Gardens theme park. Downtown Tampa is off to the left past the historic Ybor City, formerly a center of cigar-making, and now almost fully redeveloped with both entertainment facilities and multi-family housing.

Just before we land, I would like to remind Jake and Jimmy that you are on your own for lunch, as Nash and I have an appointment in the adjoining Marriott Hotel. We will meet you at the helipad waiting room in ninety minutes, or I will phone you to the contrary, if our plans change. You will find several dining choices in the terminal building."

❦

Jonas Jensen, at six-feet, six-inches tall, mid-forties in age, and carrying 250 pounds of muscle within a very fit body, looked very much like the former professional football player that he was for six years, until a blown knee finished his career. His thinning black curly hair and dark brown eyes added to his obvious African-American ancestry. Although he had been raised in Chicago, he and his family of a beautiful Italian wife and three pretty daughters, were very happy with his government posting to Tampa. They all enjoy the Florida climate.

Jensen had been sitting in the Marriott lobby overlooking the runways for twenty minutes, waiting for the brightly-colored Logan helicopter, and he was relieved to see it settle in for a landing just ahead of their appointment time at noon. He quickly identified Nash and Mark from the three passengers and went to wait for them in the corridor leading from the terminal to the hotel.

"Mr. Logan, Mr. Wilkins, I'm Jonas Jensen. I am pleased to meet you both," as he stepped toward them with his big hand out and a wide smile on his face. Both of his visitors acknowledged his friendly greeting and followed him to the Marriott dining room.

"I suggest we have lunch here at this corner table which I have reserved. They have a revolving restaurant up top which is nice for entertaining, but too noisy for a quiet discussion."

"This is fine," answered Nash. "We have been up in the sky all morning, in fact, all week. I prefer a down-to-earth lunch location. By the way, our group is all on a first-name basis. I am Nash, as in the car of yesteryear, and this is Mark."

"Great, my name is Jonas, but most of my friends call me JJ. Take your choice. Let's order from this lovely lady approaching us, and then we can get right to the subject at hand."

All three of them ordered salads of various kinds with soft drinks.

As soon as the waitress left, Nash remarked, "You certainly are a fit-looking man, JJ. I feel safe just knowing that you are in government service."

"Thank you, I have my ancestry and several years of professional football to thank for my athletic condition; chasing after three high-spirited daughters also helps."

"I bet it does," said Mark. "How old are they?"

"Let's see: twelve, nine and seven. I had to think a moment because two of them just had birthdays."

"Those are great ages. I believe I had the best times with my kids when they were in those pre-adolescent ages," replied Mark.

"Yeah, I know there will be trouble ahead from these three. But I plan to intimidate any suitors by just rising to my full size."

"That should do it," laughed Nash.

Just then the waitress returned with their drinks and salads, and both Mark and Nash turned to JJ expectantly. The big man took a couple of bites of salad and a sip of his drink before beginning to speak.

"Gentlemen, or I should say Nash and Mark, I am sensitive to the fact that we live in separate worlds. I try to catch criminals for a living, whereas you two pursue your professions with very little concern about the bad guys. I don't expect you to be excited about what I do, just as it's difficult for me to fit in your shoes."

"No question there," chuckled Nash. "Your feet must run several sizes beyond those of either one of us."

"Right, my feet are a little large for that analogy," chuckled JJ. "But, I'm sure you understand my point. Nonetheless, we are here today because you agreed to meet with me, knowing full well that I am a government agent. Frankly, I need help catching some pretty nasty folks; and you two, but especially you, Nash, are in a unique position to help me achieve my objective of putting these people in jail."

"Hold up just a second, JJ," interrupted Nash. "We don't come as a matched pair. I have retained Mark's services to teach me about Florida as a possible place to do business. He is about ten years older than me, despite his youthful good looks; and I suspect he is not as athletic as he used to be. There is no way that I want to drag him into anything that might be dangerous to his health. I, on the other hand, am more than annoyed at these people trying to intimidate me, and I have every intention of helping you nail them."

"Well then, hold up another second," chimed in Mark. "What you say about my advancing age is undoubtedly true, but I suspect that what JJ has in mind will be undertaken with all due safeguards in recognition of our civilian status. I plan to take part up to the limit of my capability."

"Dynamite!" responded JJ. "You are saving a lot of time by cutting to the chase. Let me share with you some of the background. I know that Tony gave you the basic information, but we need to be sure that you understand the men we are challenging. I am not 100 percent sure on all of this, but we believe the investors supplying money to this operation are part of the Esperanza drug cartel out of Colombia. You may or may not have heard of Francisco Esperanza, but he is a true 'drug lord' who stops at nothing to make money. We believe the money comes in from the Bahamas as large-denomination cash to Albert Siegal in Orlando. His nephew, Kurt Richter, deposits it in several savings accounts in different banks, so that none of it gets large enough to attract attention. His problem these days is to invest this money in something legitimate, as part of a money laundering process for drug sales revenues. To accomplish this, he needs reputable businessmen such as you, Nash, in order to leave your clean imprint on the money.

"Since the property-development business has virtually come to a standstill, Swift's inability to generate new investment options is causing a clog-up in the system. Money continues to arrive, but Siegal and Swift have nowhere to put it, except in more banks; and excessive balances are likely to be reported to federal agencies. All of this means that Siegal may take matters into his own hands due to Swift's lack of success (which, by the way, may cause Swift to get angry and create some trouble of his own, so some of my staff is monitoring his movements very carefully). My best guess is that Siegal, or his nephew, Kurt Richter, will contact you today or tomorrow and apologize for Swift's actions, prior to requesting a confidential meeting with you. I would like you to accept, but to retain the skeptical attitude you have displayed thus far. That is, you are not keen on his methods; but, if that's the way it is done in Florida to achieve results, then you must at least listen.

"Now, here is the tough part: I need you both to wear a 'wire'—a tiny microphone transmitting to an off-site recorder. We will be close at hand in case of trouble, but wearing a wire is still a risky business which, if discovered, tends to make criminals mad. I cannot sugar-coat the risks here.

"Let me just add two caveats: first, a 'wire' isn't what it used to be in old movies. In fact, it is not a wire at all, but a tiny pin the size of a lapel pin. Second, we practice very close surveillance, which means that our well-trained enforcement agents will be within two or three minutes from your meeting point and prepared to rescue you if things do not go smoothly.

"The objective is to record incriminating statements that will stand up in a court of law. We will give you a confidential briefing on suitable dialogue. Any questions?"

"Yes," said Mark. "Who all will be privy to this sting operation? Everyone on our yacht is aware of the confrontation to date, and I am sure that our copter pilot and Nash's executive assistant are guessing at the occupation of our luncheon companion. Do we have a cover story, or just what do you propose?"

"Sure, excellent question," replied JJ. "By the way, we were pretty impressed with the way you discovered Tim Williams. We have been on to him for some time, but it was not opportune for us to tip our hand prematurely."

"Actually," said Nash, "that scheme was Mark's suggestion and it worked like silk."

"It sure did," acknowledged JJ. "As to Mark's current questions, we cannot leave anything to chance, such as an uninformed person blundering into a delicate conversation unwittingly. Therefore, I want you to invite another person to the party."

"Oh, oh," exclaimed Nash. "We may have moved too quickly in accepting Tony's suggestion to hire Dan Houlihan for security. He and his female associate are supposed to come aboard this afternoon."

"Hmm, let me think about that" responded JJ. "We have used Dan as a contractor before, and Ling Ho is a secret weapon of enormous value. Perhaps we will just ride with them, rather than complicating the on-board group.

"As part of his security advisory services, Dan will meet with everyone aboard, including you two, and spin a plausible story for everyone to believe and act upon. I already like it better than my earlier idea. I will contact him to work out the details this afternoon. As for this luncheon, I just became a realtor with a hot piece of land to sell. Can you handle that?"

"No problem," both men said simultaneously, and then laughed at their duet.

"Great, then I am going to assume we have a deal. You two already are a team, so we just added a couple of wrinkles. Let me add one word of warning: let Siegal come to you. Don't push under any circumstances. If it doesn't happen the way I have suggested, just be patient.

"By the way, I will not be visible in this operation, but I will be in communication every step of the way. Please take your advice from Houlihan. He knows his stuff."

Their time estimate for the luncheon turned out to be about right; so Nash and Mark returned to the helipad waiting room to find Jake and Jimmy waiting patiently. Nash greeted the two men and complained that their realtor meeting turned out to be a bust. The property was not worth their time.

The four men immediately returned to the helicopter to continue their tour. Once up in the air, Mark directed Jake to fly south to the waterfront, crossing over the campus of the University of Tampa, prior to reaching Tampa Bay.

"On the left, gentlemen, is downtown Tampa, the very active center of a city of nearly three-hundred and-forty-thousand residents, and a four-county metropolitan area of almost four-million residents that includes St. Petersburg across the bay. This peninsula extending out into the bay from downtown is Harbor Island, at one point under single ownership and developed for mixed-use housing and a hotel, as a new town in-town. The tip of the larger peninsula to the west is MacDill Air Force Base which played a big role in the initial Iraq conflict under President George H. Bush. Over to the east is Tampa's port which handles the bulk of Florida imports on the Gulf Coast.

"As we head down the eastern shore of Tampa Bay, you can see the large coal-fired power plant at Apollo Beach. Just beyond is the extensive canal system at an older resort—environmental controls no longer permit canal dredging—and next to it is the popular Mira Bay community, originally planned by General Development Corporation, but actually developed by Morrison Homes, a Taylor-Woodrow subsidiary. And beyond it, extending out into the bay from the small city of Ruskin, is the high-density resort community of Little Harbor that took advantage of an existing marina and protected harbor for its high-density vacation-home development.

"Jake is now turning east to one of Florida's oldest large retirement communities, initially developed by Del Webb, considered by many as the father of retirement communities because of his huge post-War Sun City near Phoenix, Arizona, with forty-six-thousand senior residents. In 1959, his company purchased twelve-thousand acres, twenty-five miles south of Tampa, which he opened in 1962 as Sun City Center, exclusively designed for modest-income retirees who preferred one-story bungalows similar to the larger ranch homes they left up north. Ten years later, he sold it to investors, and it grew rapidly over following years to sixteen-thousand residents in 2000, when it was bought by a Florida developer named Al Hoffman. He subsequently purchased Westinghouse's WCI Communities that eventually succumbed to bankruptcy during The Great Recession.

Sun City Center is a good example of an old community that re-invented itself after thirty years, to continue its growth into a new chapter of development. So, I have arranged for you to tour it on the ground, as soon as Jake sets us down on the helipad next to the relatively-new visitor welcome center."

Their tour of Sun City Center was a real eye-opener for Jimmy Quickfoot. Even though he had been impressed with their tour of The Villages a few days previously, he found Sun City Center more amazing because it is a mature small city of seemingly 100 percent retirees whose golf carts mix with automobiles on the main highway through the community. Although there are gated neighborhoods within the complex, the overall community is open to anyone who cares to drive in off I-75 on the west or from US 301 on the east.

Unlike Del Webb's Sun City, Arizona concept of keeping nursing homes and assisted-care facilities outside the community so that they will not spoil the active lifestyle image, Sun City Center integrates them into the fabric of the community, along with shopping, entertainment, hotel and medical facilities. There is no pretense about the fact that these are people in the final stages of life, and they include an age range of over forty years—longer than many of them had worked at primary occupations. Although there are no longer any original residents from 1962, the population does include a wide range of ages in various stages of mobility who can and do live here for the remainder of their lives.

"Mark, thank you for bringing us here," said Nash at the end of the tour. "It is a real treat to see such a diverse age population, from age fifty-five to over ninety, apparently happy with living adjacent to each other despite notably different interests. This is exactly what I would like to accomplish with Logan Lifelong Living—'different strokes for different folks' within a community accommodating everyone. Even though some of the buildings are badly outdated in exterior design, the amenity facilities have been kept up-to-date for everyone to enjoy."

"You're welcome, Nash," smiled Mark. "That's why you hired me, and I am pleased to comply. I have spent my entire career advising developers; and some of them turn out better than others, but I still take pride in the positive influences I have been able to exert."

The flight to Fort Pierce was uneventful, with the conversation primarily devoted to discussing the tour activities of that day. They all were pleased when Jake announced that the "Victoria" was below, and they would land in a couple of minutes. He set the helicopter down in his usual gentle fashion, and the three passengers disembarked, with Jimmy heading down to his cabin. Mark and Nash entered the main lounge, where they glimpsed Bobbi and Linda sitting with two strangers that, by their appearance, had to be the new security force. Mark went directly over to give Bobbi a kiss on the cheek, whereas Nash greeted Linda with a smile, and turned to the two newcomers who rose to greet him.

"So, you must be Dan Houlihan and Ling Ho. There can be no mistaking you from the two separate descriptions I have received in the past twenty-four hours. Welcome to the 'Victoria.' I am Nash Logan and this is Mark Wilkins. I see you already have met Bobbi and Linda."

Houlihan, a six-foot tall athletic-looking man with reddish-blonde hair, shook hands with Nash and Mark, followed closely by Ling Ho, a diminutive woman of Asian appearance, with her black hair in a pony tail.

"I'm a little reticent to shake hands with you, Ms. Ho," said Nash with a smile as he took her hand. "Your reputation in martial arts is formidable."

"Have no fear, Mr. Logan," smiled Ling Ho, somewhat coyly. "I only attack upon command, and I understand that you are now in command." Both Bobbi and Linda burst out laughing at this quick retort, while Mark smiled quietly.

"Ah-ha, well then, my first command is that we all call each other by our first names, Ling; and, my second is that you and Dan join us for a drink."

"Thank you, Nash, we will be delighted to do so."

When Jose appeared to take orders, Dan ordered a coke and Ling an iced tea, after which Dan felt compelled to explain that neither of them drinks alcohol when on duty, and that is their position during their time with the passengers and crew of the "Victoria".

Nash then revealed that he had asked Jose to hire a launch to take the six of them to dinner at a waterfront fish restaurant in Jensen Beach a few miles south on the Indian River, and he asked everyone to be prepared to leave at six o'clock sharp. No sooner had he made this statement than Jose approached him to report that a gentleman named Siegal was on the phone, claiming he needed to speak with Mr. Logan on an urgent matter.

"Ah-ha again," said Nash. "I will take it in my study, Jose. Mark, would you please join me along with Dan and Ling?"

∽

"Mr. Siegal, this is Nash Logan speaking. I don't believe that we have met before?"

"No, we haven't, Mr. Logan," replied a soft and quite pleasant-sounding voice from the speaker phone in Nash's study, "and let me first of all apologize for interrupting your cocktail hour. I know that you are a busy man and I am reticent to phone you without an appropriate introduction. But, frankly, I just received a report from my associate, Jack Swift, who clearly botched up the simple task of presenting our interests to you."

"Well, I must admit, Mr. Siegal, that I am not accustomed to such brash behavior back in my home country."

"Of course you aren't, Mr. Logan, and nobody should have to listen to rude comments in a business presentation. I am appalled by his behavior, and I personally want to apologize for him. We did not grow to become Florida's largest equity investor in new communities by that kind of presentation."

"Well, then, I am glad that you called and I accept your apology."

"Good! Then I suggest we begin a new communication as soon as possible. But this time, I would like to meet with you personally."

"Sure, I don't see any reason why we can't do that."

"Splendid! Then, if you are free, I would like to invite you to dine with me at my club in Orlando tomorrow evening?"

"I believe I am free, but, of course any business meeting would have to include my Florida development adviser, Dr. Mark Wilkins."

"Of course, I have heard of Dr. Wilkins by reputation, and I would enjoy having him join us. I understand you are touring the state by helicopter. If you can ask your pilot to land at Herndon Airport, just north of Orlando International Airport, about seven o'clock tomorrow evening, I will have a car and driver pick you up at the terminal and drive you to the Semoran Club. He will return you after dinner."

"That sounds good to me," replied Nash. "We will look forward to seeing you then."

"Until tomorrow evening then, goodbye."

Mark waited until the line went dead before hanging up and turning expectantly to Dan.

"Well sir, that was just about perfect," said the security adviser. "It would have been nice for him to offer a little more information, but this was a good initial conversation, and your response was just fine: skeptical but curious. I like it."

"Great," said Nash. "Do you need to brief Mark and me before then?"

"Tell you what," smiled Dan. "I have brought you both a present from the DEA. Here are two new ties, red for you Nash, and blue for Mark. Make sure you wear them tomorrow evening. They both have hidden microphones woven into the pattern which transmit to a receiver within a couple of hundred feet. The DEA already has an agent on the serving staff of the Semoran Club, who will keep an eye on you as well. So, you will never be in any danger. As an extra precaution, I will ride over in the helicopter with you and arrange separate transport in Orlando. Ling will remain on the yacht to keep an eye on activities here. Does that sound like a good plan?"

"Perfect," replied Nash. "We will see you tomorrow about six o'clock then."

"Ah, not exactly, Nash! I must insist on riding with you in the helicopter through the day as well. We never know when my advisory services may be necessary."

"Okay, we can do that. I will inform Jake that we have another passenger for our morning flight. We usually gather for breakfast prior to seven o'clock, but, if there is any change, I will tell you at dinner."

The launch ride down the Indian River in the late afternoon sunshine to the Jensen Beach restaurant was a memorable occasion. A steward served drinks to the six of them—Nash, Mark, Bobbie,

Linda, Ling and Dan—and they chatted about the riverside scenery, as well as getting to know Ling and Dan.

At the restaurant they shared the round table for six that Jose had pre-arranged overlooking the river on a perfect spring evening. The fresh saltwater fish which everyone ordered was superb; and, of course, Nash once again proved his knowledge of wine by producing an excellent Sauvignon Blanc, in addition to an interesting non-alcoholic cider for Dan and Ling. All too soon, they were back in the launch for the return trip under a starry sky.

DAY 9

Saturday, April 3, 2010

Both Dan and Ling arrived before seven o'clock for breakfast with the usual group of Nash, Mark, Jimmy and Jake. Mark announced that, although this was the day for touring Planning District 9—the Southwest Florida Regional Planning District (better known as "SWIFTMUD" by locals)—he begged their indulgence for an hour after breakfast to summarize the great post-War real estate boom before starting to tour. Even though Planning District 9 is large in size, it is primarily located on the west coast, and the distance from Fort Pierce is relatively close; so he did not anticipate any difficulty in returning before five o'clock that afternoon to prepare for the seven o'clock dinner engagement in Orlando. At the conclusion of breakfast, he invited everyone to bring a second cup of coffee and gather at the corner conference table. Even Bobbi, complete with tape recorder, showed up at the last minute to join them for what she claimed to be a keynote presentation by Mark.

"Although I previously presented Florida development pioneers of the late nineteenth century, including Plant, Flagler, Disston and Sanford, as responsible for initiating destruction of a substantial portion of this state's natural environment in favor of human habitation, I believe that we must pay due homage to the entrepreneurial and marketing skills of the post-World War II land developers for truly large-scale destruction. In terms of both scale and utter disregard for conservation of natural resources, these men excelled at their craft. Of course, we also must include the well-meaning, but clearly short-sighted, officials of the state's first water management district: the Central and Southern Florida Water Control District, established in 1949. As I described in an earlier session, they did their best to destroy the eco-systems of at least one-third of the peninsula in the name of flood control.

"But today's focus is on a few large-scale land developers who elaborated upon the efforts of their forbears from the 1920s to slice and dice large parts of this state into subdivisions that we must live with through an unforeseeable future. Since you will fly over some of these creations today, I believe it is important for you to know about them in advance."

"Wow, that's pretty strong talk, Mark," interjected Nash. "Are you exhibiting a personal bias here, or are you citing clear evidence?"

"Good question, Nash. If I do sound biased in this explanation, it is because I have spent a good part of my career trying to overcome, or at least modify, wasteful land-use patterns that were created by these post-War developers. After I tell you about them, hopefully in reasonably objective fashion, you can witness some of their accomplishments and draw your own conclusions about their contributions to Florida's future.

"First, I would like to introduce you to the Mackle Brothers who, perhaps more than any other single developer, changed the landscape of rural Florida. In 1908, a twenty-five-year-old engineer, Frank Mackle, migrated to Jacksonville from Great Britain and established the Mackle Construction Company. In subsequent years, he taught the construction business to his three sons: Frank Jr., Robert, and Elliot. The family built their first one-hundred-and-twenty-five small houses (of some thirty-thousand over the years following World War II) in Delray Beach, Palm Beach County. From there, in the late 1940s, they invested all their profits in two-hundred-and-twenty-seven acres of Key Biscayne (across the bay from Miami), built a hotel, and sold bungalows for eleven-thousand-five-hundred dollars each. Their pioneer waterfront development was the first step in the eventual urbanization of Key Biscayne (the subsequent winter home of President Richard M. Nixon).

"Their next venture was 'Pompano Beach Highlands', which they advertised in national magazines for three-hundred-and-fifty dollars down, toward a full price of four-thousand-nine-hundred-and-fifty dollars, including both house and lot. But sales were not up to their expectations, and they came up with the idea of selling lots at ten dollars down and ten dollars a month—an investment plan for retirement. Houses were built only on fully-owned lots. The lot-sales installment plan was promoted in national magazines and became a huge success. However, in most of their developments, house sales never came close to matching lot sales. As a result, Florida is still marked by thousands of acres of relatively-useless land that is divided into quarter-acre lots with a few scattered houses.

"In 1954, the Mackle family acquired the eighty-thousand-acre Frizzell Ranch in northern Charlotte County next to the Myakka River, and transformed it into 'Port Charlotte', the first 'community' of the new General Development Corporation (GDC), formed in 1957 as a consortium between the Mackles and a Canadian firm. The new company staged an expensive national promotion campaign for homes/lots starting at six-thousand-nine-hundred-and-fifty dollars, with two-hundred and-ten dollars down. Later, it advertised home sites for just ten dollars down and ten dollars a month for ten years. Every lot was one-quarter acre to meet the Florida Department of Health minimum for a lot with a well and septic tank. GDC provided dirt roads and electricity and telephone lines (financed by the utility companies). In 1958, GDC sold forty-five-million dollars worth of real estate lots; and by 1959, Port Charlotte included sixty-five-thousand sold lots, but only sixteen-hundred new homes. Sales escalated by 40 percent in 1959 with a high proportion sold to former members of the armed forces who were attracted to Port Charlotte.

The Frizzell Ranch property acquisition was expanded into Sarasota County as the city of 'North Port Charlotte', and the company moved in its own employees, rent-free for a year, in order to control the resident vote for incorporation. The new city annexed an additional forty-seven square miles. Once incorporated, GDC donated to the new city a sixteen-acre park with community center and swimming pool, in addition to five acres for schools and parks. In 1974, the residents voted to shorten the name to 'North Port'. It is the Florida city with the fourth largest land area (seventy-six square miles) of any city in the state, but only about 20 percent is developed.

"The new GDC quickly expanded to become the largest land development company in Florida with large tracts at 'Port St. Lucie',

'Port Malabar', 'Sunny Hills', 'Tierra Verde', and later including 'Port St. John' and 'Port Labelle', in addition to a twenty-five-thousand-acre tract in Tennessee. Port St. Lucie north of West Palm Beach was platted in 1958 for eighty-thousand quarter-acre lots on eighty square miles of swamp and forest land. Originally intended as a retirement community, Port St. Lucie became popular with all age groups and expanded to ninety-thousand residents by the year 2000, with the surrounding developments of 'St. Lucie West' and the new 'Tradition' resort community expanding the St. Lucie County population to almost two-hundred-thousand residents today.

"In April, 1988, the federal Securities and Exchange Commission, acting upon a complaint from a St. Lucie resident, brought charges against GDC, its mortgage banking subsidiary and members of its senior management in Miami for fraud in its house pricing. In 1990, executives of the company and their appraiser were convicted and jailed for fixing prices beyond market value, but the Court of Appeals reversed the convictions and exonerated them in 1996. The company was re-organized in 1990 under Chapter 11 of the bankruptcy law as the Atlantic Gulf Corporation (AGC), which continued to receive estimated revenues of over fifteen-million dollars annually from time payments on GDC lots."

Mark explained further that "the Mackle Brothers had sold out their interests in GDC in 1962, and started a new company called 'Deltona', which engaged in exactly the same business of dividing large parts of Florida into quarter-acre lots and selling both lots and houses on the installment plan. These brothers eventually acquired over three-hundred-thousand acres of Florida real estate in seven counties across Florida. They even left their company name on a new community north of Lake Munroe in Volusia County called 'Deltona', but it remained relatively dormant until nearby Orlando exploded with Disney World in the 1970s and Deltona expanded to sixty-thousand residents by the year 2000.

"Meanwhile, the Mackles acquired thirty square miles of Hernando sand hills and platted thirty-thousand quarter-acre lots which they promoted as 'Spring Hill'. They marketed Spring Hill with a fly-buy program which attracted five-hundred northerners every winter weekend. Sales exceeded sixteen-million dollars the first year, mostly to frugal retirees (no employment centers were within easy commuting range). Today, Spring Hill has expanded beyond the initial boundaries and is home to residents of all ages, in addition to the strong base of retirees.

"The Mackles then decided to expand their consumer base to more affluent northerners; and so they purchased 'Marco Island' from the Collier family. It is located south of Naples and it is one of the largest and most accessible of the Ten Thousand Islands bordering the west coast of the Everglades. The island is six miles long and four miles wide, and the Mackles divided it into eleven-thousand lots, and added miles of canals to enable small boat access for greater value. But, in 1968, the United States Department of the Interior denied Deltona's request for a dredge-and-fill operation in one of the first environmental challenges to Florida developers. It resulted in a lengthy legal battle, in which conservation groups joined forces against the Mackle brothers. But, despite its environmental destruction, Marco Island development was approved and became a great economic success for attracting affluent residents and visitors.

"In sum", explained Mark, "through forty years of accelerated development, the Mackle Brothers succeeded in subdividing vast stretches of Florida for residential subdivisions marketed to consumers of all ages and financial status, with little regard to the future livability of most of them in terms of commercial and civic centers or long-term infrastructure. A few exceptions included 'Julington Creek Plantation' in Jacksonville that evolved into a livable suburban community with major recreation and commercial facilities, and 'St. Augustine Shores', 'Citrus Springs' and 'Marion Oaks' that are still selling lots today. The Mackle brothers sold their interests in the Deltona Corporation, which eventually was sold to a Belgian investor who continues to operate its holdings in several parts of Florida.

However, many of the Mackle land developments remain as vast empty street networks with occasional houses dotting the landscape; or, in the case of Port Labelle, the remains of deserted multi-story buildings that never attracted anticipated northerners.

"The Mackles were not alone in transforming Florida's landscape into subdivisions. Another set of brothers, Leonard and Julius Rosen, arrived in Florida in 1957, flush with success from selling appliances on the installment plan in Baltimore, and hair conditioners on the new television medium. The two brothers purchased over seventeen-hundred acres of vacant, but well-drained, land at the mouth of the Calloosahatchee River in Lee County, called Redfish Point, for six-hundred-and-seventy-eight-thousand dollars. They renamed it 'Cape Coral' and, in 1957, before beginning development, they offered lots on the installment plan to northerners in an expensive multi-media advertising launch campaign.

"The Rosens established the Gulf American Land Corporation as the developer, and hired experienced hard-sell salesmen to greet on-site visitors. Eventually, the company purchased a fleet of airplanes and established a national travel agency for fly-buy programs. They hired Connie Mack, Jr., son of the baseball legend, as the Cape Coral spokesman. At one point, GAC was fined a record nineteen-million dollars for demolishing thousands of acres of mangrove habitat. But the Rosen brothers persevered, and Cape Coral today contains over one-hundred-and-sixty thousand residents; and it also contains a high number of foreclosures, resulting from The Great Recession beginning in 2008.

"Their success at Cape Coral encouraged the Rosens to move their focus inland, and they proceeded to acquire one-hundred-and-seventy-three square miles of the logged-out portion of Big Cypress Swamp on the western edge of the Everglades. They dug one-hundred-and-eighty-three miles of canals, disrupting the flow of water through the swamp, for development of 'Golden Gate Estates'. Work was stopped there after several-thousand investors complained about their purchases of submerged lots, an issue that arose again in 1987 when Avatar (the re-organized GAC, after bankruptcy) began purchasing the formerly-submerged parcels and re-selling them to unsuspecting consumers.

"Lee Ratner was another large-scale subdivision developer responsible for changing the Florida landscape. After making his first million dollars in manufacturing D-Con rat poison, Ratner purchased the sixty-two-thousand-acre 'Lucky Lee Cattle Ranch' in eastern Lee County. In 1954, he joined with fellow Miamian Gerald Gould in subdividing the ranch into 'Lehigh Acres', fourteen miles east of Fort Myers, and began selling lots at ten-dollars down and ten-dollars per month. By 1959, Ratner's sales team had sold forty-thousand lots in Lehigh Acres, a tract of featureless land that evolved into an inland city for frugal retirees and service workers in coastal resort centers.

"Excuse me," interrupted Jimmy, "weren't there any respectable developers in Florida during this period of real estate boom?"

"Good point, Jimmy, I have been focused on the primarily profit-seeking groups that controlled the largest land tracts. Yes, there were men of foresight and quality. Let me give you a couple of examples.

"Over on the east coast, Abraham L. Mailman, took his earnings from manufacturing Persona razor blades and purchased one square mile of Broward County dairy land. In collaboration with his son-in-law, he planned to build a community of modest-price homes for working people, which he called 'Miramar'. By the 1960s, Miramar was Broward County's fastest-growing suburb; and today it is home to over one-hundred-and-twelve-thousand residents.

"Arthur Vining Davis is one of the best-known and respected post-War developers in Florida, particularly for the 1957 creation of 'Arvida', the company which bears the acronym of his name. Arvida has planned and developed dozens of quality communities in Florida, most notably in Boca Raton.

"Davis was over eighty-years of age, and one of the wealthiest men in America, when he settled in Miami in the 1940s, after founding and directing the Aluminum Company of America (ALCOA). He began by purchasing large tracts of rural Kendall on the edge of the Everglades west of Miami in the early 1950s (paying about three-hundred dollars per acre). In the 1960s, the Janis brothers, Ernest and Bernard, purchased a large tract from Davis for five-thousand-and-three-hundred dollars per acre because of their belief that growth would move westward. They proceeded to develop several modest-price 'Kendale' villages, secure in the fact that the new Palmetto Expressway would generate buyers.

It did, and this unincorporated portion of Dade County now includes some three-hundred-thousand residents. In 1956, at age eighty-eight, Davis purchased fifteen-hundred acres of land, including a mile of oceanfront and the Boca Raton Hotel and Club, for over twenty-two-million dollars, the biggest real estate deal in Florida up to that time. He then added a number of farms in South Palm Beach County and proceeded to build several high-quality developments, including the 'Royal Palm Yacht and Country Club' and 'Boca West'. About the same time, he invested heavily in the Sarasota waterfront on Lido and Longboat Keys. Long after Davis's death, Disney purchased Arvida as its development arm, but sold it after two years; and then St. Joe made it that company's development arm, eventually dissolving it during the past decade.

"John D. MacArthur, like Davis, was the son of a preacher, and he made a fortune in his lifetime selling insurance policies. At his death in 1978, he was pronounced a billionaire and, by some estimates, he was the richest man in America. His trust, set up jointly with his wife, continues to donate to worthy causes annually. His estate included two-hundred-thousand acres of Florida property, including the thiry-five-thousand-acre 'Ringling tract' in Sarasota, ten-thousand acres at 'Rocket City' east of Orlando, and forty-one square miles of Palm Beach County. He was responsible for creating many developments in North Palm Beach County, including 'Palm Beach Gardens'. Although he waged a continuing battle with environmentalists, he stimulated many quality developments both before and after his death.

Mark concluded his story by stating that these are some of the most notable developers of huge parts of Florida during the real estate boom extending from the late 1940s until the real estate bust of 1974-76. This bust reduced new development until the mid-1980s. Tomorrow, I will cover significant changes after that time, and then I will summarize our tour of Florida development on Tuesday. Thank you for your attention today. I hope you carry away some helpful information from this session."

"We sure are overcome with new information today, Mark," spoke up Nash. "I never cease to be amazed at your knowledge of this state. By the way, I do now understand and empathize with your bias against the developers you presented this morning. They were a greedy bunch, except of course for the last three. Now, how about today's tour?"

"Right, Nash, and thank you for those kind words. I'm afraid we still have some greedy real estate people in this state; and it will be important for you to distinguish yourself from them, in order to receive fair treatment from state officials."

"And with your help, Mark, I believe we can succeed."

"Thanks again. And now, I will provide a summary of today's tour. As you can see on our mounted map, we are docked here at Fort Pierce, the northernmost point in Planning District 10, virtually due east of Sarasota on the west coast. So, I propose we go to Sarasota last, after beginning in the northeast corner at Okeechobee, and heading south over the lake and the cane and vegetable fields to the southeast corner of Collier County. We can then head west along US 41 across the top of the Everglades to pass over Big Cypress and Golden Gate, as well as have a look at 'Ave Maria', the new community being developed by the Detroit pizza king primarily for Roman Catholics. Then we will swing out to Marco Island and allow you to judge the continuing argument over its development, before taking a run up to the Naples waterfront to Fort Myers Beach and then swinging back to see Immokalee, where we can drop into the local airport for another southern lunch of ribs.

Exhibit 27:
Planning District 9—Southwest.

"After lunch, I propose that we head back to the coast to view some of the high price resort communities all the way up to Sanibel Island. And then we can cut inland to get a good look at Cape Coral, and continue east past central Fort Myers out to Lehigh Acres. After Lehigh, I want to show you the 'Babcock Ranch', over ninety-thousand acres of pristine forest, wetland and farmland, most of which are deeded to the state as a permanent conservation area; and seventeen-thousand acres are being planned as a new community, due to begin preliminary development next year.

"Next, we can have a look at Punta Gorda and the vast Port Charlotte subdivision, now enhanced with a regional shopping center. Also, I will ask Jake to swing back to the coast for a peek at the exclusive 'Boca Grande Island' where the Bush family vacations. After that we will travel up the coast to Sarasota, before we have a look at the eastern part of Sarasota County and, finally, head back to Fort Pierce. Any questions? Okay, let's take off in ten minutes."

After they were seated in the helicopter ready to depart, Mark checked to make sure that both Jimmy and Nash had retrieved their Planning District handouts, so that they could more easily follow the route he had summarized on the ground.

Once Jake had ensured that everyone was belted in for take-off, he lifted off and headed southwest to Lake Okeechobee, and proceeded to fly them over the many examples of bad planning that Mark had described prior to lift-off.

They passed over the destructive farmlands north of the Everglades, and then the Seminole and Miccosukee Indian Reservations preceding the tall grasslands of the Everglades in Collier County to the southern boundary of Planning District 9 at Everglades City and the island town of Chokoloskee bordering the Gulf of Mexico and the Ten Thousand Islands of the southern Everglades. Jake continued his route to the infamous Marco Island with its beautiful sand beaches on the southwest corner of mainland Florida.

"Wow!" uttered Nash, after sitting silent on the flight up to this point. "I certainly can see why the conservationists were angry with the Mackle Brothers. This island is encompassed by wetlands on three sides. They had to destroy a great deal of it to push through two access roads to Marco Island, before they even began to install drainage canals on the island."

"You are absolutely right, Nash," replied Mark. "Marco Island was the prototype contemporary battleground between developers and conservationists. Even though the developers won this battle, it became the example for tougher legislation and regulations to follow.

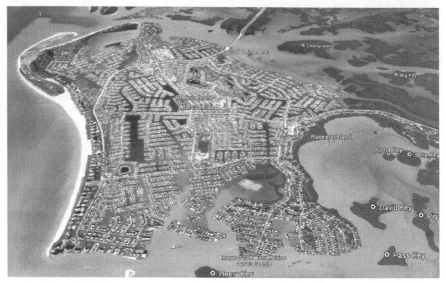

Exhibit 28:
Marco Island.

Now, I have asked Jake to fly up the coast as far as Fort Myers Beach to show you the waterfront development primarily for seasonal owners, and then swing back inland to show you intrusions on the rich farmland adjoining Big Cypress Swamp."

For the next forty minutes, the five men (now including Dan Houlihan in the middle rear seat) were focused on the waterfront condominiums and beautiful sand beaches of Collier and Lee Counties, eventually extending to barrier islands which were separated from the mainland by mangrove swamps and lagoons. The winter season was still in full swing; so the beaches were crowded with suntanned northerners enjoying the natural pleasures of Southwest Florida.

Upon reaching Fort Myers Beach on the northern end of Estero Island, Mark pointed out the historic site of 'Punta Rassa', the cattle-exporting port at the mouth of the Calloosahatchee River (by the bridge to Sanibel Island, to which they would return later in the day).

Jake then headed south down the route of I-75 to provide an overview of the dozens of gated, golf course resort communities in southern Lee and Collier Counties—a true playground for affluent northerners and foreign nationals. He followed I-75 on its eastern turn to see the Rosen Brothers' abandoned Golden Gate Estates described earlier; and then headed north on SR 29 again, to show his passengers the partially-completed 'Ava Maria' community; financed by the Detroit founder of Domino's Pizza as a new town for Roman Catholics. The cathedral in the center is truly an inspiring structure, surrounded by housing construction which has slowed down in concert with most developing residential communities. North of this site are the vast farmlands of the Florida prairie, stretching northeast into the counties of Southwest and Central Florida. The commercial center of the southwest farming community is the city of Immokalee which expands with Mexican farm workers in season.

"I have asked Jake to set down at the Immokalee Airport and hire a van to take us into a local restaurant that serves excellent Mexican food. Most of the land surrounding Immokalee is owned by the two branches of the Collier family, who have been collaborating with other large land owners to construct a bypass for I-75 around the eastern edge of Naples to accommodate through traffic to Miami. One of the family firms has planned a twelve-hundred-acre business park next to the airport, to take advantage of this new highway, as well as to invite corporate air travel. The plan also includes an adjacent new residential area and school for employees of business park tenants. So, hopefully, the rather sleepy little town of Immokalee is on the verge of transformation to a new era. In the interim, I thought you might enjoy some ethnic lunch."

At this same time, the yacht "Victoria" was moored in Fort Pierce for one more day, before departing for its next berth in Fort Lauderdale. Bobbi and Linda were comfortably settled in chaise lounges on the upper deck, where the ever-attentive Jose was serving them tall, cool drinks of his own creation.

"You are certain there is a minimum amount of alcohol in here, Jose?" questioned Bobbi, as she removed her sunglasses to look him in the eye. "I do not want to be out of control before we hit the big city."

"No problem, Senora Wilkins, I have created this fruit drink with only a dash of rum to give it flavor, no more than one-half ounce, I promise. The captain would never forgive me if I persuade our guests to drink too much. So, I am very, very careful. You can depend on me."

He ended his little speech with a big smile for both ladies, and then, as an afterthought, he added: "Besides, in one-half hour, I will be bringing you a wonderful salad lunch which I will set at the table near you. The food will absorb the tiny bit of rum in your drink, so you will be all set for another. You will see." And, with that, the little steward bowed low and disappeared down the stairway, leaving both women laughing at his charm.

"Bobbi," began Linda, suddenly adopting a more serious tone, "I have a problem that I hesitate to broach with you, or with anyone for that matter, but I must seek your advice."

"Dear sister, after all these years, I can't imagine any problem that you couldn't share with me. I believe that is what sisters are for, so get on with it. We are all alone up here and there couldn't be a better time to chat."

"Thank you. I knew I could count on you. What I would like to know is, after two years of marriage to Mark, are you completely comfortable with the age difference between you? I realize that this is very personal, but I would like to know whether there are any issues because of your fifteen-year age difference. Do you mind me asking?"

"Good gracious, no, I don't mind. I don't mind because it is not a subject that concerns me in the slightest. Oh sure, I gave it some thought before we were married, but Mark is such an athletic person and so much fun, I have trouble thinking of him as being a whole lot older than me. And, after two years, I really believe that I am aging faster than he is. Or perhaps you are talking about what happens if he becomes infirm after a few more years and I must become a care-giver?

"Frankly, I believe that is a risk all of us take at any age by devoting ourselves to another person. Either one of us could be stricken by an accident or disease at any time, regardless of age. I believe we must live for the present and let the future be a new adventure. But, wait a minute, why are you even asking me these questions? Do you know something about Mark that I don't know? Or, is this not about me at all? Are you serious about some older man? What's going on here?"

"Yeah, well sorry, I guess it is unfair for me to be so abstract. But this subject has been on my mind a lot over the past few days, and this just seemed like a good time to let it hang out. I didn't prepare anything in advance."

"So, what is the topic we are discussing? C'mon, Linda, quit being mysterious and come clean with your older sister. Ah-ha, could this be about Nash?"

"Well, yes, I must admit that I am infatuated with him, and I don't know how to handle it. After all, I was married for sixteen years and never even thought about other men; well, other than the imaginary late-night dream of an evening with Gregory Peck. Suddenly, my husband ups and leaves me for a glamorous young account executive, and here I am without any skills at dating or even flirting. Thank God, I could never have any children to whom I must explain this unhappy situation. Now I have two guilt trips—lack of children and escaped husband. I was coping reasonably well until this week; and now I have to face my unexpected exposure to a really handsome and charming man every day. I keep trying to find faults with him, like the age difference; but, so far, I think I am in trouble if I don't get off this boat before I do something really stupid, like jumping into his bed in the middle of the night."

"Wow, this is a problem. I imagine a rich and handsome guy like Nash gets propositioned on a regular basis from a wide array of glamorous and sophisticated women. And that doesn't even consider the longevity of his love affair with his wife Victoria, for whom this yacht obviously is named. She has been gone for only three years. I must admit that the real problem may be with him, rather than with you. His charm may be a genuine cover for long-term sadness over the loss of his wife."

"I know, but how do I find out without a full confession?"

"Oh-oh, here comes Jose with another delicious gourmet lunch, so we'll just have to postpone this tough topic until later."

The Mexican lunch in Immokalee turned out to be a big hit with Mark's companions, especially Jimmy, who claimed it was the best Mexican food he had ever eaten. Jake also was complimentary, although Dan responded that his forty-inch waist does not allow much leeway for food addiction. Nash was eager to get back in the air; so they hurried back to the airport and climbed aboard. Jake headed due north to overview Lehigh Acres, which turned out to be a relatively dreary pattern of regimental small boxes from the sky.

"Jake, please head due north across the Caloosahatchee River and stay on course until you come to the first paved road; then loop west and return down SR 31. Gentlemen, in front of you is the ninety-three-thousand-acre Babcock Ranch, owned by the same family since the nineteenth century, until it was sold two years ago to Kitson Partners of North Palm Beach. Sidney Kitson, backed by Morgan-Stanley financing, sold seventy-six-thousand acres back to the state for permanent conservation, including a management agreement by which he retained most of the original maintenance staff, and created a master plan for the remaining seventeen-thousand acres in the southwest corner for a new community catering to retirees, as well as to employers and workforce housing. The master plan lies partially in Lee County, as well as Charlotte County, and negotiations still pending with the former county have delayed a construction start. It promises to be a state-of-the-art new community under the leadership of Tom Danahy, former President of Lakewood Ranch Communities in Manatee and Sarasota Counties that we flew over yesterday.

"Now, Jake, please follow the river out to its mouth, to take up where we left off this morning. On the left is downtown Fort Myers and on the right is North Fort Myers, the bulk of which is Cape Coral, the most successful of the Rosen Brothers' developments. It basically is a lot-sales development, but with drainage/small boat ditches added for greater value. Although a large share of this community was built out by Gulf American Corporation, followed by its successor, Avatar, there are still ample lots available, and perhaps as many foreclosures accruing from The Great Recession.

"Beyond Cape Coral is 'Pine Island', with small developments dating back forty years, and beyond that is 'Sanibel Island', a retreat for affluent seasonal residents. The north end of Sanibel is 'Captiva Island', most of which is a resort that was prominent in the news a few years ago for Congressmen's boondoggles financed by major lobby organizations.

These islands protect the entrance to Charlotte Harbor, which is bounded by Punta Gorda on the south and Port Charlotte on the north. The latter, of course, was made prominent by the acquisition and marketing of eighty-thousand acres by the Mackle Brothers and General Development Corporation in the 1950s and beyond, as discussed earlier.

"Out toward the coast is a unique development called 'Rotunda', which was planned in the shape of a wagon wheel, but developed slowly over several decades. Its most prominent feature is its inefficient site-plan design. Just to the north of Rotunda is Boca Grande Island, a winter vacation home of the Bush family, among other wealthy residents."

"Mark," interjected Nash, "with all of the GDC homes built on septic tanks, hasn't Charlotte County been saddled with difficult sewage construction costs?"

"Yes, indeed, Nash. As I have mentioned previously, this problem of complying with state sewerage construction mandates has been particularly difficult in former GDC and Deltona developments where home sales never caught up with lot sales; thereby not providing sufficient property-tax revenue to finance improvements. Port Charlotte was obliged to place a moratorium mandate on any new construction throughout a large part of the county for several years in an attempt to re-organize its haphazard growth.

"Moving north along the coast, we next come to the city of Venice, which, for several years, held the distinction as having the oldest average age of any municipality in Florida. It supports Sarasota

County's 'oldest-county median-age' of fifty-three. From Venice north, barrier islands extend through Sarasota County and Manatee County all the way to Tampa Bay. They are virtually filled with full-time and seasonal residents. Lido Key, due west of downtown Sarasota, contains St. Armands Circle, one of the most popular shopping and dining centers in the county.

"As we complete our tour of the edges of Planning District 9, the history of Sarasota is an interesting footnote. Although Sarasota has long been considered as the winter home of elegant New Yorkers, and one of the top Florida counties in household income, its beginnings were much less auspicious. Initial land acquisition from government holdings was by a Scottish investment company named the Florida Mortgage and Investment Company, which offered lots in a new town with a golf course (the great Scottish contribution to recreation) to Scottish residents at very modest prices. The first colonists arrived in what is now Sarasota from Scotland in 1885. Instead of a town with a golf course, they found a trail and one building. Most of them returned home after a cold winter, even including snow.

"But the Florida Mortgage and Investment Company moved ahead with initial building plans under the personal direction of J. Hamilton Gillespie, son of the company president. The result was the DeSoto Hotel, a boarding house, a dock, several houses, stores, and the clearing of three miles of streets. Steamer service was inaugurated between the new community of Sarasota and Palma Sola. But no land sales occurred in 1886 and only eight lots were sold in 1887. The company's Board of Directors ordered a voluntary liquidation of its holdings. But Gillespie persevered and, in 1902, Sarasota was incorporated as a town with Gillespie as its first mayor. He promoted golf in Florida from his first arrival and through the following years, he designed and developed courses in Sarasota and other cities. This stubborn immigrant died in 1923 while playing on one of his golf courses.

"The great American promoter and showman, John Ringling, fell in love with Sarasota in the early 1900s and soon became its most revered resident. He planned and developed the 'Ringling Isles' subdivision on the barrier islands west of the town, including 'St.

Armands Key', 'Bird Key', 'Coon Key', 'Wolf Key' and two-thousand acres on 'Longboat Key' (all of which he owned). He was a strong supporter of President Warren Harding and planned to have him establish a winter White House on Bird Key, but Harding died in 1923 before commitments were complete.

"Ringling and his associates built the 'Ringling Causeway' and bridge to St. Armands Key and donated it to the city, a strategic investment as sales of residential lots on St. Armands generated over a million dollars in the first year after opening. He also donated one-hundred-and-thirty acres on Longboat Key for a golf course that still remains today. After the Ringling and Barnum and Bailey Circus moved its winter quarters to Sarasota, its annual circus programs carried advertisements on Sarasota. His Sarasota home featured a sixty-foot-high tower modeled after the old Madison Square Garden, a reminder of his sponsorship of a two-week Florida Exposition at the Garden in February, 1924, at the height of the Florida real estate boom (which crashed in 1926). Today, the John and Mabel Ringling Museum is a major tourist attraction in the area.

"As Ringling and other developers attracted increasing numbers of wealthy New Yorkers and affluent residents of other northern states, Sarasota became a no-growth county and resisted new development during the Florida real estate boom after World War II. It was not until the initiation of Lakewood Ranch in 1995, that Sarasota Commissioners voted to establish an Economic Development Department; and to retain an experienced professional to direct it. Concurrently, through the exceptional talents of the Lakewood Ranch President of Real Estate Development, John Swart, new employers poured into the Sarasota-Bradenton MSA, and Sarasota reaped the tax benefit, along with Bradenton. The resultant growth spurt caused Sarasota Commissioners to regenerate their no-growth past and adopt a 2050 Development Plan that maintains the status quo of promoting estate lot development east of I-75 and impact fees everywhere, while espousing the objective of developing affordable housing. This kind of contradictory policy pushes the availability of workforce housing beyond the source of employment to North Port in the southern part of the county, and to neighboring rural counties (including

Hardy, DeSoto and Hendry), where land is still lower-cost, in the time-honored American tradition of sprawl. The current price decline, resulting from The Great Recession, is unlikely to establish a lasting reprieve for the availability of affordable housing to accommodate a growing workforce in Southwest Florida.

"The remainder of Planning District 9 is predominantly agricultural. It remains to be seen how the parochial interests of individual counties can be meshed with the broad interests of the state to control future growth through the functions of the Regional Planning Councils."

As promised, Jake delivered his four passengers back to the "Victoria" at Fort Pierce shortly after five o'clock in plenty of time for Nash and Mark to get dressed for their scheduled dinner appointment in Orlando. Jose immediately notified Mark that the three ladies—Bobbi, Linda and Ling—had gone into Fort Pierce for a final shopping trip before leaving the next morning. They were expected back before six for pre-dinner drinks. Both Mark and Nash headed down to their cabins to dress for dinner and study their notes of prior conversations in preparation for the dinner meeting with Albert Siegal.

Mark glanced at his notes first, and then stripped off his clothes and took a quick shower and shave just before the cabin door opened and Bobbi came in and sat in a chair waiting for him to come out of the bathroom.

"Hi Bobbi, did you have a nice day?" asked Mark as he emerged in the yacht's terrycloth bathrobe.

His wife smiled up at him as he gave her brief kiss at the end of his question. "We sure did. It turns out that Ling Ho is a delightful companion, despite her constant watchfulness of everyone within eyesight. I feel supremely secure with her next to me, although I must admit that my confidence is all based on hearsay. I haven't actually seen her perform any martial arts."

"And a good thing too," replied her husband with a smile, as he settled into one of the other four chairs around the table where Bobbi was seated. "Frankly, I will be very happy to not witness conflicts of any kind, either on this yacht or anywhere else. As I hope you know, I am not a combative person."

"Absolutely, that is one of your characteristics that I like the most. Although, I must add, darling, that I adore all of your characteristics." She paused for a few seconds, as though she were choosing her next words carefully. "But, Mark, we do have a small problem with Linda, about which I would like your input."

"You bet. Does she need help with her return ticket?"

"Oh, if it was only that simple. Now please don't mention this to anyone else, especially Nash, but I'm afraid that my little sister is falling head-over-heels for our charming host and client. Since she has witnessed no reciprocal affection, except his usual charm, she has sought my advice as to whether she should quietly slip back to Atlanta and try to forget our dashing Canadian, or perhaps attempt a somewhat more pro-active attitude with him. Remember, Linda hasn't practiced any flirtatious activities on anyone except her departed ex-husband for sixteen years; she doesn't feel very confident about subtle, yet effective, tactics."

"Hmm, my love," Mark replied with a grin. "Were you able to divulge some of the clever ploys you used to snare me?"

"Very amusing! Now, be serious for a moment and give me your honest opinion. Nash must be hounded by beautiful women everywhere he goes. It seems to me that he has installed an automatic defense mechanism that manifests itself in outward charm, mixed with very guarded displays of affection. Have you ever discussed such personal things with him during your travels? I believe the two of you have bonded very well during your time together."

"I believe that you are right, my love. But our bond has been focused on professional topics rather than personal ones. Nevertheless, let me give this issue some thought, and I will try to make some suggestions to you tomorrow, our second-last day of touring. Right now, I must get dressed for our dinner with the wily Mr. Siegal. So please excuse me. I promise to respond by the end of the day tomorrow."

Mark arrived at the waiting helicopter just in time. The other three had already climbed aboard. He quickly joined them, taking his customary right rear seat and fastening his belt. Nash was across from Mark in the left rear seat and Dan Houlihan was up-front next to Jake. The able pilot wasted no time in completing his check-list and lifting off for the short flight northwest across the Florida prairie to Orlando.

"Nash," said Mark into the head microphone, as he turned to look at his companion, "you have much more experience in these types of interactions than do I. What do you expect from our pleasant-sounding Albert Siegal?"

"First of all, Mark, my guess is that your career has been full of difficult negotiations with both clients and colleagues; second, Mr. Siegal obviously is a follower of the Teddy Roosevelt school of 'walk softly and carry a big stick'. Since I have no intention of capitulating to his soft-spoken demands, I imagine that we may experience the oral equivalent of the big stick before the evening ends. Third, and of greatest importance, I believe our primary mission is to encourage him to make some incriminating remarks for transmission through our wired neckties. I may require your planning knowledge to pull this off."

"Let me interject here," said Dan from the front seat. "I believe your three points are right on target, Nash, with the third point taking its rightful priority up front. This guy Siegal is as smooth as silk when everything is going his way, but I believe he can become quite arrogant when he doesn't get his own way. By the way, gentlemen, I mentioned this before, but it deserves repeating. You will be monitored every minute of your meeting tonight, so please do not have any concern about your physical safety at any time. We have an excellent crew of federal agents on hand if anything goes wrong."

"Thank you, Dan," replied Nash. "That is good to know, but I cannot imagine any physical violence taking place in an upscale private club. My expectation is that he may well threaten us, but that we are in no danger, at least not this evening."

"Once again, Nash, I believe your estimate is correct. But, in our business, we cannot be too careful."

"Yes, of course, and we appreciate that policy, believe me. That reminds me, Dan, what time should we tell Jake to expect us back at the airport?"

"Right, I believe you should be gone about three hours, perhaps a little longer. Since I see that he is skirting the Orlando Airport right now, my best guess is that we all should be ready to take off shortly after ten tonight. Did you pick up on that, Jake?"

"That's a roger, Mr. Houlihan. Please check your seat belts, gentlemen, we are about to set down at Herndon Airport in beautiful Orlando."

⁂

A uniformed chauffeur met Nash and Mark inside the small terminal, and ushered them out to a black Lincoln Town Car for the trip to the Semoran Club. Dan Houlihan stayed with the helicopter until they left the terminal; and then he walked inside to meet a DEA agent whom he knew from previous assignments. Jake retired to the pilot's lounge, where he could enjoy snack food and soft drinks during his wait time.

Nash and Mark arrived at the club within fifteen minutes, and proceeded up the steps into the elegant entrance foyer where a short, bald man came forward to meet them.

"Mr. Logan and Mr. Wilkins," smiled Albert Siegal as he shook hands with each of them. "It is a pleasure to meet both of you. I trust you had a pleasant trip over here?"

"Absolutely," replied Nash, "and your man was waiting for us when we landed. Everything went very smoothly."

"Good, good, please come with me. I have arranged for a private dining room for the three of us, where we will not be disturbed by anyone except the waiter."

⁂

The dinner proceeded affably, with Siegal recommending the specialties of the house while they enjoyed a cocktail and made their selections to a very attentive waiter. Siegal had pre-selected white and red wine, Nash taking the red to complement his prime rib and Mark taking white with his baked sea bass. Siegal also ordered sea bass with white wine, before asking them about their travels around Florida. He professed genuine praise for Mark's geographical organization of the state for daily tours.

"So, at this point, you have flown over everything except the southeast and the Keys?"

"Yes, that's right," Mark responded. "Tomorrow, we do the four counties of the Treasure Coast, and then the final day is a relatively short tour over Miami/Dade and Broward Counties. We won't bother with the Keys, as there is no land of any scale to develop on those islands."

"Please tell me then, Mr. Logan, what criteria have you set for property selection?"

"Sure! We intend to manufacture packaged houses on-site, so we need good transportation, preferably both road and rail, as well as a natural gas line if possible. It is my concept to provide employee housing on-site at a very attractive price, and also to cater to Florida's retiree migrants. So we want to be within an hour from a major city that offers entertainment and shopping activities. Those three primary requirements, plus a modest commercial center, add up to less than twelve-hundred acres; but my adviser Dr. Wilkins recommends we look for over fifteen-hundred acres to allow for wetlands and retention."

"Very wise advice, Mr. Wilkins," responded Siegal. "Have you applied your criteria to any particular areas yet?"

"No, we don't plan to assign criteria until we finish our tours over the next two days."

"Well then I guess the entire state is open for consideration?"

"More or less, but with some exceptions, such as the Keys, urban areas and conservation areas. Is that a fair statement, Mark?"

"I believe so," replied Mark, "except for entitlement considerations, which may prove more efficient in some counties than in others. With the prospect of the 'Hometown Democracy' movement hanging over our heads, we must be very sensitive to those areas where we can make friends in the easiest and quickest fashion."

"Very sensible, Mr. Wilkins," said Siegal. "We anticipate a very busy year for entitlements despite the lingering recession. I might add that we are very familiar with those counties that tend to welcome, rather than over-control, new development. Perhaps, we could be of some assistance in this respect."

"That sounds very interesting," said Nash.

"And I will respond, but, in the interim, I recommend the Club's special dessert. Can you describe it, Carl?" Siegal asked the waiter, who immediately reacted by passing out dessert menus and then describing three of the favorites. Each of the diners accepted one of the waiter's choices, along with coffee.

Mark picked up the conversation by addressing Siegal: "You probably could save us some significant time if you had intelligence on the political climate in each of the counties where we have an interest. How could we tap into that information?"

"Excellent question, Dr. Wilkins! Our group brings four valuable assets to the development table. First, we maintain an intelligence network on the 'political climate,' as you put it, in each development-active county in the state. We actually monitor the current climate and update it quarterly. So, I can tell you on short notice whether a given county is likely to be friendly toward a new developer. Second, with due respect to your own lengthy service in this business, Dr. Wilkins, we can define and manage the fastest entitlement team in the state, regardless of the developer's special needs. Third, development operations have become much more dangerous over the past couple of years as new projects have become fewer in conformance with The Great Recession; so we have assembled an efficient security force to provide full-service insurance to our developments that provides a guarantee for personal safety, as well as for equipment and buildings. Fourth, and of greatest importance, we can supply both equity and debt financing at any level, providing we also handle the first three items to ensure that each project is efficient for our investors. In short, our group can put you on the map faster, safer, and more economically, than anyone else in this state."

The waiter then interrupted the discussion to serve the dessert and coffee to each diner. He left Siegal a small box with a button to push for additional service. Otherwise, he thanked the three diners for the pleasure of serving them. No check was mentioned.

Nash took up the discussion after the waiter left: "Mr. Siegal, your statement is very enticing; but, as they say, the devil is in the details. We need to examine each of these four segments to see what they hold. For example, what financial institutions do you represent?"

Siegal smiled brightly. "That's easy, all of our finances are privately subscribed into separate funds for each project. We simply send out the financial plan for a specific project to our private investors and some or all of them decide to subscribe to the equity and/or debt financing for that project. We are always over-subscribed for every project we undertake."

"But, who are these people? Why do they invest vast sums of money in your projects for several years, without knowing each specific developer?"

"Very frankly, Mr. Logan, why do you care? As long as the money keeps being paid on time, it seems to me your concerns are unfounded."

"Ah-ha, that is exactly the point. How can I feel certain, how can my shareholders feel certain, that the money will continue to be paid to complete the project on time?"

"Certainly, as with any financial institution, we will have a signed agreement between us that will define the times and amounts of loan payments as well as other details."

"And what is the name of the lending entity, Mr. Siegal?"

"As I mentioned earlier, Mr. Logan, a new lending entity is incorporated for each project, so the actual name will be selected when we agree orally to move ahead."

"And this investment group will provide money up-front for the new entity, or will the investors only produce cash as called upon during the course of the loan?"

"Well, of course, the investors don't like to have their money sitting idle waiting to be drawn down. They will provide funding in stages as required by the terms of the loan."

"So, Mr. Siegal, that brings us full circle. You claim to have money available, but you are unable or unwilling to reveal names or institutions that we can examine for financial viability. I really do not see how we can do business without full transparency on the sources of funds. I cannot satisfy my own shareholders' questions on financial viability without normal due diligence examinations. Frankly, I cannot see how we can do business."

"First of all, Mr. Logan, I can understand your reticence to commit on short notice. But, I want you to know that our consortium of private investors has funded over three-quarters of all the Florida developments over five-hundred acres during the past four years. I will be pleased to give you the names of each one as well as the names of the individual developers involved. Secondly, I would like to have the loan documents delivered to your yacht tomorrow morning for your personal scrutiny. You are a careful man and you will soon see that the documents contain all of the necessary safeguards. Also, you will find in these documents a clause about security throughout the entire relationship. There are a lot of unscrupulous contractors and just plain thieves in Florida lying in wait for you. It is in our interest to keep you protected at all times. Our investors, backed up by our experienced on-site team, guarantee your safety during the term of the agreement. I believe that you will find this means a great deal in today's development climate. Now, can I have your agreement to review the documents that I will have delivered tomorrow?"

"Sure, I will review them and also have my lawyers review them. But, I must warn you in advance that I am not sanguine about a positive outcome."

"No problem," replied Siegal, with a knowing smile. "I feel certain that, once you fully understand the advantages of a ready money supply coupled with a secure work environment, you will be convinced of the positive advantages of our agreement. I will not keep you any longer now, but I will contact you the day after tomorrow, when you have had time to review the agreement documents, at which time I will request another meeting with you. Until then I wish you a pleasant journey back to Fort Pierce." The little man then rose to his feet and shook hands with his two dinner companions, prior to ushering them back to the entrance of the club. "You will find the driver waiting for you at curbside. Have a pleasant journey."

The driver was waiting at the curb holding the rear door open for his two passengers. The two men remained quiet during the trip to the airport, not wishing to discuss any aspect of the dinner conversation within earshot of the driver. Upon arriving at Herndon Airport, the driver refused any gratuity and wished them a pleasant flight. Jake and Dan Houlihan were awaiting their arrival in the terminal and ushered them directly to the helicopter. Jake immediately prepared for flight, as the other three men belted themselves into their seats. Within a few minutes, they were up in the starlit sky, heading southeast over the Florida Turnpike on their way back to Fort Pierce.

"Well, Mark, what are your thoughts about our conversation with Mr. Siegal?"

"Frankly, Nash, I found him a very engaging personality—definitely not the criminal type I anticipated. I believe his four-part program has been carefully organized and would be of great appeal to developers whose primary interest is in the creation rather than the financing."

"Yes, I believe you are right. But, knowing what I do about his background, I felt definite concern about his emphasis on security at the end of our discussion. I interpreted that topic as a not-so-subtle threat to our well-being if we don't play ball with him."

"Absolutely! Despite his quiet smile, I too received that message clearly. But, I am not overly concerned, especially with the competent Dan Houlihan riding shotgun."

As if on cue, Dan broke into the conversation on the intercom. "Gentlemen, I appreciate your confidence in me, but please do not underestimate the basic cruelty of Siegal. Several law agencies list him high on their suspect lists for a variety of criminal acts, some of which have caused serious bodily harm. Believe me, both Ling Ho and I take this assignment very seriously. I . . ." Dan stopped in mid-sentence as the helicopter suddenly began to shake violently.

"Gentlemen," interrupted Jake in a calm voice, "please tighten your seat belts. We have a serious problem and I need to set this bird down for an emergency landing. Over the noise of the rattling machinery, the others heard Jake contacting the Orlando Control Tower to report his plight. And then, he switched suddenly to "Mayday, Mayday" when the helicopter turned upside down and headed for the ground. Jake fought valiantly with the controls to bring it almost upright as it plunged into the dry prairie grass.

Although all four occupants of the helicopter were securely fastened in their seats by harness belts, the angled landing caused the left strut to hit first and fracture with a sharp shift to that side resulting in all of them being jerked to the left. Jake already had released his door, allowing his head to snap left in clear air, but Nash behind him banged his head on the door frame rendering him unconscious. Dan and Mark on the right side of the cabin remained conscious, but their angled positions made it difficult to unbuckle their safety belts, especially with their minds in a state of shock.

Jake immediately observed the conditions of his three passengers, and reacted in accordance with his many years of emergency training procedures. First, he turned off the ignition to reduce the danger of engine fire, and then he jumped from his left door and managed to open the rear door and unbuckle Nash. He dragged him from the helicopter and pulled his employer fifty feet away from the wreck. As he finished laying Nash on the prairie grass, he realized for the first time that fire had broken out in the engine despite his ignition deletion. Without hesitation, he ran to the right side of the bird to aid his other two passengers: first prying open the rear door and releasing Mark's safety belt as he grabbed him by the shoulders and yanked him from the now-burning machine. After dragging the semi-conscious Mark twenty feet from the ruined aircraft, Jake dashed back to help Dan in the co-pilot seat.

Dan's two-hundred-and-forty-pound semi-conscious body was tilted away from the safety harness buckle release, making it very difficult for Jake to get it open, especially with flames beginning to extend from the overhead engine. Finally, with the aid of his pocket knife, the buckle gave way. But, at that same instant, the entire cabin exploded with enormous force as the fuel tank erupted. Now released from the safety belt, Dan was propelled out of the door at tremendous speed, knocking his rescuer to the ground under the aircraft. Dan landed unconscious some thirty feet from the explosion, whereas the brave Jake was quickly suffocated and then burned to death from the blazing fuel leaking onto him from the ruptured tank. None of the four men uttered a sound as the fire reduced the helicopter to a pile of black rubbish.

DAY 10

Sunday, April 4, 2010

Sunday morning news reports on Orlando television stations described the helicopter crash and explosion as an unexplained accident being investigated by the FBI, as well as Osceola County Sheriff's Deputies and Florida State Highway Troopers. The Federal Aviation Agency was reported to have inspectors en route to the scene, two miles north of Yeehaw Junction in the vast cattle range between Orlando and West Palm Beach.

The helicopter explosion just before 11 pm on Saturday evening had launched a huge fireball into the sky, easily visible to motorists traveling on Florida's Turnpike a mile west of the accident site. After notification by State Highway Troopers, helicopters from two Orlando hospitals raced to carry the three survivors from the scene to hospitals in Kissimmee and Orlando. The pilot's lifeless body was burned beyond recognition and transported to the Osceola County morgue in St. Cloud. For some inexplicable reason, the three passengers were found unconscious some distance from the wreck, presumably having been jettisoned from the crafts explosion. Television pictures from news station helicopters showed an unidentifiable smoldering black mound as the only evidence left of the five-passenger Bell helicopter owned by Logan Homes of Toronto, Canada. The firm's founder and president, Nash Logan, is reportedly one of the two injured passengers in Florida Hospital Orlando. The co-pilot was taken to Florida Hospital Kissimmee.

News of the accident reached Captain Franz Ericksson about an hour after the crash on the basis of information from Dan Houlihan who regained consciousness after reaching the hospital. Despite the midnight hour, the always-calm Franz awakened all of his passengers to give them the horrible news. Jimmy Quickfoot reacted immediately by using his cell phone to waken a local helicopter operator and hire him to report to the waterfront helipad within the hour, prepared to transport four persons to Orlando. He then hired a limousine service in Orlando to meet the helicopter at Herndon Airport and transport them to the two hospitals. Jimmy proposed to Franz that the passengers should be the three women—a wife (Bobbi), a nurse (Linda) and a security advisor (Ling Ho)—and himself. The captain agreed with Jimmy's arrangements and the identified passengers repaired to their cabins to dress, while Franz opened his own cell phone to call Logan Homes Executive Vice President Nathan Rosenberg at his home in Toronto. He then wakened Deckhand Carlos and Stewards Jose and Alfredo, requesting them to mount an all-night vigil in two-man shifts on the boat deck to safeguard the "Victoria".

It was after three in the morning by the time that the three women and Jimmy arrived at Orlando's Florida Hospital to interview the doctors who had treated Nash and Mark. Dan had been taken to the Kissimmee Florida Hospital where Ling phoned to ascertain that his injuries were confined to a concussion, so they were keeping him overnight for observation. Ling Ho chose to stay with her clients and contact Dan in the morning. It turned out that Nash and Mark fared rather well, given the severity of the crash. Both were sedated when the four visitors arrived, but an intern explained that none of the injuries was life-threatening. Mark had a dislocated shoulder which was in an elevated sling, and Nash had a broken right forearm and broken right shin bone. Both of his broken bones were in casts and the leg was elevated in a harness. The two men were expected to sleep through the night, but Bobbi elected to keep a vigil beside Mark's bed while the other three visitors decided to adjourn to the hospital cafeteria for a late-night snack.

By the time the two injured men awakened later that morning, Jimmy had been in contact with Franz on the "Victoria" to ascertain that no problems had arisen there; and he had spoken to Nathan Rosenberg who was catching a direct flight from Toronto to Orlando and would join them by noon. By mid-morning, Jimmy reported his activities and Nathan's pending arrival to Nash, who was wide-awake but completely immobile. A few minutes later, the two men were surprised by the unexpected appearance of Mark and Bobbi entering Nash's room, where Linda and Ling were already in attendance.

Although the visitor seating in the hospital room was not sufficient for accommodating everyone, Jimmy quickly rounded up additional chairs. Then he went into the hallway to ensure that no news reporters would be admitted (the floor nurse having already informed him that both reporters and cameramen were waiting in the lobby for an interview with the survivors).

The focus of conversation in the hospital room was on the bravery of Jake Johnson and his sad death. Nash reported that Jimmy had assisted him to send a letter of condolence to Jake's parents in Brampton outside Toronto. Then he compared his own recollection of the accident with Mark's. Both men told similar accounts of the amazing efficiency of Jake to rescue each of them, despite their semi-conscious conditions, prior to the explosion which enveloped him in flames when he was trying to rescue Dan Houlihan. Although thankful to be alive, they both grieved for their friend Jake, who lost his own life to save theirs and Dan's. Until they received their visitors that morning, both men had assumed Dan had been killed as well. They had no idea that he had been blown clear of the helicopter in the explosion. Ling informed everyone that she had been in touch with Dan by phone and, except for a nasty headache and a sore body, he was healthy and expected to be back on the job this afternoon. Both Nash and Mark expressed empathy for Dan in relating their own bruises and aching muscles.

Nash then briefed everyone on his closed door session with the orthopedic surgeon earlier that morning. Although the doctor would prefer to keep him under observation for several days, he conceded that Nash's injuries were not life-threatening. Providing Nash could arrange for round-the-clock professional nursing care, the doctor agreed to an air evacuation back to the "Victoria." Apparently, Nash had approached Linda earlier that morning about extending her vacation to accept a short-term assignment as "ship's nurse"; and, after confirming with her hospital administrator in Atlanta, she accepted the assignment with the proviso that the patient agree to obey medical orders. Nash reported that he had given his solemn promise (eliciting laughter by everyone, except Linda, who remained expressionless). Bobbi turned to Mark with a sly wink, but he quickly turned away, pretending not to notice.

A few blocks south of the hospital, in the law offices of Richter, Hansen and Morgan, the diminutive Albert Siegal was on his feet and clearly furious at the contrite Jack Swift seated at the conference table with Kurt Richter.

"This is the most idiotic action you could have taken, Swift," raged Siegal. "I told you to cause a small accident to make them aware of the danger in Florida, and you proceed to try and murder them. Are you out of your mind? How on earth do you think we can invest money with a dead man? Well, say something, don't just sit there staring at me."

"Albert," began Swift. "It was an accident . . ."

"Bullshit," screamed Siegal. "I know you hired a mechanic to cripple his helicopter. This was no accident, you fool."

"What I am trying to tell you, Albert, is that the mechanic was hired to disable the gear mechanism, so that the helicopter would have to make an emergency landing; but something went wrong and the rotor apparently stopped functioning completely, thereby causing the crash. It was accidental. I never intended for anyone to be injured."

"Look, Albert," interrupted the calm-looking Richter. "There is no question that Jack's man screwed up, but yelling and screaming is getting us nowhere. Thank God our office is closed today, so we have no witnesses. I suggest that we focus on our next steps rather than Jack's screw-up."

"Very well," answered Albert in a calmer tone, and he sat down for the first time since entering the conference room about twenty minutes earlier. "What do we do with this so-called mechanic? The feds are bound to find some clue in the wreckage and then learn of his involvement."

"I don't believe so," replied Swift. "He did his work after nightfall when the pilot was eating dinner in the terminal café. I personally kept watch from the edge of the building. There was nobody else in sight during the thirty minutes he was on the helicopter."

"Very well, but we still need him out of town as of noon yesterday. Arrange it with a couple of suitable witnesses. And make sure there are no more accidents. Do you understand?"

"Yes sir. I'll look after it this afternoon."

"Good. Now Kurt, how do you propose that we rescue this mess-up?"

It was almost three o'clock in the afternoon when three federal agents showed up at Florida Hospital Orlando requesting an interview with Nash and Mark. They had already interviewed Dan at the Kissimmee hospital; so they were seeking corroboration or conflict with his account of the accident. One of the men was with the Federal Aviation Agency and the other two were with the Federal Bureau of Investigation. They requested separate interviews with Mark and Nash. Mark had already checked out of his room; so the agents arranged for an empty office where they could meet with him privately. Bobbi was politely requested to wait outside.

Mark told them of the sudden shaking in the air at what he assumed to be at only two or three thousand feet altitude. He estimated that they began to lose altitude quickly as Jake fought to gain control of the helicopter. But, then he admitted to complete panic as the machine rolled upside down and seemed to corkscrew downward. He recalled glancing up to see Jake continuing to wrestle with his controls, and actually succeed in turning the machine upright just before a resounding impact with the ground that must have broken the left skid, because he remembered being at a forty-five-degree angle and having severe pain in trying to reach his harness release (the pain was caused, he learned later, by his dislocated shoulder). The machine's engine had been turned off, but he could smell fuel fumes and knew he had to get out. Nevertheless, he could not free himself. He watched Jake release an apparently unconscious Nash on the other side of the seat and pull him to safety prior to returning to the rear seat and releasing his harness. Jake then pulled on his injured shoulder causing him to lose consciousness from the pain. His next recollection was lying on the ground some distance from the crash site where he was able to see Jake opening the right front door and reaching in to release Dan's harness just as the explosion obliterated the scene from his sight. He believed that he must have passed out again, to be awakened by two emergency medical aides securing him to a stretcher, prior to loading him next to Nash on the hospital helicopter.

The three agents thanked him for his concise account; and then they gathered up their notes and tape recorder to head up to Nash's room for a repeat performance. Mark joined Bobbi in the waiting room where he was thankful to find a soft, upholstered chair to replace the hard chair in the office.

After asking Linda and Ling to wait outside, the federal agents asked Nash for his account. They were not surprised to learn that he lost consciousness upon impact, after reciting a very similar account to Mark's about the frightening descent. They thanked him for his cooperation and collected his identification and contact numbers for the "Victoria," before departing and informing the two women that they were welcome to return to their patient.

As they descended in the elevator, the FAA inspector turned to the FBI agents and said: "The DEA agent's report of witnessing a man on the copter at Herndon when he was tailing Jack Swift appears to be substantiated by these similar accounts of the mechanical problems—this crash appears to be no accident." The other two men nodded grimly, and one replied: "Unfortunately, his account of the apparent sabotage did not get reported prior to the helicopter crash, a critical communication lapse that will cause somebody's ass to get kicked."

⁓

After picking up Nathan Rosenberg at the Orlando airport, Jimmy Quickfoot was able to coordinate the transportation back to the "Victoria." He arranged for Mark, Bobbi, Dan and himself to return by limousine and helicopter at four that afternoon, whereas Nathan would stay overnight to visit with Nash and possibly return with Ling, Linda and Nash following morning in the hospital helicopter (to accommodate Nash's elevated leg).

The first group landed on the "Victoria" in ample time for the cocktail hour. But Mark, who was advised to refrain from alcohol while he was taking pain medicine, treated himself to a pre-dinner nap, while Bobbi joined Jimmy, Franz and Dan in the main lounge to re-visit the events of the past twenty-four hours. The conversation was focused on Dan's interpretation of the crash incident and its probable cause. However, despite his pleasant manner after his harrowing experience, the big man was not very forthcoming about interpreting the cause or the implications of the crash. He did advise Franz that a continuation of the round-the-clock vigil on the "Victoria" would be a prudent precaution.

After Nash finished his five o'clock hospital dinner (tastier than he expected), he asked the two ladies to leave him alone with his colleague, Nathan, for a couple of hours, in order to catch up on company business. So Ling ordered a cab and took Linda to one of her favorite restaurants in Winter Park for dinner. After spending all day together in the helicopter and hospital, the two women had discovered they enjoyed each other's company; so the dinner was a pleasant event for both of them. Not only was the food good, but Linda found Ling's accounts of her occupation really fascinating; and Ling, in turn, enjoyed hearing of Linda's hospital adventures. The revelation that Ling had to learn body joints and pressure points, in order to gain physical advantages over much larger people, gave the two of them a common interest in the human body and how it works, or does not. Linda vowed to learn more about martial arts, not just for self defense, but as an effective exercise program.

❧

While Linda and Ling were dining, Nash's hospital bed was transformed into a conference table for computer spread sheets and financial statements on the current progress of Logan Homes. Although the United States housing market was down because of the recession, the Canadian market appeared to be gaining ground, and Logan Homes had profited in Nash's absence. Of course, Nathan was more interested in what knowledge Nash had collected in Florida, and in how soon they could get started on their new project. The two men had been working together for six years, and both of them felt a genuine affection for the other. Although the much-shorter Nathan was twenty-five years younger than his employer, his keen intellect and seemingly tireless energy proved a match for the boundless enthusiasm of Nash Logan.

Nash admitted to Nathan that Mark Wilkins had thrown so much information at him during the past week, that he felt saturated and unable to sift it into logical decision-making units. However, he believed that Mark would end the week by coordinating it all into clear-cut categories which would launch them into a rational course of action. In the interim, however, their dealings with Mr. Siegal and his colleagues was an annoying side-issue that filtered the fun out of the development process. By the end of the allocated two hours, they had brought each other up-to-date and they were ready to concentrate on Florida. Nash asked Nathan to arrange transport over to the yacht at Fort Pierce early the next morning in time to attend Mark's morning session, in addition to other sessions over the remaining three days—they had lost a day because of this annoying hospital stay, but he hoped that they could compensate for it by a faster "summation-and-conclusions" process, now that Nathan had joined them. Nathan left just before the two women returned from dinner, only to find their patient exhausted from his meeting.

"You two should find a nearby hotel and get a good night's rest," said Nash from his bed.

"I'm afraid not," replied Ling with a smile. "I'm under contract to provide security twenty-four hours per day, so you'll just have to put up with me overnight."

"And I have just accepted a contract for special nursing services," added Linda, as she placed her hand on Nash's forehead to check his temperature, "so you will have the added pleasure of spending the night with two women."

"Well," responded Nash with a sad smile, "ordinarily, that would be an exciting proposition, but tonight I feel too tired to get excited about anything."

The two women exchanged quiet smiles and welcomed the hospital nurse who arrived with the evening pain and sleep medications for Nash. Within a few minutes, their incapacitated employer was asleep for the night.

DAY 11

Monday, April 5, 2010

Breakfast was a somber occasion for the guests of the "Victoria" without the always-cheerful Jake Johnson to set the mood. People wandered to the table over the course of an hour; and the conversation was subdued and lacking energy.

However, Mark was a paid consultant contracted to complete his assignment. So, promptly at eight o'clock, he moved to the conference table and prepared to begin the topic delayed from yesterday. The others soon joined him. But, before he began, the noise of a helicopter landing on the rear deck captured everyone's attention. Jimmy rushed out to the deck and greeted the only passenger, Nathan Rosenberg. Carlos took Nathan's suitcase to a guest cabin, and Nathan joined the group around the conference table.

"Sorry to be late for your morning meeting," Nathan announced to everyone, before directing his attention to Mark, "but I would like to substitute for Nash, who promises to join us before noon."

"No problem," replied Mark, waving his one good arm. "We had just gathered here when you arrived; so you haven't missed anything. Although we lost a full day from our schedule yesterday by our tragic accident, I am prepared to pick up today regardless of our lack of the helicopter. I plan to brief everyone on both Planning Districts 10 and 11, while I describe their features on the mounted map with my one remaining good arm. Since Nash is missing this session, I must rely on Jimmy's notes, and perhaps Bobbi's tape recorder, to provide a record for him to catch up on this session. You all should have a copy of the Planning Districts map. If not, I have additional copies you can use to follow along with me through our oral tour.

"When Nash arrives to join us later this morning, Captain Erickson will begin his cruise down the coast to Fort Lauderdale and I will point out highlights that can be seen from the ocean—not as comprehensive as touring by helicopter, but these last two districts do not offer as many development opportunities as other parts of the state. I should explain to you, Nathan, that we have been touring the 11 Planning Districts of Florida in chronological order—one district per day. Prior to the crash, we had completed tours of nine districts; so we just have these two left to examine. The reference map I passed out shows these final two districts with a total of seven counties: four in District 10, referred to as the Treasure Coast, presumably because of the shipwrecks of sailing vessels in prior centuries, but equally symbolized by the colonies of extremely wealthy people along the beachfront; and three more counties in District 11, of which two are almost completely urbanized and the third includes the sparsely-populated lower Everglades and the Florida Keys."

"Great, Mark. I understand. Please don't impede any of your presentation for special attention to my newcomer status. I will sing out if I need help."

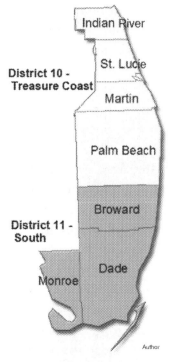

Exhibit 29:
Planning Districts
10 & 11.

"Okay, we will carry on as planned," resumed Mark. "Planning District 10 contains four coastal counties known as the 'Treasure Coast,' the location of some of the wealthiest enclaves in Florida. Palm Beach is the most famous, dating back to Flagler's luxurious hotels of a century ago, and continuing without major interruption as a winter vacation place for multi-millionaires ever since. It was the center of an exciting new form of residential and resort architecture named Mediterranean Revival, that was championed by Architect Addison Misner, although a wide range of styles and eclectic designs were generated by many famous architects. During the first three decades of the 20th Century, the world's rich and famous people paid enormous sums of money to outdo each other in palatial mansions. Palm Beach became a social playground for the wealthy. In 2000, Palm Beach County ranked third in the country for per capita income of one-hundred-and-ten-thousand dollars.

"In the southern part of the county, Boca Raton also is known as an elegant address. With fewer than one-thousand residents in 1950, the city population multiplied to seven-thousand by 1960; and it includes close to ninety-thousand residents today (despite promises to limit growth in the 1990s). Its growth was strongly influenced by Arthur Vining Davis's developments for the affluent; coupled with Addison Misner's building architecture, which was already famous in Palm Beach.

"North of Palm Beach in Martin County, the seventeen-mile-long Jupiter Island has become a valued enclave for rich people of many origins, with median home prices in the millions of dollars and personal income well over two-hundred-thousand dollars per year. Although Florida contains many communities of wealthy residents (Fisher Island in Biscayne Bay being tops in the nation), the southern portion of the Treasure Coast is best known for its concentration of the rich and famous.

"North of Martin County is St. Lucie County, which I described earlier as one of the lot-sales sites of the Mackle Brothers and General Development Corporation. Although St. Lucie does contain a few affluent enclaves, it primarily attracts modest-price and even low-price residents. This has become the case also with Indian River County, as production builders invaded this 'largest citrus-producing county' in Florida during the past fifteen years. Prior to that, the barrier island, known as 'Hutchison Island', and its centerpiece, Vero Beach, were favored by wealthy snowbirds who settled 'Johns Island' community initially, and then 'Windsor' (a 'new urbanism' site plan by Andres Duany and his colleagues), 'Orchid Island', 'Sailfish Point' and many oceanfront condominiums.

"Treasure Coast contains a total population approaching two-million residents (not counting seasonal snowbirds), the majority of whom (75 percent) are in Palm Beach County. All these counties have older populations than the overall state, with its median age above forty years (Charlotte County on the Gulf coast is Florida's highest-age county with a median age of fifty-five years). Of course, these ages are for recorded residents and exclude many of the snowbirds who maintain their resident addresses elsewhere.

"In comparison, the largely-urbanized Planning District 11 with over four-million residents (exclusive of Munroe County with only eighty-thousand residents in the Everglades and Florida Keys), contains a much younger population, with Miami-Dade having a median age under thirty-eight years and Broward County having a median age of thirty-nine years. Assuming the continuing prohibition of further incursion into the Everglades, there is no significant amount of developable land remaining in this Planning District.

"These Southeast Florida Planning Districts have led the state in growth over the past twenty-five years until they now are virtually saturated with human development, assuming conservation of the Everglades prohibits future human incursion.

"After the national real estate crash of 1974, followed by the national economic recession of 1980-1982, the Florida real estate boom continued, particularly in southeast Florida. In the early 1950s, Broward County (centered on Fort Lauderdale) was home to eighty-five-thousand residents in its twelve-hundred-square miles. Most people lived in rural villages adjacent to farmland. During that decade, a great transformation in resort and retirement communities took place, causing the population to quadruple by 1960 and double again by 1970. By 1980, Broward had reached one-million residents. Over the next thirty years, the population grew to almost two million, as available land for continuing growth had dwindled.

Broward County has twenty-nine separate municipalities. Next-door neighbor, Palm Beach County, is even more fragmented with thirty-five municipalities. Like the state itself, both of these counties contain highly-diversified populations, including residents from many states and other countries, as well as many groups with diverse ethnic and religious backgrounds. Infrastructure to service this growth has strained local and state government budgets, especially during The Great Recession of 2008-09 when government revenues declined everywhere.

"It was during this same period in the 1970s that the giant International Telephone and Telegraph Company (ITT) chose to open its planned one-hundred-thousand-acre (subsequently reduced to forty-two-thousand acres) retirement community, called Palm Coast, in the slash pine forests of Flagler County on I-95 between Jacksonville and Daytona Beach. The huge conglomerate poured money into its creation for the next twenty-five years without showing a profit, before finally selling off the remaining undeveloped properties to other developers. Currently, it has become the city of Palm Coast, with increasing numbers of younger people arriving to service the retiree residents. But, during this recession, it is experiencing a record number of foreclosures.

"In the early 1990s, Florida's one-hundred years of growth was badly wounded by the massive failures of Savings and Loan institutions across the country. Florida contributed to this recession with extraordinarily bad investments due to over-confidence in the real estate business. More than two-hundred-thousand Floridians lost their jobs between 1988 and 1993—unemployment exceeded the national average. It was considered the worst economic crisis since The Great Depression, but it was soon forgotten in the surge of optimism that fostered an even greater real estate price run-up leading to The Great Recession of 2008-09, which still has not achieved recovery.

"In 1992, Hurricane Andrew crashed through Miami, to add physical disaster to the economic recession sweeping the country. But, in reality, this environmental disaster proved to stimulate an economic recovery by massive federal assistance and insurance claims. Prosperity returned and a new wave of migration fueled the growth cycle again. New wealth poured into the state and developers jumped onto a bandwagon of bigger and better homes and new communities. Luxury was manifested in every part of the state, but especially in the south where the status of the affluent became associated with 'big.' The condominium became an integral part of Florida housing and was sought after, especially by foreign buyers who could come to fantasy land on vacation and then 'lock-it-and-leave-it' until their next visit. In the year 2000, almost five-hundred-thousand homes were recorded as vacation homes and the total number of condominium apartments exceeded one million—an estimated half of the entire nation's inventory. Florida led the nation in gated communities.

"The love affair of affluent householders with Florida was not confined to southern locations. The Florida Panhandle, re-named the 'Emerald Coast', experienced a rush of wealthy second-home buyers, with many purchasing second and third vacation and investment homes. Condominium prices along the white sand beaches soared to new heights, right up until the recession halt in the last quarter of 2007. Although many parts of Florida experienced rapid growth in the 1990s and afterward, Southwest Florida from Tampa through Naples was outstanding for its condominiums of every size, coupled with new golf course communities.

"In 1950, Collier County in southwest Florida had a population of fewer than six-thousand-five-hundred residents. 'Naples-by-the-Sea' was founded in the 1880s as a winter resort for a few wealthy northerners, mostly invalids. It did not attract large numbers of tourists until the 1950s. John Glen Sample purchased two square miles from the Collier family in the heart of Naples and developed 'Port Royal' as the city's most luxurious neighborhood. The completion of I-75 through Florida to Naples and beyond to Miami, in addition to the Southwest Regional Airport at Fort Myers, generated new growth in this southwest corner of the state. In 2000, Naples became the nation's highest-ranked metropolitan area in personal income (over forty-three-thousand dollars), even though fewer than half its residents worked for weekly wages. Today, Collier County is approaching three-hundred-and-fifty-thousand residents with many more in the winter season.

"Coastal development extends from Naples north to Fort Myers, with only sporadic vacant waterfront north of there to Sarasota County where coastal development is solid north to Hernando County, and then mangrove growth dominates the coast up to Apalachicola Bay. In Lee County, immediately north of Collier County, the extravagant 'Bonita Bay' resort community was developed next to the village of Bonita Springs and it filled up with wealthy northerners dwelling in high-rise condominiums, as well as single-family homes. The developer expanded to five other communities in Lee County before The Great Recession of 2007-09 caused its bankruptcy.

Many other gated communities for the affluent, most with signature golf courses, were generated through the 1980s, 1990s and 2000s in Lee and Collier Counties as buyers surged in from northern states and other countries to purchase vacation homes. Both luxury condominiums and single family mansions became commonplace as well as more modest-price dwellings for the status-seeking less affluent consumers. However, the development bonanza came to a sudden halt with The Great Recession, and Lee County subsequently acquired the highest rate of foreclosures in the country. Now, I suggest we take a ten-minute break, so that I can take another pain pill before I continue."

Jackson James had one special skill in his life and he had practiced it since he learned auto mechanics in high school. By the time he was twenty-five, he was widely known in Orlando as an expert in all kinds of vehicle mechanics, including airplanes and helicopters. His skills had been used by Jack Swift for several assignments over past years, and he was the logical choice for disabling the Logan helicopter. When he left the airport after performing his skill that evening, a second FBI agent had been summoned to follow him to his vehicle and record the license plate identification. He was not a difficult person for the federal agents to track down, especially since he dutifully had phoned in sick the next morning to his supervisor at the repair hangar where he was employed at Herndon Airport.

Jackson made the mistake of owning an easily identifiable, florescent green, custom-body, two-seat automobile that he proudly drove down I-4 from Orlando to the Tampa Airport the next morning, just as Jack Swift had instructed him. His ticket to Mexico would be waiting at the American Airlines counter. But he never picked it up.

That morning, no fewer than four separate Florida State Troopers reported the bright green car traveling west on I-4 in response to the all-points bulletin requested by federal officials shortly after midnight on the fifth of April. The bulletin required only notification of the vehicle's whereabouts, rather than detention of the driver. DEA agents identified the vehicle as it passed by Lakeland and initiated visual surveillance from there to the Tampa Airport long-term parking lot. As he got out of his car, he was surrounded by five DEA agents, including the imposing frame of DEA Division Director Jonas Jensen.

"Planning on a little vacation trip, Jackson?" boomed Jonas.

"So what," answered James with a smirk? "What's it to you?"

"We have slightly different plans for you, my man. Please read him his rights, Jim, and charge him with murder. Then bring him to our office for a little chat, before we turn him over to the county sheriff. I will meet you there. First, I want to phone Nash Logan to inform him of our arrest and extend our condolences over the death of his pilot."

Jonas Jensen's "little chat" with Jackson James turned out to be six hours long before the surly mechanic revealed all of the assignments he had performed for Jack Swift over a period of several years. Although none of the others had resulted in murder, they did present ample evidence of Swift's involvement in a number of extortion and blackmail cases that were awaiting resolution.

"Jensen requested an immediate warrant for Swift's arrest on the murder charge, as well as less-serious extortion and blackmail charges. It was his plan to hold Swift incommunicado while applying surveillance to Siegal and Richter, in case they attempted to flee the country. He notified Dan Houlihan to remain alert in case of possible reprisal by Siegal's drug-dealing colleagues in other countries.

Meanwhile, Mark Wilkins' conference aboard the yacht "Victoria" continued after the mid-morning break.

"Perhaps the most dispersed Florida growth since the 1980s was caused by retirees. Although the wealthiest seniors tended to locate in resort communities, a surge of modest-income retirees has located in designated retirement and mobile home communities throughout many parts of the state.

"The concept of retirement is a relatively recent phenomenon. Historically, males worked until death or infirmity. Retirement emerged with the rise of the industrial society, coupled with longer life-spans. In 1950, over half of American men aged sixty-five were still working. But, by 2000, only 8 percent of this age group was in the workforce. The impact of trade unions and pension plans for workers at all pay levels, as well as for those in government service, had made possible a new era of retirees.

"Financed old age had fostered an emergent proliferation of retirement communities, ranging from recreation communities for active seniors, to care communities providing a variety of services, ranging from congregate meals and health programs to assisted living and skilled nursing care. Definitions were confusing, since they all went under the generic title of retirement communities. The increase in life expectancy over the past century has climbed over thirty years, and it continues to grow, along with better health care for seniors.

"Florida's warm climate and modest cost of living have attracted more seniors than other states; it became known as a refuge for seniors even in the 1930s. By the 1980s, the increase of seniors in Florida had reached its zenith as a major population shift, immigrants to Florida being assisted on their way by corporate and government pension plans. According to one estimate, over two-million war veterans lived in Florida in the 1990s. At the same time, Miami became a center for Jewish migrants, primarily from New York City. Municipalities throughout the state, eager to cash in on these revenue-generating seniors, began promoting their advantages to retired persons. During the 1990s, Florida attracted three times more elderly than its nearest competitor, California.

"If Del Webb was the first developer to start a retirement community in Florida, H. Irwin Levy was the first to start an affordable retirement community, in 1968, when he launched

'Century City' on six-hundred-and-eighty-five acres in West Palm Beach. Walk-up apartments (soon to be called condominiums) sold for nine-thousand dollars, with access to golf courses, clubhouses and swimming pools—a major improvement from retirement hotels that had previously housed seniors. Although he charged for the use of recreation facilities, the low initial cost attracted new residents in large numbers, especially Jewish migrants from New York. He advertised: 'We give years to your life and life to your years.'

"Levy continued to build retirement condominiums throughout southeast Florida, completing over thirty-thousand in his lifetime. Other developers soon followed Levy's lead in new retirement communities in Florida's urban areas, as well as free-standing locations such as the huge Port Charlotte development of the Mackle Brothers. By 2000, Clearwater had the distinction of the highest percentage of residents over age sixty-five and Venice had the highest median age of almost sixty-nine (10 percent of Venetians were over age eighty-five). But, over the past twenty years, major urban retiree centers have faded away, as cities like Miami Beach and St. Petersburg have transformed their waterfronts into more vibrant attractions catering to younger adults. Retirees, most now originating from low-density suburban areas, looked for more peaceful surroundings and found them, especially in Central Florida where gated communities emerged like vegetable crops dedicated only to active seniors. The most successful, as described earlier in our tour of Planning District 6, is The Villages, that now spreads over Lake, Marion and Sumter Counties, with room for over one-hundred-thousand residents. It is touted as a recreation paradise, with sixteen golf courses and over four-hundred social clubs and shopping opportunities within a short drive of every resident's golf cart. The land was formerly a mobile-home park on US 27/441, and named Orange Blossom Gardens, when Harold Schwartz purchased it in 1982. It became the fastest-selling community in the country within twenty years.

"Florida is projected to continue expanding its elderly population, with persons above age fifty-four reaching over ten million by 2030, and continuing at a faster growth rate than that of the state's overall population. Current projections for this growth of seniors reach almost 38 percent of the state population by 2030, compared with 27 percent in 2000. The over-eighty population rises from under 17 percent to over 20 percent of seniors during this period.

"In sum, Florida will contain the most seniors, and it will have the highest median age, of any state in the nation. The age of new home buyers also will increase, thereby escalating the number of potential consumers at a faster growth rate than the overall population.

"The retiree migration to Florida thus far has been primarily a white movement. Up until recently, most African-Americans did not enjoy the longevity or income to participate. Of course, up until the 1980s, they were specifically not welcome by lingering remains of racial segregation. Lack of health insurance among seniors of all races was also an impediment to Florida migration up until the introduction of Medicare and Medicaid. By 2004, Florida had the highest per capita Medicare enrollment in the United States.

"The popularity of mobile-home parks and seasonal recreation-vehicle parks for active adults expanded exponentially in the 1980s and 1990s, as the combination of economy and mobility appealed to growing numbers of modest-income seniors. Since the 1936 opening of the country's first 'trailer park' in Bradenton, the custom of leasing pads for mobile homes provided a lower housing outlay (vehicle cost plus monthly rent), and it set the example for increasing numbers of long-term land trusts for land rental, to decrease the costs of permanent housing today. However, the fear of hurricane damage, coupled with the increasing value of well-located mobile-home parks for alternative uses, has reduced the expansion of these living environments for retirees. Nevertheless, Florida still records over three-thousand such parks. In addition, most of these parks require car travel for shopping and recreation activities, which has contributed to Florida having the unenviable state record of the highest number of elderly drivers killed in vehicle accidents.

"Although other states increase their immigration of seniors, Florida still leads the nation. Despite rising costs and hurricane damage, Florida's combination of warm climate and low cost still proves a strong magnet. Clearly, the Logan plans to create a better living environment at reduced costs should be a welcome addition to this state. Nash's objective of creating better living conditions for all income groups could set a new standard for other developers to pursue, and thereby improve Florida's environment for all residents."

The sound of a helicopter approaching in the morning sky caused Mark to smile before concluding his remarks: "I am truly astonished to complete my remarks concurrently with the arrival of our mutual employer. But it's true, and I suggest we all gather on-deck to welcome him back to his nautical home."

The medical evacuation helicopter landed on the rear deck of the "Victoria" just before noon. The disembarkation of Nash was preceded by that of Ling and Linda, as well as the helicopter medic, who enlisted the help of Carlos and Alfredo to transfer Nash in his wheel chair down to the deck. The audience of onlookers broke into applause at the return of their host and employer. Then Linda took charge and wheeled her patient into the main lounge dining area in preparation for lunch. She made it clear to Nash and his colleagues that he would need to retire to his cabin for a rest after lunch. Dan Houlihan requested a minute alone with Nash to report that Jonas Jensen had phoned him to report the arrest of the suspected saboteur, Jackson James. Captain Ericksson then made an appearance to confirm his cruise plan with Nash, prior to everyone being seated at two tables and lunch being served by Jose and Alfredo.

The "Victoria" left the Fort Pierce dock at one-thirty that afternoon after Nash had been safely carried to his cabin and the leg elevation apparatus erected. Linda sternly insisted that he swallow sleep and pain medications, prior to a minimum of one hour's rest. She left him alone for that period, subject to an alarm buzzer which she had purchased in Orlando for him to summon her if necessary. Mark also took this opportunity for a nap with the aid of pain and sleep medication. As Linda anticipated, the hour passed without interruption, allowing her to sit on the upper deck with Bobbi and Ling, to enjoy the view as the "Victoria" proceeded out to sea via the channel through Hutchison Island. Captain Ericksson then set a course south, parallel to the shore, so they all could view the coastal development of Southeast Florida.

At two-thirty in the afternoon, Linda and Bobbi went below to awaken Nash and Mark. Mark immediately went to the bridge and asked Franz to notify everyone aboard that he and Nash would gather on the stern deck outside the main lounge to comment on shoreline development (he assumed it would be too difficult to carry Nash to the upper deck). Franz reported, rather hesitantly, that Carlos and Alfredo were occupied on another task, so Mark recruited Dan and Jimmy to go below to carry Nash up to meet Mark on the stern deck.

"Ladies and gentlemen," began Mark, as soon as everyone was seated, "we have been traveling along South Hutchison Island, the major barrier island along this coast, and we have already passed the Florida Power and Light Nuclear Plant and a variety of condominium developments, the last one on the south end of the island being the upscale community of Sailfish Point, developed in the 1980s by the Mobil Land Company, complete with a large, sheltered yacht basin and a championship golf course.

"The charming city of Stuart, with its own executive airport, is on the mainland. We now are passing a state park to reach the Hobe Sound National Wildlife Refuge and then Hobe Sound Beach with the small village of Hobe Sound on the mainland—the home of golfer Greg Norman and several other wealthy residents. Immediately south of Hobe Sound is the seventeen-mile-long Jupiter Island which also houses many wealthy inhabitants. You can see their mansions as we approach the island."

"This is extraordinary," commented Linda. "I had no idea so many wealthy families congregated north of Palm Beach."

"Yes, you might consider Jupiter Island and Hobe Sound to be the Palm Beach overflow area. Remember, the island of Palm Beach was virtually filled up prior to the 1950s. So these rich people moved north to equally pleasant beaches and yacht harbors. We are just passing the border between Martin and Palm Beach Counties and we are coming up on Jupiter Inlet that provides access to a large area of inland waterways for yacht mooring. Ahead is the lengthy Juno Beach leading to Palm Beach Shores, the initial overflow from Palm Beach. North Palm Beach and Riviera Beach adjoin these coastal communities inland. The city of West Palm Beach is opposite the island of Palm Beach to the south."

The ostentatious display of wealth in the mansions lining the beachfront over the next several miles was overwhelming for the onlookers aboard the "Victoria." Most of them just gazed in awe, without making comments of any kind. Mark, too, elected to remain silent and let the extravagant Palm Beach scenery speak for itself. The barrier island narrowed south of Palm Beach, allowing them views of the mainland communities of Lake Worth, Lantana, Boynton Beach and Delray Beach, before the resumption of showpiece architecture in Boca Raton.

Exhibit 30: Palm Beach Waterfront.
Photograph courtesy of The Palm Beach Proper and Michael Kagdis

It was about this time that Mark noticed the yacht's direction was taking them farther from the shore. He asked Jimmy to go up to the bridge and inquire of Captain Ericksson why he was headed farther out to sea.

When Jimmy returned some ten minutes later, his face appeared pale as he asked for everyone's attention. "Ladies and gentlemen, the captain has asked me to inform you that our yacht and everyone on it are under the direct control of Mr. Albert Siegal and his colleagues, who sneaked aboard just before we left the dock in Fort Pierce. They have imprisoned Carlos and Alfredo, leaving only Pierre, Marie and Jose to prepare and serve food. He also told me to tell you that they have searched all of the cabins and confiscated cell phones and computers, except for missing phones belonging to Mr. Houlihan, Ms. Ho and Mrs. Wilkins. They have instructed me to collect these phones, along with weapons from Houlihan and Ho, and deliver them to the bridge. Everyone else is to stay seated until further notice. Please note the armed guards keeping watch from the upper deck."

Everyone looked up to confirm the presence of two men with automatic weapons looking down upon them from the upper deck, the same two men who had accompanied Swift on his visit a few days earlier. Although Dan and Ling were visibly embarrassed by this silent hijacking of the "Victoria" while it was under their protection, they had no choice but to surrender their weapons and phones to Jimmy. Bobbi added her phone without comment, and Jimmy gathered them all in his arms for the return trip to the bridge.

"This is outrageous," fumed Nash. "How did these gangsters come aboard without anyone seeing them? And where do they plan to take us? Jimmy, please tell Siegal that I must speak to him immediately."

"Yes sir, Mr. Logan. I will convey your message right away." Jimmy left for the bridge with his contraband phones and weapons.

Prior to the departure of the "Victoria" from Fort Pierce, a group of six agents from the DEA and the FBI met in Jonas "JJ" Jensen's conference room in Tampa. Their request for local police agencies in Orlando to find and detain Jack Swift, Kurt Richter and Albert Siegal on suspicion of murder had produced no results, despite accompanying alerts to all railway, bus and airport security officials across Florida, including notification to executive airports and immigration services. All three men had disappeared overnight without a trace. Police searches of each of their homes revealed that the wives of Swift and Richter (Siegal lived alone) knew nothing of any travel plans. Automobiles registered to each of the men had been located at their offices and their secretaries appeared equally uninformed of their whereabouts. A search of records at rental agencies and limousine services revealed nothing. During the morning of the fifth of April, the three men had simply vanished.

"Ladies and gentlemen," said Jonas, "there is no question that our three perpetrators were helped by accomplices who drove them and/or flew them somewhere. They did not leave the country through normal channels, but they could easily be in another state in this country by now. And we have no vehicle identification with which to trace them."

"What about a boat, JJ?" offered one of the two female agents at the table.

"Yes, Siegal owns a forty-two-foot sport fisherman moored at New Smyrna Beach, and, according to local police, it is still moored there. The other two don't own boats. We have State Police checking on South Florida boats owned by known Esperanza drug contacts, as well as charter services throughout the state—nothing to report thus far. I keep coming back to transport out of Orlando. Somebody drove them somewhere."

"Absolutely," responded the senior FBI agent at the table. "I believe we must identify all of their known accomplices in their land financing operations and begin an interview process without delay."

"You are right on target, Milt," said Jonas. "Let's focus on this potential by sending two of your agents to the offices of Swift, Richter and Siegal. Gather all the relationship info available and meet at the FBI office in Orlando tomorrow afternoon to compare our lists before hitting the pavement." Everyone around the table nodded agreement with the DEA Director, who added: "See you all there."

Albert Siegal had agreed to meet with the passengers in the main lounge of the "Victoria" and everyone had moved inside. Linda had been able to push Nash's wheel-chair without difficulty, although she had not resolved the future problem of moving him to his cabin below without Carlos and Alfredo. Siegal arrived with the two large men who previously had accompanied Jack Swift and described as Jones and Johnson. Siegal took a chair on one side of the corner conference table and his two bodyguards stood behind him surveying the unhappy passengers.

"Good afternoon everyone," began the diminutive Siegal. "First of all, I must apologize for commandeering your yacht; but, as a famous man once said, 'Desperate times call for desperate measures.' As some of you may know, my name is Albert Siegal, and I have the pleasure of knowing Mr. Logan and Dr. Wilkins from our dinner Saturday night. Unfortunately, one of my associates made a stupid mistake, and we are now being sought by the police. So, we must borrow your yacht to avoid unpleasant penalties.

"We have no intentions of harming any of you; unless, of course, you should attempt something foolish to keep us from our objective. This is a reasonably fast vessel and we should arrive at our destination before morning when we will leave your yacht. You will then have to negotiate with local officials for your return trip to Florida. I am sure you will have no difficulty. In the interim, I have left your cooks and steward free to prepare and serve meals. Captain Ericksson and our group will dine and sleep on the upper deck and bridge; so you will be free to socialize on the other decks. We have removed all communications equipment from the lower decks and from your individual keeping. There is no opportunity for heroes. I understand that we have crossed the twelve-mile limit and, therefore, we are now in international waters, so you cannot anticipate a miraculous Coast Guard rescue. Do you have any questions?"

"Yes," replied Bobbi. "I have two questions. First, are Carlos and Alfredo injured? If so, we would like to offer care to them. Second, where are we headed?"

"Excellent questions, Mrs. Wilkins. Your two crew members are in good health, but detained in the crew quarters to prevent them acting foolishly. There is no need for you to be concerned. Second, since your clever mind will soon figure it out anyway, I will tell you that we are headed for the port of Matanzas on the northern coast of Cuba, where we will be met and flown to another undisclosed destination. As I mentioned, we should arrive before morning and you will be free to return tomorrow. Now, I must leave you to ensure that your captain stays on course. Please remain calm and peaceful during the remainder of our cruise together."

"Well, folks," began Mark after Siegal's departure, "We are in an unfortunate situation that is frightening for all of us. However, I am sure that Nash agrees that we have no option except to sit tight and hope for the best."

"Absolutely, Mark", responded Nash. "Much as I would like to subdue these criminals, now is not the time or place. Please do not attempt any heroics that could endanger all of our lives. In fact, as a diversion from our predicament, Mark, I suggest that you continue with your description of Southeast Florida."

"Sure thing, Nash! I regret that we cannot examine additional South Florida waterfront, but I trust that you learned something from your cruise down to Boca Raton. Hopefully, you can see more on our trip north tomorrow or the day after. Although Nash and I are still in considerable pain from our injuries, we are determined to complete our mission on this cruise.

"Tomorrow, regardless of where we are located, I plan a brief wrap-up of development along the Atlantic Ridge—the southeast coastal area that you have been viewing—prior to presentation of a location-decision matrix within the parameters of the ten planning districts we have described and visited on this trip. This matrix should establish the basis for selecting a more specific location and defining parameters for proceeding with the new community on our final-day cruise back to Jacksonville. Since it is now the beginning of the cocktail hour, Nash and I wish you all cheers from us non-alcohol patients on pain pills."

"Mr. Jensen," said his secretary, "I am sorry to interrupt you in the middle of your research, but I believe the phone call I just received may have some bearing on the Siegal investigation."

"Sure, Mary, what have you got?" replied Jonas, looking up from his desk.

"I received a phone call from your brother-in-law, Tony DiMartino, a few minutes ago. He told me that a Mr. Duncan MacTavish, the General Counsel for Logan Homes in Toronto, phoned him to report that he is unable to contact Nash Logan or his Executive Vice President, Nathan Rosenberg, by cell phone or ship-to-shore phone aboard the yacht 'Victoria.' Mr. MacTavish wondered if Tony might have some insight as to why communications are down. Tony told him that he would look into it, but he also was unable to communicate with anyone aboard the 'Victoria.' And, in addition, he learned that the captain of the 'Victoria' cancelled his mooring reservation at Fort Lauderdale for tonight. Now, Mr. Jensen, I certainly don't want to advise you on this investigation, but these issues seem too major to be coincidental."

"Mary, you are a gem," shouted Jonas, as he grabbed his phone and hit a speed dial for the U.S. Coast Guard. "Hi Jack, it's JJ, and I have some urgent business for you. I have strong reason to believe that a two-hundred-foot yacht named 'Victoria' has been hi-jacked by one or more murder suspects from Florida who are connected to the international drug trade. It left Fort Pierce early this afternoon and it has blocked all communications, both in-coming and out-going. I want these guys badly, Jack. Will you get back to me ASAP? I will not leave this phone until I hear from you. Thank you, my friend."

JJ then hit another speed dial: "Hi, Milt, it's JJ, and I've got a strong lead that the Siegal group may have hi-jacked the Logan yacht out of Fort Pierce. I have contacted Captain Jack Stuart at the Coast Guard and he is investigating. In the meantime, could you get someone over to Fort Pierce and see what we can pick up from that end? Thanks Milt."

JJ then hit a third speed dial: "Hi, Tony, it's JJ. Your phone call was right on target. The safe passage I promised your friends from

Toronto is in jeopardy, but I've got the Coast Guard and the FBI on the job. Thanks for your quick action, good buddy."

Mary stood at JJ's door: "Captain Stuart is on the other line."

"Thanks Mary. Hello, Jack, let me put you on the speaker so that Mary can take notes."

"JJ, we have a satellite fix on your yacht. It is located twenty-five miles east of Miami and headed due south at top speed. It will not respond to our communications. Can you give me a typed directive that suspected United States' murderers are aboard? By the way, this yacht is registered in Toronto, so I am already on to the Canadian Consul in Miami for clearance to board. She should give me a formal positive reply as soon as I can copy her on your directive. I also have lined up a detachment of Navy Seals in Key West to make ready for action."

"Is that all? What took you so long? I will email the murderer directive to you within fifteen minutes. I love you, baby."

"Okay, get me the directive and we should be in the air before sunset."

"I'm on it."

After typing out a draft of the directive for the Coast Guard and sending it to Mary for finalizing and transmitting to Captain Stuart, JJ hit yet another speed-dial button to a friend at Mac Dill Air Force Base in Tampa: "Hi, Murph, it's JJ. I need rapid transit for a murder arrest at sea. It is a yacht with a helipad, currently twenty-five miles east of Miami and heading south at high speed. Jack Stuart at Coast Guard is coordinating the drop. A Seals detachment is ready to go pending final paperwork . . . Okay, I am leaving the office now for arrival at Mac Dill in twenty minutes. Thanks, buddy. I owe you."

Dinner that night aboard the "Victoria" was earlier than usual because of the cold buffet offered while running at sea. The cocktail hour was a somber occasion and dinner was equally quiet. Conversations were muted and focused on evaluations of their danger. Most voices tended toward severe fright rather than a positive resolution. After all, these invaders were part of a drug cartel and charged with murder. And, furthermore, Americans are not exactly beloved in Cuba, where they could be stranded, without sufficient fuel to return. The situation did not look good.

Jose was serving coffee and tea after dessert when the attack arrived. Suddenly, the sunset air around the yacht was filled with the noise of six large Navy helicopters, two firing automatic weapons above and into the bridge, while two others were unloading troops down rope ladders to the bow and stern decks, and the other two aircraft hovered above for back-up support if needed. It was not.

The two bodyguards carrying automatic weapons were initial targets—both collapsed from bullet wounds before raising their guns. Siegal, Richter and Swift had sought cover on the deck of the bridge, prior to the yacht coming to an abrupt stop, as the engines went from top speed to idle in seconds. The always-alert Captain Ericksson had spotted the approaching helicopters and he dropped to the deck of the bridge just prior to the shooting, grabbing the ignition key as he fell.

The sudden change in forward motion caused the diners and their beverages to be propelled forward, along with loose furniture. Linda grabbed Nash around the neck and braced herself against a column to save his wheel chair from heading toward the stairway, and Bobbi hung on to Mark's one good arm while wrapping her legs around another column. But, Jimmy and Jose, who both had been standing, were catapulted into the stairway together. Ling and Dan were seated to one side with Nathan, and the three of them ended up against the forward bulkhead. Fortunately, everyone escaped further injury during the few minutes of deafening fighting up above, after which there was an ominous silence, broken only by the sound of the Seals busy securing all levels of the vessel.

Within minutes of the well-orchestrated Seals attack, an Air Force helicopter landed on the rear deck and the large figure of JJ Jensen rushed out of the rear seat in the setting sun and entered the main lounge to check for casualties. Everyone was in the process of picking themselves up off the floor and nobody noticed JJ's entry at first. Finally, Nash, who had just extricated himself from Linda's headlock, looked up and said: "JJ, what are you doing here?"

The big man smiled down at Nash and replied in his calm voice: "Just dropped in to check on your progress, Nash. But I see that you're all wrapped up with a beautiful woman, so I'll only stay a minute." Then, he noticed Mark getting up with the help of his wife. "I told you we would be only minutes away, Mark."

"Holy mackerel," muttered Mark. "You guys sure play rough."

"Yes, we do, but only when it's absolutely necessary," replied JJ.

Dan Houlihan came over to shake hands with him, and said: "Thanks JJ, for your usual rapid-fire response. I don't know how you found us, but we are sure glad that you did."

"Amen to that," shouted Jimmy, as he helped Jose climb back up the stairway.

Then Ling rushed over and gave JJ a big hug: "I can't remember when I've been happier to see anybody. You saved us from a real messed-up assignment. Thank you, JJ."

"As I'm sure all of you are aware," spoke JJ in a louder voice, "there were dozens of people involved in this operation from several federal, state and local government agencies. And frankly, we were at a dead end until your colleague, Duncan MacTavish, phoned Attorney Tony DeMartino from Toronto to complain that he couldn't communicate with the 'Victoria.' That's when it dawned on us that Siegal and his men had hijacked you as their getaway plan. So, thank Duncan for producing the clue that broke open the case. The important thing for us is that all of you on the 'Victoria' escaped injury during this kidnapping. We apologize for getting you involved with these bad guys, but I am thankful that it worked to nail them. Now, I must go topside and see what we have left to take home."

As the "Victoria" began to turn back toward Florida under the command of slightly bruised, but still standing, Captain Franz Ericksson, huddled in a raincoat to keep warm from the wind whistling through the broken windows of the bridge, his crew and guests were quietly celebrating their release in the main lounge. The Seals had released Carlos and Alfredo from their locked quarters, and the two men had joined Jose in restoring the main lounge furnishings to their normal locations.

Only the upper deck of the "Victoria" had been damaged by the attack, with bullet holes evident in all of the top structure and all of its windows broken. The two bodyguards had both been killed in the brief firefight, and Swift and Richter both suffered non-life-threatening bullet wounds. They were bound and lifted into hovering helicopters along with the efficient Seals. Within minutes, the Seals' commanding officer reported to JJ that the yacht was secure and ready to return to Florida. He was assigning two of his six helicopters to accompany the yacht while the rest of his force would return to Key West with the two prisoners. His parting words to JJ were "We'll package these boys up with medication and deliver them to you in Tampa in the morning. Thanks for the opportunity to participate." JJ responded with a bear hug for the smiling officer.

Siegal was not harmed in his position beside Ericksson on the bridge deck, so JJ personally hand-cuffed him and escorted him down to the Air Force helicopter for a direct flight back to Tampa for imprisonment on several charges, now including kidnapping. Thus, JJ could close the file on the biggest money-laundering operation in Florida history, with the aid of a visiting Canadian (a fact that he could not make public for fear of potential revenge by the Esperanza cartel).

Some of the bridge equipment was damaged in the one-sided firefight, but not enough to prevent the vessel from being controlled from the bridge. Ericksson was able to start the engines and get underway back to Florida with no difficulty. Jose, Carlos and Alfredo had finished restoring the main lounge furnishings and Jose, once again with his charming smile, announced that the bar was open.

"Well, Mark," said Nash with a wan smile, "I was looking forward to beginning a wrap-up with you this evening, but I must admit that I am exhausted from all of this action. I believe that I will ask Carlos and Alfredo to return me to my cabin. Jose can bring me a light supper before I turn in for the night."

"I totally understand," replied Mark. "I am also feeling tired, perhaps worsened by the pain pill I swallowed a few minutes ago.

You and I are fortunate that these two sisters saved us from further physical damage. I had no idea of their strength before, but they managed to hold onto both of us successfully."

"Yes, indeed. Thank you, Linda, for your quick action, or I'm afraid I would be a tangled mess at the bottom of the stairs."

"You are most welcome, Nash, but that's why we nurses are trained for physical defense. C'mon, Carlos and Alfredo, let's transport our patient back to his cabin."

By the time the "Victoria" reached a mooring in Miami, only Jose, Carlos and Alfredo were on hand to assist the captain. Everyone else had retired.

DAY 12

Tuesday, April 6, 2010

A beautiful morning sky revealed the injured "Victoria" moored at the public dock on Biscayne Bay, separating Miami from Miami Beach. But most of the occupants aboard the yacht were still asleep, recovering from their harrowing experience of the previous day.

Nash Logan had been awake before daylight and ready to go, despite the continuing aches in his leg and arm. As he lay in his large bed, he decided that he was already bored with these injuries, and he certainly was tired of peeing in a bottle. But, regardless of his boredom, the leg harness was fixed to the bed frame and he could not move the right side of his body. Just as he was contemplating whether it was too early to buzz his always-smiling nurse, she walked in the door without knocking and wished him a cheerful good morning greeting. Nash summoned up his spirit and loudly replied with a pleasant "Good morning to you." He was just about to ask her to sit down and chat for a minute when he realized that she had gone right past his bed to the bathroom (or 'head' as she was learning to call it). She emerged in a couple of minutes with a bowl of water and washcloth ready to clean him up for the new day. As she began to soap the washcloth, he raised his left arm in protest.

"Damn it, Linda, I am perfectly capable of washing myself, you know."

"I see," she replied with another smile, "you mean my work is not satisfactory Mr. Logan?" She even managed a brief pout at the end of this remark.

"No, of course not! I don't mean that at all. What I mean is that I am not used to a woman washing me. That is, I . . . well, the truth is that a beautiful young woman like you massaging an old cripple like me is . . . well, it's difficult to explain, but I find it disturbing . . . in a pleasant way, you understand."

"Yes, I think I do. You are telling me that you would like to trade me in for an older and uglier nurse, perhaps even a male nurse."

"No, no, that's not it at all." Suddenly, Nash raised himself up to a sitting position. "The fact is that I don't want to trade you at all. But I'm afraid you think me rather old for a serious suitor and I don't blame you. After all, I will turn sixty-two in another two months and you are likely still in your thirties. Sorry, I just kind of let that all hang out. Please forgive me. But, even if you don't forgive me, don't leave me. I couldn't bear to go back in that hospital again."

Nash was interrupted by a knock on the door, which Linda promptly opened (secretly prepared to murder the intruder). It was the always-smiling Jose.

"Sorry to interrupt, Mr. Logan, but you asked me to tell you when breakfast is served, so here I am to tell you. You want me to get Carlos and Alfredo to carry you up top?"

"Yes, of course, Jose. I will join the others." After the little steward left, Nash turned to speak to Linda again, but she had gone out the door ahead of Jose.

Now that Nash was back on board, early attendance at breakfast appeared suddenly expanded, with many showing up for an opportunity to spend time getting acquainted with Nathan Rosenberg. But, for most, the end of the Florida tour was upon them and they had increased their interest in this southern state with all its past mistakes and potential future opportunities. They looked forward to the climax of this two-week discovery program and the final location that would emerge for the Logan Lifetime Communities.

At seven-thirty, Linda appeared in the main lounge to request, on Nash's behalf, that the program for this morning be delayed until eight o'clock so that Nash could join the discussion after his bedside breakfast. Promptly at that hour, Linda re-appeared ascending the stairs, followed by Nash in his wheel chair with the elevated leg extension, carried by Carlos and Alfredo. He smiled at everyone before wishing them a loud and cheerful "Good Morning" that was echoed by several voices as the group moved to chairs around the corner conference table.

"Ladies and gentlemen," began Mark. "I am truly humbled by your attendance for this wrap-up session on our tour of Florida. I must admit that the rather hectic activities of the last couple of days were not in my work schedule, although a helicopter crash followed by a yacht hijacking certainly adds new experiences to my lifetime adventures. As we reach the end of our Florida tour, I realize that Jimmy is the only person here who has been with me throughout each day, but I trust his notes will provide a good record for Nash and Nathan to review back in Toronto. The primary purpose of my role is to provide Nash with an informed foundation for deciding on the best site for his new community, which I have begun to think of as 'Lifetime' in commemoration of his slogan: 'Logan Lifetime Communities.' If you object, Nash . . ."

"On the contrary, Mark, I think that it is a brilliant name. However, as Nathan knows, I have found it wise to submit names to both our marketing and legal experts, prior to falling in love with any of them. I have lost more of those contests than I have won."

"Good, we won't spend any more time on name choice. Yesterday, Nash, before our astounding hijacking and rescue escapade, I summarized the development pattern in Planning Districts 10 and 11. Although District 10 contains ample potential for further development, land cost is higher than in other parts of the state. District 11, on the other hand, contains virtually no undeveloped land of any scale suitable for your purposes. Even the islands are filled up. Today, then, I would like to finish up with a brief summary of the Atlantic Ridge, that part of Florida providing the bulk of early coastal development along the southern east coast, prior to summarizing my assessment of our location options.

"The Atlantic Ridge was described earlier as a narrow peninsula of limestone extending down the east coast of Florida, parallel to the central peninsula foundation. It provides elevations up to forty feet above sea level along the barrier islands. The coastal rivers provide excellent irrigation and drainage for these oceanfront areas, making them historic prime agricultural lands for citrus and row crops. But the elevation also made these coastal areas a primary transportation corridor and settlement area even before Flagler's railway and subsequent highways. Beginning with Palm Beach County and extending south through Broward and Dade, small communities grew into big communities and the big communities merged with other big communities until the rich farmland gave way to urban settlements at an increasing rate. It is an indisputable historic fact that, when two uses compete for the same land, the higher value use will prevail.

"An excellent example of this transformation is the vegetable farms that covered most of Broward County during the first half of the twentieth century. Small rural communities like Dania and Pompano, extolled for their tomato and bean crops, began to grow at exponential rates in the 1950s and 1960s, quickly overrunning the vegetable fields with houses and infrastructure. In west Broward, Bud Lyons had amassed a huge vegetable farm, reportedly the largest bean farm in the United States. He sold nine-thousand acres to Westinghouse's Coral Ridge Properties, which launched a new community in the 1960s that quickly became the fastest-growing city in the country. The city of 'Coral Springs' now contains over one-hundred-thousand residents.

"In the early 1960s, the Graham Dairy Farms sprawled over a large portion of land beyond northwest Miami. In the 1950s, the family patriarch, United States Senator Graham, decided to convert the farms into a planned community which he called 'Miami Lakes'. Although both his sons took an interest in the project, one brother preferred politics and became well-known nationally as Florida Governor and United States Senator Bob Graham. Bob's sister, Katherine, married a newspaperman in Washington and ended up managing *The Washington Post*. Their brother Bill managed the development of Miami Lakes, and then enlisted his son 'Young Bill' and his three daughters in the business. Third generation Young Bill took over the helm of the Graham Companies from his father in the mid-1980s and decided to expand their original holdings with a new community of diverse detached homes called 'Lakes-On-The-Green', about three miles north of Miami Lakes (a modest-price, six-hundred-home community which sold out in under three years).

"By the 1990s, Miami Lakes was replete with thousands of single-family homes and rental apartments (owned by the Graham Companies) and included two golf courses and a retail center with a Miami Lakes Hotel. Young Bill's three sisters and two brothers-in-law also were involved in the management of the company. The Grahams convinced the respected coach of the Miami Dolphins football team, Don Shula, to sponsor the restaurant in their country club, and later the hotel in Miami Lakes, now known as the Don Shula Hotel. The Graham family was one of a new breed of land developers who devoted their efforts to superior living environments, rather than maximum profits. They established a model of excellence that became a standard for many Florida developers to follow.

"This same transition story was repeated dozens of times in southeast Florida until very little agriculture land remains. The megalopolis of Miami/Fort Lauderdale/Palm Beach is composed of some eighty municipalities blended together in a constantly-moving mass of residents and visitors living, working, shopping and playing together with little concern for the land that they have consumed.

"Yet, by intruding further into the edges of the Everglades, Palm Beach County was able to devote more acreage to farmland than any other county (six-hundred-and-fifty-thousand acres). Even Dade County maintains over ninety-thousand acres of tropical fruit production in the southern part of the County. Broward County, too, despite Arvida's ten-thousand-acre new town of 'Weston' on its western edge, still manages to preserve cropland from former Everglades land drained through the diligence of post-war water management 'experts.'

"Although the anti-growth Martin County has been a holdout to massive growth, its northern neighbor, St. Lucie County, was divided up into quarter-acre lots by the General Development Corporation to initiate a haven for workers escaping the higher prices of West Palm Beach down the road.

"Indian River County, north of St. Lucie, the largest citrus producer in Florida, is quickly being transformed into low-density housing developments, and Brevard County is progressing somewhat more slowly toward urbanity because of the threatened slowdown of the space industry.

"Florida is no longer a young state, either in terms of development or population age. Its land is wrinkled from countless maturing experiences. Its framework is worn from migrant and visitor overload. In this, the fabled home of the 'Fountain of Youth', it seems fitting that we can re-invent our growth practices to provide incentives for conservation rather than penalties for destruction.

"Last night, I made a small matrix on my computer and made copies for each of you. For those who have lost, or never received, the map of Planning Districts, I made additional copies.

"Everyone can follow along as we retrace our tour through the ten (of eleven) Florida Planning Districts and summarize the twelve key-location criteria for each. I have marked my estimates on the handout matrices, in terms of plus, minus, or a neutral zero; and I have added up the plus signs for each of ten districts. As you can see, results range from five pluses in District 10 to nine pluses in Districts 1 and 4.

"However, there is room for one additional criterion at the bottom to be scored by Nash Logan (noted on the matrix as 'NL')—it could, of course, dominate the other scores.

"If we begin at District 1, you can see I scored it nine out of twelve, with the only negatives being lack of existing sewage capacity and entitled land, in addition to lack of a major city (although Pensacola and Mobile contain many of the advantages of large cities). Major transportation ways and extensive available land characterize most of the Districts; and positive politics are also common, except for the overzealous regional planning staff in District 10. The railway is an additional problem in District 10 because of its proximity to heavily developed coastal areas without existing access to undeveloped land areas. What questions do you have about this matrix? Nathan, you look perplexed?"

"Yes," responded Nathan. "I am surprised that District 6, containing Orlando and the Space Coast, didn't rank higher. Can you explain?"

Location Criteria	Planning Districts										
	1	2	3	4	5	6	7	8	9	10	11
Freight Railway	+	+	+	+	+	+	+	+	+	0	
Interstate Highway	+	+	+	+	+	+	0	+	+	+	
Undeveloped Land	+	+	+	+	+	+	+	+	+	+	
Clear Land	+	+	+	+	+	+	+	+	+	+	
Dry Land	+	+	+	+	+	0	+	+	0	0	
Climate	+	+	+	+	+	+	0	0	0	0	
Major City 1 hour	0	0	-	+	-	+	+	+	0	+	
Water Supply	+	-	-	+	0	+	+	+	0	+	
Sewer Plant	-	-	-	0	0	0	-	0	0	0	
Land Cost	+	+	+	0	0	-	+	-	+	-	
Entitled Land	-	-	-	+	0	0	0	+	+	-	
Positive Politics	+	+	+	0	0	0	+	0	0	-	
Sub Total +	9	8	8	9	6	7	8	8	6	5	NA
Total (with .5 for 0)	9.5	8.5	8	10.5	8.5	9	9.5	9.5	9	7	
Intangible (N Logan)	X			X			X	X			
Total (for land study)	10.5			11.5			10.5	10.5			

Exhibit 31:
Location Decision Criteria.

"Sure! The cost of undeveloped land in East Central Florida is higher than in other parts of the state, other than the southeast. This situation might shift with the returning economy, but not at present, so development has been deferred. In comparison, District 7, southwest of Orlando, has been a popular new development area, and it benefits from the planned CSX intermodal terminal in Polk County. This county contains large tracts of entitled land suitable for multi-use development, but it has no large-scale development plans except for the partial entitlement of Clear Springs encompassing the city of Bartow. Thus, because of this available potential, it rates slightly higher on this matrix than District 6.

"Let me add, at this point, that you probably should consider hurricane frequency. Many people apparently consider this danger to be a very good reason to stay away from this state during the months of July through November. However, some parts of the state are much more prone to hurricanes than others. Note that the northeast part of the peninsula is rarely bothered by these storms—a rather handy marketing benefit for locations in that area. I thought that you should take it into consideration in your deliberations. For example, I have been a resident in Northeast Florida for over four decades, and I am pleased to say that I have never experienced a hurricane.

"This is a very useful piece of information, Mark," said Nash. "I never gave any thought to hurricanes in Florida. Sure, I knew they happen. I guess that I just thought that they wouldn't bother me. But, of course, they are an important factor for hazard insurance and structural cost, as well as for personal safety. Thank you."

"You're welcome! Now, getting back to our focus on narrowing down your location options, this is a crude location-decision matrix on two counts: (1) the districts are relatively large and diverse, and (2) the category measures are broad. It is best used to eliminate districts rather than choose among those that rank high. In terms of rapid large-scale entitlement, the areas around Tampa (District 8), Orlando (District 6), and Jacksonville (District 4), appear to have the greatest potential for the purchase of land that is already entitled. I should add the large Southwood tract at Tallahassee (in District 2) that was entitled by the St. Joe Company, but demand proved well below projections."

"This is not bad," interjected Nash. "We can live with examination of four or five sites simultaneously if we move quickly on performing due diligence. Don't you agree, Nathan?"

"I do, Nash, but I don't know enough to be comfortable about Mark being right on the overriding criterion of entitlement speed."

"Ah-ha, my friend," replied Nash. "That information was presented on the very first day of this program. It is called Amendment 4 to the Florida Constitution, and it is better known as the Hometown Democracy Amendment. I will lend you a pamphlet to read tonight that will blow your socks off. Essentially, it would make every land use change subject to local referendum."

"You're joking!"

"I wish I were, but it is a serious proposition with a good deal of money supporting it. Our best bet is to purchase an existing approved development and revise it as needed down the road."

"Holy moley!"

"Exactly. Let's have lunch."

⁓

The Joint Task Force of federal agencies headed by JJ Jensen had enjoyed a very successful time in examining the offices of Siegal, Richter and Swift. Investment monies did not come from many sources, as stated by Siegal in his taped conversation with Nash and Mark; but rather it all came from a single bank in Nassau, Bahamas. Some rapid arm-twisting by the Bahamian government convinced their local bank officials to open their records; and, to nobody's surprise, deposits were tracked through other offshore banks to the Esperanza drug cartel in Medellin, Colombia. The loop was complete, and the DEA seized all bank accounts maintained by Siegal and Richter.

Freezing the investments already spent in several Florida developments was more complicated. But the office records clearly showed the specific properties with investments owed to the companies established by Siegal and Richter. Of greater interest to Florida authorities, the records also identified the monies paid directly to local government officials for services rendered in ensuring the passage of entitlement approvals. State troopers made simultaneous arrests of local government officials in several parts of the state. The governor was ecstatic to announce this clean-up of corrupt officials, especially since the publicity would argue against the need for the Amendment 4 referendum. The governor issued a statement affirming that government can effectively police its own dishonest officials.

As spokesman for the federal task force, Jensen was hounded by reporters for the latest information on arrests. He was able to report that the three men arrested for controlling this network were being held without bond, but that they had been cooperating with authorities in unveiling what some are calling the biggest money-laundering scheme in history. Although Jensen would not estimate how much money had been placed in Florida over the previous five years, it appeared that hundreds of millions of dollars were involved in development investments that now would go to public auction.

Reporters eagerly awaited an opportunity to interview the civilians who had infiltrated the investment syndicate, but Jensen refused to divulge their names, as he had promised Nash and Mark. Luckily, reporters had not connected the fatal helicopter crash with the drug-related money-laundering scheme.

After lunch on the "Victoria," the Logan Homes group re-convened around the conference table and the mounted map of the state of Florida.

"Mark," announced Nash, in an authoritative voice, "I have given this issue a good deal of thought, and I believe that we should begin a site search without delay. Now that we've got rid of the pesky crooks, we should be able to proceed more efficiently. I would like to begin tomorrow in the four top districts you have indicated first: West Florida (focusing on the area surrounding the new airport in Bay and Washington Counties—primarily St. Joe land ownership, but I learned from a recent article in *Florida Trend* magazine that the Knight family owns fifty-five-thousand acres in adjacent Washington County); second, Northeast Florida (focusing on existing DRI approvals west and south of Jacksonville); third, Central Florida (focusing on land close to the CSX multi-modal terminal and Clear Spring entitled land); and, fourth, Tampa Bay (focusing on entitled land in Pasco County). I am open to comments and criticisms from everyone."

"Frankly, Nash," replied Mark, "despite your protests about information overload, I believe you have hit this nail right on the head—an excellent summation."

"Hold on a minute," said Nathan. "I know that I am the least-informed person here, but I am interested to know about transportation access to each of those areas?"

"An excellent point, Nathan," responded Nash, "and a very important one. The basic answer is 'yes'. But we are still dealing with broad generalities in terms of the railway line capacity in each area and also in terms of the availability of land with access to the railway. These latter points can only be resolved when we examine specific properties; and, even then, the issue of weighing different strengths and weaknesses of comparative sites will prove difficult. But that's why we are here and that's why we hired Mark Wilkins to guide us through this process."

"Okay," said Nathan. "I can buy into this process. But how do you propose finding and screening potential properties in each of these districts? There are only three of us here and you are in no shape to travel around."

"Quite right! But I have given this issue some thought as well, and here is what I propose. We now have a reputable attorney in Florida, by the name of Tony DiMartino. He is the same fellow who quickly discovered the real background on Jack Swift and company. I suggest phoning Tony this afternoon and to tell him that we want to hire four honest Realtors in four parts of Florida, and who will each accept a base fee of five-thousand dollars to explore our needs in strict confidence. If we purchase a piece of land identified by any of them, they will receive the buyer's share of the commission in addition to the base fee. We need results in three days. What do you think?"

"Sounds like a good plan to me, Nash," responded Nathan. "But we need to tell them the parameters for the property, and also how we want the information submitted, so that we can compare it with other options."

"I agree, Nathan, and here is my answer. We invite the ladies to go out shopping for the remainder of the afternoon, and the four of us—you, Jimmy, Mark and me—address the site parameters in concise fashion. Of course, Dan also will be here, as a non-participant to keep an eye on us. But, first of all, we get on the speaker-phone with Tony and set him to work selecting and contacting the best Realtors for us in these four sub-districts. Let's make Jimmy the contact point for each of them; and, Nathan, you will undertake the comparative analysis to avoid bias from either Mark or me. Today is Tuesday, so we tell them that Friday is our absolute deadline. While you and Jimmy coordinate these guys and analyze their information, I will work with Mark on developing clearer objectives for our site plan. Mark, how be we invite Tony to cruise up to Jacksonville with us tomorrow and discuss the entitlement approval process?"

"That sounds good to me, Nash. But, there is no longer any air service between Jacksonville and Orlando, so we have a problem in getting him back home."

"Damn, I miss Jake already. Okay, Jimmy, figure out how to get him on-board—we will be at sea in the morning—and back to Orlando from Jacksonville."

"Excuse me," said Bobbi in a loud voice. "If you plan to dismiss us three ladies, then I suggest that you get on with it, so we can have some quality time in Miami."

"Absolutely! Jose, please arrange some transport for these ladies into Miami."

"Yes sir, Mr. Logan. I'm on it." The three women all rose together and headed to their cabins in anticipation of an early departure.

"And Jimmy," continued Nash, "please phone Tony DiMartino and ask if he can spend fifteen minutes with us on the speaker-phone." Jimmy pulled out his cell phone and stepped out on deck to make the call. But, within minutes, he was back inside setting up the speaker-phone, after telling Nash that DiMartino was available immediately. The phone rang.

"Hello, Tony?"

"Yes, indeed, Nash. I am sorry to hear of your mishaps. I hope you are feeling better."

"Thank you, Tony, and thank you especially for the part you played in helping discover our kidnapping. We could be in Cuba now if it wasn't for your call to JJ."

"Believe me, I was pleased to have the opportunity to help. After all, I bear some responsibility for getting you involved with those gangsters."

"With respect to my health, Tony, I hurt all over; but that's no reason to delay our purpose for being here. Now, I know you are a busy attorney, so please tell me if what I am about to ask is too big a burden, and we will devise another plan. But, here is what I have in mind."

"One moment, please, Nash. If you don't object, I would like to record your statement so that I do not miss anything."

"No problem. As you know, we have spent the last two weeks getting acquainted with Florida. Mark has done a magnificent job of explaining every part of the state to us and I feel comfortable about proceeding to a purchase decision. We have narrowed down the regional choices to four districts, and now we need your help in moving to the next step. We want you to identify four quality real estate brokers in four areas of the state, who can put other priorities aside and go to work for us immediately in locating a tract of fifteen-hundred to two-thousand acres that is entitled, or in the entitlement process, for mixed-use development. We will pay them each a retainer fee of five-thousand dollars to conduct a property search within three days; and one of them will be able to receive a sales commission. The four areas are: (1) Panama City area, (2) Jacksonville area, (3) Lakeland/Winter Haven area, and (4) Pasco County north of Tampa. We will supply parameters for the property, but we need knowledgeable people on the ground. We are going to purchase only one property, and we intend to do it quickly. Assuming that you can set up four competent brokers this afternoon, I would like you to join us on a cruise up to Jacksonville tomorrow to define the parameters. We will transport you to and from the yacht. What is your response?"

"Wow! That's a tall order. But I like it. Here's what I propose: let me go to work on the four brokers first and I will call you back before five o'clock on the cruise participation."

"Okay, done! Put us on the clock, and we'll talk to you later."

"Fine, I will phone you back. Good bye."

Jimmy clicked off the phone and joined the others in looking at Nash for direction. Mark pulled out his laptop and plugged in his portable printer.

"Nash, last night I began playing with some concept organization parameters. Let me print out copies of a diagram I prepared for an article on this topic a couple of years ago. We can use it as a checklist for everyone, as a starting point to structure a discussion."

"Perfect, I knew I could count on you to get us moving in the right direction, Mark."

Within five minutes, Mark had printed four copies of a chart which he passed out to Nash, Nathan and Jimmy as well as keeping one for himself.

"As each of you can see on this chart, I have defined five major components of a new community. Each of the sub-components may not be part of every new community, but the five major components are necessary for any community in this country. Because of your key interest in establishing the package housing factory, I suggest that we begin with the Commercial component, and then proceed counter-clockwise through Infrastructure, Housing, Leisure, and Institutional."

"Sounds like a good idea," responded Nash. "Let's get started."

"Okay, I further suggest that we begin at the bottom of this list with 'Industrial' as our first sub-component. By the way, in case you hadn't noticed, there are a total of thirty-six sub-components on this chart, so this is not a brief exercise. I anticipate that we may be at this table well into the night. To begin, I would like to hear Nathan's parameters for the housing factory."

"Very well," said Nathan, "although I am sure that Nash would be equally capable of defining them."

"Yes, but we heard from Nash early in this exercise. He gave you primary credit for creating this concept. So, it would be would be beneficial to get your definition," stated Mark.

"Sure, but before describing the factory concept, I believe I should give you some insight as to the basis of this idea. I have been working with Nash for several years. I began as an architect and proceeded to re-design Logan dwellings to make them more efficient and attractive. I even won a national design award. When I went to Ottawa to accept the award, it suddenly occurred to me that I really wasn't worthy of this award. Sure, I designed a better house than others who competed, but none of us really had added significant improvements to the standard North American, or even the worldwide, house. Look back one-hundred, or even two-hundred years. Except for plumbing and electrical features, the house is basically the same structure: a foundation of masonry or concrete with walls of masonry or wood frame holding up a roof of wood frame. We are using the same natural resources that the Vikings used to build shelter in a world that is being depleted of its natural resources at a terrifying rate. There must be a better way. We learned to build automobiles and airplanes out of synthetic materials, and consumers admired and used them as much, or more, than wooden carriages and kites. Why can't we do the same thing with houses?

Exhibit 32:
New Community Components.

"This became more than a rhetorical question when my wife and I shared a vacation cabin one summer with my brother and his family. David, when he is not vacationing, is a chemical engineer who rose to become a senior executive with a major chemical firm.

So, I was genuinely surprised when he answered my question with a question of his own: 'why did we rent this cabin?' 'Don't be silly', I replied. 'We wanted a recreational spot beside a lake to enjoy part of the summer with our kids.' 'No,' he answered, waving a finger knowingly at me. 'We rented this place because our two wives fell in love with the picture of this log cabin. And that,' he said, 'is why house construction has not changed in hundreds of years.' I was astounded. But of course, my wise older brother was correct. Auto makers are well aware of this emotional appeal. They are careful to change their designs only at the margin—drastic innovations like the Studebaker or the Tucker are not acceptable to customers who make emotional decisions on major purchases. So, that summer David and I discovered the essential idea for a completely innovative new house that would be acceptable to our tradition-bound consumers.

"As my brother and I chatted about the stagnant nature of housing construction, David suddenly jumped out of his chair and started pacing the floor. 'What's going on?' I asked, and he replied that he might have the answer to our quandary over housing construction. He told me that his company had developed a non-petroleum-based plastic that contains some amazing properties, including the ability to harden beyond the range of reinforced concrete, with the addition of a catalyst that his scientists had discovered. At that point, it was still in the highly-classified stage until they acquired a patent, but he set up a little test case for me at their Toronto plant, where we designed molds for a small-scale playhouse which we replicated with varying surface features. We used photographic images of lap siding, red brick and stucco to dress our playhouse in three different styles. I brought along some pictures to show you the degree of realism we attained in this initial experiment." He passed the pictures to his three colleagues, two of whom expressed absolute amazement, while the third, Nash, just sat back in his wheel chair and smiled smugly.

"When I showed these photographs to Nash for the first time three years ago, he literally jumped up and down with excitement; and he got even more excited when I showed him numbers on the modest cost of the material and processing. The very next week, he bought an abandoned warehouse outside Toronto and directed me to produce prototype houses. We have completed three different houses with three different exterior appearances, in addition to an apartment unit ready to plug into a multi-story building. I told him we are ready to go into mass production; so here we are in Florida with both Canadian and U.S. patents."

"This is truly an astounding story, Nathan," said Mark. "I would get up and jump up and down if I wasn't crippled. Seriously, I am genuinely impressed by the Rosenbergs' invention and I am humbled to be part of the launch crew. However, at this point, I would like you to define the factory you need to construct these house packages."

"Okay," replied Nathan, "here goes. I visualize the factory as consisting of five interactive elements. First is the 'Mixing Center'. This includes reception of all basic house ingredients; so it must have access to major transportation, preferably by both rail and highway. These products are placed on distribution conveyors to different sectors of the production process; for example, raw structural ingredients go directly into the mixing tanks, along with coloring for a particular house type; whereas the air-handling unit and appliances move to the latter part of the process, for installation in the completed structure.

"Second is the 'Molding Center' where the liquid structural ingredients are poured into specific molds for different types of houses. One particular mold may be used for several house types, whereas another may be used only for one or two house types. The beauty of the design is that we mix large structural components to make a new house, whereas traditional methods use very small components such as pieces of lumber and sheets of drywall. The shortcoming is that the same color appears on both interior and exterior surfaces, with the color appropriate to the exterior surface that is patterned by the mold. However, the finished material accepts normal paint applications for interior décor and the structural material contains strong insulation factors. The exterior never needs further maintenance, unless the owners choose to paint it a different color.

"The third major element is the 'Production Line' where the structural molds are fitted with the smaller house parts, including windows, doors, exterior porches, and mechanical/plumbing/electrical systems—these systems fit right into slots provided in the mold process, so their attachment is very efficient.

"The fourth element is the 'Finishing Center' where we apply interior finishes and cabinetry by hand (the slowest part of the whole process).

"The fifth element is the 'Control Center' where administration of the entire operation is coordinated along with marketing and sales activities."

"I assume you have a conceptual plan of this building?" asked Mark.

"Absolutely, but I did not bring it with me in my hurry to fly down here. I estimate a building, or perhaps buildings in this climate, to produce up to five hundred dwellings (including apartments) per year, when fully operational, will be approximately two-hundred-thousand square feet. It would require a site of about twenty-five acres, including outdoor storage of completed houses and a loading area for trucks and possibly railroad cars, as well as employee and visitor parking. We anticipate a large number of visitors, so the building design includes special accommodations for them to view the process without disrupting production.

"I should add that we haven't yet solved the issue of multiple plants, if our houses turn out to be as popular as we anticipate. So, if our production reaches capacity, do we expand this plant, or start a new one in another location? I like the second option because it provides the opportunity to build another new community; but, to be on the safe side, I believe our initial site should be about forty acres. We can always sell the surplus land in future years if we opt to have multiple factories."

"This is really impressive, Nathan. I admire your attention to detail and also your vision of where this new process could lead. Did you design the production process as well as the dwellings?" asked Mark.

"Yes, but I received a good deal of help from my brother David, the chemical engineer, and also from Nash who peers over my shoulder on a regular basis."

"Darn right," interjected Nash. "That's why I only hire short men and women, so I can always see over their shoulders."

After everyone afforded Nash a little chuckle for his joke, Mark continued. "Okay, so one of our parameters, Jimmy, in addition to the size of the factory, is the need for direct highway access, so that we do not disrupt the rest of our community with trucks and visitors to this site. Clearly, a rail link is a means of reducing highway traffic. This is important because of the state impact fees linked to external traffic. We will receive credits for having employees work on-site and not generate off-site commuting trips, but these will be somewhat offset by commercial traffic to and from this factory. What about other factors, such as excess energy demand and concerns about safety? And, are these product components combustible?

"Good questions, Mark," replied Nash. "This production process does not require excessive energy. It uses electricity to heat the mixing tanks and to run the equipment, but not in exorbitant amounts; and the non-petroleum-based plastic we use is not flammable. The big cost is in the price of the capital equipment. The process itself is highly automated and non-hazardous. It should be a safe and healthy environment for employees, as well as for the surrounding community."

"Okay, great. I think that covers the factory, at least in terms of acquisition parameters.

Let's discuss other industrial and office development." Mark looked alternately at Nathan and Nash for a response. As he expected, Nash took the lead.

"As I mentioned when you brought up this topic earlier, Mark, Nathan and I believe that we will attract several support operations to our site. Despite our primary reliance on the liquid plastic, we probably will not prove a big enough consumer to attract a chemical company, and that's probably just as well, considering common distrust of such companies' safety and pollution reputations. However, we should attract smaller specialty operations for doors, windows and interior finishes. An operation of our size may also attract offices for advertising, office services and the like. All together, we estimate occupying some two-hundred-thousand square feet of additional ground-floor building space that could occupy another thirty to forty acres at a ratio of 25 percent building coverage. If you allow 20 percent for roads and pathways, the total industrial park should be ninety-to one-hundred acres in size. Earlier, in our initial discussion, I estimated one-hundred acres for this land use and I still believe it is a safe number."

"Fine, although you need to beef up this argument with some more detail on allied industries, because this taxable industrial space is a major political selling point that will be questioned in detail. Developers have been known to exaggerate this land use to make a stronger case for political approval. Although, I believe you have a strong case on the basis of your new house invention, I do suggest that you put an economist to work on industrial potential, as well as on employment and payroll, to present the strongest possible case for approval with or without the passage of the 'Hometown Democracy Amendment'. This taxable property with low public service demand and new employment is the key to widespread popularity."

"By golly, Mark, you do know a thing or two about this business," smiled Nash with genuine admiration in his voice. "Let's move on to the next topic. We've covered only one sub-component with thirty-five left to go."

Bobbi, Linda and Ling were enjoying the elegant shops of central Miami. After two hours, each of them had satisfied her zest for purchasing new possessions: Bobbi picked up a truly elegant Vera Bradley summer purse, as well as new style of silk blouse by Gypsy 05 "Fay"; Linda also bought one of the new Gypsy silk blouses, in addition to a handsome leather picture frame on its own stand that she planned to package as a gift for Nash along with a picture of "Victoria's" passengers prior to the helicopter crash; and Ling was excited about the locally-designed Cuban ear rings she found in a small handicraft specialty shop.

So, each of the ladies had two or three packages in their arms, when they decided to pause for a drink at a small tavern before catching a taxi back to the yacht in time for the daily pre-dinner cocktail. Because most of the tables in the tavern were taken, they decided to sit on stools at the bar. The efficient bartender wasted no time in serving them two Margaritas for Bobbi and Linda, and a soft drink for Ling. They no sooner had taken the first sip from their drinks when a husky-looking man of about forty years of age sauntered up behind Linda and put his arm around her shoulder.

"How be you and I get acquainted, little lady?" said the newcomer, with a slight slur in his voice, indicating he may have been in the tavern for some time.

"No, thank you," replied Linda, clearly annoyed. "And please take your arm off my shoulder."

"You've gotta be kiddin', baby," he replied. "You and your friends should join my two friends and me at the corner table. Whadda ya say?" And he proceeded to pull Linda off the bar stool with the seeming intent of actually dragging her over to his table.

"Hold it, fella," shouted Ling, suddenly standing in front of the newcomer. "I don't want to hurt you, but I will if you don't disappear in three seconds." The man stopped pulling Linda and stared with astonishment at the seemingly fragile Asian lady in front of him.

"Is that so?" he said, as he reached his other arm out to embrace Ling. That turned out to be a major error, as she grabbed his wrist with two hands and twisted it sharply downward, before yanking it up, with the result that the big man was suddenly laying flat on his back on the floor. He shook his head in surprise and muttered some unintelligible curses as he quickly got to his feet and started to attack Ling. She calmly stepped aside, pulling his arm with her and administered a Karate chop to his neck that sent him back to the floor, apparently unconscious. But, in the interim, the man's two burly companions had rushed to the fray with the intention of grabbing this foreign-looking woman and rescuing their friend. The bartender, after phoning 911 for assistance, rushed around the end of the bar with a baseball bat; but, he was too late. With what appeared to be a sudden flurry of arms and legs, Ling sent the other two men to the floor with their companion, and then resumed her seat at the bar, leaving the bartender standing over the three men with his baseball bat raised, just as two policemen charged through the front entrance.

"Harry, I hope you didn't kill any of these guys," yelled one of the officers. "It's bad for the tourist trade."

"Kill them? I didn't even touch them," replied the astonished bartender. "They attacked these ladies at the bar and this one small lady floored the three of them before they could raise a fist. I've never seen anything like it." Suddenly, the other patrons burst into a rousing round of applause, while Ling modestly sipped her drink.

"Lady," said the bartender to Ling, "you are welcome in here anytime, and the drinks are on the house. Believe me, you are better than any bodyguard I have seen, and I have seen a few barroom brawls in my day."

The two police officers just shook their heads in disbelief and proceeded to help the three men off the floor, before handcuffing them and leading them out with a friendly wave to Harry the bartender.

"Bobbi turned to Ling and said: "I wondered when you were going to show us your skill. We had to drag you into a bar to see it; and, believe me, it was worth the price of admission. You aren't even sweating, and those three thugs were down for the count."

"All in a day's work," replied Ling with a smile. "I'm glad to be of service. Besides, I haven't managed to get a lot of exercise on this assignment, so this was a good opportunity for a much-needed workout."

The other two women just stared at her in admiration.

Back on board the "Victoria," Captain Ericksson was settling the charges with workmen for replacing the windows in the bridge that had been broken in the previous day's attack at sea. Dan Houlihan kept a watchful eye on the workmen from the sidelines. Earlier in the day, the Captain had enlisted other workers to replace some damaged bridge controls and to patch up the bullet holes. He also entertained the Coast Guard inspector who arrived to write up a report on the incident and damage to the vessel. With the addition of fuel expected to be delivered by tank truck due within the hour, the "Victoria" appeared ready for its cruise back to Jacksonville during the coming night and day.

In the "Victoria's" main lounge, the four men around the conference table had completed defining the six Commercial sub-components as well as the six Infrastructure sub-components of a new community. Nash was impressed with the detail which Mark introduced for discussion of each sub-component. The retail, entertainment and office sub-components were closely related to projected resident needs, and the infrastructure systems were routed for optimum efficiency. He was particularly intrigued by Mark's ideas on the integration of parks and pathways with residential and commercial land uses, in addition to the potential cost-effectiveness of unmanned electric jitneys that could provide alternate transportation for work, school and shopping trips within the community. In fact, they could shift the customary focus of public planners away from internal trip generation to the evaluation of impacts on air pollution and energy consumption, assuming the substitution of low energy-using bicycle and jitney transport for automobiles.

"Mark, this exercise is really getting exciting. I only wish I could get up and pace around to stimulate my concentration on all of the ideas you are throwing at me. We have been focused on our new house innovation without giving due consideration to all of the potential improvements we can introduce to the land use plan. Do you agree, Nathan?"

"Absolutely! I can hardly wait to start on the Housing component now that we are equipped with the truly innovative ideas Mark has introduced for working and shopping, as well as for the communication and circulation linkages. I believe we can really show the citizens of Florida an 'Innovation' in a living and working environment."

"I agree, but we better take a break for dinner before beginning Housing. I see our three ladies are arriving through the door with packages in hand. Welcome back, ladies. Did you have a fun afternoon?"

"Fun doesn't begin to describe it," laughed Bobbi. "The absolute highlight was seeing Ling in action when three yo-yos decided to manhandle us. Believe me, her rapid demolition of those three large men was a thing of beauty."

"Wow," exclaimed Mark. "Did these men harm you?"

"They never had a chance," added Linda. "As soon as they started to get physical, Ling went into action like a human tornado. Bobbi and I just looked on in amazement. Thank you, Nash, for hiring Ling to protect us."

"You are welcome," replied Nash from his wheel chair, "and I would like to add my thanks to Ling for protecting our lovely sisters. Both Mark and I are most grateful."

Ling paused a minute before replying: "This is what I do for a living, and I am particularly glad that I could settle the little ruckus downtown, because I was feeling somewhat embarrassed about doing nothing to prevent the hijacking. At least, both Dan and I can feel better that we have contributed some genuine protection. Now, please excuse me while I change out of my fighting clothes." With that, she disappeared down the stairs, followed by Bobbi and Linda.

Within minutes of the ladies' departure, Jose appeared with a mobile phone for Nash. "Excuse me, Mr. Logan, but Mr. DiMartino from Orlando is on the phone. He says that it is important that he speak with you immediately."

"You did the right thing, Jose," said Nash with a smile, as he grabbed the phone with his one good operational hand. "Hello, Tony, I hope you had a pleasant and successful day. Just hold a second while I put you on speaker so that Mark, Nathan and Jimmy can hear your report. Good, they are all listening."

"Good afternoon, gentlemen. I am pleased to report that I have engaged four of the top real estate brokers in Florida on a retainer of five-thousand dollars each to pursue available property in the four geographic areas that you defined. They will begin preliminary research, but await further definition on your needs, prior to defining specific potential sites. I told them that I would respond within forty-eight hours and that we needed results within seventy-two hours after that. All four agreed to those terms, and they have sent me written acknowledgements by fax and email."

"Excellent! Mark told me that you are the best. Now how about joining us for a little cruise tomorrow?"

"Yes, I have made myself available to do that. Just tell me when and where."

"Jimmy, have you got details?"

"Yes, sir, I can answer both those questions," replied his assistant instantly. "Mr. DiMartino, I have taken the liberty of booking you a private flight on Harris Helicopter Service at Herndon Airport, scheduled for eight o'clock tomorrow morning. I hope that time is convenient for you. They are prepared to contact the 'Victoria' and land on the stern deck helipad, subject to favorable weather. If the weather is bad, Captain Ericksson is prepared to seek the nearest port and pick you up there. But he tells me that the forecast is for fair weather and mild seas. I have arranged to have you flown back to Herndon from Craig Field in Jacksonville on the next afternoon by charter plane. We will confirm the departure time after we dock in Jacksonville."

"That sounds perfect," replied Tony. "I will look forward to seeing you all tomorrow morning."

"You bet, Tony. I am looking forward to a productive day cruising the Atlantic," said Nash. "Thanks for your cooperation. Bye." Nash turned off the phone and smiled contentedly at his three companions. "I love it when a plan comes together. Since my nurse isn't here to control my bad habits, let's all have a drink before dinner."

The atmosphere at dinner that evening was more cheerful than at any time since the helicopter crash. The confrontation at the tavern was re-told several times by Bobbi and Linda as they thought of different perspectives, and consumed another glass or two of Burrowing Owl wine for support. They all stayed away from the topic of ending their group camaraderie the next day, but it was a fact obvious to everyone; especially to Nash who listened to Bobbi and Linda's re-enactments with the increasing realization that he did not want to say good-bye to his beautiful nurse.

After dinner, the four concept definers found that they had an attentive audience gathered near their conference table to listen to the new community parameters being addressed. Even Ling joined the audience, although Dan returned to the bridge with Franz, who had announced that he planned a midnight departure for Jacksonville on a moderate sea. Clearly, Dan intended to keep a sharp lookout until the "Victoria" was safely at sea.

The Housing discussion proved to be a lively debate, with Nash and Nathan arguing for traditional segregation of house and lot sizes; versus Mark's fervent plea for a return to the small-town atmosphere of a century ago, where housing density varied from block-to-block, and zoning segregation of land uses and lot sizes had yet to be adopted. Jimmy kept discreetly quiet and concentrated on taking notes. The resultant strategy was a Logan compromise between the two points of view. Whereas Nash was concerned about the risks of mixing lot sizes and densities, he admired the logic of Mark's argument that people really live happier lives in socially-integrated communities. Mark had undertaken a great deal of research on this topic and he presented some excellent examples to support his housing-and-land-use integration recommendations.

On the other hand, Mark criticized the 'New Urbanism' principles of forcing center-city housing densities into small-town centers to support the viability of commercial establishments, particularly the traditional center-city pattern of housing over commercial establishments—a type of housing that had not fared well on the ownership market in new communities (although rental apartments did appear successful in many cases). Instead, he argued that community land use interaction should be distributed throughout the community by ease of transport, through his notion of a low-cost automatic rubber-tire jitney system to link activity centers. He argued that this system's costs could be kept low by using an electronic guidance system along paved rights-of-way, with a single-system controller able to increase and decrease the frequency of nine-person jitneys (three seats of three persons) depending on levels of activity on various parts of the system. Each jitney would have an automatic braking system for emergency obstructions and passenger accidents. The 'New Urbanism' standard of using a quarter-mile walking radius to define a high intensity center was not germane to a vibrant community with a safe and free transit system. Mark described it as similar in concept to the high-volume rail systems in Disney World and the Atlanta Airport, where horizontal access to activities is mandatory; that is, carnival rides and airplane terminals cannot be stacked vertically). Such a community would have limited automobile traffic, and no school buses for the elementary school (middle and high school students could gather at a central pick-up point for travel outside the community).

Nash was impressed by the logic of Mark's arguments, most of which depended on the economic viability of the electronically-guided jitney transit system. With the proviso of an immediate engineering and economic study of the jitney system (Nash instructed Jimmy to mark it with an 'urgent priority' in his notes), Nash dictated a modified concept of varying neighborhood densities and related jitney service to special-purpose activity centers; the neighborhoods would contain similar populations based on household size, ranging from neighborhoods with activity centers (and jitney stops) at radii of four-to-five-thousand meters (about one-quarter mile) up to lower-density neighborhoods with activity centers at radii of eight-to-ten-thousand meters. The latter would tend toward the periphery of the property and contain larger houses with larger lots for families who could afford their own personal Neighborhood Electric Vehicles (NEVs), ranging from individual 'Segues' to two/four/six-person electric carts, to transport them to the nearest activity center.

Mark concluded that Nash's realistic solution would very likely require a site that should approach a circular shape rather than a long-narrow or multi-arm shape. Therefore, the four real estate agents should only consider sites that accommodate approximate circular plans, within the normal (for Florida) constraints of small wetlands. Other shapes will not be considered. Nash and Nathan agreed with this conclusion and, after two hours of debate, agreed upon another site parameter.

The other Housing sub-components of house features, pricing, and locations for Multi-family and Congregate Care housing, were deferred as they did not affect the site acquisition decision.

"Super," exclaimed Nash enthusiastically. "This exercise is turning out to be far more productive than I imagined. Thank you, Mark, for your expert direction. Now, let's all take a fifteen-minute refreshment break."

∽

The four primary definers, still accompanied by their fascinated audience, convened around the conference table again after the refreshment break to tackle the fourth major New Community Component: Leisure.

"Welcome, everyone, to our definition discussion on the fourth major component of a new community: Leisure." At this point, Mark paused to pass out additional copies of the "New Communities Components" chart to those who had not received it previously. "We already have covered Commercial, Infrastructure, and Housing in our discussions, leaving Leisure and Institutional topics yet to complete. So let's dig into Leisure this evening."

"Excuse me for interrupting," said Nash, "but is it your intention to cover both Leisure and Institutional tonight?"

"That's up to you," replied Mark, "but I thought that we could finish Institutional in the morning. However, if you choose to keep going into the night, I am available. Now let's get started with Leisure.

"One of the major issues in planning a new community is the extent to which you can add appealing amenities, without driving the cost up to the point of exceeding consumer financial capabilities. As we have mentioned previously, Florida's Community Development District Legislation has allowed developers to bond both infrastructure and amenities, and thereby separate their costs from initial land expenses. Although this deferral of costs for both infrastructure and amenities has reduced the encumbrance on initial lot prices for consumers (but sometimes added to developer profits, rather than passed on to the consumer in lower prices), it does encumber residents with bond repayment over many future years. This practice has caused a very large number (well above one hundred) of Community Development Districts to default on bond payments because of house foreclosures, developer bankruptcies, or both. Many Florida communities are encumbered with debt burdens that residents cannot resolve. You may recall, earlier in our discussions, that Nash suggested the CDD concept may be terminated because of these untenable debt situations arising from The Great Recession."

"Absolutely," added Nash. "I believe this idea was a developer-support concept that has been misused, in many cases, to defer community debt without the full understanding of new residents buying into these communities. Of course, full disclosure is required, but the emotional commitment of purchasing a home often causes buyers to overlook future payment obligations. My objective is to build a new community with all development costs incorporated in the land price; but then to spread that land price over fifty or more years in lease agreements that will remain constant with the cost of money, throughout the lifetime of each resident who chooses to age in place within this community.'

"Good, Nash, and I understand and applaud your objective," replied Mark. "But reaching this objective puts even greater pressure on the balance of amenities with developed land costs as passed on to your purchasers in either purchase or Land Trust lease rates."

"Mark," interrupted Bobbi, "I know we are just spectators to this discussion, but could you clarify the long-term land-lease concept for those of us who are uninitiated?"

"Sure, good point, Bobbi. A Land Trust is a community-based non-profit corporation that owns and manages land for the benefit of those who use this land. They often are used by public entities to establish land conservatories, either through easements on land owned by others, or by acquisition under a limited-development scenario, whereby a portion of the land is protected and the remainder is available for development, according to specific use criteria. A Land Trust can be established for an entire neighborhood, or to an even larger area, where each resident can lease his lot or share of condominium land over a long period of time, assuming the Land Trust can secure long-term financing on the land's acquisition and development costs. The most common example of land leasing, although not usually in a Land Trust, is the mobile home park where the resident owns the mobile home, but leases the land from the owner (usually the owner of the mobile home park) for a monthly fee. The major difference between this mobile home park example and a Land Trust is, as the name implies, a non-discretionary pact on the lease of the land over a lengthy time period for residential use (that is, the land cannot be sold for another purpose). By this means, long-term financing can be established at very low rates of interest which encumber the homeowner with separate payments on a house mortgage and land lease. These payments can be substantially lower than the monthly payments on a mortgage for a house on a purchased lot, particularly if the price of that lot excludes CDD bond payments for infrastructure and for amenities that must be paid separately to the bond holder, in addition to mortgage payments and ad valorem taxes to the local government jurisdiction. Such a land lease can be transferred to another party who purchases the house from the original owner. I hope that explains the Land Trust concept that Nash is planning for this community; but, if you want more detail, I can cite some references for you when we return home."

"Thank you, I believe I understand the concept now," answered Bobbi.

"Returning to our major topic, we must define leisure-time facilities that meet the needs of a diverse-age community, as well as ensure that the costs do not exceed the spending capabilities of potential residents. In the final analysis, this blend of appealing amenities with affordable housing land must be submitted to a computer model of costs and revenues; but, at this stage, we simply must be sensitive to the issue when defining leisure-time facilities. Sometimes, we can solicit a special-purpose entity (such as the YMCA) to locate in the community as a relatively low-fee provider of these services, particularly indoor services; and frequently we can collaborate with local school districts on joint use of outdoor facilities (and possibly even indoor facilities for community meeting rooms outside school hours). However, since we are starting from scratch on an unknown site, I suggest that we do not assume any of these relationships, but rather that we concentrate on essential needs."

"Sounds good to me," added Nash. "Let's do it."

"Leisure-time activities are, of course, related directly to the characteristics of the proposed residents of our new community. In this case, we anticipate a mix of younger singles and couples with families of all ages and also older couples and singles—a diverse-age group of residents with a wide range of interests and athletic skills. Florida has a year-round outdoor climate for recreation activities; and our first priority is to plan a system of parks and playgrounds for all outdoor activities, both organized sports and individual pursuits. I suggest fifteen-acre active playgrounds be located convenient to every five-thousand households. The elementary school-yard can count as one, with three others distributed proportionately. Each can feature a special sport, such as soccer, baseball, softball and flag football; as well as smaller area sports including tennis, pickleball (deck tennis) for older persons, swimming pools (including a competition pool of Junior Olympic size, a shallow entry pool for young children, and a constant depth pool for aquasize), basketball courts, volleyball courts (sand), an adventure park with climbing apparatus for pre-teen children, and tot-lots for young children.

"These playgrounds should be supplemented by passive mini-parks, best linked by pathways and assigned special features including gazebos for small gatherings, flower gardens of specific varieties (for example, a rose garden) with benches and picnic tables with barbeques for picnics. Dog parks have also gained popularity, with a fenced paddock for letting dogs run without leashes. Outdoor 'hang-out' centers for teen-agers have proven popular in some communities (basically, a small sculpture garden with group benches of concrete which becomes a focal point gathering place). Some developers refer to this mini-park system of parks as a 'charm bracelet,' with each charm being a special-interest mini-park on the pathway system."

"How do these parks and mini-parks fit into the residential greenway system you have proposed earlier for linking the rear yards of houses?" asked Nathan.

"I was hoping you would ask," replied Mark with a smile. "The answer is that the two are integrated with the 'charm bracelet' extending through the various neighborhoods, offering new residents the opportunity to live on the pathway, and even adjacent to a charm park, or to live separate from it, with easy access by sidewalks. Choice is an essential part of the community which I propose. But once you are on a pathway, you soon learn that it leads to outdoor and indoor activity centers related to the age group of the majority of residents in that neighborhood.

"For example, families with young children will normally prefer to live near the elementary school or a pre-school facility whereas older couples often prefer to live within walking distance of a meeting and health center for their age group. So, our housing densities and types should be planned in accordance with those preferences, always with the caveat that a minority of each age group will prefer to select a location designed for a different age group. For example, some seniors prefer to live in a neighborhood where they can mingle with young children, even though the majority of their age group will prefer to be separate from children. The choice is theirs in the type of community I propose."

"So, what about indoor facilities?" asked Nash. "Clearly, unlike in Canada, here we can spend a greater part of the year outdoors, but there is still a need for heated and cooled facilities."

"Absolutely," answered Mark. "We do need two types of facilities indoors: fitness centers and meeting rooms for a variety of gatherings, from card games to lectures, as well as entertainment and group dinners. I recommend two such facilities, assuming we do not negotiate joint sponsorship from the YMCA or the school district: one, for all age groups which should be located centrally; and a second, targeted to older persons, and located central to the neighborhood housing for this age group. Both require fitness facilities, a large meeting room with a catering kitchen and furniture storage (for changing the seating and tables to accommodate different functions), one or more smaller meeting rooms for cards and other hobbies, and an office for a coordinator (either paid or volunteer), in addition to washrooms. A porch or covered deck for extending events outdoors in pleasant weather is also a nice feature, especially if it is linked to the food and drink preparation areas.

"The primary principle of this network of amenities is that their location provides both easy-access from the immediate target neighborhood, as well as access from other neighborhoods via the automatic shuttle system. Residents of all ages can attend events at any of these locations without ever taking their cars out of the garage."

"So, how do these great ideas affect the site selection?" asked Nathan.

"Excellent question! Theoretically, the 'charm bracelet' and shuttle system can be adapted to any shape, but your basic high school geometry lesson indicates that the most efficient overall shape is a circle or square; it provides the shortest distance to all points from any given location. So, we should attempt to find a site approximating this shape and avoid long narrow sites or irregular-shape sites if possible.

Now, I'm not sure about the rest of you, but this has been a long day for me. I vote that we head for our respective beds and tackle the last plan component—Institutional—first thing in the morning. How does that sound, Nash?"

"It sounds like a good plan, if I can just get a couple of strong arms to carry me down to my stateroom, so my nurse can tuck me in for the night."

"No problem, sir; Carlos and Alfredo are standing by for your signal," smiled Linda.

Half an hour after the meeting in the main lounge had ended, Nash had been carried down to his cabin, and Alfredo assisted him with his toiletries and with changing into his summer pajamas and silk bathrobe, prior to helping him over to a sit-up position on the right-hand side of his king-size bed. This allowed him to keep his broken leg and broken arm on the edge of the bed for easier departure in the morning. Alfredo then left him to receive his medications from his nurse, Linda, who noted that, rather than swallowing the pills immediately as he usually did, Nash placed them on the bedside table—no easy task with his right arm in a cast up to his elbow. She was questioning him on this move when a gentle knock interrupted their conversation. Linda opened the door to reveal the smiling face of Jose behind a tray holding two wine flutes and bucket containing a bottle of Dom Perignon champagne on ice. He marched past Linda and deposited it on the bedside table next to his boss. Then he executed a little bow and slipped out the door without a word.

Nash looked up at Linda standing at the foot of the bed, and said: "I thought perhaps you would like to join me in a celebratory drink before you retired."

"That sounds great," replied Linda with a smile, "but what are we celebrating?"

"Ah, let's see: the last night of our cruise, or the end of my elevated leg period; or, frankly, just an opportunity to visit with the most beautiful woman I have ever seen. The naked truth is, Linda, this is my last chance on this cruise to see you alone, and the champagne is just a prop to ask you to stay with me and talk for a while."

"Well, that sounds like lots to celebrate. Let's start." She then kicked off her shoes and curled up on the foot of the bed opposite her patient.

Nash immediately twisted around to grasp the bottle of champagne and held it with his left hand while reaching back for the two flutes Jose had left beside the ice bucket. Then he paused for a few seconds in a quandary as to how to hold the glasses while he opened the champagne.

"Wait," said Linda, "let me help." She then crawled across the bed and took the two glasses from his right hand, allowing him to place the bottle between his knees and pry open the cork with a loud pop. He then managed to tip it, using both hands, while Linda held each glass in position to receive the bubbly liquid. Nash managed to return the bottle to the bucket, before twisting back around to face her and accept one of the two full glasses.

"Here's a toast to my nurse, who has completely beguiled me for the past ten days with her professional skills, as well as her stunning beauty." And he tipped his glass toward her, before sipping his wine and gazing at her over the rim of the glass.

"That's pretty strong talk for a crippled man confined to a wheel chair," replied Linda, after tasting her own glass of champagne. "In my experience, those are the kind of compliments men use to coerce a girl into bed."

"Ah, but you're already on my bed, so I don't need to coerce you. The truth is that I haven't done any coercing for a long time, so I'm probably not very good at it. I needed this champagne as a prop to manage that carefully-rehearsed toast. You see, I was a happily-married man up until three years ago when my wife suddenly died with no advance warning, and left me with three grown children. I was a straight-arrow husband who kept his nose to the grindstone of building this business, so I drowned my grief in hard work and rarely even thought about other women until you walked onto my yacht. Now, I've reverted to being a teen-ager in my awkwardness to express my feelings for you. I realize that you're probably young enough to be my daughter and I have no right to approach you, and . . ."

"Hush," she interrupted. "You're running off at the mouth. First of all, I am not young enough to be your daughter, unless you were impregnating women as a teen-ager. I just turned forty-four years old, and, as you probably are aware, my husband ran off with a co-worker; so I recently got divorced after sixteen years of marriage. My sister married an older man three years ago, and she is completely happy. Like you, I have no recent experience at flirting with the opposite sex. If I did have any, I would have used it on you long before now, because I am strongly attracted to you. In fact, since we are being so open with each other, I think I will just slide over closer to you and make pretend that you coerced me with this wine."

Linda then drained her champagne and put the empty glass on the bed-table before crawling close and putting her arm around Nash's neck.

"Here is my toast to you Mr. Logan," and she proceeded to cover his mouth with hers to which he immediately responded in what quickly became a passionate tongue-twisting kiss that neither party seemed anxious to end. After a lengthy interval, they both came up for air and stared at each other with unblinking eyes, as though each one could not believe the other was equally attracted. Then they resumed mouth contact, this time with her body pressing against his while he reciprocated by putting his good left arm around her body and squeezing her even closer. It was a long time since Nash had felt the soft breasts of a woman pressed against his body, and the excitement left him speechless.

"So," she said with a twinkle in her eye, "was that a good toast or what?" He just stared at her for a moment before replying.

"It was a remarkable toast. I am virtually speechless . . . and, I also am frustrated by my inability to roll over and smother you with the passion I feel, but cannot physically express."

"Well then," she giggled, "I guess I will just have to smother you with my passion," and she proceeded to crawl on top of him with her elbows resting on his chest so she could look down at him. "There, do you feel suitably impassioned?"

"I am breathless with passion."

"You mean that I am too heavy on top of you."

"Don't you dare move," and then he suddenly started to laugh.

"What's so funny?"

"I just had a sudden thought that this activity is what they teach in nurses' training school. I never dated a nurse in my younger days, so I am not familiar with nursing procedures."

"Very funny, Mr. Logan, but the truth is that I just invented this move for you alone, and I like it up here where I am definitely in charge (as a good nurse should be)."

"Have you ever been to Toronto?"

"No, but I understand that it is a beautiful city, and that it is definitely a place I would like to see."

"How about day after tomorrow?"

"Oh, Nash, you've already rushed me off my feet. If I don't get back to work, I won't have a job to go back to, and . . ."

"Okay, I understand. But, when I regain the use of this leg and arm and then fly to Atlanta and pick you up, will you promise to come with me?"

"Well, let me give that some careful thought . . . yes," she replied by throwing both arms around him and beginning another kissing marathon. After a while she looked him in the eye again and asked: "But what about tonight? Are you in need of nursing care for the whole night?"

"Don't even think about leaving. I am in desperate need of major care . . . but, I don't think I'm capable of consummating this relationship in my present condition."

"Not to worry, my sweet, we'll improvise. But right now, I want some night clothes to replace these day clothes, so I will be back in fifteen minutes. Don't run away."

On the bridge of the "Victoria", the captain, still accompanied by Dan Houlihan, was directing Carlos and Alfredo in securing the lines on-board as he steered the big yacht away from the mooring and headed into Biscayne Bay and on out to the Atlantic for their fourteen-hour cruise to Jacksonville. The night was clear, with a half moon shining across the calm sea.

"What a great night for a cruise, Franz," said Dan. "We couldn't have ordered it up any better."

"You are absolutely right, my friend. The weather man says that we will have nothing greater than a two-foot sea all the way to Jacksonville. You can sleep well in this weather."

"I'm sure I could, Franz, but I plan to spend most of the night up here with you. If I do get tired, only then can you expect my lovely replacement."

"In that case," smiled Franz, "I'll arrange for some sleeping pills in your coffee."

DAY 13

Wednesday, April 7, 2010

"Do you see that vessel down there?" asked JJ Jensen as he put down his night binoculars. He addressed the question to Coast Guard Captain Jack Stuart, who was flying the two-seat military observation helicopter at almost ten-thousand feet of elevation over the eastern coast of Florida. They had been in the air trailing the "Victoria" for two hours, and it was now almost three o'clock in the morning.

"I see it all right, JJ. It looks as though your hunch is paying off. That seventy-five-foot 'fast boat' is tracking the 'Victoria' just as you suspected, and I will bet you a case of beer that one of Esperanza's sons is at the helm with a big load of cocaine down below. They love to take over a big yacht for a delivery into Jacksonville—always a hot spot for distribution."

"Well, I'm sure as hell not going to lose a case of beer when this chase was my idea in the first place. You must be on dope yourself."

"Just testing," laughed Jack. "You've been pretty quiet lately, and I wanted to make sure your mind was still functioning."

"So, how are we going to play this, Jack? I don't want to risk any more danger to Nash Logan and his guests."

"No problem, old friend. I've got two vessels in the water already on the basis of my faith in your hunch: a coast guard cutter is heading south out of Fort Pierce and the USS Vinson frigate is coming north about five miles behind us. But we must wait until the druggists try to board their target carrier so we have a solid case of hijacking to fall back on in case they manage to dump their cargo. We are five miles off Palm Beach right now and I suspect this is their target area—very quiet out here at this time of night. In terms of strategy, I have already contacted Dan Houlihan on board the 'Victoria' and he and Ling Ho will be ready to repel any borders, but we plan to have the very fast Vinson frigate alongside the drug boat at their moment of arrival. The coast guard cutter will close fast from the north when we advise them that it is going down."

"Sounds like a good plan to me," responded JJ.

♾

On board the "Victoria", everyone seemed to be sleeping peacefully, with the notable exception of Dan and Ling who were instructing Carlos and Alfredo in preparing for the potential arrival of unwanted boarders. They stationed the two crew members on the upper deck with shotguns from the Victoria stores. He and Ling planned to take cover on the lower stern deck with their service revolvers as the first line of defense. Any boarders that the two of them did not stop would be fair game for the two crew members, but he insisted that they both stay under cover unless they spotted a raider coming forward. Both Carlos and Alfredo had taken instruction on the use of the shotguns when they first joined the crew, but Dan revisited the procedure so there would be no slip-ups.

After positioning the two crew members under cover on the upper deck, Dan returned to the bridge, leaving Ling on-deck for visual surveillance. Upon Dan's arrival, Franz pointed to the radar screen which clearly showed a vessel closing the distance behind them at a high rate of speed. Dan immediately went to the ship's radio and turned to a pre-arranged channel.

"Hello Sky Dog, this is Mother. We estimate visitors within fifteen minutes at new rate of speed. Do you copy?"

"We copy you Mother," said Captain Stuart's voice over the bridge amplifier. "Our team is in the game on schedule. Please hold your course and speed."

"Roger that, Sky Dog. I am leaving the bridge now for defense position. Captain will be alone for duration."

"Understood! Captain, please prepare to slow vessel to stop when friendly vessels arrive."

"I understand and I am prepared," replied Franz calmly.

♾

In the Coast Guard helicopter high above the coastal waters, JJ had his night vision binoculars focused on the suspect fast-boat, which was gaining rapidly on the "Victoria".

"The bad guys appear to have five men on deck crowding the port rail," JJ reported to Jack. "Assuming two more bad guys at the helm, that makes a rather formidable raiding party."

"It does," replied Jack. "But, if everything goes according to plan, the USS Vinson should be pacing them about three miles south and it will catch up rapidly as soon as our target slows to the speed of the 'Victoria'."

"Yeah," said JJ, "if everything goes according to plan? Hold on, I believe your projection is on target. The bad guys are now abreast of the Victoria and slowed to her speed. I see a figure with a battery-operated megaphone aimed at the 'Victoria'."

"Ahoy, 'Victoria', please slow your speed. We wish to come aboard." But no sign of any recognition could be seen on the Victoria. The captain continued on his course without changing speed. So, the speaker tried again: "Allo, 'Victoria,' please slow down right now or we will be forced to open fire on you."

In response, the captain of the "Victoria" raised a hand-lettered sign in the starboard window of the bridge which said: "Go Away." A rifleman on the bandit boat immediately fired a bullet through the side window and the sign, but the experienced Captain Eriksson was already crouched on the floor and steering with one hand.

The bandit boat then moved closer to the Victoria and began riding the bow wave at a level well above the rear deck. Grappling hooks were thrown from the smaller boat to firmly grip the stern railing. Then a deck crane with two armed men in a container basket was swung over the side of the smaller vessel and the men lowered to the Victoria's stern deck. At the very second the basket touched the deck, two shots from a secure position on the rear deck caused both raiders to collapse, and return firing immediately commenced from others on the bandit boat.

Simultaneously with the firing from the bandit boat, the USS Vinson pulled alongside the smaller vessel and launched a side-ramp from which a raiding party of U.S. sailors swarmed aboard the bandit boat firing automatic weapons at everything that moved. Two sailors attacked the bridge of the attack vessel and one held the two occupants at bay while the second turned off the engine. Other sailors attached lines from the Vinson to the bow and stern of the bandit boat, securing it firmly to the larger vessel. As instructed, Captain Eriksson stopped his engines as well, successfully waking any of his passengers who had not already been awakened by the gunfire. Dan and Ling, as well as Carlos and Alfredo, wisely chose to stay under cover until the bandit boat was fully secure. Floodlights from a small helicopter lit up the rear deck as it lowered to a landing on the helipad. JJ jumped out of the co-pilot seat to embrace Dan and Ling with giant bear hugs of celebration. The three of them went up to the bridge to check on Franz. They found him on the internal ship phone explaining the action to Nash Logan in his stateroom and cursing the bandits for shooting out two of the windows that he had just replaced in Miami.

After Carlos hurried down from the upper deck to secure the helicopter, Jack Stuart checked in with Captain Ericksson on the bridge, and then joined JJ in going below to the owner's cabin to report the incident to Nash. While on the bridge, they had received word from the captain of the USS Vinson that his crew had captured Antonio Esperanza, one of the three sons of Francisco Esperanza, the notorious leader of the Esperanza drug cartel. The ship was casting off to allow the just-arrived coast guard cutter to take charge of both the prisoners and their fast-boat.

Down below, every passenger on the yacht was awake and anxious to learn what was going on. Within minutes, Nash's cabin had filled up with the other passengers, most of them in night clothes, eager to learn about the cause of all of the excitement.

With everyone talking at once, only Bobbi noticed her sister slipping out of the room in her dressing gown. She immediately followed Linda to her room and grabbed the door before it closed.

Once inside, she smiled secretively at her sister, and said: "Do I detect a rather smug look on your face little sister?"

"What on earth do you mean," replied Linda, with a look of genuine surprise?

"I mean, my dear, while everyone was rushing into Nash's cabin, you were the only person rushing out. If I didn't know you better, I would guess that you were actually sleeping with a patient."

"Well," said Linda, suddenly blushing and smiling simultaneously, "you would be right. Mr. Logan and I had a meeting of the minds last night, and, even though he was crippled with two casts, we managed to consummate our new relationship. Oh, Bobbi, I haven't been this happy in my entire life. I truly love this guy and I believe he loves me as well." The two sisters embraced for a full minute, only to discover that each one was crying.

"I am really happy for you, Linda. I sure hope it works out, because you don't deserve any more bad luck. But, remember, it gets really cold up in Toronto."

"I sure hope so," replied her sister between sniffles, "because I found just the right guy to keep me warm at night. And just think, if he is this great with two casts, I can't imagine how thrilled I will be with him in good physical condition."

As dawn broke over the eastern horizon, Captain Stuart and JJ bid everyone a cheerful goodbye after the big federal agent assured them that they would experience no more trouble with the drug cartel. The Coast Guard helicopter quickly took off and headed toward the coast. Smiling Jose then appeared on deck and invited everyone inside for an early breakfast.

For this final morning of the two-week cruise, while continuing their course back to Jacksonville in a relatively calm sea, the husband and wife chefs, Pierre and Marie Bouvet, elected to perform their skills tableside with omelets and other concoctions prepared at a portable electric grill on wheels. Despite the short night experienced by everyone on board, the two cooks endeavored to wow everyone with a special breakfast which they served to each person by request as they arrived in the main lounge.

Although everyone appeared to be cheerful about the capture of a major drug dealer, they could not help feeling sad over the absence of Jake, who they knew would be leading cheers for the cooks' culinary efforts. His death had been a big shock to everyone on the "Victoria".

However, all of them noticed that Nash was particularly cheerful that morning. He had summoned Carlos and Alfredo immediately after the helicopter left, and asked them to help him don some morning clothes, and then to carry him in his chair up to breakfast. He told everyone present (exclusive of Bobbi and Linda, who Mark reported were sleeping late) that JJ had advised him the previous day that the drug dealers might try to use his vessel to smuggle cocaine up to Jacksonville from their hideaway in Cuba. JJ told him that he was working very closely with the Coast Guard to monitor their trip and ensure that they would have the right forces on hand in case that his hunch proved accurate. His reasoning was that, after the prior hi-jacking of the "Victoria", Antonio Esperanza would assume correctly that the yacht was completely clear of any smuggling suspicion and therefore represented a perfect opportunity to be a carrier into the United States. He was carrying a large shipment for transfer to the "Victoria" (along with four of his men to ensure delivery in Jacksonville) that JJ estimated had a street value of over two billion dollars. JJ also figured that Antonio or one of his brothers would accompany such a large shipment to ensure it would be transferred safely. So, despite JJ disturbing his new Canadian friends a second time, he made the biggest haul of his career, and with the bonus of capturing one of the major principals in the Esperanza Cartel. Nash raised his coffee cup in salute: "Here's to our friend JJ, may he have continuing success nailing bad guys."

Everyone joined Nash in his breakfast toast, just before they noticed the yacht beginning to slow down. They all looked at each other in surprise, thinking that yet another incident was brewing, until Jimmy jumped up from his chair and announced that Tony

DiMartino was arriving by helicopter from Orlando right on time. Once Tony was served some breakfast, they could convene at the conference table.

∽🙰∽

Although several of the yacht passengers had conversed with Tony DiMartino by phone, nobody except Mark and Bobbie knew him in person. Mark immediately greeted him and welcomed him aboard, before introducing him first to Nash, and then to the others. He was a handsome man of middle-age and average height and stature with dark curly hair, who appeared to have a contagious smile for everyone. There seemed little question that his personality would fit well with this group.

Despite his right arm still in a cast and sling, Mark was fully prepared to chair the final session of new community components, prior to starting the planned session dedicated to site selection parameters. The attorney already had heard about the night-time incident on the radio news in Orlando while driving to the airport, and Nash filled him in on the details while he was eating breakfast, so he was all set to participate in the new community discussions.

"Gentlemen," Mark began, noticing that none of the ladies had arrived from their morning slumbers, "we dedicated today's session to discussing site selection parameters with Tony, but first we must reach consensus on the fifth component of our proposed new community: 'Institutional Land Uses'. For Tony's benefit, I should mention that we have been using this guideline diagram with five components of a new community," and he handed a diagram to Tony.

"We began with Commercial Land Uses yesterday and worked out way around the diagram to reach consensus on Infrastructure, Housing and Leisure before turning in for our abbreviated sleep. So, we now must tackle 'Institutional'. Any questions?"

"Yes," spoke Nathan, "I would like to check with Jimmy on his note-taking. We covered a lot of ground yesterday and I would like his assurance that he can summarize it for us when we return to Toronto."

"Absolutely, Mr. Rosenburg, my trusty computer contains all of the salient facts, which I will have translated and on your desk for review when you arrive back in your office."

"Thank you, Jimmy," smiled Nathan. "Please don't take my question as being in any way doubtful of your competence. But, with all the excitement last night, I just realized that I had not taken adequate notes myself, and I wanted to reassure myself that you have everything in hand. Let's move on."

"Right," said Mark. "Institutional includes six sub-components, with the two most important being Education and Health, and, at least in this state, the biggest land user being Spiritual."

"Wow," exclaimed Nash from his wheelchair. "Are you telling me that we will end up with more land for churches than for schools?"

"Actually, Nash, this is your choice to make. But the demand will be there from religious organizations, and they are prepared to pay the same price for land as commercial enterprises. So, most developers are glad to accommodate them."

"That blows me away," replied Nash. "I never would have expected such a big religious demand. I thought Florida was south of the so-called 'Bible Belt' as well as filling up with northern migrants."

"In fact, Nash, we are south of the 'Bible Belt' and Florida does attract a large number of migrants from a wide range of origins" pronounced Mark. "However, the majority of our working class migrants and our retiree migrants come from religious backgrounds, and the well-entrenched religious institutions in Florida compete strongly for religious market share. If the community developer does not allocate sufficient land for this demand, religious groups will simply purchase parcels outside the community boundary. The biggest issue for this land use, in my view, is architectural control. We are no longer in the great church-building era, and some of these buildings can be detrimental to our streetscapes if we do not maintain quality design standards.

"However, let me return to education and health, two mandatory ingredients of any community that also are major generators of traffic during weekdays in competition with employment commuter trips. The potential for eliminating school buses is my first plea for your attention. We discussed the concept of an internal automatic jitney transit system yesterday and you agreed to it subject to cost. It is the answer to replacing expensive and traffic-generating school buses, albeit just for elementary schools, but we can even reduce their routes for middle and high schools through efficient design of the jitney system. If we subscribe to the population mix we discussed yesterday, I foresee a need for only one elementary school. Assuming we locate the majority of young family housing within convenient distance of this school, and plan our jitney system adequately, I believe we can avoid buses at the elementary level. Let me also attempt to pre-empt questions of security by suggesting that current expenditures on school-crossing guards should suffice for ensuring safety on our jitney system. However, please remember that these issues are subject to the opinions of elected school boards in Florida, so this subject becomes a site selection issue with respect to the proven progressive policies of the relevant county school board."

Nash held up his one good arm and said "I must admit, Mark, that you are quickly winning me over to the idea of solving a number of issues with this automatic jitney. I only hope that it is not cost-prohibitive."

"Excellent point," replied Mark. "We cannot prove the cost-effectiveness of this concept without an engineering study. My plea is that you will agree that the benefits are sufficient to fully explore this option."

"As I said, you are convincing me to join the advocacy group. So, let's move on."

"Very well, let's return to health care. Our delivery systems for health care are already undergoing great change in this country. The current new federal legislation will accelerate this change. Neighborhood clinics and specialty surgery centers are already commonplace, as fewer and fewer procedures require hospitalization. The size of community we are proposing does not warrant a full-service hospital, but we must plan for clinics, particularly in proximity to our housing for older persons. And, we must be sensitive to current or planned full-service hospitals convenient to the selected site. This parameter is a priority for site selection that must be on the agenda for our next session. I would appreciate it, Jimmy, if you would ensure that it is raised."

"Will do," Jimmy responded, without looking up from his computer.

Mark then described other issues in the Institutional component that bear upon the activities promoted in the county to be selected for this community. Arts and culture activities as well as community support for less popular programs such as special needs groups are always more cost-effective if the county is well-managed by progressive leadership. An example is the variation in education throughout Florida. This issue used to center on racial disparity, but today, in addition to pockets of racial inequity, there are still entire districts (counties) that resist advances in education. The charter school concept, often sponsored by a forward-thinking developer is one response to this problem, but many aspects of Institutional facilities and services are a lot easier if the new community is in a county with a progressive administration. "I believe this is the key conclusion to be carried over to our next session. Tony, do you have anything to add to my conclusion?"

"Thank you, Mark, for including me in this select group as well as asking my advice on this particular subject. As most of you know, my sister chose to marry an African-American and they have three inter-racial children attending school in Hillsborough County encompassing Tampa. They searched for many weeks before purchasing a home in that county because, although the county school board was progressive, individual schools had policies that differed substantially from county directives. In short, despite being a major urban county with intelligent people elected to public office, significant disparity existed in schools throughout the county because of the influence of local citizen groups on school principals and elected representatives. My brother-in-law is a big man and usually swings a great deal of influence on the basis of his size alone, but he confessed to me that their first home in Hillsborough was an unhappy situation for their daughters because of neighborhood church groups that took strong stands on issues with racial undertones. Since he holds a senior government position, he was able to seek advice from county officials and they soon moved into a neighborhood with a higher ratio of college-educated residents who lobbied for progressive school policies. My point in telling you about JJ's problems is that site selection requires examination of local politics at the sub-county level as well as the county level, and I suggest you hire some intensive market research prior to your final decision."

"That is excellent advice, Tony, and also a convenient segue into our site selection session," replied Mark. "I suggest a brief washroom and coffee break before reconvening."

During Tony DiMartino's remarks, Bobbi and Linda had quietly joined the group, followed shortly by Ling and Dan. Several spirited discussions erupted during the break period in which the three women were involved. It seems that Tony's remarks touched off similar experiences by several of the participants that provoked different viewpoints. Mark experienced some difficulty in convincing everyone to return to the conference table to begin the site selection discussion. Finally, with everyone seated, he exhibited his friendliest smile before beginning.

"Welcome back, everyone. I note that Tony's comments before we adjourned stimulated some lively discussions during the break, which indicate that we may have a productive seminar through the rest of the day. Hopefully, that will be beneficial to our objective of setting optimum guidelines for selecting the site for the Logan new community. Since we only have an hour left before lunch, I would like to use that time to agree on the parameters for site selection. Somehow, I feel confident that one or more of you will break in if you have a contrary view. But, first of all, I have asked Jimmy to refer to his computer notes to headline the parameters that we revealed during our discussions yesterday and this morning. I will serve as his assistant by writing his key words in magic marker on this new easel pad Jimmy found for me in Miami."

Jimmy was scrolling back through his computer notes, on which he had added some red comments to highlight key parts of yesterday's discussion. "With the exception of Tony," Jimmy began, "most of you will recall yesterday's discussion at which Mark introduced the five major components of a new community, followed by focusing on each of the major components, beginning with Commercial. This subject first involved Nathan telling us about his concept of the housing package factory and its location requirements. My headline notes indicate, first, adequate electric power supply, second, Interstate Highway access, and, third, railroad access. Does that cover it, Nathan?"

"Excellent summary, Jimmy," replied Nathan. "You are assuming, I suspect, that water and sewer lines are available to the industrial park, but perhaps they should be listed as important location elements. Also, although I don't recall any specific discussion yesterday, we need to ensure proper zoning for industrial use, especially if we should follow the suggestion of acquiring an existing community site that is entitled."

"This is a good point, Nathan," said Mark. "I am listing industrial zoning along with the four infrastructure requirements. Were there any other location parameters that related to the Commercial discussion?"

"Perhaps not," added Nash, "but I am wondering whether we should assign weights to these parameters. The access elements are absolutely essential for our community, whereas we might be able to negotiate the zoning issue."

"Another good point," replied Mark, "but I suggest that we defer the priority ranking until we have a complete list in front of us. Does that seem reasonable?"

"Absolutely, Mark," replied Nash. "We should follow your call on procedure."

"Alright, Jimmy, let's move on to Infrastructure," suggested Mark.

Jimmy continued with his summary. "The Infrastructure discussion was centered on Mark's ideas for internal people-mover automatic transit which, as I understand it, would be most efficient if the community was in a square or round shape overall rather than a long or angular shape. Therefore, my headline word is 'circle' to imply overall site geography. Does that sound clear?"

"It does to me," replied Mark, as he wrote that word on his easel pad as point six.

"Excuse me," said Tony, "but I need a little clarification here. I believe you all are aware that Florida is pockmarked with wetlands, that, for the most part, cannot be infringed upon for development uses. Therefore, I assume, Mark, that you are referring to a circular site as being ideal if wetlands did not cut across it to spoil your efficient transit line? What I am suggesting is that the word 'circle' may not suffice to make your point."

"You are right, of course," answered Mark. "The concept is to define the shortest possible line linking all neighborhood activity centers. And, although your non-infringement constraint is generally correct, we have frequently been granted approval to route boardwalks and other linkages through wetlands. So, I would beg your indulgence on the wetlands issue with regard to the overall shape of the site. Although a circle may not work because of wetlands, it is still a good guideline in comparison with linear or angular shapes. However, you have raised a separate issue which we should address, so I would like to add 'wetlands' to our list as a constraint that could negate a site that is simply too expensive for efficient development."

"Can we tell from initial aerial photographs if the wetlands are too severe," asked Nash?

"In a great many cases, the answer is yes," replied Mark. "The nature of the tree growth is a good sign of the land underneath. However, we may well have questionable situations that require further study. Since, our time is short, even these may be deleted. But, in any event, the addition of wetlands to our list will keynote this parameter."

"Mark," interjected Nash. "I see that Jose is making nervous hand signals that his hot soup for lunch is cooling off, so I suggest we break for lunch and resume in an hour."

The relatively calm sea allowed the cooks to serve a delicious clam chowder soup for lunch, along with small salmon sandwiches and a light salad. Everyone seemed to have an appetite and Jose had to send down for more sandwiches. But, clearly, the somber mood prevalent since Jake's tragic death had given way to spirited conversation, especially apparent at Tony's table where lawyer stories seemed in vogue to entertain their newcomer. Although a few people returned to their cabins for a few minutes after lunch, the majority moved directly back to the conference table, where they soon were joined by Mark and Nash for a continuation of the discussion on site selection.

∽

"Now that we have gathered once again after that delicious lunch," began Mark, "I would like to pick up on the identification of site selection parameters. You will recall that, this morning, we identified seven parameters from our discussion of Commercial and Infrastructure components. I have written them on this easel pad for reference. Now I would like to turn to the third of our five community components: Housing. Jimmy, from your notes on our prior discussion of this topic, do you have any site selection parameters?"

"My notes indicate that our Housing discussion focused entirely on issues internal to the site," replied Jimmy. "But, I may have missed something."

"No, I don't think so," added Nash from his wheelchair. "I distinctly recall Mark concluding that Housing could be accommodated without affecting site location."

"Yes, I believe that is correct," said Mark. "Tony, can you think of anything in the Housing component that might affect our site selection?"

"My only comment, Mark, would be on the cooperation of the local government appointed and elected officials on some of the construction and site planning innovations you appear to be planning. I believe you are more likely to receive a positive reception from a larger and more urbanized local government than a smaller more rural one. Now, I realize that some of you may believe me to be somewhat arrogant in that remark, but the fact is that there is proven correlation between higher paid officials in larger governments and innovation."

"I think that Tony makes an excellent point, Mark," added Nash. "I suggest you add a note on innovative local government, but without the proviso on size. It could well be that there are smaller governments that have exhibited a welcome reception for innovation, perhaps under the influence of an individual leader. Although I accept Tony's observation on the relationship between size and professional staff capabilities, I don't believe we should accept it as definitive. Let's keep an open mind on size while noting the importance of positive attitude on innovation."

"Well stated," added Tony. "I agree."

"So be it, then," said Mark. "I am adding point eight as 'government innovation' which I am defining as government acceptance of innovation, but shortening it to fit my pad. Anything further on Housing? If not, I would like to turn to Leisure and once again refer to Jimmy for his notes on this topic."

Jimmy took a minute to review his computer notes before responding. "Mark, my notes indicate that, once again, we appeared to refer to the capacity of local government to provide or supplement Leisure activities in similar fashion to accepting innovation in Housing."

"Ah-ha," interjected Nathan. "There may be a significant difference between these two possibilities. "We could have a local government that has, for whatever reason, generated some fantastic facilities for leisure activities, such as a major regional park, but still be quite naïve, or even hostile to housing innovations. So I would suggest to you that these are two separate selection points."

"By golly, you are absolutely right Nathan," replied Jimmy. "I jumped to that conclusion far too quickly."

"No problem, Jimmy," smiled Nathan, "but I do believe it important to differentiate these two local government issues."

"Very well," said Mark. "I will add a new point on local government facilities, either existing or planned."

"No," interjected Nathan, "I believe that is too restrictive. Please scratch 'local.' We could have such facilities provided by state or federal branches of government."

"You are absolutely correct," acknowledged Mark. "Point nine will be simply government facilities. Are there other Leisure issues that we should consider? If not, let's move on to Institutional which, to some extent may overlap with the other components in terms of government receptivity and facilities. Jimmy, do you have notes that will help us here?"

"Oh yes, we did discuss both local government and non-government organizations being involved in this issue. The subject of innovation was mentioned with regard to the elementary school and the possibility of shared facilities. We also discussed the future of health care with respect to the growth of out-patient clinics under the new federal health care legislation and its likely impact on local delivery systems. But, of perhaps greater importance for a new community is the level of existing care and safety facilities in proximity to a proposed site. Finally, we discussed other regional programs in the arts and cultural areas that could supplant new facilities required in the new community."

"Wow," exclaimed Nash. "That's a bunch of stuff, Mark. How do we synopsize all of it into decision factors?"

"Good question, Nash. It seems to me that we were talking about the social fabric of the existing regional community and how it might impact a new development inserted into its midst.

I am reminded of a case right here in Florida, where the announcement of a new community stimulated a local hospital to approach the developer for a low-price site (which was granted), whereas negotiations with the regional symphony orchestra for a magnificent lakeside site fell through because of the opinions of a couple of major benefactors. My point is that such opportunities are more likely in an urbanized site location than in a rural situation. So is this a single criterion or several more specific criteria? Tony, what's your view?"

"Frankly, Mark, I believe you have summed it up quite well," replied Tony. "Clearly, you have more opportunities for supply partners in an urban area, but at the same time it seems likely that you may need to compromise some of your own planning objectives to fit in with the objectives of such partners. I believe this topic to be a single criterion which is strongly related to the urban development of the area. It is both good news and bad news, depending on your skill and luck at negotiating with the existing institutions of that particular area."

"So," added Mark, "Tony opts for a single point that covers all of the public and private institutions of an urban area versus the relative simplicity of a rural area. However, he did not take a stand on whether this is a good thing or a bad thing for your particular community plan. I'm afraid, Nash, that your advisors are dumping that decision into your lap."

"I hear you," replied Nash with a smile. "But I don't hear any of my own colleagues going out on a limb to take a stand on this absolutely critical issue. Therefore, I suggest that you mark it down as 'urban/rural?' without conclusion and that we open the bar to loosen tongues. What do you think, Mark?"

"Well," replied Mark with a smile, "I am almost always in favor of opening the bar, but I trust that you are fully aware of the gravity of this tenth point. It overpowers many of your other issues in determining where you buy land."

Nash smiled back at his new friend. "I do understand, but I don't know the answer, so let's throw it around some more over a couple of drinks and maybe it will be clarified. Or maybe it will get more complex and then we will need additional drinks."

"Very well, let's adjourn for refreshments and plan to gather again after dinner."

Everyone started to chat with their immediate neighbors and a few wandered over to where Jose and Alfredo had set up the bar and a variety of canapés for the guests. It looked like the meeting had ended without a conclusion. But, Mark had no intention of allowing two weeks of effort to end on an inconclusive note. He adjourned to his cabin for a personal review of his notes to prepare for a decisive evening session.

After another great dinner created by Pierre and Marie Bouvet in the yacht's small kitchen, Mark urged everyone to bring their coffee and tea to the conference table where he had copied the ten major site location parameters on a fresh page of the easel pad.

"Now we need to weight this list in terms of priorities so we can apply these parameters in rational fashion to the alternative sites being identified for us," announced Mark. "This exercise is, by definition, rather subjective. But, an advance set of priorities will help a great deal in comparing our options. So, I suggest we begin with identifying the absolutes in this list; that is, those items that we cannot live without. Let's start at the top and work our way down."

"I would suggest," offered Nathan, "that the first five points are all absolutes. We simply cannot proceed without power, Interstate access, rail access, water and sewer, and industrial zoning."

"With all due respect to Nathan," said Tony, "the last two are somewhat more flexible than the first three. We are not about to influence changes in the power grid, the Interstate highway system or railway lines. But, we can influence water and sewer systems as well as zoning changes. Before anyone pounces on me, let me add that I am well aware of the time issue, but the fact is that the last two priorities are lower than the first three."

"I agree with Tony," interjected Nash, "that, despite the time issue, we have somewhat more flexibility in changing points four and five than the first three points."

"You're right," laughed Nathan. "I was too quick on the draw."

"Okay," said Mark, "we appear to have consensus on the absolute necessity for points one, two and three. Let's attempt to rank the other seven points in relation to these three absolutes. Unless anyone disagrees, I will mark points four and five as number two priority—not absolute, but important."

"I believe that's right, Mark," responded Nash from his uncomfortable wheel chair, "but I believe that your point number eight, Innovative Local Government, should be right up there with them. We need a partner in this undertaking who is positive about new ideas and ready to join with us in finding better solutions to community land use and housing than we have had in the past. In fact, I suggest that we make any offer to purchase contingent upon successful interviews with both key staff and elected officials."

"Excuse me," interrupted Tony, "I thought that I detected an open-end contract item floating in the wind."

"First of all," exclaimed Nash in a much stronger voice, "there isn't any wind in here, and, second, Tony, you had better get used to my non-legal nature. In this case, I am trying to recruit the seller and the selling agent to become our advocates and use their influence with the local officials to welcome us into their jurisdiction. Now, this objective may be difficult to spell out in precise legal jargon, but the reasoning is sound and I believe you have the word skills to make it happen."

"Well then, by golly, if you believe I can do it, then it will be done," answered Tony with a genuine smile of acceptance. "But, frankly, Nash, I anticipated your concern about local government and I took some time yesterday to solicit opinions on the jurisdictions we are exploring. So, regardless of contingencies in the purchase contract, I believe we can answer this question to your satisfaction in advance. That is not to say that I have a problem with the interviews. On the contrary, I endorse that idea. But, I have some pretty good intelligence on the public officials in each of the target jurisdictions."

"Great, Tony," Nash smiled and spoke in a milder tone, "I look forward to learning more about this topic at the appropriate time."

	Priority
Electric Power Supply	1
Interstate Highway Access	1
Railroad Access	1
Water and Sewer Supply	2
Industrial Zoning	2
Circular Site Shape	3
Modest Wetlands	3
Innovative Local Government	2
Existing Government Facilities (e.g. Parks)	4
Urban vs. Rural Environment Issues	5

Exhibit 33:
Site Selection Priorities.

"Excellent," chimed in Mark. "We are agreed that the Innovative Local Government parameter is a second priority selection point. What about the other four points?" "Mark," spoke Nathan, "I thought you made an excellent case for the site to approximate a circular shape, and the wetlands issue appears to be a related issue. I would propose that these two points be accorded a higher priority than the remaining two issues. In fact, let me go further to propose making those two the third priority and points nine and ten the fourth and fifth priorities in that order."

"Any other thoughts," asked Mark?

"Then, I assume that you are in agreement with Nathan's suggestion. That gives us five sets of priorities out of the ten selection points. We have reduced the site selection decision by half. I am going to leave this easel here for us to re-address in the morning when Tony brings us information on the available sites. He should have his messenger here between eight and nine o'clock. I look forward to seeing you then, and I wish each of you pleasant dreams. Good night."

During the evening discussion, Captain Ericksson had skillfully guided the "Victoria" into the mouth of the St. Johns River and up the river fifteen miles to downtown Jacksonville, where he had reserved the same berth that they had enjoyed at the outset of their Florida adventure. After directing Carlos, Alfredo and Jose to set the dockside fenders and secure the mooring lines, the weary captain closed down the engines and retired to his cabin for a well-earned rest.

As was customary in port, the three crew members each took watch shifts through the night. Carlos volunteered for the evening shift and took his post on the upper deck, while Alfredo and Jose retired to their bunks prior to their shifts later that night. Despite a cool breeze, the long hours at sea proved too much for the sturdy deck-hand, and he soon dozed upright in his deck chair. He never noticed two late-evening visitors slip up the gangway.

The master cabin in the yacht "Victoria" had the dead bolt carefully secured to guard against any unexpected visitors to the newly discovered love affair between Nash and Linda. She was sitting cross-legged on the foot of his bed revealing her childhood experiences, while he was comfortably propped up with pillows against the headboard. An open bottle of champagne in a bucket of ice was on a tray between them and he sipped from his glass listening to her story with a contented smile on his face.

Linda and Bobbi had spent most of their childhood in the Atlanta suburb of Marrietta where their father was a family physician. Although they lived a relatively normal suburban lifestyle, their parents did take them on some exciting vacations to Europe and South America during their teen years, so they both experienced other lands and cultures at an early age. Nash responded that his youth was consumed by work experiences and, even after marriage, his time was devoted to developing his home-building company. Vacations were mostly at summer cottages in the lakes district north of Toronto, in addition to annual ski-weeks, primarily at Canadian resorts in Quebec and in the mountains of British Colombia and Alberta.

Linda's parents also enjoyed snow skiing, so both of their daughters spent a week every winter with them in various Colorado ski resorts. At this point in her story, Nash was able to interject his own love of skiing with his children, and they drifted into a comparison of ski resorts that they both had experienced. He mentioned that he used to rent a cabin for his family at Mont Tremblant in the Canadian Laurentian Mountains north of Montreal for several winters, and Linda was excited to report that she and her husband had spent a delightful week of skiing at the same resort just a few years ago. The fact that all of their vacations had been with other mates caused both of them a little embarrassment initially, but they soon became accustomed to the reality that they had enjoyed other companions. Besides, it helped both of them avoid the obvious topic of how their new relationship might develop in future.

Eventually, after leaning forward to re-fill their glasses, Nash ventured into a more delicate discussion topic: "You should know, Linda, that last night was a very special experience for me. No, I am not referring to my difficulties in attempting to make love with these casts on my body, but rather I'm talking about emotions that I have not felt in many years. You have completely bewitched me, and I'm afraid I cannot respond adequately by either words or physical actions. Frankly, I am as frustrated as a young boy on his first date."

"Me too," she responded quietly. "But, I am more concerned about your immense wealth than your casts. It would be a lot easier for me to fall in love with a poor man than a rich one. I have never known any rich people and I don't know how to act around them. You surprised me with your reciprocal attraction last night and I just charged ahead without thinking. But, today, I began to have second thoughts about my brash behavior. You may be accustomed to women throwing themselves at you. Perhaps I should have remained more aloof and let you decide how to proceed. Damn, I think I need psychiatric counseling."

"Hey, slow down," Nash laughed. "I forgot to tell you that I'm a highly trained professional counselor. Not only that, but my fees are very modest. If you will be good enough to move that tray off the bed and move closer, I will exhibit some of my counseling skills for you. And I absolutely promise that you will be impressed."

"Oh yeah?" she replied, as she proceeded to follow his instructions. "Well, this better be good, because I can't go back to work with a nervous breakdown."

"Just cuddle up here and put your head on my left shoulder. Good, now just relax and I will tell you how I believe you should behave around rich widowers. Listen carefully."

"I'm listening."

"Good, the first hurdle is covered . . . getting your full attention. Now the major point to remember about rich people is that they come in two flavors. First are the inherited-wealth people who have been rich since birth. They tend to be the model for all rich people since they are the personalities shown in movies and described in books as aristocratic snobs who truly believe that they are born into a life of privilege and that everyone around them should recognize their special status in life.

"Second are the self-made millionaires who devoted their lives to an invention or a business which prospered and rewarded their hard work with a lot of income. Although some of these people adopt the characteristics of the inherited wealth people, most retain the personality that they had prior to their good fortune. If they were grumpy introverted people before they made money, chances are that they remained that way afterward. However, if they spent their lives motivating other people to higher production through positive actions, then they should remain that way. Since I am of the latter group, you have nothing to fear. I am the one who must, by my very nature, motivate you to positive thinking; which, of course, is the whole purpose of this little counseling session. So, do you feel more relaxed now?"

"Well, to tell you the truth, Nash, I think you are full of baloney, but I must admit that I am more relaxed listening to your fairy tales than fretting about my own behavior. So I guess that your counseling session must be considered successful. That being said, I am therefore going to my room and put on my love-making clothes, after which I will return to my brash and aggressive behavior again. Let the chips fall where they may."

And with that little speech, Linda jumped off the bed and strode toward the door, unlocked the dead bolt, and gently opened it and closed it behind her. Nash smiled to himself as he returned to sipping the champagne. There was no doubt in his mind that Linda was the best thing that happened to him in recent memory, perhaps even in long memory. Regardless, he was determined to keep her close by for the indefinite future. Life was unbelievably good.

When the door opened again, Nash looked up in anticipation, only to be shocked beyond belief. For, instead of the beautiful Linda in night clothes, the person entering his room was none other than Jack Swift dressed from head to foot in an orange prison outfit and holding a deadly black handgun pointed directly at the Canadian. Closely behind him was the former Victoria Chief Engineer, Tim Williams.

"What the hell are you doing here?" Nash shouted angrily.

"Good evening, Mr. Logan," responded Swift with a vicious smile. "I'm afraid that the authorities failed to keep me incarcerated, and my friend Tim provided transport up here to Jacksonville where I have some unfinished business with you. In case you are thinking about making a fuss, let me first inform you that Tim and I have disarmed and imprisoned your deck crew along with Houlihan and Ho; and also, the lovely Linda Cummings is tied up in her cabin hoping to escape unharmed. And she will be unharmed if you do exactly what I tell you."

"You bastard, Swift, if you harm that woman, I will hunt you down like the dirty dog you are. What on earth possessed you to return here anyway?"

"Very simple, my dear man. You still have a portion of the cocaine shipment hidden aboard from our first hijacking. The Navy people were so anxious to arrest us and Antonio Esperanza, that they did not conduct a thorough search of the vessel. Now, you and I are going to sail off into the moonlight with our precious cargo. Your cooperation is mandatory."

"Alright, you have the upper hand, Swift. What do you want me to do?"

"Very simple, Mr. Logan, just press the button on your phone for the captain and ask him to come to your quarters immediately."

Nash grabbed the phone off the bedside table with his left hand and pulled it over to the bed, where he dialed Captain Ericksson's number and apparently woke him from a sound sleep. He replied to Nash's request with a question on the nature of the yacht-owner's problem at this hour of the night, but Nash simply repeated his request for the captain to report to his cabin.

Linda was both mad and very uncomfortable. Swift and Williams had surprised her just as she was entering her cabin to change clothes. Williams clamped a chloroform-soaked gag on her mouth and rendered her unconscious. When she awoke, she quickly realized that they had bound her with bed-sheets and tied her hands firmly to the bed's headboard. A cloth gag taped across her mouth prevented her from crying for help.

Her cabin was furnished in the same fashion as Mark and Bobbi's cabin across the passageway: a bathroom and closet at the entry hall, and a double bed in the major space, with its headboard fastened to the partition wall of the adjoining cabin forward in the yacht. In addition to bedside tables with reading lamps and a telephone, a small table and four chairs, as well as a built-in set of drawers, were adjacent to a large window with drapes closed for the night.

The adjoining cabin, she knew, was occupied by Ling Ho, whom she assumed was now asleep. Linda's mind was focused on how she could wake up Ling and enlist her help to escape her bonds. Although not an athlete, Linda kept her body in trim condition with daily workouts at the hospital rehabilitation center. She slipped off her sandals and attempted to twist sideways on the bed to reach the telephone with her toes. Remembering Ling's phone number from prior instructions, she eased the handset off its cradle and then used her big toe to push one, zero, four on the keypad. She could hear the rings, but no answer.

Linda proceeded to bang her heel on the bedside table as hard and as fast as she could manage. Obviously, she needed a Plan B. So, she disconnected the phone and, using her toes again, she was able to push the four digits for Bobbie and Mark's cabin. Bobbie answered almost immediately in a sleepy voice: "Hello, who is calling, please, hello . . ." The only answer Linda could manage was to continue pounding the table with her heel. Then Bobbie disconnected, and Linda heard the frustrating sound of the dial tone. In desperation, she managed to swivel her hips around even farther until she could stretch both feet to the wall above the bedside lamp. With extraordinary effort, she began pounding on the wall with both heels. But, her strength diminished after a half dozen tries, and she lay back on the bed exhausted. Her efforts appeared hopeless.

Just as Linda was gathering her strength to attempt renewed wall-pounding, she heard the sound of a key in the door lock, so she quickly resumed her prone position. But her fear that her attackers were returning quickly turned to relief when she saw Ling and Dan appear at the foot of her bed accompanied by Bobbie and Mark. Franz Ericksson was close behind.

It turned out that Bobbie had been sufficiently disturbed by the unanswered phone call, that despite Mark's pleading for her to return to bed, she donned her dressing gown and went in search of Dan or Ling. After receiving no response from knocking on Ling's cabin door, she headed up the stairway toward the captain's cabin behind the bridge. She was surprised to meet a sleepy Captain Ericksson descending the stairway. Since he was concerned already about Nash's terse phone call, he suggested to Bobbie that the two of them use his master key to enter the cabins of Dan and Ling.

In Dan's cabin, they found the two of them bound and gagged on the floor. Bobbie and Franz quickly released them and learned that, much to their further embarrassment, they had been captured by Jack Swift and Tim Wilson in the main lounge where they were discussing the strange saga of the past few days. Their captors wasted no time in disarming and binding them in Dan's cabin. Once free of her gag, Ling added that she had heard banging coming from Linda's room, and she suspected that Linda also may have been restrained by Swift and Wilson. So, the five of them rushed to open Linda's cabin door.

"Well," proclaimed Ling, with her hands on her hips, "this is a strange way to sleep. C'mon, Dan, let's get her untied." The two of them quickly went to work freeing Linda's bindings and removing her mouth gag. "Now, Linda, please tell us what's going on. How did you get in this mess?"

"I have no idea what's going on," Linda replied breathlessly. "I was unlocking my door to, uh, retire when two men attacked me from behind and shoved a chloroform-soaked cloth over my nose and mouth. I woke up bound up like you found me and struggled to get your attention."

"You succeeded admirably," said Dan. "Ling complained that she couldn't possibly sleep with all that noise coming from your room. But how did you manage the telephone to wake Bobbie?"

"With my big toe," replied Linda with a giggle. "I may have discovered a whole new exercise routine. But, enough of me. Nash may be in trouble. We must find these attackers."

"Right," stated Dan. "But, we must move cautiously. While Franz was unlocking your door, I contacted JJ and told him to send in the local reserves, but let's see if we can clean up this problem before they arrive. We do not know how many attackers are on board, but we do know that one or more are in Nash's cabin where they apparently ordered Nash to summon the captain. And I suspect that they began with Nash. That's the reason they assaulted Linda, to claim her as a hostage for gaining his cooperation. They must have seen you come out of his cabin."

"But, how did you know that I was in his cabin?" asked Linda.

"Please, Linda," replied Ling. "I doubt if there is a single person on board this yacht that isn't aware that you and Nash are, as we say in the south, keeping company."

"Really? I thought we were being very secretive."

"You can't keep love a secret," added Dan, "especially on a yacht at sea. But, enough chit-chat, we must go to work. Ling, let's split up. I will make my way to the bridge with Franz to acquire new weapons. You take on the master cabin. If Linda is willing, you can use her to get you in the door without an all-out frontal attack. I suspect that there is only one, or perhaps two persons, with Nash. Our big problem is how many total attackers. So, if we can free our main client, then, we can concentrate on the rest. Have him phone the bridge as soon as you gain control. I will make my move to clear the upper decks when the phone rings. Mark and Bobbie, please lock yourselves in your cabin until we clear up this attack. I will see you all shortly." And Dan slipped out the cabin door with Franz.

"I am ready to follow your orders," stated Linda defiantly to Ling.

"Okay, here's the plan," replied Ling, without hesitation. "I want you to knock on Nash's door. If someone asks who it is, simply reply normally. A little naïve tone in your voice would be appropriate. I will be flat against the wall next to you. When the bad guy opens the door, look astonished and step back. I will take it from there. If, for any reason, I don't succeed, in gaining control over that cabin within two minutes, please do not be a hero. You'll only complicate matters. Run back to your room and lock the door. Do not open it for anyone accept your sister or me. Are you okay with this plan?" Linda nodded her assent and proceeded toward the cabin door.

Their assault on the master cabin was completed in short order. Linda knocked on the entrance door and called out softly, "Nash, it's Linda. May I come in?" The door opened quickly to reveal Jack Swift in his orange prison outfit staring at her in surprise. She stepped back, as instructed, and Ling attacked Swift with both arms and legs moving in a lightning strike that put him on the floor in an unconscious state within sixty seconds, whereupon she applied similar tactics to Wilson who was too surprised to offer resistance. She then disarmed both of them and pulled two sets of handcuffs from her back pocket and tied them to their ankles with a length of nylon rope that had been tied around her waist. Barely puffing she turned to the wide-eyed Nash and asked him to phone the bridge to report peace and quiet in the master cabin.

During the final stages of restraining Wilson, Linda ran across to the bed and apologized to Nash for taking so long in returning. He calmly replied that he had not been bored during her absence, but he definitely preferred her company to that of Jack Swift and the traitor, Tim Wilson.

After Nash's phone call, Dan Houlihan proceeded quietly to search all of the public areas of the yacht from the top down, and then freed Carlos, Alfredo and Jose from the crew quarters. He asked them to stand watch for any more uninvited intruders. Within a few minutes, two police cars arrived on the Riverwalk followed by an unmarked car with federal agents. Dan and Ling transferred Ling's two prisoners to the police cars and the federal agents asked and received permission from Captain Ericksson to begin searching the vessel for the cache of cocaine reported by Nash from his prior conversation with Swift.

About this time, Jimmy and Nathan appeared from their cabins to inquire about all the noise that had awakened them. Bobbie extended somewhat sarcastic apologies to them on behalf of the entire group, and suggested that they return to bed for a quieter morning ahead.

Then, additional federal agents arrived with trained sniffer dogs who quickly located two one-hundred-pound packages of cocaine in upper deck storage containers, which had been hidden by Swift several days previously.

The excitement was quickly reduced when Jose announced the availability of freshly-baked sweet rolls and coffee in the main lounge. Carlos and Alfredo carried Nash up to join the morning party, and receive thanks and good wishes from the federal agents.

"So," concluded Nash, with a twinkle in his eye, "I am deeply indebted to government officials for finding this contraband cocaine on my yacht, which was put here by the criminals you introduced to us earlier in our Florida adventure. Thank you all, and thank you in particular for conducting these activities late at night so we don't miss any daylight hours conducting our normal work. Please excuse me for not escorting you to the dock, but the adventure appears to have incapacitated me for stairway travel."

All of his new guests laughed at his humor and gave him a round of applause for his help, before leaving to hunt down more bad guys. Nash then received a phone call from JJ, who apologized on behalf of the errant jailers who allowed the escape of Swift, and he assured Nash that his door is open to assist him anytime he needs help of any kind in Florida. Nash replied that, much as he enjoyed JJ's company, he sincerely hoped that such a request would not be forthcoming.

DAY 14

Wednesday, April 8, 2010

It seemed unbelievable that two weeks of almost perfect weather should conclude with a rainy day, but that was what greeted the "Victoria's" passengers as they gathered for breakfast after the night's excitement. On this the last day of their cruise along the coast of Florida, most of the passengers confessed to enough frightening experiences to last a lifetime. The vessel was moored once again along Jacksonville's North Riverwalk, but this time the visibility did not allow them to see the tall buildings on both the north and south shores of the St. Johns River. It was an unseasonable wet and grey day.

Since everyone had experienced a very short night of sleep because of the Jack Swift attack, conversations appeared to be in muted tones and most passengers were walking slower than usual. But Nash, in his new location in the main lounge, urged everyone to enjoy a hearty breakfast so they could concentrate on the important wrap-up sessions scheduled for this last day. "The capture of Swift and Williams was yesterday's excitement. Today's greater excitement is planning our new community. So please gather at the conference table ready to contribute."

Within a few minutes of Nash's urging, the entire group had settled into chairs around the corner conference table.

"Before we become immersed in this wrap-up session," began Nash, "I want to reinforce some important ground rules. As most of you are aware, I am over sixty years of age and I believe this project to be my major goal for the rest of my life. Although profit and loss are always a major part of my thought process, this project will have an overriding goal of cost-effective innovation. This means that, from now on, everyone working on this new community will have a big 'I' stamped on his or her back; an 'I' that stands for innovation being the major interest of the person exhibiting it. In short, everyone is responsible for innovation in everything that he or she works on throughout this project. And, everything means the design of our infrastructure through to the implementation team undertaking the construction. If you are not here to create innovation and to listen carefully to someone else's innovative ideas, then you are not here.

"The whole idea of this new community began with Nathan's original idea of a new way to design and construct houses. He stimulated me to start dreaming about a new community where we could make his idea come to life. Since then, Mark has intrigued us with his space planning and internal transportation ideas that make all sorts of economic sense as well as promoting convenience and safety. I have no idea whether all or any of these ideas will prove feasible. But, until someone proves that they are not physically or economically feasible, they are to be considered part of the plan.

"Jimmy, I want you to prepare a separate list of innovations that we have discussed thus far and any others that are introduced today. This will be an ongoing assignment that will continue until we achieve buildout. Please give me the first draft one week from today for my review before circulation among the team members in this room; plus a confidential copy to our chief lawyer, Duncan MacTavish, for legal review.

"Before we leave here today, I want to accomplish two objectives: first, settle on first and second priority sites for immediate acquisition negotiations. Tony DiMartino will be representing us for this and other legal matters in Florida. I will arrange for Tony and Duncan to get together within the next month either here or in Toronto. My second objective is to extract the best early innovative ideas from each of you to strengthen Jimmy's initial list. For that purpose, I am going to call upon Nathan right after lunch to present his ideas of the optimum future house, and I would like to follow him with Mark to present his ideas of the optimum future community. I know that each of you would like more time to draft your ideas into presentation format, but I also know that both of you can speak extemporaneously. So, we will settle for unstructured statements, hopefully punctuated by a few great ideas from your audience.

"So that's the afternoon program. This morning, we are waiting to hear from Tony on available sites for our new community. I know that his messenger arrived an hour ago, so he has the information at hand. We will give him a few more minutes to get organized while we all take a coffee break. Are there any questions or comments?"

"Yes," spoke Linda, raising her hand. "Although I am just a visiting observer on this voyage, I would like to make a suggestion."

"By all means," replied Nash with a warm smile. "I am certain that everyone here is interested in your thoughts; although, after helping subdue the angry Mr. Swift early this morning, I doubt if anyone will refer to you as an observer."

After taking a moment to restrain a blush at Nash's reference to their early morning adventures, Linda spoke clearly: "Your introduction on innovation was both admirable and marketable. I would like to invite comments from my sister and others experienced in marketing, but I believe that you have just introduced a fabulous name for your new community. Innovation can set the theme and the spirit for achieving your new community goals, and I suggest you adopt it as your own."

"Brilliant," exclaimed Bobbie. "Innovation is a distinctive and inspirational name. I know that Nash submits all such ideas to his marketing team, but I strongly endorse Linda's suggestion and urge you to put this name at the top of your list."

"Wow, Nash, these ladies are right on target," added Nathan from his chair at the back of the group. "We may need to take them on as outside consultants."

"Are you kidding, Nathan?" said Bobbie. "The past two weeks of dining and cruising, coupled with adventure vignettes, have been reward enough; right, little sister?"

"Absolutely," added Linda, "I have enjoyed the best time of my life," and her face lit up with a demure smile directed at Nash.

"Well, I am overwhelmed by this immediate exhibition of innovation," replied Nash, returning Linda's smile. "I will email our marketing people with Linda's suggestion without delay. Now let's all take a twenty-minute break before we hear from Tony."

∾

The entire group was back in their seats prior to the end of the twenty minute interlude, apparently eager to learn the results of Tony's site search. But before Tony began, Nash steered his wheel chair to the front of the group and raised his hand for attention.

"Attention, everyone. I am pleased to announce that Mark and Bobbie Wilkins, accompanied by Linda Cummings, have agreed to visit us in Toronto on the last weekend in April. I also have asked Tony to join us at that time, but he is uncertain of his availability on those dates. I have confirmed that Nathan will be available that weekend to lead a tour of our plant in Ajax. We will make all of the travel arrangements and confirm them with you. I am making this announcement now because Linda must catch a flight back to Atlanta this afternoon and will not be able to stay with us through the afternoon session. I want to take this opportunity to thank Bobbie for inviting Linda to join us. She has been a cheerful companion in addition to volunteering to serve as my nurse through my initial recovery period. Thank you, Linda, for all of your help, including your inspirational name suggestion for our new community."

"Believe me, Nash, and everyone," replied Linda, with her most charming smile, "this has been the trip of a lifetime. I enjoyed it all, even the scary parts. I am grateful to be included. And, I am looking forward to seeing Nathan's housing prototypes in Toronto later this month."

"Okay, Tony, the floor is yours," concluded Nash.

"Thank you, Nash. As everyone can see, the table in front of me is covered with maps and other information about potential acquisition sites in the four areas that Nash decided to pursue last Tuesday. I have written them on the easel pad as Lakeland/Winter Haven (one site), Pasco County north of Tampa (two sites), Bay County north of Panama City (two sites), and metropolitan Jacksonville (four sites)—a total of nine qualified sites. I have indicated on the pad the number of sites meeting our criteria in each location. Let me say at the outset that, although all of these sites meet the size and access standards we prescribed, only three meet the entitlement requirement. The others require entitlement under the Florida Development of Regional Impact regulations. One of these sites is a special government site requiring no DRI regulations."

"Wow, Tony, how is it possible to have a site of this size without DRI regulations?" interrupted Nash. "You and Mark both told me that DRI is mandatory for large scale projects."

"And so it is," replied Tony. "But we have an unusual situation here in Jacksonville, in which the state has granted special status to the Cecil Field former military base that was deeded to the City of Jacksonville by the federal government. After several years of aborted attempts to initiate new development, an industrial park developer from Dallas negotiated the current set of regulations to make the developable portion of this property attractive to potential investors. The new regulations include exempting it from state DRI regulations for development of commercial facilities that will stimulate economic development, including new employment. Although, your proposed housing factory fits these parameters, the concept of a planned community with housing does not. However, our real estate broker here in Jacksonville engaged in some rapid discussions with key local and state officials within the last twenty-hours, with the result that he has oral commitments at both levels of government to make the necessary changes to allow your new community concept to be allowed into the designated thirty-five-hundred acres of uplands of the planned Commerce Center at the established discounted land prices. There can be little question that some additional political arm-bending is required, but our broker believes that the door is open to this land use modification. My own advice, as your attorney, would be to place options on two sites and proceed with two plans until we are certain that approval is assured."

"What's your opinion, Mark?" asked Nash.

"Clearly, the Cecil Field opportunity sounds exciting in terms of rapid intergovernmental cooperation. However, I share Tony's caution and I believe a two-track approach may be the best way to proceed."

"How about you, Nathan?" said Nash, turning to his younger colleague.

"I too believe Tony's advice is sound. It is an expensive process to proceed with two sites, but we are facing an even more expensive and time-consuming process if we are delayed by the 'Hometown Democracy Amendment'. And a recent news article calculates a 50 percent chance of passage. I don't like those odds, so I vote for the two-track approach, at least until we have confidence that the Cecil Field alternative is a winner."

"Okay," resumed Nash. "It appears that the potential for intergovernmental cooperation, coupled with the road and rail access and ample upland availability, pushes the Cecil Field site into top position. Let's examine the alternate sites for a second option."

"Alright, the Polk County site between Winter Haven and Bartow is part of the seventeen-thousand-acre Clear Springs planned community which was approved under a variation of the DRI process called the Florida Quality Development legislation, which included only five such developments in the state. However, because of its pioneer legislation, the process for Clear Springs has been very slow, and the principal investor does not appear to be in any hurry. The planned industrial park will open this year with development of a vocational education arm of the community college on land donated by the developer. The land has good rail access, nearby interstate highway access and adequate upland, but no current provision for a mixed use community. I estimate that approval of your concept plan on this site would require two years, even with direct support from motivated county leadership."

"So that site is not a strong contender because of processing," commented Nash. "How about the Pasco County sites?"

"Both Pasco sites are entitled communities that were initiated prior to the recession and then allowed to sit idle for the past two years. They are residential communities with commercial zones sufficient to serve their own residents. In order to accommodate your concept, either one would require a 'Substantial Deviation' to the DRI approval which customarily takes as long as the DRI process itself. In addition, rail lines through Pasco County would require extensions and property acquisition to serve either site. I estimate this process to be as long, or longer, than the Polk County approval."

Okay, three down," said Nash. "What about Panama City?"

"We have two sites in Bay County north of Panama City, both owned by the highly influential St. Joe Company and both in the entitled mixed use development encompassing the new airport which is about to open for business. St. Joe is moving its headquarters from Jacksonville to this development as one of the initial buildings in the business park. The good news is that both sites have access to rail, and Interstate 10 is a few miles north. Both sites fall under the very large mixed use DRI approval and local and state government are very cooperative in stimulating new development interests. The bad news is that north-south interstate access is only available by I-75 at Lake City, far to the east, or I-69 at Mobile, far to the west. But, save for this distance penalty, both of these sites are contenders for you."

"So, that leaves Jacksonville."

"That's right, Nash. Jacksonville had a great deal of land entitlement activity progressing prior to the recession and it contains about twenty-eight-thousand entitled lots in the four-county area around the city. The major issue for your needs is that, except for a couple of major cases, all of the DRI approvals contained residential and modest small scale commercial uses. The exceptions are a large holding near the southern boundary of St. Johns County with frontage on I-95 which was approved for a large industrial park and the twenty-three-thousand-acre Cecil Field which has defined thirty-five-hundred acres of upland as a commerce park. Unfortunately, neither of these two plans includes any residential component. However, the unsubstantiated view that city officials might provide support to occupy almost half of the Commerce Park could be the right fit for you."

"I agree, Tony. You proved your worth in organizing all of this information in record time. We are all most grateful for your efforts. The conclusion is clear. We need to mount immediate planning efforts on the Cecil Commerce Park and one of the two St. Joe sites. I would like you to prepare options for both sites and recommend two separate planning teams. I will leave it to you to select the best St. Joe site for our needs. Please make it clear to the planning principals that we are looking for both speed and excellence, in addition to our new watchword: Innovation. I would appreciate it if your good friend Mark would be willing to critique your planning team selections prior to forwarding them to me. I need them on my desk in Toronto prior to Mark's planned trip to visit us on the last weekend of this month. Is that doable?"

"Consider it done," replied Tony, without hesitation.

"Great, then let's have lunch," responded Nash, as he wheeled himself away toward the large circular table with place settings for all of them. Bobbie took note that Linda followed quickly to ensure a seat next to Nash.

⁂

The "Victoria Group," as they had begun calling themselves, was in excellent spirits as they shared their last meal together. Although they all were aware that this was the end of their combined adventure, there was an aura of camaraderie that overcame any sadness about the end of the journey. Clearly, they enjoyed each other's company and respected the great talents that Nash had assembled on this yacht in such a brief period. Of course, Nash insisted that everyone join him in a glass of Burrowing Owl wine in memory of their fallen comrade, Jake Johnson, a moment that brought a complete halt to the luncheon revelry.

It was an excellent time for Linda to bid her farewells to everyone. She gave everyone a warm hug and saved a special embrace for her host. She whispered to him that she expected to see him walking by the time she arrived in Toronto in two weeks, and he confirmed that she could count on it. Then, with Carlos carrying her single suitcase, Linda waved a goodbye and left for the waiting taxi on shore.

"Okay," announced Nash, "let's talk about innovative housing, Nathan." He wheeled himself back to the conference area, and the rest of the group followed.

Nathan paused a moment to allow everyone to settle before beginning to speak. "Planning to develop a new community is an intimidating task. We are making decisions that will affect the lifestyle of inhabitants for decades in future, even farther if we consider the children who are raised in our community and transmit their lifestyle to other communities. But, I suggest to you that designing new types of housing is even more intimidating, because the decisions we make will affect even more lives and in the most intimate fashion. House builders have been making these decisions for their consumers for hundreds of years. They decide how their consumers will live in terms of the spaces and relationships they design into their houses. With the exception of a tiny proportion of people who can afford to employ an architect and design their own home, or craftsmen who construct

339

their own homes, the vast majority of people of all kinds throughout the world purchase or rent one of the few housing choices that is provided for them by persons who specialize in construction.

"Of course, I recognize that an emergent group of architects has devoted themselves to the design of the small house. And many of them are excellent at their craft. They study the latest opinion surveys of consumers and modify their design parameters to adapt to changing consumer needs and preferences. But, at the end of the day, they must satisfy the directions of their clients who are the builders trained in construction rather than design. Every year, an increasing proportion of our new homes are built by public stock companies—Pulte, Horton, KB, Lennar, Toll Brothers, Richmond-American and others—businesses answerable to their shareholders. Like automobile manufacturers, they dare not make major changes to their products for fear that their consumers will rebel. The 1947 Studebaker and the 1970 Edsel are often cited as examples of unsuccessful major changes that did not find consumer acceptance. So, builders make small changes that add small improvements to their houses, usually tried as options at first to gauge public acceptance, and then incorporated as standard items to increase their competitive advantage over the other large builders. Items like granite countertops, tile flooring, packaged hardwood flooring, zone air-conditioning, are recent examples. Of course, the other builders soon follow suit and upgrade their own standards. It is a copycat business. Thus, the price of housing continues to escalate, or at least it did until this Great Recession reduced land prices to a share of their former worth.

"Over the past year or two, we have seen a new builder trend, stimulated by The Great Recession. They have returned to competing by price rather than quality features. The surplus of discounted foreclosures and 'short sales' has inspired builders to lower their price per square foot to levels that even have surprised them. They are purchasing cheap lots and building smaller dwellings with lower standards of quality to appeal to first-time buyers who are not constrained by existing home ownership. Everything in our business, including wages, became cheaper and cheaper in what has been a mad rush to out-price the competition. But, despite these changes, American new home sales in 2009 were only one-third the volume of average annual sales in the first half of the last decade. Although more than 10 percent of the labor force was unemployed and could not afford to buy, the other 90 percent was reticent to buy because of lack of confidence in the economy and their uncertainty about the lowest level of prices: 'maybe they will get cheaper still and I will be sorry that I paid too much.'

"When my brother David and I first started discussing the stalemate in new home construction, we realized that the Edsel syndrome is still present. People still feel comfortable looking at a house as if they have known it from childhood. If we are going to reduce the cost of housing and add features to support new lifestyles, we must find a way to do it in incremental fashion. So we developed design molds for what are essentially plastic houses, but plastic from a non-petroleum source that has the strength and elasticity to conform to virtually any appearance. Like a chameleon, we can change our colors and texture to fit in to our surroundings; and we can produce look-a-like houses at a much lower price than constructing them piece-by-piece on the site. We know we can do this. We have done it. But, of course, selling them is a separate issue.

"Are there any questions on the structure?"

Mark raised his hand. "I have a dozen questions, Nathan, but I believe it makes more sense for me to wait until I see your prototypes in Toronto for that discussion."

"Thank you, Mark. I can do a much better job of explaining both the system and the costs when we have examples in front of us. Perhaps, we should take a ten-minute break at this point before I introduce the much more difficult issue of dwelling interior innovation."

When the small group re-assembled, Nathan was ready to continue. "Our population is changing their lifestyles at an amazing rate—from radio to television to personal computers to cell phones to brain-directed robots. We cannot be certain of what new device will be on the market next year. The pace of discovery is mind-boggling. Most of these improvements find a way into our homes and we adapt our living space to them. But, it doesn't always fit.

"The most interesting change in terms of dwelling spaces is the interaction between television and computer. Long gone are the days when the Ozzie Nelson family would sit down together in a living room and listen to a radio program, or later, watch a television program. Now each of us has his or her personal interests. Dad wants to watch a sports event on television, Mom wants to watch a cooking show on another television, daughter Mary wants to play games on the computer, and son John wants to communicate with his friends by texting on his cell phone. If they all undertake these activities in a single room, be it the living room or family room, the noise level increases as each one attempts to hear his or her own activity. Do we need this large living space? Many homes are designed with a living room and a family room, but the former usually contains no communication gadgets so everyone congregates in the family room with its conflicting noise sources. Now, technicians have developed directional speakers that can confine sound to very small spaces, so it is possible to avoid sound competition even in a single room. But is this defense mechanism the best solution. The big question on my mind is how to design interior spaces to complement the individual pursuits of each family member?

"A great many families are so concerned with individual pursuits that they no longer dine together. Conflicting individual schedules are not compatible with standard dinner hours, let alone breakfast or lunch. Do we need a dining room with table and chairs for the whole family? Do we need it for guest dinners or even annual religious and festive occasions? I would suggest to you that the major reason that new homes have dining rooms is that the builder is scared to remove it; that is, 'my mother had one so I guess I should have one.' Many small homes have three or more dining spaces, but find themselves using only one—commonly the one closest to the kitchen. Larger new homes also feature oversize master bedroom suites which have sitting areas as well as sleep and dressing areas. The sitting areas certainly provide a niche for adult quiet time, but at considerable space expense. These are but two examples of questionable spaces generated by builders to attract consumers, spaces that require re-examination in light of increasing costs and more frugal consumer attitudes.

"A few years ago, a national production builder headquartered in Orlando enlarged the bedroom hall with a niche called 'imagination space'. It became popular with young families and other builders in Florida copied it. Depending on the age of household children, they could use it for favorite games or a shared computer. By the next generation, this became a space without a purpose as computers became cheap enough for each child to have his own computer and it was portable and wireless for use anywhere—a specific station was unnecessary.

"Today, builders are experimenting with many interior planning concepts. The most common combination is to design space for living, dining and kitchen in a single 'great room' often linked to an outdoor lanai to increase both the perceived and functional space. Builders also frequently provide a study or office adjoining the great room to provide a separate activity room for one or more family members. Another appealing plan links this study to the master bedroom suite, thereby adding a second sleeping room for a partner with recurrent sleeping problems (usually in addition to one or more guest bedrooms). The addition of directional sound speakers to this space-efficient dwelling plan facilitates relatively private personal activities for a household of two or more persons in a smaller overall area than most dwelling plans of the past. And, since the 'great room' excludes definition of specific functions, owners can incorporate one or multiple dining arrangements as well as other flexible use areas to their own personal tastes—the builder does not dictate uses. So, we believe these types of flexible space plans will be the most appealing to consumers over the next several years and we are designing variations of this theme with several exterior options.

"My point in citing these examples is that our houses as we have known them are not readily adaptable to current individual interests. They still use planning components from the days of unified family activities. Furthermore, we are uncertain what our future interests may be, so we can't easily design for the unknown. I do not yet have the answers to these issues, but I feel strongly that we should provide answers in our Innovation community. What do you think?"

"Congratulations, Nathan, for flooding us with useful examples," responded Mark. "I do not have answers either, but I absolutely agree that we need to keep searching. In fact, this type of searching could be an organized activity in the community, sponsored by Logan Homes. You have enough material to organize some great study groups. They could even be of various age groups, and perhaps videotaped for other age groups."

"That's a great idea, Mark." added Jimmy. I could relate to that type of activity when I was in high school, and now I would like to know what those younger people are talking about. Although they do not represent adult consumer interests, they can broaden our perspective on future space issues with respect to priorities among young people."

"Okay," interjected Nash. "Much as I would like to continue pursuit of the dwelling space planning issues that Nathan has introduced, I am more interested in ending our two week study adventure with issues on all parts of the community. Thank you, Nathan, for challenging us with some truly perplexing issues on housing. I know that you will be leading lengthy seminars on this topic over coming months, and perhaps years. We are determined to keep our company in the forefront of housing innovation, and Nathan is our point man.

"But, now, for the remainder of our time, I would be grateful if Mark would lead us in a discussion of innovation throughout the community. He already has presented his innovations on internal transport and activity nodes, but I hope that he can expand on these ideas to share some of his ideas on a truly optimum community for the future and incremental steps to achieve it." Then, he motioned to Mark to take over the leadership role.

"As you know," Mark began quietly from his chair, "I have spent my entire career trying to create improved environments for better living conditions. Never once in all that time did a developer, or even a government official, offer me carte blanche in terms of creating an optimum community. Everyone involved with new development was immersed in cost and regulatory issues, occasionally swayed by emotional pleas from evangelical environmentalists committed to preserving our natural resources. This is not an admission of failure on my part, or on behalf of many colleagues devoted to better living conditions at all economic levels, both in this country and in less developed nations where I was employed. We did accomplish improvements of many kinds, but, like Nathan's story of incremental change in automobiles and housing, our development plans and construction achieved incremental improvements in all of the five components of community development.

"Let me just repeat those five components for anyone whose memory may be blocked by the fine food and drink we all have enjoyed: Infrastructure, Housing, Leisure, Institutional, and Commercial. The order is not important. But every new community of scale must incorporate each of these components to some degree. External impact costs are reduced to the extent that travel to and from the community is minimized and daily needs are provided within the community. The provision of these needs becomes more difficult as the community gets smaller in size because most needs require a minimum market size. For example, a modern elementary school requires about three-thousand average households to generate over five-hundred students and a traditional supermarket requires at least five-thousand average households.

"Customarily, a proposed new community is on a specific site which can accommodate a calculated number of households and related land uses. However, in the case of Logan Homes, the site size is calculated from the concept of supplying housing for factory employees on-site, in addition to an estimated number of retirees attracted to living in this community. Obviously, retirees do not generate school children, so the support for an elementary school must be generated from employee households. That is why, at the beginning of this study tour, I recommended sufficient industrial and retail land to support at least twenty-five-hundred households of employee housing, exclusive of demand for retiree housing.

"So, the first point of importance in planning a new community is the numbers. They drive the land uses and the land uses determine the site size. You may recall, at our first all-day session, I felt obligated to disagree with the initial site area estimates provided by Nash and Nathan. The reasons were twofold: first, the proportion of wetland and required retention in most parts of Florida, and, second, the scale of residential development required to support desirable commercial and institutional needs.

"However, please note that numbers are relatively useless without creative interpretation. You may have heard the story of Albert Einstein's sign in his office at Princeton University. It read 'Not everything that counts can be counted, and not everything that can be counted counts.' In short, it is vital to have good numbers describing a proposed development, but it is equally important to retain a creative and experienced interpreter of numbers."

"Excuse me just a moment, Mark," spoke up Nathan. I am a little concerned about enlarging our planned workforce without designated employers. We calculated a reasonable production program for the Logan Homes Package Plant, but attempting to forecast the presence of related employers is akin to 'skating on very thin ice' as we say in our country."

"This is an excellent point, Nathan, but I submit to you that the risk factor on projecting future development is tied to the success of your new housing venture first of all. I know that you are very positive about its success, whereas a banker might take a much more conservative viewpoint. So, I would use a saying from your British roots: 'in for a penny, in for a pound.'

"My argument is quite simply to approach this development from more than one perspective and then fiddle with the overall projections until they support the community facilities that all of you believe are essential in a new community. Education is a good example. You can support an Elementary School by increasing your base population at the margin, whereas it would take a doubling in size to support a Middle School and High School. Therefore, I do not believe you can rationalize a community of that size, and I am aiming for the Elementary School. My plea to you is to become sensitive to these key community facilities and their support populations as you move ahead with master planning and base your decisions on a full range of knowledge."

"Okay," replied Nathan with a smile. "I take your point, and it's a good one. We must learn a great deal more about this business in short order to prepare the best possible plan. I assume that Nash will be working on you to continue helping us, so I will not interfere with his plans. But the knowledge you bring to the table for this undertaking is enormous."

"Thank you for those kind words, Nathan, but we will introduce you to some very knowledgeable planners who understand this business as well as I do, and, in addition, they are much younger and more energetic than this old body. But let's put that topic aside and let me return to the subject of an optimum community."

"Yes, Nathan," interjected Nash with a smile to his colleague. "I am working the staffing side of the street. Please concentrate your superb skills on the physical stuff."

"To recap, then," continued Mark, "the first point of importance in planning a new community is the numbers: people numbers, dollar numbers, acreage numbers, et cetera. These form the parameters for everything else and you will need a skilled numbers man on your team.

"The second point, and the most fun, is the physical arrangements of manmade components in relation to the natural features of the land. In most parts of Florida, including the two areas you have selected, the natural features are not very dramatic, so the manmade additions are of even greater importance than in areas with substantial topography and/or natural waterways. This is the topic that is bogged down in decades of regulations and customs that unnecessarily limit our creativity, so the success of our endeavors is very strongly associated with how good we are at getting outside historical precedents and inventing new solutions to old problems.

"Earlier in our discussions, I introduced some of my thoughts on internal transportation and related land use. Now I would like to return to these ideas from a somewhat different perspective. Most urban planners through the ages conceptualize a new community in its final form, and then define the growth of the community through phasing the components of the overall plan. I would like to suggest to you that you establish land use priorities for your community as the first step, followed by efficient implementation of each priority on the overall site area. This organic approach to community planning ensures a functioning community at each growth step rather than deferring the viable community until growth objectives are complete.

"For example, let me return to the example of the elementary school. Historically, we taught all elementary classes in a one-room schoolhouse because we could not physically transport our students longer distances to larger urban centers. Teaching all elementary students in one classroom was discarded when school buses evolved to provide efficient transport to central school locations serving a larger population base. These central schools became sized according to the efficiency of the physical plant and the travel time radius.

"But, what if we took a different approach from the arrival of the first employees in our industrial park and the provision of housing for them? One of the needs of these arriving families is education for their children. Assuming that the majority of parents are not interested in, or capable of, home schooling, then what is the solution to schooling at initial population levels, and then increasing levels as our community expands? Busing to existing schools may not be a viable, or even desirable, solution if the distances are great. Other alternatives can and should be explored.

"Another issue of importance is shopping for convenience goods. In recent years, we have witnessed large supermarket chains develop smaller stores to make them more accessible to low density neighborhoods. It is a trend likely to continue as customers discover that these smaller stores still provide sufficient variety of goods at competitive prices to satisfy their weekly needs. Travel distances are reduced as cost-sensitive customers surviving The Great Recession compare travel costs with the costs of convenience goods. Developers of some small communities have experimented with local 'general stores' to serve even smaller neighborhoods; an expansion of the convenience store concept that has become popular around the world.

"These two examples illustrate the developer obligation to provide services in the initial community, regardless of the potential in the ultimate master plan. The trade-off for consumers is travel costs and time between limited-choice local facilities versus greater choice regional facilities. The trade-off for the developer is happier residents in the initial community versus a higher proportion of on-site employees who opt for other residence choices closer to necessary or desirable goods and services.

"In the nineteenth century, major industrialists like Lever Soap in England and Cannon Textiles in North Carolina and Hershey Chocolate in Pennsylvania sponsored housing close to their factories so that employees could walk to work. The so-called company town evolved as a cost-effective solution to ensuring a satisfactory labor force in an era of slow transportation. Such towns became less popular with the advent of automobiles and buses to increase the convenience of commuter travel. But, in this century, our vehicles have multiplied faster than lanes of roadway with the result that the daily commute has become an increasingly costly primary annoyance for growing numbers of employees in developed countries. In short, if we can re-invent the company town to remove the stigma of subsidization and look-alike housing, I believe our industrial park will fill rapidly with employers eager to locate in a community devoted to both economy and convenience.

"So, I am arguing for a planning process that focuses on the comfort of local employees at each level of community growth, from the very first resident onward to completion of site development. Clearly, the costs of development must be lower than the sales of land revenues, and each developer-paid improvement must be cost-effective. But, I am convinced that the innovation theme advocated by Nash at the beginning of this session can provide solutions to the incremental resident satisfaction program that I am advocating."

"Excuse me a moment, Mark," interrupted Nathan. "I am impressed with your argument for multi-level planning of community services, but please give us an example of how you visualize the launch stage. How much must we spend on the initial improvements to achieve the goal of a comfortable environment from Day One?"

"Excellent point, Nathan," replied Mark with a smile, "and that is why I emphasized at the outset that a creative numbers man is an essential member of the planning team. Front-end costs will be considerable, and they must be recovered with a logical margin from land sales revenues within a reasonable time period. This is the challenge of all land development. However, please keep in mind that a key ingredient of both costs and revenues is time—the faster that land sales proceed, the lower the cost of debt service. Therefore, the initial attraction of the community in portraying an appealing lifestyle for residents is paramount in fueling the pace of development. I should also add that you are launching this development on the heels of The Great Recession, which promises a prolonged period of economic growth ahead. You must capitalize upon this growth period prior to the next economic downturn, and the best way to do that is to accelerate your development from the beginning.

"Let me try and exemplify what I have in mind. First of all, you have a special problem insofar as you must have employees to operate your factory before you can produce housing to accommodate these same employees—unless, of course you enlist conventional homebuilders to construct initial residences simultaneously with construction of the factory . . ."

"Wait a minute," interjected Nash. "That idea seems to fly in the face of our objective to make 'Innovation' a prime example of our new housing technique."

"I kind of figured that I would stimulate such a response," replied Mark with a grin. "But, this is a real conundrum that you must resolve in the near future. Jimmy, I urge you to feature it in your notes for high priority attention. A number of solutions occur to me, but all of them require advance action well before initial construction of the new community, and at least one may require acquisition of a parcel of entitled land outside the new community site, perhaps even in a potential competitor's site."

"Are you suggesting some type of multi-family housing complex for employees as temporary housing which can subsequently be marketed as rental or condominium housing?" asked Nathan.

"Yes, that is at least one alternative worth considering," answered Mark. But, let me return to the primary topic of the initial stage of development in Innovation. It seems to me that you are going to be under intense public scrutiny prior to and after opening the factory. A proven public relations firm, and possibly an experienced staff publicist, must be at work to turn this scrutiny into an asset from the time of your initial site acquisition. I suggest that the primary focus of attention should be on the community rather than the new housing technique. That is, you have come to Florida to build a better community, not just to sell a new type of housing."

"That makes sense to me", said Nash. "But it means that we need to have a better community to show off from the get-go."

"Precisely," replied Mark. "This conclusion has a major bearing on the front-end investment you need to plan for the initial stage of

Innovation, an investment that will have a significant negative impact upon your project cash flow. Let me now suggest some preliminary ideas on this subject.

"Previously, I mentioned to you the 'Charm Bracelet' which had its origin in linking places of interest ('charms') along a pathway through the community, so that residents would experience more enjoyable walking adventures. Now, I am proposing that we carry this concept to a new level in making this bracelet into a low-speed transit link connecting all the key activity centers in the community. The technology is perfected for unmanned rubber-tire vehicles to travel along an electronic pathway safely, at slow speeds, with programmed stops at each center and un-programmed stops whenever something or someone interferes with its pathway. Each vehicle might accommodate eight or twelve riders on bench seats with roll-down weather shields for rain or cold (but basically open-side vehicles in the Florida climate). Such a system can be operated with a single person monitoring the progress of the vehicles in a control center and a contracted maintenance team for potential breakdowns. I visualize it as a hard-surface pathway that is dedicated for this purpose, but not fenced, because of the safety stop mechanism built into each car. The electronic guidance line would be placed in the paving to prevent vandalism. The pathway should have night lighting in addition to lights on the vehicles. The number and timing of the vehicles can be varied according to the rider demand at different population levels and at different times of the day.

"The transit route can match the stage of development, beginning with a loop to link the first neighborhood center with other recreation institutional and retail facilities, as well as the employment center and a terminal for middle and high school buses external to the community. As the community grows, additional neighborhoods and activity centers would be linked with an expanded pathway and/ or a new loop interconnected with the first. Each vehicle could travel the entire multi-loop system so that transferring would be minimal (depending on the size of community and ride-time limitations).

"Instead of relying upon an untrained school bus driver to control children on their way to school, parents probably would take turns riding with their children both to and from school. Those parents whose work limited their ability to be available for this service could substitute another volunteer task. Education costs would be lower and parent involvement would be higher. School buses would be limited to middle and high school students who would congregate at one or two stops for the entire community rather than cruise local streets.

"In sum, the system I have proposed should reduce local car travel throughout this community to a fraction of what it is today in most communities. For those residents who are employed in the industrial park, commuting costs could be reduced to zero and they would not be restricted by car pools or public transportation schedules. For example, the transit vehicles could operate on a fifteen-minute schedule and increase the number of vehicles during high travel demand periods. Such additions could be handled readily by the control operator by having extra vehicles stored on an electronic siding which can be accessed from the central control.

"In terms of planning, this transit system route becomes the essential first priority in designing the master plan. Assembling activity centers along this route must be addressed simultaneously so that the transit route is the shortest and most efficient pathway in the community. By the way, with respect to pathways for walking and cycling, they could be planned in parallel with the transit line but not sharing the same pavement—the movement of walkers and bike-riders would trigger automatic stops of the vehicles.

'In the past, roadways have been the priority component for community planning, although, in Florida, wetlands often take precedence. Acceptance of the transit system, more properly addressed as a people-mover, would relegate roadways to a secondary role; one which is still of prime importance in serving individual residences with owner and service vehicles, but not the shortest route between residences and activity centers."

"But Mark, you haven't mentioned costs," interjected Nash. "I am mesmerized with this concept, but can we afford it and still meet our primary objective of modest price housing."

"Excellent question," responded Mark. "The real answer is that I don't know the answer. The technology has been available for many years, but it has been applied only in recreation theme parks and airports with very heavy people traffic issues. The very low volume application I have proposed has no precedents. We also know very little about the trade-offs of reducing automobile traffic and school buses. My low-volume transit recommendation must be accompanied by a parallel recommendation that you assemble a multi-discipline study team to examine the costs and benefits of this concept. I further suggest that you approach the United States Department of Transportation and manufacturers of these kinds of vehicles to pay for this research. This is a first priority of pursuing this recommendation.

"Fair enough," said Nash. "Jimmy, please set this up as a high priority action item for my immediate attention after I return to the office."

"Yes sir, it will be done," replied Jimmy. "Would you like me to copy anyone on this?"

"Absolutely not," said Nash in a strong voice. "Except for the people in this room, in addition to Duncan MacTavish for legal issues, I believe it critically important that we keep these ideas confidential until we employ a public relations firm to release them according to a specific marketing strategy. If the numbers on Mark's concept are realistic, we may have an enormous tiger by the tail. Let's make sure that we don't give it away."

"I agree with you, Nash," interjected Nathan. "But we also are dealing with a critical time issue here, or at least it could be critical depending on the success of the Hometown Democracy movement. We cannot afford to tackle these issues in sequential fashion."

"Your point is well taken, Nathan. I propose that we try to engage Mark to define this concept in as much detail as possible to present to our two planning teams as a guideline, and that we activate our cost-benefit study simultaneously. In short, we proceed on a veto basis, assuming that it will work until proven wrong. Granted, that could be expensive if I am wrong, but it is too exciting to sidestep. Do you agree?"

"I do."

"Then, Jimmy, please set up this parallel study approach as a policy which Nathan and I will sign as another top priority."

"Yes sir."

"So Mark," continued Nash, "what more can you load onto our plates before we leave here?"

"Thank you, Nash, for your vote of confidence," replied Mark. "The low-volume transit system has been a dream of mine for a long time, but, up until now, I could not sell it to anyone who has sufficient funds to make it happen. I accept the engagement to define the concept at no fee because of my dedication to this idea. And furthermore, I will complete it over the next week in advance of your selection of planning teams."

"That's great, Mark, but we will discuss fees in a separate session."

"Thank you. Let me just conclude this session by referring back to Nathan's earlier reference to the 1947 Studebaker. I actually remember it being announced. His point that we cannot jump to the future and expect to win the support of the American people is accurate. In the case of community planning, we have recognized our mistakes of the past in relying upon automobiles to resolve our local travel needs. The reaction of city planners always has been to create greater residential density in order to induce our residents to walk more and drive less. But this solution, as attractive as it may seem, has not proven appealing to the majority of Americans. We continue to manufacture cars faster than we build roads to accommodate them. Higher densities continue to attract less than one-third of our population. My recommendation is actually a compromise, insofar as it acknowledges the single family dwelling as the most desired residence type among Americans, but it attempts to coerce them into low-volume transit as a means of reducing car use.

"Let me carry the argument one step further. The potential of locating our activity centers along the nodes of this charm bracelet provides incentive to consider locating related activities around the same centers. It may give new definition to the neighborhood center which historically has been a definition for primarily commercial retail activities, but could be reborn as a rich mix of institutional, commercial and residential activities. For a community of the size we are considering, it could well be that there is no dominant center, but rather a series of centers containing both distinct and common facilities. With the acceptance and common use of a low-volume transit system, the common practice of defining markets in terms of numbers of households within a prescribed radius of the center may no longer prove valid. A terrific tavern, or a popular medical clinic, is likely to attract transit riders from other neighborhoods only a few minutes away by transit. Consequently, there may be decreasing demand for a singular community center, or town center, or even city center. The transit line can make several centers within easy access.

"This potential of dispersion of activities, rather than centralization, is somewhat foreign to our society's history of hierarchical organization. But those who struggle with the congestion of ever-larger urban centers may find it appealing Of course, it flies in the face of segregation of land uses left over from the early twentieth century, but I believe it to be a natural evolution of human preferences. If we provide the opportunity for more convenient local travel, I believe that we may find related conveniences occurring as well. We planners and developers must be prepared to build sufficient flexibility into our plans to accommodate changing patterns of consumer demand. So, I fervently hope that the costs of low-volume transit will prove feasible and thereby open the door to new patterns of community living that are more efficient, more convenient and safer for our residents.

"Early this morning, I made a preliminary list of plan parameters that I will leave with you as a starting point for the design of the community master plan. The list which I am passing out to each of you now only contains eleven points as guidelines to begin the plan, but each point is a parameter that we discussed over the past few days as an opportunity for innovation. I have endeavored to list them in priority order, because it does make a difference where you begin on a blank sheet of paper.

"I am leaving this list with you to as an initial starting point when you meet with your site planners as summary results of the discussions we have held during our time together. It is my fervent hope that each of these parameters will be given the most careful consideration in designing the site plan.

"As you all are aware, the normal procedure for beginning a site plan exercise is to map the natural characteristics of the site and then delineate the areas of developable land, minimizing any potential wetland mitigation requirements. Many planners then indicate connector points to link these developable parcels as the initiation of a vehicle circulation system which becomes the key guideline for the resultant plan. My plea is that you assign first priority to the public transit system as the key parameter and fit the vehicular streets in later as a residual that necessarily will take a longer route. Thus, I leave you with this list of parameters in order of priority, emphasizing internal transit as your major guideline.

Objectives	Plan Components	Phase	Notes
Live Close to Workplace	Planned Employment	Launch	Logan Packaged Home Factory
Play Close to Residence	Planned Play Facilities	Launch +	Nhbd Ooutdoor, Community Indoor
Shop Close to Residence	Planned Shopping Centers	Phases 2 & 5	Nbhd Convenience, Comty Center
Public Transit	Efficient Links to Work, Retail, Civic	Phase 3 +	Automatic Electric Jitneys
Residential Integration	Linked Neighborhood Clusters	Phase 1 +	Mix Village Housing Size, Price Range
Residential Density	Mixed Densities	Phase 1 +	Building Exterior Design Compatibility
Community Center Uses	Retail, Office, Civic, MF Housing	Phase 5 +	Vertical Office, Town Hall, MF Apts
Infrastructure: Pathways	Optimum Distance Connections	All	Surface Use, Width Criteria, Safety
Infrastructure: Streets	Minimum Total Area	All	Access Points Parking
Infrastructure: Underground	Efficient Routing	All	Efficient System Connections
Infrastructure: Electronic	Wireless Communitywide	All	Innovation

Exhibit 34:
Logan Community Plan Parameters.

"Let me just add that, despite my broken arm, the past two weeks have been an exhilarating and memorable experience for me, and I believe that I speak for Bobbi too in expressing our heartfelt gratitude to Nash for sponsoring what has turned out to be an outstanding seminar on the history and potential of new community development in Florida. Thank you all for your participation."

With the exception of Nash, who was still confined to his wheel chair, the entire group rose as one to extend Mark a well-deserved round of applause.

"Goldarnit, Mark, I wish I could jump up and exhibit my personal appreciation for your contribution to our planning session," said Nash. "Harold Abrams underestimated your value when he told me you are the best. You go well beyond the best, and I feel both humble and proud to have you with us, and opening our eyes to the possible. In fact, I feel so good that I believe we all should have a toast to each other before we leave. Jimmy, would you mind finding Jose?

Mark and Bobbi lingered with the "Victoria Group" for another hour to participate in champagne toasts and accepting and passing out compliments to everyone, before Carlos appeared to tell them that their luggage was in the limousine that Nash had ordered to take them back home to Fernandina Beach. They found it difficult to depart, but Mark's assignment was complete and a new "Innovation" was about to start in Florida.

EPILOGUE

Two weeks after the "Victoria Group" dispersed in Jacksonville, most of them met again at the Logan Homes headquarters in the Toronto suburb of Richmond Hill. Mark and Bobbi Wilkins from Fernandina Beach, Florida and Bobbi's sister Linda Cummings from Atlanta, Georgia, along with Tony DiMartino and his wife Marcie from Orlando, were flown to Toronto by an executive jet chartered by Logan Homes. Jimmy Quickfoot met them at the airport and drove them to the Logan Building on Yonge Street in Richmond Hill. Nash was on his feet with a cane when they were ushered into his large office. Linda showed no hesitation in embracing him along with a lengthy kiss, while Bobbi and Mark waited their turn for affectionate hugs. The DiMartinos settled for handshakes.

Although Nash relied upon Jimmy to personally show them the office and meet friends from the Florida trip, as well as a first personal meeting with the venerable Duncan MacTavish, he gathered all of his executive staff in the conference room to introduce his new southern friends. Of course, everyone present had heard about the successes and perils of the Florida adventure, and they all wanted to shake hands with the reputed planning guru who taught them about Florida's development history as well as its future potential.

Nash had invited the Florida contingent to stay at his home only a few miles from Richmond Hill. They arrived after six o'clock and, after being shown to their rooms to freshen up, they assembled for drinks on the patio at seven, followed by a sumptuous dinner prepared by Nash's housekeeper, Ginny Sullivan. Two of his grown children joined them for dinner, Megan and Scott, both of whom were employed at Logan Homes and lived in their own apartments near Richmond Hill. Nash's other son, Alexander, lived in New York, where he was employed as a bond trader. Nash apparently had advised his children about his feelings for Linda, because they made special efforts to befriend her throughout the evening.

After dinner, they moved to a sitting room from which they could see the Toronto skyline some twenty miles south, highlighted by the CN Tower soaring well above Toronto's many tall buildings. Coffee and tea, along with after-dinner drinks were served by Megan and Scott, both of whom seemed comfortable in the host and hostess role they inherited after their mother's death. It was after ten when Mark announced his bedtime and everyone took his cue to retire. A half hour later, Nash limped into Linda's bedroom attired in a maroon silk dressing gown. She also had changed into night attire, and welcomed him with a warm embrace. They wasted little time in climbing into the double bed to spend their first night together without casts on his right arm and leg.

The next morning, after a buffet breakfast was served on the patio overlooking the swimming pool and extensive rear yard, they were picked up by two limousines for the drive along the multi-lane Expressway 401 to the suburb of Ajax east of Toronto. Nathan Rosenberg met them at the entrance to the unidentified factory, and proudly showed off their completed model homes inside an adjoining warehouse before guiding them through the complete factory. Nash excused himself from the tour and waited for them in a conference room.

Although the factory was not operating, the various stages of production that Nathan had explained to them in Florida were more fully explained here. When they finally adjourned for a catered lunch with Nash in the conference room, each of the Florida visitors expressed congratulations to Nathan on what appeared to be a major breakthrough in manufactured housing. Bobbi was particularly enthusiastic, and eager to know when she could publish an article about the process. Although Nathan deferred to Nash on timing, it was quite clear to everyone that they were months away from factual publicity. In fact, Nash suggested that it would be combined with planning approvals for the new community in Florida.

That afternoon, after Nash returned to his office, Nathan took them on a tour of two Logan Homes' subdivisions under development east of Toronto near the former farming center of Markham. They visited furnished model homes in both subdivisions and posed for a company photographer to commemorate their visit for a future news article.

That evening, after returning to Nash's home for cocktails and a change of clothes, they attended a dinner in a private dining room at the original Four Seasons Hotel (the initial hotel of the worldwide luxury hotel chain founded in Toronto) located a few miles south of his home. All the senior executives of Logan Homes were present to visit with the honored guests from the United States, and several descriptions of their yacht adventure were presented by various speakers, including Mark, who proposed a minute of silence in memory of their fallen comrade, Jake Johnson.

After another night in the Logan home, where Linda and Nash continued their love-making in a guest room (he could not bring himself to invite her into the bed that he had shared for so many years with his deceased wife, Victoria), the American visitors enjoyed another breakfast on the patio. At ten o'clock, the limousine arrived to take them back to the airport for their flight back home to Atlanta, Jacksonville and Orlando. Each of the five passengers on the plane expressed excitement about the new breakthrough in housing that they had witnessed in Ajax and about the advent of the new community of "Innovation" in Florida.

A few months after the Toronto trip, both Florida and Atlanta newspapers carried the story of murder convictions upheld by the District Court in Orlando to Jason Jackson under hire by Jack Swift, Kurt Richter and Albert Siegal. The latter three also were convicted of cocaine smuggling and received total jail terms of thirty years each. Jackson was given a life term in prison for the second degree murder of Jake Johnson.

The residents of Florida rejected Constitutional Amendment 4 (Hometown Democracy) by a two-to-one majority in November, 2010. During that same election, a new Republican Governor was elected, Rick Scott, who immediately rejected a two-and-one-half-billion-dollar federal grant for launching high-speed rail between Tampa and Orlando. Subsequently, he abolished the Florida Department of Community Affairs and approved a revised Community Growth Act that simplified state and regional regulations for developers, despite stiff opposition from conservation groups.

Additional Readings

Brown, Robin C. (1994). *Florida's First People: Twelve Thousand Years of Human History*. Sarasota, FL: Pineapple Press.

Chandler, David Leon (1986). *Henry Flagler, The Astonishing Life and Times of the Visionary Robber Baron Who Founded Florida*. New York, NY: Macmillan Publishing Company.

Derr, Mark. *Some Kind of Paradise: A Chronicle of Man and the Land in Florida*. Gainesville, FL: University Press of Florida.

Fernald and Patton (Eds.). (1985). *Water Resources Atlas of Florida*. Tallahassee, FL: FSU Institute of Science and Public Affairs.

Gannon, Michael (Ed.). (1996). *The New History of Florida*. Gainesville, FL: University Press of Florida.

Lanier, Sidney. (1875). *Florida: Its Scenery, Climate and History*. Philadelphia, PA: J. B. Lippencott & Co.

Mormino, Gary R. *Land of Sunshine, State of Dreams: A Social History of Modern Florida*. Gainesville, FL: University Press of Florida.

Nozzi, Dom. (2003). *An Introduction to Sprawl and How to Cure It*. Westport, CT: Greenwood Publishing Group.

Oppel, Frank and Tony Meisel (Eds.). (Reprint 1987). *Tales of Old Florida: 1870-1910*. Secaucus, NJ: Castle.

Pritzker, Barry M. (1998). *Native Americans, Vol. 2*. Santa Barbara, CA: ABC-CLIO, Inc.

Small, John Kunkel. (1929). *From Eden to Sahara: Florida's Tragedy.* Lancaster, PA: Science Press Printing Company.

Smith, Patrick. (1992). *A Land Remembered.* Gainesville, FL: University Press of Florida.

Stephenson, R. Bruce. (1997). *Vision of Eden: Environmentalism, Urban Planning, and City Building in St. Petersburg, Florida, 1900-1995.* Columbus, OH: Ohio State University Press.

Waldman, Carl. (2006). *Encyclopedia of Native American Tribes.* New York, NY: Infobase Publishing.

Zietwitz, Kathryn and June Wiaz. *Green Empire: The St. Joe Company and the Remaking of Florida's Panhandle.* Gainesville, FL: University Press of Florida.